ADVANCE

"The imagery and character development in *Water* pull you deeply into the protagonist's metamorphosis of body, mind, and spirit. You'll agonize with her pain and celebrate her self-awareness, and you will be changed by this story. It's a tale of a woman with many gifts battling sexism, trauma, fear, and the world's unenlightened deadness. Yet she emerges a courageous, creative empath who will inspire you to dance with your inner vitality and stop settling for less."

—Gail McMeekin, author of *The 12 Secrets of Highly Creative Women*

"Emotional and gripping, *Water* is set against a time of great social change. The novel flows into uncommon metaphysical territory, making the invisible real, spirit palpable, and the quest for healing the driving force behind the soul's purpose. *Water* quenches our collective thirst for authenticity."

—Rev. Judith Laxer, author of *Along the Wheel of Time: Sacred Stories for Nature Lovers* and Founding Priestess of Gaia's Temple

"Caroline Allen has written an eloquent and succinct guidebook to healing the dark night of the soul. If you have anxiety, you'll recognize yourself in these pages and know once and for all that you are not alone. I wish I had had *Water* tucked beside me when I was going through my own dark night."

Ellen Newhouse, author of the memoir *Nothing Ever Goes On Here*

Merry Christmas, Leslie!

Love, Jin

12-25-2020

WATER

BOOK FOUR OF THE ELEMENTAL JOURNEY SERIES

CAROLINE ALLEN

Publisher: Art of Storytelling
Inquiries about permission should be directed to info.artofstorytelling@gmail.com.

Cover design: Greg Simanson
Cover concept: Caroline Allen
Editor: Caroline Clouse

PRINT ISBN: 978-0-9975824-6-8
EPUB ISBN: 978-0-9975824-7-5

This book is dedicated to the misfits, the oddballs,
to all of those who simply do not fit.

"Dark river beds down which the eternal thirst is flowing,
and the fatigue is flowing, and the grief without shore."
—Pablo Neruda

O
THE FOOL.

CHAPTER 0

The Fool

Nobody wants to hear about the despair. Dark nights of the soul. We beat around that burning bush, beat around and around and around. Don't poke it. Don't stir it.

In a rundown duplex near Aurora Avenue in Seattle, a block from the whores, I've been twisting and turning on this futon for days—weeks, months, centuries. The year is 1991, but there's no time here. I'm twenty-eight but feel like I'm a thousand. The futon dominates the only real room in this godforsaken studio apartment. Beaten, crooked hardwood floors, cobwebs in the corners, a broken light fixture filled with lifeless flies.

I moved back to the States two months earlier after a decade living abroad. I'm back "home" in a country I no longer know, in a city I've never visited. I'm home and have never felt more homeless.

The bitch has always snarled, torn at my trouser legs, but now she wants my entrails. For years I've suffered the black dog, fits and starts of depression. This is different, though—

darker, scarier. They used to last awhile, then the clouds would part and clarity return, but this one has been going on and on and on. This despair is me, and more than me. I swear I am also picking up somebody else's mutt, absorbing the entire world's mongrel.

Waves of it lift my body from the futon and crash it down. I take fistfuls of the bedsheet and arch. I'm a fish being scaled and gutted, the skin torn from my body. The despair mixes with my dreams, and I'm living inside a nightmare from which I can't awaken.

I hadn't expected it to be so hard to return to the States. *Takers. Takers. They are all takers. They take and take and take.* I hadn't expected home to feel so foreign. I hadn't expected the reverse culture shock. I hadn't expected the takers—the *taking; taking, taking.*

I dream I'm walking on the bleached bones of the dead. My hair falls out as I walk, skin sloughs, muscle and fat tear away. I become bones, bones walking upon bones.

When I say that I am bones walking upon bones, you think I'm speaking in metaphor, in dream language. You're waiting for the real story to continue, the story of the futon, the story of sweat.

What you don't understand is that my dreams—not just my nightmares, but all of my dreams—are as much the story as that mundane reality. Metaphor is the missing legend. We live in a world that has lost its metaphor, its poetry, and without it, we are plunging into ugliness. The dream world is as real to me as your Starbucks, your children, and your husband who no longer wants to have sex. Metaphor is as real as reality. How many times have you seen a shadow and jumped or stopped driving, thinking the shadow was a thing that could tear your car in half? How often has a shadow been a dark pit in the middle of the road that you could fall into? Plato was wrong. The prisoners in his allegory of the cave were right. The shadows have meaning. The darkness is a thing. The dark dream is a thing.

If I'd been born in another time, in the time of the Aborigines, or during the Dark Ages or the Renaissance, or perhaps in ancient Greece, would my metaphor, my dream world, my visions, this dark night render me chosen, a goddess, a priestess, an oracle to be honored? Here, in this spiritual wasteland that is "home," I'm fucked up, a mess, mentally ill.

Something else exists in this dark night, some calling, something I'm required to do or be, but I'm so weighed down by the heft of it I can't take hold of it.

As my dried bones stand upon dried bones, my skeleton crumbles to a fine powder. Dust to dust. I know a single drop of water will revive me, just one dollop. A drop of water will mix with the dust I've become and re-form me. I'm desperate for that one tiny blessing of holy water. The metaphoric sky turns dark and rumbling and threatens rain. I beg skyward. I open my mouth for a drop. Please, just one damned drop!

Noise outside jolts me into the present—a bang as a door is slammed. Someone wants to get in—someone wants to get out. I listen. It is a reminder that there are people out there living in the "real" world, people out there existing, surviving, thriving.

I focus on my body, do a scan, try to parse the pain. Aching toes, yearning knees, pulsing hips, fisted shoulders. When I was young and a long-distance runner, I learned to parse the pain. I could run miles. When asked how, I would say that pain isn't pain. It's pressure. It's contraction. It's protraction. It's emotion. You have to study it.

What is this pain in my joints? This fatigue? This curdling stomach? Do my body parts have dreams of their own?

By day ten, or is it twenty, I'm not sure, I decide that I must figure out a way to separate myself from this black dog or fall completely into its jaws. I must find distance from it. I think of my journalism training a decade ago, how they taught us to separate ourselves from the story. Who, what, when, where, why? Stand outside the story, be an observer, untangle, pull back. I try this, try to stand outside myself and see this moment of despair dispassionately, but the current is deep and strong. If I'm not pulled under, I'm on the surface, a tiny boat pitched and thrashed by roiling waves.

What do the Zen Buddhists teach? We have a kind of second self, the observing self. Who is the "I" observing me going through this? Who is the "I" having these thoughts?

I'm able to pull myself from the ocean for a blink and see myself from above. Below me, I writhe on the sheets like I'm drowning.

I see from this perspective that the depression is a force that's not just me. It's not "my" depression. It's "the" depression, a blackness that rumbles across nations, circumnavigating the globe, seeking a place to land. It's a fisted cloud that refuses to rain. But my distance can't last, and I crash back down into my torturous body. Some entity is standing at the bottom of the futon taking my ankles, lifting me up, and shaking me, again and again in waves.

During the day, sunlight hits the standing lamp in the corner, and its shadow works as a sundial across the room, shifting positions to mark the passage of time in a place where there is no time. I feel my ancestors. They appear in the shadow and in the cartilage of my body, my great-grandmother lodged in my glowering intestines, great-great-grandfather in my calves. This soul shadow has been building over centuries in the bloodstream. The experiences of my ancestors are in it, a reckoning in the DNA.

I count the cracks in the ceiling. Count and recount the cracks. My head throbs, my body aches, even my hair hurts. I have no one to call. I left my friends behind in London, and in Tokyo before that, and going back further, Missouri. Now our realities are so divided, even when we do talk, across oceans and years, we are no good for each other. Anyway, I'm too deep now for any call to any friend to really help.

I will never tell anyone I'm this messed up. I won't go to a doctor or a therapist. I know if I go for help, they'll make me crazy. Label me crazy and then *make* me crazy. It's this world that's mad, that's creating this internal torture. I'm the world. Why would I go to them for help? They refuse to see how insane the world is and how it's making them insane. They project it onto anyone who has the gall to call the world out for its madness, anyone who is sensitive and broken down by its crazy. I cannot let them script my story. I must hold on. They'll write you in as mad if you allow it.

Tossing on the disheveled sheets, I think, *Is there a world where this dark night is danced? Is there a blue song for this underworld place? A group of people to wail, to tear hair, to rend garments? Must I go through it alone?*

Rope will be easy to purchase. In my mind's eye, the tree and its sturdy branch appear. The scene unfolds like a movie. Me, the rope, the tree. The end.

The visual of it takes over and fills the room, breaks through the walls, envelopes the weedy abandoned lot next door, blossoms out into the broken street, waves to the whores who know it well, cups the city, rises up to the stars.

This is a bad sign. To see something so clearly is to make it a reality.

"The decision is yours. To live or die. *You* have to decide," a voice says. Whose voice, I do not know. The voice does not judge or sway. It states matter-of-factly.

Live.

Or die.

Your choice.

Shit or get off the pot. Die already, or choose to live, but a choice *must* be made.

I know that my death is bigger than just me, affecting generations both backward and forward. It will change the timeline. Like time travelers who go back in time, kill one insect, and change the trajectory of an entire civilization, my death will have consequences. My bones ache with the responsibility, the karma.

I choose, then, to live.

Rage wells with the decision. The anger grinds my bones, burns in the center of my chest. *Fuck you to have to live in this fucked-up world. To have to force myself to face a people so skewed they're intent upon destroying themselves. Fuck you that I have to smile and nod my way through this bitter world, bobbing my head in agreement with everything I abhor like some dashboard dog. Fuck you, world that has lost all of its metaphor.*

"Good," the voice says. "Rage is progress."

I want to smash the voice in the face.

"If I have to live," I say out loud toward the spidery ceiling, my voice cracking after so little use, "I will only do art. I will live only if all I do is art."

I'm not an artist. I don't paint. I don't draw. I don't play music. It doesn't make any sense. Delirious, I plunge into sleep.

When I awaken midmorning, the "fever" has broken. My bones are jelly; I'm cleaned out. I lie there in nothingness—no money, no family, no friends, no job. It is just me. I cross my hands over my naked heart. *All I have is myself. All I have is my integrity.*

Integrity is the word that remains with me. I struggle aboard it like a life raft. I promise myself I'll hold onto integrity for the rest of my life, the only thing that floats in a sea of chaos.

I get up. In the junk drawer in the kitchen, I find the Post-it notes and a pen. Back on the edge of the futon, I write "Get out of bed every day" on a pink Post-it and place it on the window where I can see it.

"Make the bed every day," I write on a lemon note. This too goes on the window.

"Brush your hair every day." I take the few steps to the bathroom and place the lime note on the doorframe. My thick black hair is difficult at the best of times but now is hard, matted, and tangled.

I sit back down, tired. "Brush your teeth every day." I put this sapphire square also on the bathroom doorframe.

"Did you shower today?" Orange, bathroom doorframe.

"Change your clothes." Violet and on the closet door in the living room, which is also my bedroom.

A long, narrow hallway leads back to a small kitchen. I place at intervals along the hallway:

"Eat every day."

"Did you have breakfast?"

"Did you eat enough today?"

"What food have you put into your mouth today?"

I pepper other multihued Post-its throughout the tiny apartment. "Clean the kitchen." "Sweep the floor." "Do laundry."

I lie back on the futon. I cannot move for an hour. Finally, I reach over and grab a stack of Post-its, write "Get out of bed" again. On ten more Post-its I write "Get out of bed." Still lying down, I reach to place them on nearby surfaces: bed frame, wall, side table, hardwood. I understand that this decision to live will take more than just an idea. I know that living will require concerted participation.

Later I wake up from a dream where I'm told to add one more note: "Drink water. Lots of water." I write it on a powder-blue Post-it and put it on the fridge.

I look around. My home has become a rainbow of messages willing me to survive.

I
THE MAGICIAN.

CHAPTER 1

The Magician

A warehouse of psychics: clairvoyants, palmists, numerologists, astrologists, pet mediums. Fluorescent lights throw fat shadows on an industrial carpet of outdated geometric shapes. In my warbled mind, it's a hall of mirrors and everyone has flat heads, enormous hips, dwarf legs.

It's one month after the dark night. I've gotten off the futon every day. I've taken my few possessions—a sari from India, shadow puppets from Bali, the dolls Usui made for me in Tokyo, photos from the travels through Asia, photos of friends in London—and decorated the apartment. I don't hang photos of Finn. I keep that lost love buried deep in the box.

I work odd jobs. I shower. Most days I eat. Every day I get up and fake my desire to be alive. Fake it till you make it, they say. Every day I work to tame the mongrel.

Two dozen psychics sit at folding tables. Crystal healers, spirit photography, aura photos, rune readings. I've come to this psychic fair because normal isn't working. I'm here because normal wants me dead. Brochures for psychic surgery, alien abduction, reading your pet. I try not to bolt out the door. Many of the readers wear some version of purple, a couple are in quilted jester's outfits. It's like a circus without the monkeys. I pass a woman staring at a muddied Polaroid of her aura, and at a table a man clenches a woman's face and stares intently at her left eyeball.

Goods are for sale on long tables covered in purple fabric. Tarot cards, incense, candles, crystals, jewelry, wands, and objects I don't understand. I browse the pop-up bookstore. The covers of the spiritual and metaphysical self-help books and memoirs are in lavender with swirling spiral designs. I've always wondered who made the decision that the covers of metaphysical books always have to be purple and have swirls. Everywhere the smell of patchouli, essential oils, and competing incense.

A spiral-bound book at a main table has the bios and pictures of the psychics in the room. I choose randomly, a face I like. It costs thirty dollars for thirty minutes, most of my food money. Maslow's hierarchy of needs, with food at the bottom and self-actualization at the top, but I'm sure that's not right. My soul is so malnourished it's killing me. I have an hour wait to see the psychic, so I stand against a wall and watch.

I've spent years hating psychics. We made brutal fun of them in the newsrooms where I worked in London and Tokyo. Hucksters. Charlatans. White-trash wack jobs. Circus sideshows, no better than bearded ladies or the world's fattest woman. That I'm even *at* this fair proves how desperate I am. Just because you survive the dark night of the soul doesn't mean you're happy. Doesn't mean you have answers.

She wears Prussian blue, Rayne. Her hair is wavy and so black it's purple. A light exhales around her. Her hands are bejeweled. Opal rings, bracelets with bells, fingernails of lush burgundy. My nails are bitten and scratched up, my skin thin and leathery. Veins pop out of the backs of my hands, working-class hands. Dirt hands.

Tarot cards rest in her palm. *She spends her days using her hands this way*. I was born to farmers. Hands shoveled, picked, weeded. Hands did dark things, the killing of animals, the brutalizing of souls. As a journalist, my hands were for regurgitating the world's trauma. *Extra, extra! Hate, war, rape, murder! Get it here.*

Her cards are blue backed and covered in white stars. She hands them to me to mix and then asks me to divide them into three piles and choose one. She rests her chin on the cards' edge, closes her eyes. She smells like musk. Chunks of amethyst, citrine, agate, rose quartz circle a candle. I think of the forest rocks my father used to collect: canary gypsum, streaked limonite, black feldspar and, in a hidden drawer, a bulbous lump of gold. It's the first time I've thought good thoughts about my father in a long time.

Rayne asks my name. *Aren't you supposed to be psychic?* "Pearl."

"Have you had a reading before?" She throws the cards one by one onto the table. Kings, queens, and knights. The sun and the moon. Why do I feel like a starving kid at a banquet, begging for crumbs?

"Yes." I lean forward, elbows on my thighs beneath the table, my face close to the table's surface. I'd met psychics in Japan and Asia, a turbaned seer in India who cast his spell.

"So you know the drill."

I don't, but I nod.

"OK, let's see what we have here." She sits up straight, fans out her fingers over the reading. "Well, they're happy you're here." She laughs.

"Who are 'they'?" I ask.

"Your guides. You're being awakened to your Divine Feminine. Do you know what that is?"

Trying not to roll my eyes, I shake my head and look toward the exit. The desire to run is strong. I palm the pack of Marlboro Lights in my pocket.

"OK, let's start with a solid description of the Divine Feminine. First, we're not talking about men and women here. We all have feminine and masculine traits. Right now, the world is tipped heavily toward masculine traits, like taking action, competition, individualism. The Divine Feminine is more receptive. It's about creation, intuition, community, sensuality. We honor our feelings instead of our brains. Do you understand?"

I nod.

"It shows in the cards that you've been in a very masculine career. What is that?"

"Journalist."

"Can you see how masculine that is? The focus just on the brain? Nothing about sensuality and creativity?"

She makes my head hurt.

She continues, "We've been in a masculine paradigm for many years, and the lack of balance is wreaking havoc. Environmental disasters, violence, suicides, mental illness. You understand this. I know you do."

I nod again.

She reaches out a hand across the table. "The call often starts with despair, especially for those who are highly sensitive. To find oneself, one must lose oneself. Everything must go. We have to sit raw and open like a newborn baby."

"What do I do? What are these people who are being called supposed to do?"

"Build a better world, my friend," Rayne says.

But how? I want to ask but can't seem to say the words.

Rayne stares at me. "It takes a while to figure out what our individual paths are to fulfill the calling. Follow the heart. Follow the intuition. Deepen into your inner goddess."

I want to gag. It's like I have two choices, the brutal world out there or women who use the word "goddess."

Rayne takes the cards off the table and hands them to me, and I mix. She throws ten new cards. The conference room is filled with milling people and low-grade chatter.

"It is like you are two people, one divided from the other. There's a side of yourself you've disowned, and this journey in Seattle is about owning that other side." She looks at me full in the face, her eyes like pools of dark chocolate. "The body must be taken care of to house such a gift. Do you understand? The body is exhausted and filled with poisons."

I begin to hear other voices above and beyond the crowd, a chanting, speaking, and singing. I kneed my cigarette pack. I cannot go into a vision now. Not *now*!

I tell her about the visions I've been having all my life. The first one happened when I was thirteen, but I may have had them since I was little—I'm not sure. The energy takes me like a lover, and I see spirits and they tell me things. I've spent my whole life trying to manage them. I've spent my whole life just trying to be normal.

Rayne looks excited, pulls up the reading, mixes the cards, and throws a few down with a great flourish. She laughs. "You're psychic!"

I cringe. I don't want to feed the monster.

"You've been resisting this for years. It's time to stop resisting."

This came up in the dark night of the soul, this side of myself I've always kept at arm's length. My face must be conveying my dread, because she adds quickly, "I know accepting it feels like being in an ocean, dissolving into it. Ceasing to exist."

I cry, "I am trying to exist!"

She points to a card that has a skeleton on it. "This is the Death card. What you're going through is a death."

I don't respond, shaken.

"OK, you've had this mysticism your whole life. Why are you so intent upon resisting it?"

I hold up my fingers and count off the reasons. "I'll go mad. Two, I'll go broke. C, I'll be a loser. Three, normal people will stone me to death. E, I'll die. I'm terrified I'll die."

"From what I can see, you're already broke. Why not take that list and flip the script. I'll go sane. I'll be rich. I'll be a winner. I'll be honored. I'll live a beautiful life. I'll really live."

I tell her how I don't fit anywhere, not in Missouri where I grew up, not as an expat in Asia and Europe, not anywhere on this ever-lovin' planet.

She pulls a few more cards and tosses them on top of the others. "Yes, you don't fit. It's true." She wobbles her head, touches a card. "What if 'not fitting' is the point? What if by not fitting you go on to build a new system, something that replaces the old?"

I think of Dr. Linda Dunn, a therapist I interviewed in London for an article. She also said that not fitting might be my purpose. How being an expat, traveling the world, and living outside the culture, the not fitting anywhere, could actually be a person's raison d'être. I think about the repatriation I'm going through now and how much I don't fit into the American way, how I may never fit back into my home culture.

"I can't live in this world."

"You're right, you can't."

"That's not what you're supposed to say." I curl my fingers. I have rage toward her.

She looks at me with doe eyes. "It's not working."

"What's not working?"

"The world. As is. Honor these dark feelings. They are truth. Wisdom. Honor the bones.

"Your hatred of your visions, Pearl, your dislike of psychics—in effect, you're hating yourself, but the wild thing is this. The psychic side isn't the only side you're resisting. There's another gifted side that you're holding at bay. It's exhausting expending all of this energy to keep your authentic self down."

I cross my arms, tighten my body. I feel she's trying to convert me to something I don't want. *I refuse to be you. You will NOT turn me into one of you. Over my dead body!*

She picks up the cards, mixes and throws. "You are one of a group of people who are being called right now to stand up and create a paradigm shift." She puts her hands up, holds her own hands, rows of thick, fat rings. Her way of talking sounds like singing, and it's soothing my rage. "This is too long of a discussion to have here. I feel the natives getting restless behind me." She holds up one adorned finger. "First you must find your voice. Who are *you*? What do *you* think? But, most importantly, what do *you* love?"

"My entire life I've just wanted to be normal."

A sudden laugh like a raven's caw. "Oh, my friend, that ship sailed lifetimes ago." She holds up a card. The picture on it is of an exploding tower. People are falling from the top of it.

"We're coming to a time when all must fall apart. Everything *will* fall apart. The earth cannot sustain this system. We can't sustain it. We must rebuild from scratch.

To go forward you have to go backward. This is not just you. Many of us."

"Why do I have to be one of the people making a difference? Why can't I just be happy?"

"Who says the two are mutually exclusive?"

I snort.

"Normal never ever existed for you in the first place. But it's bigger than that. Normal isn't working. There is no home in normal."

The woman behind me clears her throat. When I don't turn around, she clears it again.

"So I'm cursed."

"Stop calling it a curse. This loneliness you feel—you miss yourself. You've banished the self to a closet of discarded items, and you miss her. You have to choose how *you* want to live within your sensitivity."

I point at the cards. "How *do* I want to live within that sensitivity? Please tell me." A loud cough behind me.

Rayne hands me her business card. "Call me."

As I stand, the woman behind me grips the back of the chair and pulls it away from me. Rayne says to me, "Wait, Pearl. I don't usually do this." She picks up a rose quartz crystal from the table and places it in my palm. "A gift."

The woman takes the chair and sits as I say thank you. I put the stone in my pocket with my cigarettes.

I roam the vendor stalls, deep in thought. I know it's time to stop resisting, and I'm terrified. At one table, I use my final twenty dollars to buy a tarot deck from a long-haired guy wearing a fool's hat.

★ ★ ★

I get off the bus a few stops past mine on Aurora. It's pissing down and I become soaked as I walk, pondering the riddles Rayne has given me. I find the building, an ugly warehouse with yellow metal siding, a chain-link fence. I join a line of people already waiting in the rain. It's backed up across the parking lot.

I start crying. The sky's so heavy, and the rain so consistent, I think maybe the other people can't see I'm crying. I put up my collar and try to disappear beneath it. People pass with bags of food.

I'm finally proving my mother right. I'm at the food bank because I cannot survive in the real world. I'm here because I need food, and I feel like I've fallen so low.

They give me a brown paper bag full of canned vegetables, mostly black-eyed peas, and a massive frozen chicken in a plastic bag. It's not like I'm ungrateful. Of course I'm grateful. It's just that food banks are for poor people, not people like me.

As I walk the two miles back to my apartment, the chicken grows heavier and heavier. It's so frozen. Its life and death on some overcrowded factory farm, its frozen-solid body in a plastic bag like some kind of omen. All existence is this chicken: a grueling life and an insensitive death. I pass two women working a street corner, smeared lipstick and fishnet stockings. A car pulls to the curb, and both lean into the window. I think, *This chicken is so heavy, I could swing it and kill somebody. This chicken could be a murder weapon.*

Whitman Street in Wallingford is named after Walt, but its leaves are blackened and sickly, its grass full of burrs and weeds. The area is a down-and-out strip of low-rent houses, broken fences, and weedy vacant lots.

Gem is on the porch, framed by the duplex's flaking indigo siding. She's my neighbor, her apartment on the other side of my wall. She sits on a metal chair at a flimsy metal table on the crooked porch.

When I first met her, she told me her full name was Gemini. "Hippie parents. Kill me now."

When I told her my name, she said, "Oh I get it. Like the black pearl, everything grates on you, wears on you, annoys the shit out of you, but it all turns you into a precious thing." I laughed. I liked her, but she scared me shitless.

As she sits on the porch now, she has her arm crooked out in the rain, and her elbow is soaked. Her lips are thick, her lipstick deep purple, and the cigarette she's smoking dips deep into the dark crevasse.

"What's that you got there?" she asks.

I hold up the frozen chicken. "I went to the food bank." I don't tell her that I cried. I don't tell her going to a food bank feels like hitting bottom more than anything else that has happened.

"Give it here," she says. She grabs the bag and nearly drops it because it's so heavy.

"I didn't even know it was a chicken at first, it was so frozen, and the frost is so thick on the bag," I say.

"Heavy," Gem says, and swings it around. She has a tattoo of a snake around her skinny wrist.

"On the way home, I kept thinking it was so heavy it could be used as a murder weapon. I could spin it around and bash someone's head in with it."

Gem laughs. Loose pigtails frame her face. She's dark and smells of sex. Men come and go from her side of the duplex all the time. "Then you could come home, boil it, and eat the murder weapon."

I go into my apartment. Before I can nudge the door closed, Gem follows. It's the first time she's been inside my side of the duplex. She looks wide-eyed at the dozens of Post-it notes. She walks around and reads them.

I put the damp, disintegrating paper bag of canned vegetables and the frozen chicken on the travel crate I use as a coffee table. I look at the chicken and again feel the poor beast's hard life and its even harder death. *Me and you, chicken. We're no different. Your dark night is my dark night.*

"Look, I'm tired," I say to Gem.

She ignores me and goes down the hall reading the notes.

I call after her, "I'd like to lie down if you don't mind."

She comes back. "Sit." She points at the futon sofa.

I do as I'm told, massaging the tarot deck in my pocket. She has a magnetism that I can't seem to resist. She circles her arm, motioning to the kaleidoscope of notes. "Explain."

I give her an abridged version of the dark night, the recurring despair, the reading with Rayne.

"Well, I knew you weren't exactly Miss Happiness when I passed you on the porch." She looks down at me.

I look up at her. I don't know what to say.

"Come," she says, and walks out the door.

I sit and stare at the open door, but then she yells, "Come!" and I get up and obey.

On the porch, she holds the door to her side of the duplex open. "Enter."

I walk in and rear back. It's like a bomb went off. Boxes and bags, tins and crates. A box of computer keyboards, a bag of plastic eyeballs, a cup of bottle cleaners, tins overflowing with wooden buttons, severed arms and legs from dress dummies. Hundreds of thread spools, dozens of squirt bottles, a steering wheel. There seems to be just one chair. This is a studio apartment, and I don't see a bed. Where does she sleep?

An aversion creeps up on me. I'm messy, but this is anarchy and it scares me. My mother hated my mess, shamed me for it. I work hard to keep myself in check. Something boils in my soul in seeing Gem's absolute disregard for decorum.

She holds her arms out and spins like she's flying. "My woman cave. I use found objects to make art." I have to stop myself from cleaning up.

It's no surprise to me that I live next to an artist. It's happened all my life. First with my half-sister Meghan and with my childhood friend Jason, and then Yuriko, my Tokyo friend and roommate, who left paint tubes all over the tatami. Yuriko, though, didn't trigger me like this.

There was also my brutal father. Gem's found objects take me back to the basement corner where he kept objects he found in the woods, old railway ties and turquoise glass breakers, and how my mother did everything to control the mess from getting upstairs into the house. He never did anything with them, just collected forest junk like a person would collect stamps.

"My motto? Don't hold it. Let it out. Give the girl something to do. Purge that shit. Let the bitch run free over the wild Serengeti."

I bark a laugh, the first time I've laughed in months.

A guy comes out of her bathroom—tall, so thin his chest is concave, a loose hoody over a khaki singlet, low-riding jeans, high-top sneakers. He's hot.

"When will I see you again, love?" he asks in a British accent.

Gem is looking at me and not him. She doesn't answer. The guy looks at me. "OK," he says. "I'll call you." He puts up his hoody. As he passes me, he puts his hand on my arm. "What is it with you?"

I watch him leave, confused and turned on by his touch.

II
B
J
TORA
THE HIGH PRIESTESS

CHAPTER 2

The High Priestess

My shrink in London, Shirley, had talked me into leaving London and moving back to the States only a few months ago.

"You must find the lost parts of yourself," Shirley said. "You will not find them in London, I assure you."

I didn't disagree with her. I'd been abroad for a decade. The rural upbringing of hunting and butchering, a scholarship to journalism school in the American Midwest, then Tokyo, travel through Asia, London. I was no longer American, but I wasn't English either, a woman with many countries and no home.

I needed the cues, the stench, the thick consistency of reality that was my home country. I was a puzzle with missing pieces. When you live abroad, you're able to live disembodied from the past. Little exists to trigger you. No TV show, no conversational twang, no cultural reference applies to you. You live walking a few feet above the cultural pavement. You get a free pass. But freedom has its consequences.

"And who knows, Pearl, there may be a whole world of new ideas you'll come into contact with when you go back that you simply cannot get here. You're leaving the old world for the new. Perhaps there's something in that."

Shirley had long silver hair and hairy ankles, and I loved her. She was a soft, heart-based woman in a culture that was intellectual and critical. Far outside the British stiff-upper-lip norm, she emanated hope and trust and something like faith. She studied alternative energy work and held spiritual circles in her therapy space. Every time I disembarked at Elephant and Castle, as I came to her street and walked toward her building, my heart would melt, and I'd feel soft, and I'd feel something close to "home."

For the year I saw Shirley, she was always trying to get rid of me.

"I can't help you, Pearl," she said more than once. "Let me find you someone else."

"No," I would beg her. "Please, no." I trusted her. There were not many people I trusted.

"I'm just not qualified," she'd say, leaning forward in her wicker chair. She was a counselor, not a licensed therapist, and she worried that I needed serious help.

She knew about the visions. That they were sudden and physical and full of information I had no idea how to process. We'd already spent a lot of time discussing the visions. How they were different from intuition. How they took me over and thrust me into a different reality. She helped me learn how to manage them better, but they never fully went away.

It wasn't the visions that Shirley couldn't handle—it was my depression. I first came to see her when I'd broken up with Finn and the loss had triggered a well of abandonment. I grew so skinny you could count my ribs, dark circles beneath my eyes. I looked haunted. I was too broken. Too upset. Too lost. She first threatened to refer me to someone more experienced, and when I wouldn't go, she threatened to have me shipped off to a mental health facility if I didn't gain some weight. I clung to her like a life raft.

This time, when she said she was sending me packing to the States, I had to agree with her. It was true. I needed to go home.

"As a kid," I'd told her, "I promised myself I'd be healthy, that I'd do whatever it took to be healthy when I grew up." And I didn't mean physically healthy, I meant I would be mentally and emotionally healthy. As I told her this I was twelve again, standing in the pasture, looking at the cows, and making my solemn promise: *I would grow up and be healthy.*

"I also promised myself I wouldn't do the traditional marriage and kid thing. People just kept passing on the trauma generation after generation, and I promised myself I wouldn't do that."

As a child, with each trauma around my father's rage and my mother's denial, with no one to turn to, fragments of myself, balls of light, had spun from the top of my head and flown up and out. With each loss, I became more of a shell. I knew even then that at some point, I'd have to figure out how to retrieve the parts. I'd have to go find the lost pieces, put them all out in front, connect the dots, create a constellation. Re-form myself from the dust and light of the universe.

Shirley and I had agreed, though, that although returning to the States was important, settling back in the Midwest was not a good idea, no matter how many of the broken pieces of me could be excavated from the soil there.

"You'll have enough to deal with just getting settled in a new country," she'd said.

I had no idea where to move in the States. I'd lived in the middle of Missouri and only traveled to Iowa, Kansas, and Illinois. I knew much more about Japan, Southeast Asia, and Europe than I did about the States.

"The plan was to get as far away as possible from everything American," I told Shirley.

When you're gone for years and it's time to come "home," you have no idea where home is. The traveling life is no longer home, the man you broke up with is no longer home, the birthplace you left is no longer home. Where, then, is home? When you're moving to a country you don't know, what do you do?

With Shirley's help, I ended up choosing Seattle. It was West Coast liberal and cheaper than California. It felt like throwing a dart at a map and seeing where it landed.

"Home has become a random act," I'd said to her.

"Or has it?" she replied, and lit some incense.

We talked about my stopping off in Missouri.

"Do you really think it's a good idea to do that? Why not travel on directly to Seattle? I'm worried about you being retraumatized just at the point when you're already dealing with one of life's biggest stressors—moving abroad."

"I have to." How could I explain? I grew up in wild nature. I left the forests and rivers, the cacophony of creatures that blossomed in the pitch-black night. I left it all for big cities. When you've traded earth for concrete for a decade, you need the water of your ancestors. You need the land, the grit of the soil. The mud. You need the soaked forest that fed your child soul. You needed blood.

Still, home was a scary place. I told Shirley, "There's a magnetism and a revulsion." I couldn't smoke in her office, so I took out a cigarette and rolled it in my fingers. "It's like when you visit an old lover. The love's still there, but you know the pain this person is capable of inflicting."

Love was what always got me in trouble. If I could just stop loving things so heavy. I loved the midwestern earth, but I was raw from the torture the place had inflicted upon me.

She'd tried but couldn't talk me out of the Missouri visit. She with her roots. She with her family just down the road. So tired of people with families giving me advice, trying to protect me. I had my legend, my story: ugly, misshapen, twisted. Hard truth written in the flesh. How could I continue my narrative if I avoided the roots?

When it was time to go after my last session, Shirley had opened her arms and I fell into them. I wasn't a toucher or a hugger growing up. It just wasn't done, but I was learning. She didn't wear deodorant, and I fell into the citrus and musk sweat of her. I let my head rest on her shoulder. I could feel I was too heavy for her. I knew I was too heavy for some people, but I let myself rest there for one moment, and another. We were both wiping away tears as I opened the door and merged with others on the busy street.

It'd been so long since I'd driven a car, and big wheelers and trucks on I-70 slammed by at eighty miles an hour. The drive from St. Louis to Jason's was two and a half hours, but only if you drove at top speed. I had to pay attention, but the land kept pulling me.

The way the earth sings the song of the frozen river no matter how far you travel. The way the icy north wind cuts through your coat and breathes the old you into your cold soul. The way oak bark ices over, becomes the flesh of your flesh. The way you can leave but never escape the deep freeze of home.

Big sky, frozen fields, frozen cows dotted along virgin snow. The earth was beaten down by winter, bent like an old woman—vicious snowstorms had pummeled it for centuries. When the Germans and Irish had settled the cantankerous land here, only the ornery survived.

I read the Bible as a kid, in secret in the upstairs bathroom, cover to cover. There were no books in the house, except the Farmers' Almanac, and once for a brief time a tattered *Curious George*. I fantasized about a house with a library, or even a house with bookshelves. Even that. I was voracious for story.

As I devoured the Bible, I saw the Midwest as the Old Testament, an eye for an eye. Retribution. The back of a hand. A fist. The Dark Ages. I'd left because I thought the New Testament was "out there." I'd been traveling the world looking for this gentler New Testament, and I still hadn't found it.

For hours I drove, deeper and deeper into a rooted world that held the old, the discarded. Me.

Memories flooded back, stitching themselves together like a rag quilt: the younger me who loved to run through the woods, talk to trees, collect lightning bugs then let them go. A girl who hated butchering animals, but did because there was no choice, whose whole life was a gritty relationship with the land. Darker memories too, of a terrified mother and father whose only language was the violence they themselves had learned as children—dark squares on the quilt that went back generations.

I finally pulled up to the fence that was still damaged, the yard that was still weedy. A dog bombed through the screen door, slid on the icy steps, and flung himself at my car. Jason followed. I'd called from a gas station ten minutes away and they'd been waiting.

He was the old Jason, the red hair, the leanness, the paint-spattered clothes. He was one of the few people in the world who knew me, really knew me. As I got out of the car and stood next to him, I felt sixteen again, and Lady Luck was still alive, and Jason and I were still. Us.

"Lady, chill out for God's sake," Jason said as I got out of the car and the dog jumped on me.

"This is Lady. Lady, meet Pearl." I put out my hand and she put up her paw. I bent, cupped her mug, and kissed her cold, wet nose. Dogs held the stories of families. Dogs carried generations. Years ago, my family had owned a dog named Lady Luck. He was male, but Father liked to gamble, and named him as a joke. Lady Luck held the narrative of generations of my kinfolk in his gut. If the dog represented the man, then Father hated himself. Lady Luck was tethered in the dirt, in mud, in stifling heat, in bitter snow.

He was kicked and beaten up and cursed. It destroyed me watching a dog chained like that and taking boots to the gut. It was a metaphor for generations, for my childhood, a life lived tied up, an existence only as long as the expanse of a short chain. A childhood of being punched in the gut.

One day I saved Lady Luck, carried him and myself out of the muck, deposited us both at Jason's house. Then Lady Luck and Jason's mom fell in love. I was in Asia when Lady Luck died. Jason told me about it over a bad telephone connection somewhere in Nepal. He'd gotten Lady soon afterward.

Jason bent for a hug. I couldn't feel him through the thickness of our coats. The mist of my memory cleared and I saw he wasn't the old Jason after all. There was a distance. He smelled of mothballs. He wouldn't look me in the eye. His goofy smile was gone. Time had not stood still for Jason. When you leave your home because you cannot take the crazy, you leave the people who have known you all of your life. You leave being *known*. You carry a snapshot of what once was, and in your mind as you float around the world, the people stay the same, never grow up, and never change.

Inside the house, it took me a while to figure out what was missing. I lived in this house with Jason and his mom during my last year of high school and into college. They were a second family to me. Or a first. The dining room had always been full of easels, art tubes, canvases, and brushes, spilling into the living room. Now there was no art and no easels, and it worried me. Art was who Jason was.

He brought me a tall-neck MGD from the fridge. I sat on the same sofa I'd sat on ten years earlier. He sat in the one armchair.

The last time I saw Jason, we'd made love in my favorite clearing and he'd begged me to stay. I tried not to think of it, but the images of his torso and thighs took over my vision. We looked at each other, and I swore he was thinking the same thing. We made small talk about the flight. He didn't ask me about London, about the life I lived there. It was the challenge of being an expat—old friends didn't really ask you about your life abroad. They didn't know what to ask.

After an awkward silence, he blurted, "Mom's bedridden."

"Oh I'm so sorry, Jason."

"For months now." He took a hard swig of his beer. "I'll show you." He got up and led me down the hallway. "She still drinks, but now she gets only a six pack of Bud a week."

"That was what she used to drink every day, besides the wine," I said.

"I know." Jason opened a bedroom door. I was surprised by the beauty of the room. Her paintings hung on all the walls. It was like entering the womb of a gifted madwoman. She was a plein air painter, and her vibrant landscapes were messy and crooked. The room smelled of lavender, and speckled cold light dashed through lace curtains. A bouquet of sloppy flowers sat on a dresser.

"What a lovely room," I said.

"We fix it up special, don't we, Ma?" Jason said, going over to the bed. Mrs. Paulson was so diminished she was like a child lost deep in pillows, comforter, and mattress. "We know how important beauty is, don't we?"

"Beauty," his mother whispered from deep within the pillows.

I leaned over to say hi, and the light came into her face. "Pearl Elizabeth Swinton!" she said. Her hand emerged and grabbed two of my fingers, like a toddler holding onto its mother. "We lost Lady Luck, Pearl." Tears welled in her rheumy eyes. "He was a good dog. You saved his life."

"You did," I said.

"He saved all of our lives," she said.

"Ma, Lady Luck is right here," Jason said, just as Lady came bounding into the room, tail flipping in eager joy.

"Son, I'm not an idiot. I know that's not Lady Luck. You think I'm an idiot, but I'm not. I'm a drunk, there's a difference."

I burst out laughing. Mrs. Paulson looked up at me, startled. "Wait, are you really Pearl?"

I squeezed her hand. "Oh, I'm Pearl, Mrs. Paulson. Trust me."

"I'm not an idiot. That's not the same dog. And you're not Pearl." She looked me up and down. I was hungover and jet-lagged, and my clothes hung on my skeletal frame. I'd looked better. "We lost Pearl years ago," Mrs. Paulson said.

I extracted my hand.

"Ma, be nice," Jason said.

She looked at me. "I'm not an idiot, son." Her voice grew softer. "Whoever you are, you need beauty." She closed her eyes. "Lots of beauty. Every day." She fell asleep.

As we left the room, Jason whispered, "I should've warned you. Today's the one day of the week she doesn't get her beer. It makes her crazy." He shook his head. I agreed with her. I did need beauty. The problem I was having was how to find it in a world that was so full of ugly.

Jason stopped at the basement door. "Want to see my studio?"

"Of course!"

As we maneuvered down the narrow stairs, I said, "I was wondering if you'd given up art, because I didn't see all of the easels and supplies in the dining room. I didn't even know the house had a basement."

"Yeah, it was pretty trashed. Took me months to clean it out. Found decomposing critters beneath tarps and shit."

It was cold. I still had my coat on and hugged it to me. The space ran the length and breadth of the house and was filled with easels, studio lamps, shelves of paints, coffee cans of brushes, special shelving for the finished canvases, other canvases in process. Paint was spattered everywhere. It smelled of turpentine.

"It's like a rainbow hit the basement and exploded," I said.

I roamed in wonder. There had to be a hundred finished canvases stacked against different walls. My pulse raced as I touched them. A group of finished canvases leaning on the back wall caught my attention. I stood stock still, mesmerized by the work, unable to move or breathe.

"Are you OK, Pearl?" Jason asked. "Is it a vision?" I didn't answer. "Pearl?"

"No," I said. "No. It's not a vision." I tried to breathe.

"Are you still having them?"

"Yes, but I'm better now at gauging when they're going to happen and going to the bathroom or finding another private place."

"I still can't believe you have these premonitions and still choose to go and travel. That's crazy brave of you, Pearl."

"It's your art, Jason. That's what was moving through me," I said.

"I just had a show in St. Louis." He took the stack I was looking at and lined the canvases side by side against the wall. He'd evolved, become a different artist from the one who used to paint the sky. He'd become a different person. I'd locked Jason into the age when I left him. He wasn't the teenager in my imagination anymore.

In front of us were portraits of rough characters, the wizened, the old, the redneck, and they were painted as saints. Borders with vines of leaves and flowers like illuminated manuscripts, and the people wearing halos. Some had miniature angels and devils flying toward the canvases' corners.

"They're icons," he said. "I'm fascinated with the art of Orthodox churches, going way back. Medieval. I'm basically doing medieval icon portraits of the people in my life."

The people were not attractive. Midwesterners sometimes were good-looking in a healthy, big way, but often they were not. Often they were peasants with ratty hair, far-set eyes, fat faces, and bad teeth.

The figures had a two-dimensional perspective, like early paintings before they discovered perspective. He'd used gold paint on the borders and halos. On some, he glued gems and stones at the corners. One painting was of an older man with a handlebar mustache. You still see guys in my hometown with staches they'd curled up with hair gel.

"That's my uncle Mel." A small black devil was pulling on one side of Mel's mustache with a rope.

There was a portrait of a young boy with hooded eyes, a golden angel in the corner of the blue background. One was of Jason's mother, a halo like a large, flat golden plate behind her head. Her cheek was nestled against a wine bottle.

"What was the show called?" I asked.

"Iconic Pathways. The most common subjects for icons were always Jesus, Mary, saints, angels. I wanted to swap that for normal people. That's the whole point, right? That we're all holy. Or should be, I guess."

I loved the medieval. I was drawn inexorably in Europe to the old corners, to the grit of filth in the cracks of an age-worn world. I'd spent my years in London at the art galleries, pulled always to the art of the Middle Ages, to the darkness. In Jason's basement, I stood back and saw the whole studio like an old-world church, a temple, a clearing in a forest of towering redwoods. Something deep was going on here. Holy.

I didn't want to feel the love. I didn't want my heart engaged. Not here. Not in the Midwest. Love was dangerous here. Love left you open to the abuse they didn't know they were handing you. It was harder to leave love, to extricate the tendrils. Anger was easier. Resentment. Old wounds.

In the evening, Jason and I huddled around a fire pit in the backyard. It was too cold, but Jason was insistent. The sun was low, deep between the branches of a leafless oak. Shadows were long. Lady was at Jason's feet. It wasn't just the visuals of the life you left, it was a dog bark in the echoing distance, the smell of wood smoke in your hair. It was the cadence, the aromas. The rough and raised textures.

Jason put a grill on top of the fire, and he was grilling fat burgers on the edge of the pit, blood dripping and spitting. He'd plopped an empty tub between our lawn chairs, filled it with handfuls of snow, and wedged in bottles of MGD.

I sunk down into my coat. His orange truck was in the driveway. It used to be my truck. I'd sold it to him when I left. "How have you kept this thing running?"

"I like old things. I fix them." That was the difference between us: I wanted to be done with the old. I wanted the new.

"I miss cruising in that old thing." We'd taken that truck to the clearing that last time. I looked at Jason in memory. He jerked his eyes away and poked the fire.

I stood, ran my hand down the back of his coat. He looked up at me, eyes shaded, half his face red from the fire, the other half freckled like the color of the dirt. He was like one of his paintings, half devil and half angel. I leaned and kissed him. He responded.

He stood abruptly, put both hands on my upper arms and pushed me back. He grabbed the grill fork and took the meat off the fire. "I'm with someone." He was breathing erratically.

I said nothing.

"Her name's Molly. She's a teacher." He piled the meat on a plate.

I said nothing.

"Second grade."

He took the plate to the picnic table and assembled the burgers with sliced cheese, ketchup, and buns. He took chips out of a bag, put them on a plate, came back, and handed me a plate. He pulled a beer from the tub and took his plate and beer to his chair. He twisted off the cap and downed half of it. I took a beer too and drank. The plates sat untouched on our laps, the warmth comforting through my jeans.

"Does she know I'm here?"

"Oh, yeah." He took a drink. "She kept asking if you were pretty." He took another drink. "I told her, 'Ugly as a mutt. Disfigured. Obese.'"

I laughed.

He sat. I sat. We ate in silence. The beef was red with blood. You didn't get beef anywhere that was as good as beef in Missouri.

"You have the saddest eyes of anyone I've ever met, Pearl." I looked to see him staring at me.

I touched his hand. He didn't move it. He said, "I'm only going to say this once. I'm begging you not to do this, Pearl. You come into town and you do this and you leave. You always leave. And you mess me up for years . . ."

I removed my hand. *Jason can't survive my love*, I thought. *It isn't my love he can't survive, it's my perpetual abandonment.*

"Do you love her?"

He wobbled his body and head and I wasn't sure if it was a yes or a no, or if he'd rather not have me ask that question.

In most stories, this was where the boy realized his old soulmate had returned home. This was where the girl realized she'd found home again in this man from her past. This was where backstory met front story and healing happened. This was where two friends on either side of a tub of cheap beer, watching a fire spit and hiss, found each other again. This was where I found the missing parts of myself in Jason and sang them into my soul and recovered.

This was not such a story. This was a different kind of love story.

As we hunched in the cold over the burgers in our laps, I knew he would marry this Molly. He would have children with her. I saw his legend unfold. I loved him. I wanted the best for him. The way the fire turned his red hair into gold.

We sat and watched the rising moon. We reminisced.

We stayed there freezing into the wee hours, feeding the fire, laughing at life's stupid things.

The next morning, after a sleepless night on the couch, after I said goodbye to Mrs. Paulson and to Lady, after I said farewell to Jason on the porch, after a quick hug, after I got into the rental car, I turned to wave, but he was no longer there. He didn't wait to watch me drive away. It was the end of a book, a story I didn't want to end, but I knew I had to close the cover.

And move on.

Shirley had been right. Coming to Missouri was a bad idea. Overwhelmed with emotion, I had to pull into the gas station and use her breathing exercises to calm myself. There was no way I could face my mother. I didn't have the strength for it, with so much unknown on the horizon. I went to the pay phone and called her, left a message that I wouldn't be coming after all. I told her that after I got settled in Seattle, I'd come for a visit then. It'd already been years since I'd seen her and we'd rarely spoken—what did another few years matter?

I sat in the car, unable to move. Not seeing my mother wasn't just that I didn't want to be reminded of the difficulties of childhood, the abandonment, the verbal abuse, the neglect, the denial. I'd run so far to get away from that. It wasn't just the pain that was stopping me.

It was the love I also could not revisit. That childhood life wasn't just full of woe. It had joy in it. It had the earth in it. A vault of memories. It was a life where a little girl's love and hope were still locked away, like a princess who needed to be saved.

As I drove out of town, I didn't expect to turn left at Holy Cross, to drive past the church and the elementary school where I'd spent thirteen years of my life, down the steep incline to the convent. I didn't expect to enter the nondescript, low brick building, to seek out Sister Alice amid the smells of lemon cleaner and musty books, to be surprised to find her still there after so many years, and then to be sitting in her spartan room, on top of a handmade rag quilt on her single bed, while she sat across from me on an upright wooden chair. I didn't expect my trip to end with religion.

Sister Alice was a spirit from my past, with googly eyes and wide feet. She was a woman who'd once saved my life when my father's brutality crushed me, my mother abandoned me, my visions overtook me, and I ended up on a psyche ward. She'd reached down inside me and pulled me back to the surface. We'd written letters sporadically while I was abroad, although they'd tapered off over the past few years. In her last letter, she'd written she'd been moved to the Holy Cross convent.

She gave me a worried once-over. "So, tell me about your journey."

"Not over yet, I hope." I held a tall glass of water that Sister Alice had given me and looked down into its clear depths. I could smell the Vicks VapoRub on her. She sat up, looked you in the face, and held the room with the confidence of someone beautiful, and she was quite ugly.

I told her about my journalism career in Tokyo, the year through the Philippines, Nepal, Thailand, and India. I told her about Finn, but not much, because I wasn't ready to talk about him, to remember him. I explained to her my life in the journalists' cooperative in London. I did not tell her about the article we wrote, the article I was most proud of, about the abuse in homes for handicapped children, and how the managers had just moved the abusers to a different home. I didn't tell her because it was too close to what was happening with the Catholic Church and was one of the things that made me lose all faith. I told her I was moving to Seattle, with no job and no friends after ten years abroad.

She sat up as if she'd just thought of something. "You!" she exclaimed.

"Me?"

"I have something." She laughed and said under her breath, *Our Lord Jesus, it was her the whole time. Thank you for guiding her to me.* She went to a dresser, rooted around in the top drawer.

"How could you have something for me? You didn't know I was coming."

She came back with something wrapped in a white cloth. When I didn't take it, she put it in my lap and flipped opened the cloth. Inside was a wooden cross, painted a deep red with gold inlay, the paint chipped. It looked medieval.

"I got this when we went on sabbatical to the Holy City. The only time I've ever been abroad." She looked off for a moment. "The world is so full of depth and beauty," she said. Her eyes were full of the universe when she turned back to me. "I brought it back and just knew it was going to be for someone special. And here you are. And there you go."

I rubbed the texture of it like a talisman and felt suddenly sad. For the life that I had left behind, for the world, or both. She came over and sat beside me on the single bed, and our hips touched.

"You're upset."

I nodded back tears.

"It's an upsetting world," she said. "One with so much beauty, though."

I felt more understood in five minutes with Sister Alice than I felt with all of the journalists I'd known, with the global travelers I'd met on my journey, with my shrink, with Jason, who had known me all my life.

She said, "You know how they say 'Many are called but few are chosen'?"

I nodded.

"I've always thought that you are one who has the call in them." She'd said this to me before, lifetimes ago.

I laughed. I thought maybe she was talking about a spiritual calling, like being called to become a nun. I was pretty sure if she knew about all of my boozing, drugs, and sexual escapades she wouldn't be saying that.

"Will you like me less," I asked, "if I tell you I want nothing to do with Christianity? I don't want to answer a call from a mean, male God." I used air quotes when I said God.

"I don't think the call has anything to do with our notions of God."

I gave her a hard, dark look. "The world is so fucked up." She flinched at the F word. "Sorry," I said. "But I can't live in that happy denial place."

"What if living in that dark place is the actual denial you're referring to? What if God wants you to be happy?"

If it wasn't for Sister Alice's energy, her integrity, I would've gotten up and left. Her words could be so facile. I hated Catholic churches, had panic attacks when I tried to enter them. I'd spent seventeen years in Catholic schools, was forced to go to Mass three times a week. Shirley called it spiritual trauma. I really didn't know what I was doing at this convent. The nuns used to beat us with yardsticks. We were small children, abused for our simple curiosity. I had no faith in nuns. When I'd met Sister Alice at the psych ward, it'd taken me a long time to really trust her.

"Where does God fit in all the abuse scandals in the church?" I asked. "What about that denial?"

"Don't blame God for that. That's man. Man."

I'd never seen her upset. She straightened her blouse and took a breath, then another. "I agree with you about the abuse," she added more calmly, "but let's save that for another conversation, OK? I don't believe there's only one way to get to God."This time she used air quotes around God, then stopped herself and wiped the air like she was clearing a white board. "Being called doesn't mean you have to be Christian, Pearl. It doesn't mean you have to be Catholic. It doesn't mean you have to be religious at all."

"I don't want any of it." I wiped the air like she had done.

She sat quietly beside me. I felt horrible that I'd offended her. I didn't come here to get into an argument with Sister Alice. I was led here by the memory of her love.

"I think they have that saying wrong," she said, playing with the hem of her shirt. "I think it shouldn't be, Many are called, but few are chosen. It should be, Many are called, but few *choose*. I think you're going to have to make a choice soon, Pearl. A big one."

"I can't be what you want me to be," I said. I tried to hand the cloth-wrapped cross back to her. She was the one person who'd really gotten me, and now she was trying to turn me into some kind of God freak.

"Oh no you don't. You don't get to choose whether I give you that gift, and you don't get to choose whether God gives you a gift, either." She looked me up and down again. "Oh, I can see how much you've grown. You've seen the world. It's in your eyes. You're more sophisticated, harder. But really you have not grown up very much."

She stood up, leaned over me, and wrapped my hands around the cross. She put a hand over my heart. The mentholated scent of the rub brought back memories of my mother.

"Pearl, you have one of the kindest hearts of anyone I've ever known. Don't be so scared to show who you really are."

I felt tired. So tired. I wanted to curl up on her single bed in that simple room and sleep for hours, or generations.

I had the evening meal with the nuns in the dining room: breaded fish and a head of lettuce cut into strips. I was too tired to chat, but it was OK—most of them ate in silence.

Afterward I was shown to another room, like Alice's, small and sparse. I fell hard into sleep. I had to awaken at four the next morning and get on the road to make my flight.

As I was leaving, I stood in the doorway of that dark room with its single bed, one dresser, and single chair. It reminded me of van Gogh's painting *Bedroom at Arles*. I wanted in the depths of my being to stay, to drop back into my past, to live in the old world, to exist between these simple walls, to have nothing to do with that outside world. To live a life of innocence, before I'd witnessed so much. To take on a spiritual life and leave the mundane world to its monsters.

But I couldn't.

III
THE EMPRESS.

CHAPTER 3

The Empress

In Seattle, after the dark night and the reading with Rayne, I'm a soul pitted against itself. I sit in my apartment for weeks, veering between peace and fear. A deep calm, then a sudden backlash of dread.

Tranquility. Terror.

Calm. Fright.

I feel like I'm losing my mind. I feel like I'm jumping out of my skin.

There is some kinetic energy around my body that I cannot control. I go into grocery stores and loaves of bread fly off the shelves in my wake. I'm at the temp agency filling out paperwork, and frames fly off the walls. Inside me, I too am flying and falling. I cannot get my footing.

Some of it is repatriation, but not all. The social withdrawal, depression, anxiety, the inability to connect, alienation, disorientation, disenchantment—yes, they are all there. I'm not a fan of the big, the loud, the American. I've been through so much, and repatriation is hard, but it's not what is challenging me the most.

There's something that wants to be born from me. It's rattling at my cage as if it absolutely refuses to be tied up any longer. I have no idea what it is or how to let it off its leash.

One day it's so bad, it feels as if I'm being blown into the cosmos. I rush out and run to a park a few miles away and cling to a tree. Afterward, on a park bench, bereft, the questions spiral through my mind: *What is going on? Why won't this stop?*

A small voice says in my ear, as clear as if someone were sitting beside me, "This depression is important. This soul tumult is the most important thing that has ever happened in your life. Pay attention to it. Take it seriously."

More information comes to me: "What is happening is a perceptual shift. You're losing your mind because your thoughts must transform. The ego is being stripped from the body. This 'call' is not just about you. The world must shift or it won't survive."

A calm descends, all-encompassing. Doors inside me open. Universal doors open, behind them a profound peace. I see for a moment that everything just "is." I sit in the isness.

It doesn't last.

Fight or flight. I cannot flee from myself, so instead, day after day, I turn to fight it. I grapple with spirit like I'm fighting a bear. You will not have me. You will not own me.

The call is a spiritual one, and I want nothing whatsoever to do with religion. I fear if I answer the call, I will become a right-wing nut job Christian American. Religious trauma after religious trauma dredges up, memories of Holy Cross, the nun beatings, the shaming, the guilt. The oppression.

How can I answer such a call? I grapple with this as the black dog nips at my ankles. Still, as I struggle, some part of me wants to answer the call, but the doorway in is filled with monsters.

I look haunted. In the mirror, my eyes dominate my face. A black smoky mirror seems to surround me. I'm walking in Belltown at night, and a young man in black jeans and a black shirt with a skull on it passes me. He's on heroin—I can see the drugs in his veins. His eyes are dark and otherworldly.

He looks at me and stops. "Whoa," he says. "Death."

He sees it in me and he's right. I am in denial, angry, bargaining, depressed. I am punching and kicking. There is no way I will accept whatever it is that's happening to me.

She has lovely gardens, Seattle. Her landscaping is exquisite. She knows how to dress it up. Ferns, lupine, bugbane, asters, cypress, mountain laurel. She has her native side, too. Bleeding hearts, Scotch broom, Pacific dogwood, vine maple, salmonberry. She wears them well.

Seattle says all the right things. She's socially correct. She speaks up for the right causes. When I was in newsrooms abroad, my journalist friends and I decried American political correctness, a mind-control technique from a dominant white culture that had the time for such nonsense. And here I am now, hoping to fall into her nice, compromising arms.

Every day I roam the neighborhoods to get to know my new home. The old haunts the new. I miss London, travel, friends, Finn. The past pulls me back until I'm more there than here, but still I force myself outward. The future is a door I'm desperately trying to force shut, but still I force myself into the world.

Everywhere there are lakes and bays and rivers, the city an isthmus cushioned on all sides by water. Water beside, water above, water below, water within. Puget Sound, Elliott Bay, Union Bay, Duwamish River, Montlake Cut, Portage Bay, Lake Union, Fremont Cut, Shilshole Bay, Bitter Lake, Haller Lake, Green Lake—water is not an adjunct to the terrain, water *is* the terrain. The land does not define the waterways, but the waterways the land.

These waters are shapeshifters. It isn't just that each lake or river or bay is different from its peers—each has a shifting personality, a face that changes with the winds. Rain spitting against cheeks, wind gluing strands of hair against neck, I feel myself shapeshifting with the water.

Water is to blame when I get lost on my long meanderings. I use a glistening sliver of lake or bay in the distance as context to know where I stand, but then turn and mistake a glimpse of another body of water as the same entity. One day, I walk for eight hours, feet throbbing, and find myself so distant from my apartment, I have to use much-depleted resources to take a cab home.

The rain itself has a personality. It drizzles and stings, it pours. If you're a true Pacific Northwesterner, I am told, you don't use an umbrella, and when the rain hits your eyes you don't blink. A sky so laden and heavy sometimes, the dark of clouds meet the dark of the water's horizon with no distinguishable difference. The weather's moods become your moods. It leaves you sodden. It pulls you under.

A city is like a person. It has chemistry. Krakow was my best friend the second I landed in Poland. London, too, took a seat in my heart and lodged there. Tokyo was so foreign it took a while to even begin to understand her, except I knew the geishas instantly, their bundled gait, their porcelain faces. I'd been a geisha in some other era, some faraway time. Paris was another story. We'd had a bad past. I did not like her. I could not forgive her, and she still blamed me.

Seattle is a melancholic spirit. She drips green with meaning; she forces you down inside yourself. She's far-off and moody, full of misty vistas. Still, there is something agitating beneath the surface in Seattle. Some ancestry that is kicking and screaming and has yet to be resolved.

When I first arrived, when the plane descended into deep, dark clouds toward SeaTac, when the taxi drove me to a bedsit I'd let temporarily in Belltown, I felt no connection. *What am I doing here in this isolated, wet town in the middle of nowhere?* As the taxi passed Lake Union and Gasworks Park in the midst of a sideways-spitting rain, I knew I would have to believe I was led here, that I was here for a reason, because I felt absolutely no connection to this new place I was supposed to call home.

I'm in Fremont walking the canal, hypnotized by the drops of rain making concentric circles on the water, when the vision hits. I throw myself down on a bench so others won't notice. The telltale buzzing at the base of the skull, the way the energy slams into me. Head back, eyes rolled into another dimension.

In this vision something is buried beneath the perfect landscaped lawns, some story, some denied narrative. That something comes alive, a rising up of Native nations, in front of me the faces of so many. Below me in the canal, I can see Natives floating face down, arms locked. It's not that they're drowning, but more that they see themselves as no different from the waterways. They are the water. I look deep into the canal, and the interlocked bodies float in layers, layer upon layer. I'm separate from these people, separate from the water, disembodied from the land, an interloper. We are all interlopers here. The ones who came before wove their legends within the water, dissolved their stories into the lakes and rivers, into the rain, and the interlopers changed the plot. The interlopers thought themselves separate from the rain. They built a life and moved away from the water.

I have the same feeling later that night as I stand outside the duplex on the concrete sidewalk. I don't know why I'm there, standing in the pouring rain without a raincoat, barefoot. Perhaps I want to be cleansed of the vision earlier in the day. A feeling of such confusion overtakes me. The rain seems to be seeking its forest, but it only has this spread-out city to fall upon. A woman walks by with a broken rainbow umbrella and laced thigh-high boots and we stare at each other. I stand for an hour trying to understand this feeling, trying to understand why the rain feels so lost.

One day, I'm roaming Queen Anne and come upon lines of people walking downhill toward Seattle Center, the Space Needle. I join the throng as we stop traffic and move as one body toward the grounds where thousands have already gathered.

People wear flannel and dirty trousers, and many are crying. It's a mini Lollapalooza without the good mood. A six-year-old boy, holding his mom's hand, has on a formal black suit like he's attending a funeral or a wedding. Groups of people play Hacky Sack. A teenager holds up a boom box and plays "Rape Me."

I ask a white guy in dreads and a rainbow Rasta hat what's going on.

"Kurt Cobain committed suicide, man." He has a bag of colorful jelly beans and holds it out to me. I shake my head. "He was pure love, man. Even when he was shooting up, he was looking for love in the heroin, in the *vein,* man. Love was in his *blood.* The heroin was a substitute for love."

I look at him. I can't stop thinking of my own dark night.

"No really. The Dalai Lama *said* so." His face, and the faces of the others who have stopped to listen, are skewed up and dark, like a Goya painting. "Cobain, man, he couldn't survive in this crazy blasted-out-of-its-mind world, man. He was too *pure*, man." He puts his face close to mine and it contorts in pain. "He's *dead*, man."

I roam around. Cobain certainly wasn't one of the politically correct. There is a bar near the duplex that I've gone to many nights since my arrival in Seattle, the Salty Dog on Aurora, and they play his songs a lot. I was not that familiar with his music before Seattle. He was one of the interlopers who knew he was an interloper. His death feels like an omen, like the plot is changing in the once-grunge city. The sorrow of the collective weighs too heavy on my chest, and after twenty minutes in the massive crowd, I have to leave.

That night as I drink at the Salty Dog surrounded by junkies and old men, the jukebox *only* plays Cobain. "I wish I was like you, easily amused."

Me too, Kurt, me too.

Frustrated with my walkabout, I feel like I still don't *get* Seattle, haven't connected to its roots. I've learned this from living in other countries: the first and most important thing to do is make the new city your home.

I ask the bartender, "Do you know where I might go to meet local Native Americans?"

He is not a talkative guy. He shrugs as he wipes the bar. "Pioneer Square?" A drunk geezer at the bar snorts a laugh.

The next day, I find the right bus to Pioneer Square. I have to look it up, not knowing it's downtown. About twenty-five minutes into the ride, the driver yells, "Pioneer Square, next stop." We're on First Avenue South, smack in the middle of downtown Seattle, swamped on both sides by buildings and hemmed in by narrow streets and too much traffic. Between buildings, I can see a sliver of the dark waters of Elliott Bay. We're stuck in traffic before the bus stop, so I watch the goings-on through the window.

The cobbled square is filled with homeless people. I try to look closer. Are these the Native Americans I've asked to see? They're sitting, kneeling, lying in the square, on park benches, on the sidewalk. Homeless. Drunk. Drugged.

I get off the bus at the stop completely confused. Pioneer Square is a cobbled square edged by art galleries, the abstract paintings glowing amid the human toll, with restaurants and trendy coffee shops pumping out smells of baked goods. At least three dozen homeless Native people sit or lie on benches around the square, and more on the sidewalks in all directions. The food smells mix with the tang of vomit and feces. I don't understand why the bartender sent me here. Is it some sick joke? I feel like someone has punched me in the solar plexus.

I think of Usui, my old friend in Tokyo, his homelessness, his piece of cardboard at Yoyogi Park. I've always wondered if the people who become homeless are some of the world's most sensitive souls, barometers of how badly we are treating the earth.

What had I expected? Was I that green? Did I think the bartender was sending me to some village of teepees where

Native Americans dance, weave baskets, string beads, make colorful clothes out of animal pelts, and offer me a peace pipe? People who hunt their food? We hunted when I was a kid in the Midwest, gutted, scaled, dismembered. Am I looking for something I lost as a child?

I'm overcome with guilt and grief. *How much am I part of this decimation? This genocide that every white person walking by tries hard to ignore? How entitled am I, even in my thoughts? What can I do about it?*

It's more than this. Ever since I was a child, I felt I was no different from a tree, a creek, or a river. I felt I was no different from any person. Missouri folk would say when they saw someone downtrodden, "There but for the grace of God go I." I never thought that. I thought, *There go I. There go I. There go I.* As I stand in Pioneer Square, I feel I'm no different from the people around me on the benches. I am them and they are me. Does that make me entitled? I don't know. I can clearly see I am not living their life now. I can see that I don't have their challenges, but this connection between us is something deeper that also feels like truth.

A Native woman in a wheelchair approaches and hits my ankles with her chair, rolls back a few inches, and hits my ankles again. It hurts.

"That hurts."

She's holding out something in her palm. She has long gray braids, pouches under her eyes, and a fanny pack hanging sideways over her shoulder. She says something, but there is a buzzing in my ears, a vibration in the back of my skull.

My head swims as the square warbles and shifts. I'm going into another vision and I cannot stop it. I'm no longer standing in a city, but in a dense forest. I'm dwarfed by massive cedars, limbs heavy with moss. Fallen trees have other trees growing from them. Roots as big as your thighs. A blanket of ferns underfoot. The forest is thick, dark, dripping, mythic. I've walked into a fairy tale. Sounds of bird chatter, skittering creatures.

The wheelchair woman is here and she can walk now, or it is someone who is her kin. I cannot be sure. Two children run wildly, chasing, laughing. The woman is holding up the front of her dress and gathering mushrooms, berries, using a tool to dig up roots. I follow her as she leans and picks and digs and palms deftly, slips everything into her dress. Through the trees I catch glimpses of the bay. We seem to be walking parallel to Elliott Bay, the woman bending and picking and digging in poetic choreography. Ahead in the forest, I catch glimpses of others collecting forest food too.

We pick our way over root and log for a while and come out of the forest at a river. On the shore a man is bracing one leg against a giant cedar log, scaling off wood chips using a D-adze, a canoe emerging flake by flake beneath his hands. A long cedar lodge sits back by the tree line, next to it a two-story rack where fish hang to dry. More people here, and I look closely at the clothing, strips of cedar woven together. Cedar is their home, their clothing, their transportation.

Dozens of men, women, and children line the river. We get closer. The group is collecting salmon from nets. I help too, the fish fat, slippery, and silver, with deep watery eyes. We hand the salmon back to people who are cutting and hanging them. I understand that this is one of a series of catches that will feed these people all winter.

I feel a relief here. Fish, berries, roots, everything *from* the earth and *of* the earth. A cornucopia, an abundance available to all. The smells are fishy, earthy, sweaty, and the deep mud scent of the river.

No *I*, or *me*. Just *we*. Such a respite in the *we*. Such relief.

I awake on the ground, leaning against the Native woman's legs. She's holding something under my nose, something for me to look at. It takes a second to fathom where I am. The smell of booze and the sound of horns honking in the distant bumper-to-bumper traffic. *Takers, takers, takers*, I think low and harsh.

Sitting there on the cold, hard cobblestones, I miss the *we*. It's not just *we* the people, but *we* the blade of grass, *we* the river, *we* the forest. The *we* of the people who came before, and the *we* of those of the future. The *we* of the stream, the fish, and the shore.

The woman is pulling dollar bills out of my purse. I grab her wrist. She leans forward, looks in my eyes. Is it her trauma or ours I see in her depths? She shakes her palm under my nose, and finally I look. She's holding a small wooden carved fish.

Still holding her wrist, I take it between thumb and forefinger. A salmon. The body is thick, round, and smooth, the tail curling slightly, carved lines on face and fins. There is an energy to it.

The woman has five ones in her fingers and says, "For the fish. You need the damned fish. Now let me go."

I let go of her wrist. I palm the salmon, rolling it around in my hand. Two people on the edge of the square call to her, and she shoos me away.

Shuffling back to the bus stop spent from the vision, I clutch my wooden talisman. The visions always require something of me, but I'm never sure what.

As I walk, I avert my eyes from the modern hustle. I'm seeing too much. I'm seeing the present so clearly it's as if I'm seeing the future. One thing becomes clear deep in my gut: If things changed from that bucolic scene at the river to this fist of buildings and cars, if they changed this quickly in less than two hundred years—from forest myth to this polluted chaos—if the taking, taking, taking resulted in this in such a brief time, how quickly will they change in the future? How much time do we truly have left?

I seek journalism jobs but no one will return my calls. I haven't been employed in the States for years, so unemployment benefits are not an option. Not that I would want assistance anyway. It's bad enough that I'm going to the food bank. It just wasn't done when I was growing up. You got up, and you worked. If you were sick, you worked. If you were injured, you worked. I'd been making my own money since I was ten years old. Babysitting, paper routes, ice cream parlors, grocery stores.

I decide to go back to freelancing, thinking about the success of my work with the journalists' cooperative in London. I find an old computer and keyboard at a yard sale and a folding table at a garage sale and set up a workstation in the cramped kitchen. I pitch but do not hear back.

I understand why. The way I see Seattle is too far outside the cultural paradigm. This outsider's look at the city may be successful if I can pitch it right, but to pitch it, I have to be inside the paradigm enough to know how to present it. I'm vibrating at a different frequency than everyone else. I know from being an expat in other countries, leaving one and entering another, that aligning with the vibration of the new place takes time. So much time.

The idea for "Church Hopping" appears in a dream. I see myself in the dream go from church to church to explore this thing called faith. I wake from the dream and stare at the ceiling. I figure I can do it if I avoid the Catholic Church and its trauma.

Faith is not an easy concept for me. What does it even mean? Faith in what? The decency of people? I didn't even have that kind of faith as a child, or if I did, it was knocked out of me. Faith in life? I have no proof that life is anything worth believing in. Faith in myself? Belief that I could live someone else's version of who I should be? What does faith even mean? Faith in a white man's bearded God? A Catholic upbringing scared all of the faith right out of me.

As a girl, oh how I loved Jesus. I stood on tiptoe on the kneeler at Mass and sang high and mighty, feeling the joy and love. Even as a kid, dogma seemed absurd to me, limbo and purgatory and such. But I could feel the spirit of things—in a leaf, a blade of grass, in handfuls of water from a creek, in a single beam of colored light coming through a stained-glass window.

The dream comes again, so I decide to try it. I understand that this is the beginning of my journey to owning this spiritual life, and I must start with what I know.

I pitch magazines, suggesting I spend the twelve Sundays going to twelve services and write an article about things like inclusivity, attendance, and the themes of sermons. One magazine is interested. I sign a contract. It's barely enough money for two weeks of groceries. But the idea sparks something in me, gets me out of the apartment, and sends me on an entirely new walkabout through the neighborhoods of Seattle.

Unitarian, Episcopalian, Presbyterian, Baptist, Lutheran, Quaker. I avoid Catholicism but don't tell the editor. I pick the religions arbitrarily and do not include Buddhism or Judaism, and only later ask myself why.

The majority of services remind me of my Catholic upbringing. No one greets you as you enter. We read rote messages from prayer books. The priest is a man. The sermons don't move me.

Still, I'm impressed with the turnout. Almost every service is full. This itself is worth the walkabout, this understanding of the number of people searching. Even if they are just attending church because that's what their parents did, even if they aren't really delving into their souls, something is drawing them, some search for meaning, even if they aren't conscious of it. It surprises me to see so many people filling the pews.

I start to notice that I can feel the vibe as I walk up to each church well before I go inside. Unitarian Universalism is a liberal religion characterized by a "free and responsible search for truth and meaning." They assert no creed but are unified by a shared search for spiritual growth. It sounds perfect.

As I approach the community center, I don't understand why I feel so disconnected. The minister is a man, but I know from their website they have numerous women ministers, so that is not the reason for my disconnect. I just feel no fit here. I'd have to be a different person, and I truly cannot fathom why that is, or how my core would have to be different to fit in here. The service is spiritual but not religious. The people are dressed nicely and are perfectly fine people, but when I look at them, I see no recognition between us.

The sermon is about finding meaning in the mundane, about being socially responsible when you purchase products, and I agree with everything he says, but nothing here is touching my heart.

Surrounded by the others, head down, I contemplate my disconnection. I finally realize I worry I cannot be ugly here. The dark sides of myself are not allowed here. I worry I would have to disown a whole edgy side of myself to fit in.

Afterward at home, I grapple with this experience. When your whole life you feel like you don't fit in, and find a group of people who are supposed to be like you and you *still* don't fit, it stirs deep confusion.

When I approach a humble brick Presbyterian church near Green Lake, I feel shy, like a child, humble. In the pew, I notice the congregation is more mixed than usual. In front of me is an elderly woman in a pillbox hat and next to her a rough guy with tattoos. There are gay couples everywhere. The pastor is a woman. The inclusivity fills my heart.

As the pastor preaches, a love washes out over the crowd. She's talking about inclusivity, about how we must welcome everyone into our hearts, but something bigger than her words emanates through the pews. I hold my fists tight and my arms by my side, doing everything I can not to break into sobs. I know the people on either side of me can see my body shaking with the effort.

I feel so alone. I want to turn to the person next to me and fall into their arms. *I'm so alone.* I barely hold myself together until the end of the service.

I'm left only with love after this service, and with the knowledge that an institution *can* create a culture of love. That it is possible. But how do I write this in a journalism article? Love is not something they teach you how to write about in journalism school.

I'm learning as I go from church to church that Jesus is not my bag. I have nothing against him as a prophet but cannot get behind God as a man, always a man. What did this do to a girl's self-esteem, when she's bombarded with a male as the God figure? What did it do to her sense of self, to her belief in her own nature? What did it do to her voice? When I was little I felt the energy. In the woods, especially, but in other people, too, of something bigger, something greater than the sum of our fleshy parts.

I believe in the energy, just not the dogma. Using the word "god" invokes a white man with a beard, and I want nothing to do with that.

My final service is at the Quakers Friends meeting house in the U-District. As I approach, I can feel excitement in my soul. I read up on them beforehand. Founded in the seventeenth century, they wanted nothing to do with the rituals or the fire and brimstone of other Christian religions. They're called Quakers because they quake when they feel spirit. I quake when I have my visions. I quake all the time.

In their foyer, there's a flyer inviting the gay community to the meetings. On the wall next to the flyer, a list of their beliefs: Integrity, social equality, pacifism, silence. I love them.

The documentation I pick up in the lobby says this is the largest unmonitored meeting in the Pacific Northwest. No one leads us. Inside the meeting space on simple wooden benches, a group of about twenty people sits in silence.

A peace wends its way into my soul, a blessed relief. Later, the floor is opened so that people can speak. If someone is moved to say something, they raise their hand. A few raise their hands, discuss conundrums in their daily lives and how to live in more integrity. A man talks about his reconnection with his estranged son, who is also sitting in the meeting. Again I feel the tears well up.

I stay after the meeting for a discussion on their community involvement. They are starting a homeless initiative and discuss installing a Porta-Pot and showers behind the building. I'm impressed. They're willing to get their hands dirty.

The joy of freelancing, and the reason I like it better than working for newspapers, is that you get time to contemplate the meaning of the piece. With newspapers in Tokyo, I oversaw five pages daily, commissioning articles and photos, editing, writing headlines and captions, and there was no time for any air to flow through the narrative.

I sit with the walkabout and explore faith. I think how I could write a whole book on faith, on my childhood immersion in Catholicism, in the Buddhism and Shintoism I encountered in Japan, the Hinduism in India. My best friends throughout the world who were Jews, atheists, Taoists.

What is my path to faith? I understand again how I do not like dogma. I have never believed in an organization telling you what to believe.

I think about a childhood of being forced deep into myself to find meaning, to find what I believed in a world I didn't believe in. How moving abroad was an extension of this, how not fitting at home became a lifestyle of not fitting, and how that forced me even deeper into my beliefs.

And now, back in my home country, not fitting again, and again I'm forced to find the bedrock of my belief.

I find myself one evening reading an article from a free alternative magazine. In my research to become a freelancer, I collected stacks of local and regional publications. The article is in my hands and I'm reading it before I even know how it happens.

It's on mysticism. There is an energy to it that is greater than the words on the page. It's about personal and direct connection with the divine, about being a channel for the information outside normal reality.

For the first time, I feel I've stumbled upon an answer of who I am. I remember the books on Catholic mystics Sister Alice gave me, and I knew then, when I was a teenager, but the knowledge hadn't stuck.

I feel a veil lifting, a door opening. Dare I walk all the way through that open door?

In the end my article isn't much. The final edited copy contains nothing of my personal reaction to this search for faith. It is a list with addresses, a few notes beneath each listing. I don't argue with the editor. I've been trained this way too, to separate the person from the experience. Deep down, I know this is bogus. Journalism tries to be objective, but everything is subjective, even down to the churches I chose to attend for the article. Everything is subjective. Even our presence affects everything that is around us. Quantum physics tells us this is so.

For months afterward, I go back again and again to the Friend's Meeting House, to the Quakers, and sit in silence in exchange for nothing but silence. No one taking. No one giving. No one lecturing. All of us simply being. It is as close to mysticism as I can find for now.

Weeks later, I receive a check for a hundred fifty dollars for the article. I have to get a proper job.

IV
THE EMPEROR.

CHAPTER 4

The Emperor

When I went to journalism school at age eighteen, I thought I'd died and gone to heaven. It was only thirty minutes from where I grew up—who knew nirvana was just a handful of miles away? From a family where conversation didn't exist, where dinnertime was an enforced, tense silence, to a group of people my age from around the world who loved to talk about current issues. I couldn't believe I was still in Missouri.

In journalism school we were taught to separate ourselves from our story. We were taught distance and objectivity. We were taught to question everything. We were taught by some of the greatest journalists in the country.

Journalism school opened up a world of ideas for me. It had gotten me a degree I loved; it had launched me out of Missouri. It helped me travel the world. It'd gotten me newsroom jobs in Tokyo and London. It'd helped me work for some of the greatest newspapers in the world. I'd come from parents with little education, and I'd traveled the world with a dimensional career.

Now, in Seattle, no newspaper or magazine will hire me. I send out dozens and dozens of resumes and can't get an interview. Depressed and at the end of my financial rope, I interview for corporate copywriting jobs and do not get them. I apply for program manager jobs and never hear back. Finally, hopeless, I go for receptionist jobs, which I also do not get. People complain about the job market in Seattle, but never in my life have I found it that difficult to find a job.

Finally, with no other choice, I accept an entry-level position working on a boat in Elliott Bay. We ferry tourists. The pay is minimum wage. *How low can I go?*

Daily, I swab decks, check the engine room, greet tourists. It is a painful and dumb job, stacking Reese's peanut butter cups at the snack counter, cleaning up half-finished cups of Diet Coke. It's the kind of job I had when I was fourteen. I show up for tit on time and do good work, but inside my soul is dying and I don't understand why this is all happening to me.

Elliott Bay smells like exhaust, oil, and fish entrails. At least the new boat job is outside. It's a job of shifting centers, of docks that sway and boats that rock. The white caps of the hazy Olympic Mountains march on the horizon. Elliott Bay has depth and breadth—a waterway whose stories go back millennia.

The tugboats move like old men, and the ferries like ancient hotels, plying back and forth. Some days it's so dark, you can't tell the above from the below. Other days, the sun throws thousands of stars across the water's surface and into my eyes.

I start to see some benefits of doing this work. Most of my journalism jobs were in smoky, badly ventilated open-plan offices. Cigarette tar stuck to the windows and blocked out the light. We rarely had time to leave the room, let alone go outside. We sat at computers for twelve hours, fourteen hours. But here is earth, air, and water.

I've been working on the boat for about a month when I see the posters. They're up everywhere near the dock. A photographer has been following our boat taking pictures. The boat, the link of mountains in the background, the shimmering water.

Our captain is around forty and probably used to be handsome, but now the booze has made him chubby and washed out. He's had sex with most of the female staff and has been touching me too much lately. He comes up behind me as I'm looking at the poster. I can feel his chest against my back.

"That's you!" He shoves his arm by my face to point at the figure standing at the rails, staring wistfully out to sea. "That's you standing there."

"We all wear the same uniform—how can you tell?"

"Because I see you standing there every day." I lean in closer to look. He leans in behind me. "Why do you think I'm a sea captain? There's something about being out on the water you just can't get on land."

I'm surprised by how small I look. Gentle. How my hair blows up and back with the wind and how that feels like love, like the wind is loving my face and my hair. I merge with the elements. This young woman is not at all confused and depressed. On each poster, I'm standing at a different spot, so I must be doing this all the time.

I turn in my time card inside the main office, and they have other photos, postcards, and brochures, and in each one, I stand looking out to sea. Watching myself watching the ocean, it is my first hint that maybe I needed this dumb job, this open-air cleansing. Maybe this dumb move to this isolated enclave at the farthest Pacific Northwest corner of the United States, and maybe this job swabbing decks are helping me heal. Maybe the universe isn't against me after all.

On the boat I try to make friends, to connect with people, but nobody wants to hear the stories of my life before. I strike up conversations, and no one seems to care. My mother used to say when I was a girl: "You gotta let Pearl talk. She's gotta be heard. The only thing that girl can't stand is being ignored or interrupted."

Each workday, the other workers swab away from me as I talk. They go below deck to avoid me. They find something that suddenly needs to be done elsewhere. I'm tired of hiding what I know. I discuss the treatment of women in Japan, the poverty in India, hiking the Himalayas. They keep moving away.

I become invisible. It reminds me of my childhood, this invisibility, of the things I could see and the things that I knew, and how I was forced to shut up by a raised fist. I can talk to Gem, but there is no one else. It isn't just trying to find community that matters, it's who I am, my identity.

In Tokyo, a British friend of Finn's went back to London and then came back and told us this, that no one wanted to hear his stories. They couldn't relate. He said, "You feel like an outsider in your own country." When you're abroad, you're special. People don't expect you to fit in. You go home and you're just another person in the crowd. When you're abroad people aren't sure of your social status, so few judge you by it. When you go home, you're just some weird person who doesn't fit in. He talked about the depression, too. How you had to work to fit in when you didn't even want to.

I pick up one of the boat staff one night and take him to the Salty Dog. We neck in a dark, dank corner, and I bring him back to my place. I light candles and incense and show him my Indonesian puppet. It comes alive in my hands like another person in the room. He laughs, backs up nervously, makes some excuse, and leaves before we do the deed.

I know the puppet is haunted. I know that I'm haunted. The past is building in me with nowhere to go. I know that I'm weird, that they see me as odd. But still I reach out my hand.

I find El Capitan easily. The sharp corner of the massive building is like the bulwark of a ship sailing the waves of Capitol Hill.

It's spitting rain. I ring the buzzer but no one answers. I ring and ring like a person drowning, like a man overboard.

I check the card in my backpack again, and yes I have the right address. I smoke a cigarette in the dripping rain. As I wait, I think of the dream I had the night before. I was in a white space with no objects and no edges, and I was told to take a step forward.

"Into what? Where?" I asked, flustered.

"Take a step forward," the voice came again.

I moved forward. My body painted a colorful mosaic behind me. My shoulder swiped a line of blue, my hips a patch of orange. My fingers created line and form like colored pencils. When I stepped forward, azure tiles came up to meet my feet. In the dream, there was this white nothingness in front of me, but when I looked behind me, the colors were spectacular. My movement created a path of beauty.

"Hello." I turn to see a frazzled Rayne loaded down with groceries. "Sorry I'm late," she says, smiling and fumbling for her keys.

I take two of her bags.

"Thank you," she says.

Seeing her as a human being and not a fortune teller behind a folding table is disconcerting. We enter an old, narrow elevator and stand awkwardly side by side. She smells of sweat, peppermint, and the trailing essence of sage.

Her living room is painted deep purple. Dark like menstrual blood. I want to curl up on the Persian rug. Golden frames of mystical art, candles. Lush fabric on the sofa and chair. It's whimsical. I live like a bachelor—shoes on countertops, clothes strewn on the floor. I took apart the vacuum cleaner to clear out its hoses and still haven't put it back together. I moved it and the parts to the edge of the main room. Part of me wishes I could be more like Rayne, and part of me knows she's not me.

In the kitchenette, we put the bags on the counter. There is a tiny table and two wooden chairs by the rain-spattered window overlooking the gray, snaking streets. She lights the candles and incense. Smoke wafts like signals.

I'm impatient while she makes tea. I'm not doing particularly well today. I'm waiting for a happy self to kick in, waiting for the turning point in this move back to the States to where I feel normal again, like a human being, seen and heard and at home. But it's a roller coaster, and today I'm at the bottom of the double loop.

As soon as she puts the big red mug next to me, I blurt out the issues I'm having with finding a journalism job. How that career had driven me for so long and given me purpose. My identity had been tied to traveling the world for a decade—

now who am I? A deck swabber? A poor person in a rundown duplex? I'm used to picking up the phone and important people calling me right back. Now I pick up the phone and even the unimportant ones don't return my calls.

She's still a bit frazzled, and I can see she's trying to get centered. She does the ritual as before, holding the cards beneath her chin, closing her eyes, whispering prayers. I couldn't hear her before with the noise of the psychic fair; now I hear her faintly: *Spirits of the Earth, Air, Fire, Water be with us now. Spirits of the Earth keep us grounded. Spirits of the Air bless our breath. Spirits of the Fire light the way. Spirits of the Water deepen our connection to spirit.* It's like a prayer, and more like a song. She's singing the elements. I think about my dark night of the soul and how I wanted a group of women to sing the despair, to turn the pain into a chorus, how in other worlds, my dark night would be operatic.

Spirits of the Center keep us aligned now, in truth, in love. I feel my soul limping to life, and the world begins to echo poetry and possibility, and not all this loneliness.

She hands me the cards. I mix them quickly and give them back. She asks me to use my left hand to divide them into three piles, then to choose a pile.

Gathering them all up, she pulls ten, turns them over onto the lavender tablecloth. Incense wafts and dances. I see the characters moving on the cards as if they are alive, and I try to shut it down. *Not now.* I haven't had a vision for weeks. *Go away. Leave me be!*

She studies the cards, touching each with the pads of her fingertips. She looks at the cards with such love. "There is so much to say here, I don't know where to even begin. You want to know your calling. Well it's not journalism anymore."

"Then what is it?"

"It's a learning process for a lot of people, Pearl. We're talking about creating new systems with new rules. I know you can feel what I'm saying."

My body is vibrating with the truth of her words. "I just don't know how it translates to reality."

"You just have to stop resisting who you are. The psychic side of you. You're a channel." Visuals of a white-trash woman reading fortunes fill my head, and I shudder.

"But there's more here in the cards. You're an artist." Her voice is musical, lilting.

"I'm not an artist." This angers me. The dark night of the soul brought this message. I don't draw. I don't paint. I don't do art. This is ridiculous. What am I supposed to *do* with this?

"I'm *trying* to get a proper, well-paying job," I say too loudly. The steam from the tea is annoying my face, and I shove it aside, spilling some on my hand. "No one will hire me. There's this well-worn path for journalists in this country," I say. "From small-town paper to regional paper to city paper. So I'm screwed because I haven't followed their path. I haven't followed anyone's path."

"What if you counted it as a blessing that you cannot find a journalism job? What if that's the universe's way of breaking your addiction to it, so that the new way can enter? Remember your reading at the fair, when we discussed the Divine Feminine? The call of the Divine Feminine will take you away from the mainstream. The mainstream is not working anymore."

On one level, I know she's right, but it terrifies me. How am I supposed to make a living?

Rayne studies the cards and moves her head as if she's having an internal discussion with them. She pulls more cards. Studies them. "This says you're an artist."

She looks at me and shrugs.

I put my chin in my hand and slump, scowling at her.

"I'm. Not. An. Artist," I say. *There goes sixty fucking dollars.*

"Look, it's like life in general. You can surrender to it, or you can fight it."

"I need my career back." My teeth are clenched because I'm trying not to lose my temper.

"It's like the ocean. You're familiar with the surface. The surface is comfortable for you. It's all you know. You're rowing your boat along the surface right now. It's cloudy. You feel like you don't have a destination, just floating along the surface. Below that is a world of color and texture and form that is just right there, even though you can't see it!" I'm transported to Finn and me snorkeling in the Philippines and how I'd had no idea such beauty existed just below the surface. Whole worlds, the neon colors of starfish and tropical reefs. After that, for a while I saw the entire planet as fake surface, and a few inches below was the fantastic, bejeweled alternate reality.

"How is being an artist, when I'm not one, supposed to help me right now as I apply to an endless string of humiliating odd jobs? How is it supposed to put food on the table? And even if I accepted the idea, what does it mean? *I don't do art!*"

She reads more cards, but I don't listen because I'm battling with the demons in my head.

Sixty dollars, I think as I hand over three twenties at the end of the reading. *Sixty fucking dollars.* I traipse around Capitol Hill in the rain with my hoodie up. I smoke cigarette after cigarette. I window shop. I see all the fancy things for sale behind thick plates of glass. I feel like those things, but not fancy. I'm a cheap thing for sale.

Artist. I grunt. *That's just what I fucking need.* I stomp my cigarette into a puddle.

The weather is stormy, tumultuous. I'm on the boat at Lake Union greeting the tourists as they embark. The sky is black and the wind and rain a sideways smack.

I register the number of tourists on board on a clipboard in the wheelhouse and hear the captain arguing over the radio. He doesn't want to risk taking the boat out. The woman on the other end makes him wait while she goes to speak to someone. She comes back and says, "Affirmative, the boat needs to do its normal run." He argues, she makes him wait, then comes back and says, "Affirmative. Affirmative. Make the normal run." He hangs up the mic, turns to me so close I can smell the alcohol on his breath, and says, "Well, I guess greed wins today."

Lake Union is fine, despite the heavier rain and blackening sky. Everyone is in good humor huddled below deck, looking out rainy windows at murky views.

"What did you expect, folks, clear skies?" The captain laughs into the intercom. "This is Seattle."

He points out Chihuly's glass studio at the water's edge. As we approach the Ballard Locks, he gets on the loudspeaker and gives everyone too much information on the infamous salmon run through the locks. I run to the bow to work the locks, not minding being in the blustery rain. I tie the lines and watch as the locks are opened, river water rushes out, and we descend to sea level.

When we motor out into Shilshole Bay, the weather is ugly. High winds whip up massive waves. I'm drenched when I get down below deck.

The captain says over the speaker, "Batten down the hatches, folks, it's going to get messy. Just think, you'll have something to tell your friends when you get home."

As we move into open water, the waves are nothing like I've experienced in my months on the boat. The ship rises, hovers there, then slams down. Rises, hovers, slams, again and again and again. Some of the tourists downstairs are openly crying. A few are puking.

The bucking ship brings something feral out in me. Something is pulled up in me after Rayne's reading. I leave the enclosed area and go out into the driving rain. It's impossible to walk, so I hold onto the walls as I move.

I grab onto the railing and swing my way up the stairs toward the upper deck. I'm hit by waves that flush down the stairwell, and I slip and fall and get up again.

At the upper deck, the waves are so high they're washing over everything. I pull myself post by post to the middle of the deck. Palming a post, I pull myself up to standing, reach my other hand out in the wash of waves to grab another post. I stand, arms outstretched, rising up with the ship, my knees bending as we slam down. Waves rise over the railing and slam into my chest, my face, my thighs. Up, hover, slam, splash. Up, hover, slam, splash. I want the waves to bash it out of me. Each wave knocks breath from me, wrestles hair and clothes into a frenzy. It feels like fucking. I'm fucking water.

Two people are struggling up the metal stairs. They are soaked, tumbling and fumbling with every buck of the boat. Two women in their forties. They slip and slide across the deck and take up positions on either side of me, hands holding posts, bodies open to the waves. The three of us in a line, taking wave after wave after wave.

"Bring it, bitch!" one of the women yells. Up, hover, slam, splash.

We take up the chant. "Bring it! Bring it!" Up, hover, slam, splash. After about five minutes of this, they laugh and point downstairs. They can't take any more of it. They wave goodbye as they slip back across the deck to wrestle their way down the stairs. I ride the bucking boat and take waves to the face and chest all the way to the docks.

It is my job to help the tourists off the boats once we dock. Drenched and wild, I descend the stairs, jump from the ship to the dock, tie the line to the massive grommet and, as the captain docks, get the doors open. The customers, nauseated and beaten by the ride, waddle as they pick their way off the boat. I feel like baring my teeth, like pounding my chest.

There is a lesson in it. Let it slam into you. Cry for it.

A tourist pukes a few feet outside the door.

I wish it were that easy. One just stands in the power of the wave. One just lives the power of the sea. Instantly you're Neptune, controlling the depths. Within a week, I'm fully in overwhelm mode and find myself back in Rayne's kitchen.

The workaday world chips away at the soul. It's a seesaw, an extreme ebb and flow. Freedom. Fear. Openness. Terror. Dichotomies of a tricky mind.

Rayne makes tea. It's only been two weeks since my last reading. I feel like I'm in a Catholic confessional. *Bless me Goddess, it's been two weeks since my last confession.*

I stomp my foot like a child at Rayne as she pours steaming water into thick mugs. "The artist reading doesn't make sense. I demand that you make sense!" After taking the wave pounding on the boat, I have been filled with energy I don't know how to release.

"Pearl, I stick by my message. What kind of messenger would I be if I didn't honor the message?"

I do another petulant stomp.

"I'll read on any other subject. I don't doubt the guides. Doubting the guides has consequences."

I insist. I demand. I tantrum. Finally she gives in. I sit in the chair by the window. It's so rainy and foggy that the view out her fifth-floor window is an abstract painting of gray-and-red-peppered dots from the far-off streetlights.

She looks at the cards a long time, moves her head this way, that way. She views the reading from different perspectives, like she's looking for a way in. She holds her head sideways and squints at the cards. "You need to sit and write every day," she says.

My clothes are itchy. I pull at them.

"Write. Write it all out," she says again.

My scalp is scratchy. I put my hands deep in my hair and yank at it.

"Writing is your way *in*." Her fingers, sporting those precious stones, move over the cards. "Writing will come first. Art will come in a secondary wave of creative outpouring." Her voice is the color of blood mixed with purple, sultry like the deep painted walls.

I rend my garments, tear at my hair.

"Are you OK? Why are you so bothered?"

I start crying. She looks at me, perplexed.

"Why are you crying?

"I can't. I. Cannot. Do. It."

"I don't understand. Weren't you a journalist? Didn't you write all the time?"

I'm now blubbering so hard I can't respond. She watches me, then looks back at the reading.

She throws more cards. She studies them. She says, "Oh!" like a sudden epiphany.

"OK, I get it now. So interesting. The writing you're being asked to do is a self-determined, self-focused level of writing. With journalism, editors told you what to write. Or, even if it was your idea, the story was outside of you. It wasn't *your* story. You had this little window of space to tell a story in. You had to disappear completely from the story!" She's elated.

I rub my temples.

"Your guides want you to write *your* story. For newspapers you had to write about what was going on out there." She leans over the table and points out the abstract window at the abstract city beyond. "Now they want you to write about what's going on in here." She points at my heart. "This is the very essence of the Divine Feminine, a woman telling the truth about her life."

I wail.

"Pearl, why are you still crying?" she asks plaintively. "Why does this need to be so hard?"

I lift my hand to show her my fingers are shaking. "If I open that cage, the monsters will get out."

"Monsters?" She offers me a box of tissues. The clock behind her is ticking like a time bomb. She throws a few more cards, shifts in her chair.

"OK, this is . . . " She throws more cards. "Your spirit guides are constantly looking for a way in with you. This is why you have so many dreams, so many visions. They're trying to get through to you, and sometimes they resort to shouting." She holds up a card with a woman in a turban on it, and she's wearing a necklace of coins. "Nine of Coins. It's a weird message."

I take a wadded tissue from my pocket and blow my nose, a loud snort in the small kitchen.

"Go get the materials to build a cage."

I stop crying. "A cage?" I hiccup.

"Build it and put it under your desk."

I stop crying. I'm like a two-year-old having a temper tantrum one minute and distracted by some shiny idea the next.

"When you're ready to write, sit at your computer, open the cage, and let the monsters out. When you're finished, put the monsters away and close it."

I wipe snot on the back of my hand. "I love that idea," I say.

"Write every single day."

I nod. Sniffle.

"Every single day. I mean it."

I start crying again. I can't breathe. I put my head between my knees. "The monsters are already getting out!" I gasp as I look toward the floor. She puts her hand on my back. "I have to be able to function," I say in a tiny voice. "I have to be able to work. I have to be able to do my dumb job, help the dumb tourists, pay the dumb landlord."

When the panic attacks started in London, Shirley taught me how to breathe in through my nose to the count of six, hold for six, and breathe out through my mouth for six. I do this now between my knees.

Rayne pulls cards as I count. "Six, five, four, three, two . . ."

"Water seems to calm you," she says.

I nod against my knees. Lying completely submerged in a bath was the only thing that had ever helped with my panic attacks.

"All right, this is your homework besides building the cage. Take an Epsom salt bath. Your upper chakra, the visions, is very active, and we need to ground you by connecting you to your body. That should help with the visions and with this fear you're experiencing. Sometimes trauma we have as children forces us out of our base chakra and into the upper chakras to survive. So you're strong in the part of you that receives these visions, but weak at the base. Does that make sense?"

It does. It is the closest thing to truth I've heard about myself in a long time.

"Good. We're going to reconnect you with your body. So you're going to take a bath, and in the bath, you're going to touch your different body parts and thank them and tell them you love then. Touch your toes. I love you toes. Thank you toes. Your feet, ankles, calves, all the way up the body. I love you scalp. I love you eyelashes. Thank you for what you do. That sort of thing. Can you do that?"

I nod. My breath is ragged as I sit up.

"This is not the universe picking on you, I promise. We're all so far away from who we really are. Most people have no idea about their authentic selves. Lots of people live quiet lives of desperation. Some of us find it harder than most to live in this normal world. We live in the same desperation—we just cannot do it quietly." She leans over and puts her warm hand on my arm. "It's just about owning who you really are. That's all." As usual, she gives me a cassette tape, a recording of our session.

"Write!" she orders as I pay her.

I wander, lose myself in the wet reflections on Broadway, roam up the steep hill, hoodie up, smoking a cigarette that fizzes in the rain. Crimson, lemon, and lime streetlights reflect in puddles and darkened shop windows. I see my reflection, and I look like a skinny boy. I'm gloomy, and I know I have to do something. I have to stop resisting and listen to Rayne. Something has got to change. On the way home, I duck into three different thrift stores to find a boom box.

That night, I put in the tape and get the weed out to roll a fat joint. Gem is my supplier. Thanks to my ex Finn, I can roll perfectly. A cigarette burns in an ashtray overflowing with butts, and an ice-cold MGD sits on the coffee table. I roll the joint with one hand. In the UK, I was used to adding tobacco, but Gem tells me in the States you just use grass.

I put the blinds down and push play. When I'm stoned I travel to far-out places. This time I find myself in the Himalayas with Finn. We are on the slippery slope to the Everest base camp, a primordial place of blacks and whites and grays so deep you can feel death inside them. I can summon the place as if I'm back there sliding up its slope.

Rayne's voice acts as the voice-over to my trek on Mount Everest. I hear myself muffled on the tape, speaking between my legs, trying to breathe. I ascend the mountain, toking deeply on the joint.

I look about, straddling two worlds. I'm holding a joint in one hand, a beer in the other. I'm in a tiny apartment in Seattle *and* I'm on the Everest slope. The mountains here do not care if you live or die. The air is so thin. The air is so cold. I have no hands to hold on, to stop myself from falling into a crevasse or sliding down the mountainside to my death.

Each world—the world of Nepal and this apartment in Seattle—is drawn on a piece of tracing paper, one paper layered over the other so that both worlds seem as real as the other to me.

I slide over to the bathroom in my apartment. I can see the wind blowing wisps of snow off the peak. I lift the toilet lid. I will not survive with my hands so busy and my body so full of toxins.

I dump the beer. Flick the joint into the bowl. I go back and grab the ashtray. Blasted by the searing wind of Everest, I dump the lit cigarette and the butts in the toilet. I take the pack from my pocket, crumble each, one by one into the bowl. I flush the toilet and watch the swirling mess of ash, butts, and piss-colored beer swirl away and disappear. The snow blows like angels off the Everest peak.

Later, as I fade to sleep, coming down now, so far down, I realize that when I wake up I will start a life of sobriety. I will be sober for the first time since I was fourteen years old.

V
THE HIEROPHANT

CHAPTER 5

The Hierophant

I run the water as hot as I can get it in the giant claw-foot tub, pour in bubble bath and Epsom salt, and gingerly climb in. I lie for a while looking at my toes and thighs and arms. This is so weird.

"Hello toes," I say tentatively, bringing my foot up and touching my toes one by one. "Thank you. I love you ankles. Thank you knees."

I look at my soapy fingers. "Thank you hands." I think, *What do I use these hands for?* "Thank you thumb. Thank you knuckles. Thank you pinkies."

The past decade has been about living only in my head. How easy it is to ignore the body. How I used to be a runner when I was a kid. How I used to bike everywhere. How my fitness defined me, and how that changed when I moved abroad and lived in big cities with so little space to breathe. I put my palms over my eyes. "Thank you, eyes. Please help me to see things differently."

I have an urge for a cigarette and clench and unclench my fists. The tobacco withdrawal has been something out of a horror film. My face has broken out. Even baths like this don't seem to clear the awful stench of my sweat. I shit out decades of toxins in gooey trajectories. My clothes are ruined. Did they always smell this bad? The leather jacket I bought in Bombay has to go. The stench of ugly sweat in the leather sends me reeling. The cravings are cellular, my body tensing with need. I can't imagine giving up harder drugs if cigarettes are this intense. I have been drinking water, lots and lots of water, to try to dilute the purge.

Gem asked me if it was a good idea to give up smoking when I was already going through such intense stuff in my psyche, and I told her that I'm just going to do all the shit, all at once, bear down on it all with strength.

I place both hands over my heart. I close my eyes and submerge my head. My heart beats beneath the surface and it's as if the water itself has a pulse. I cannot at first seem to thank my heart—it hurts too much. How do I thank it for hurting? *Thank you heart, for loving so much.* I sit back up in the tub, reach for the towel, dry my eyes.

"What the fuck!"

Gem is sitting on the toilet seat.

"I knocked."

I try to cover my breasts.

"Oh please, it's nothing I haven't seen before. They're spectacular, by the way."

"I'm sorry I *ever* gave you that emergency key."

"I felt compelled. Like something very interesting was going on in here."

"Hand me another towel."

"Prude." She obeys.

I drape both towels over me and unplug the drain. Covered in sopping towels, I sit back as the tub drains.

"Do you think those wet towels are *less* provocative than when you were nude?" Gem says and whistles.

I try to cover myself. "I was doing an exercise that Rayne gave me. Thanking my body parts."

Gem laughs.

"You think it's stupid?"

"No, be my guest. Anything that works."

I get out of the bath holding one of the dripping towels, grab my robe, take a new towel to dry my hair, and comb the rats out with my back to Gem. In front of me is the Post-it that says "Brush your hair." The brush will only go through a few inches of my thick and difficult mop, and then it becomes an all-out fight.

Something is changing in my face. I see it in my eyes as I look in the mirror. They're less troubled. But something else comes to me, as well. "Gem, do you think you and I kind of look alike?"

She doesn't answer. I turn around. She's gone.

"Bye then!" I yell, and it echoes down the long, empty hallway.

I measure beneath my folding-table desk in the kitchen. At the hardware store, I purchase a roll of chicken wire, a trowel, a hammer, nails, and loose wire. I have the guy cut the two-by-fours and a piece of plywood to size. Gem sees me building the cage on the front porch. I explain to her awkwardly what it's for, and she throws her head back and barks out a deep laugh.

"I like this Rayne person. She's wack!"

She gets on her knees and takes over. We make a base with the plywood and two-by-fours and use the chicken wire to encase three walls and the ceiling. The most work comes around building the little door, but Gem has a way with figuring stuff out. She even adds a little latch. She stands back and surveys the finished product. "For your monsters," she says, and laughs again. "Fantastic!"

I carry the cage inside and put it beneath my desk.

The next morning, I get up at six and sit in front of my computer. I take a deep breath, lean down, and open the cage. "Monsters, you may come out," I say.

I hover my hands over the keyboard and break into sobs. The keyboard gets soaked with tears. I want to be seen and heard. I've always only wanted to be seen and heard. Out the window, a view of the moss-covered roof of a red shed. Hours go by. I write one paragraph. I give up.

Again the next day, the crying. Again, one paragraph. And the next day.

One day I write two paragraphs between the tears. A week later it goes up to three. Slowly, I stop weeping and start doing more and more writing.

I write snippets. Vignettes. Flashes of a life. I write about bad things I want no one ever to know, cut them into small strips, and burn them one by one in a pan on the stove. I write about love and put the pages in the freezer to stop time.

I pen strange stories. A woman who sits with her head in her hands, and when she sits back up, her head doesn't come with her. She carries her head like a sack of potatoes under her arm for the rest of the story. Another where a small girl is nailed to a cross in the garden, a scarecrow there to keep away the crows. The stories are weird and dark. I open the cage and let the monsters have their say.

★ ★ ★

My unopened tarot deck has been sitting on the scarred travel trunk for months. I haven't even unwrapped the cellophane around the box. Day after day I walk around the deck and view it from different angles like a deer circling food, wary it's a trap. Sometimes I hold the deck in my palm, like I used to do with my pack of smokes. They attract and repulse, a love and a fear. They carry a power, or I do, or both. I fear what ogres will be released if I engage them.

I read the history of the deck in the pamphlet that comes with it. It's called the Thoth deck. Painted by Lady Frieda Harris, commissioned by English occultist Aleister Crowley, the cards incorporate imagery from disparate disciplines: science, philosophy, a variety of occult systems.

One night a few weeks after I've started my writing routine, curtains drawn and candles lit, I decide to take them out of the box. Once I pierce the plastic I know there's no going back. I slip them out of the box and hold the deck without looking at the images for several minutes.

Slowly, I turn each card over. One card called Art fascinates me above the others, a two-faced woman, one side dark, one light, pouring an elixir into a giant cup flanked by a lion and an eagle. The symbology and the archetypes burn something deep in my groin. On the Universe card, a woman rides a snake and blasts light into a giant third eye. The Devil card has balls.

Pandora's box. Now I know I won't be able to put the secrets back. For the next week or so, the cards remain scattered across the travel trunk as I come and go, as I cook or write in the kitchen, as I move the trunk to the side at night to open the futon. I dream of the Art card night after night. Her dark side like my dark side.

Soon the deck is in the futon with me, scrambled across the deep-green sheets. I awake to a Knight stuck to my thigh, an Ace of Cups plastered to my cheek.

There must be a discipline around learning how to use them. I spend weeks staring at each card. There are seventy-eight cards in the deck: twenty-two that are major cards, like the Sun, the Magician, and the Fool, and then fifty-six minor cards that mirror a deck of playing cards.

I start with the major cards and get to know them one by one. The little booklet that came with the deck is no help, both too impersonal and too old world. I spend hours studying the expressions on faces, the use of color, the things they carry: lanterns, scales, swords, wands, flowers, scepters, fruit. The figures start to appear in my dreams, silent entities running through my consciousness like underwater earthquakes, like hidden storms, tip-tapping like rain, leaving traces of their knowledge speckled on my flesh.

Awake, I ask them questions. *Why can't I find a journalism job? Why am I in Seattle, for what purpose? What is my purpose?*

The questions are too big. The answers too complicated. I can't read them. I go smaller. *What will happen at my job interview?*

I pull a card or two from the major cards and record what I can see in them in a journal. After the interview, I jot down what happened and compare the notes. I do this for question after question, fill up a journal with the queries and with the cards' responses. I record the outcomes. Compare.

Then it starts to blossom. I'm given answers awake and in my dreams. I can start to discern as I look at the cards what is my ego response and what is intuition. There is a flavor to intuition, an energy that differentiates it from thought. Mere thought is full of tension and desire. It is selfish and clinging.

When I'm receiving higher answers, when the archetypes speak to me, my heart beats a little faster, my breath rushes with excitement, there are goosebumps. If it's really on target, my genitals pulse like I'm about to have sex. The answers seem to come from an energy field around me. The energy in an intuitive hit feels free, not constricted and fisted, not selfish like my thoughts.

This goes on for months. My skin clears up. My psyche clears up. Without the fog of booze, I start to notice things: stamen of a flower, dew on a blade of grass, patterns on the wings of a bird, differences in the pulse of the wind. Without cigarettes, my smell and taste come rushing back. It's as if there was this vivid world I'd been missing out on. The aroma of lemons at a kid's lemonade stand, the tang of a Fuji apple at a farmer's stall at the downtown market.

I only noticed these things before tangentially, as a backdrop of a bothersome life, but now they've become vivid entities. As if my clear attention is breathing life into everything around me and they in turn are breathing life into me.

On a soft spring day in May, a breeze moves the curtains at the open window, a finch moves in the weeds outside, and the whole game irrevocably changes.

On the boom box, Pachelbel's "Canon." I'm cross-legged on the hardwood floor, shuffling the deck. Something wraps itself around my torso, a generosity, an abundance, something new and fresh and perhaps as old as time. It flows around my head and softens my vision.

In a trance, I pull the Prince of Wands first and stare at it in my palm, mesmerized. The Prince comes alive in my hands. He releases one leg from the confines of the card, then another, and stands up. He prances to the edge of my hand, leaps, and hits the ground like a dancer. He looks at me and holds up both hands as if to say, "What now?"

I pull more. The Queen of Cups slips from my fingers in a billowing dress and twirls into form.

The Prince extends his hand to the Queen to dance, but she turns her back. He taps his foot, crosses his arms, and looks to me because he wants more. I pull. The Queen of Swords brandishes her blade and throws it down between my fingertips, and the tip embeds into the hardwood. She jumps with a thud to the floor. The Page of Coins follows, shy and unsure, rolling the coin in front of her like an old tire. The Jester has cynicism written all over his face.

The group transmutes into actors playing out a skit, which I understand that I'm meant to interpret. The Queen of Swords grows critical of the Jester, and the Page of Coins is having an affair with the Devil. The Prince tries to make nice with everyone, but his cohorts are too self-involved.

It is a passion play, a harmonizing Greek chorus, a backdrop to the legend of my life. They cavort, caper, frolic, and prance. A side of me so long hidden is flowering into form, a world beyond anything I could've imagined.

At night with the blinds drawn, I throw readings. For now, this is my little secret. I study the actors and record the passion play in my journal—my personal mythology, the metaphor and symbol of the psyche. I begin to keep a record of my wild and provocative dreams and visions, too, the hieroglyphics of my soul.

It is strangely satisfying talking to the cards and confiding in my journals. I spend money I don't have to buy gorgeous receptacles for my thoughts: handmade, threaded at the spine, hand-torn pages, covers that are engraved and embedded with jewels. Soon, several are filled up and stacked on the shelf. They feel like an ancient friend, like someone rich beyond belief.

I buy more decks. Cards painted for Italian Viscounts, or with Egyptian imagery, or modern renditions by collage artists. I have a deck in every room. The kitchen deck, the bathroom deck, the traveling deck I keep in my backpack.

Relationships with the different decks are like relationships with different friends. They have wildly varied personalities. Speaking to the collage deck is like talking to a hippie on acid who has flashes of genius. The Italian decks are fanciful and moving, like a period film, but ever so hell fire and fury in their message. Thoth is full of some carnality that boils at the base of my spine.

Something happens as I keep reading. An empathy flowers, an understanding and love for people. It is me, but it's bigger than me. I keep getting the phrase *The Great Compassion.* The phrase stays with me. My vision of the world softens.

A red scarf over the standing lamp throws a menstrual glow. Gem and I have cleared enough space to sit on the floor of her side of the duplex. I'm going to read tarot cards for her, my first reading for another person, and I'm nervous as hell.

"I don't mind you using me as a guinea pig, just don't turn me into a Stepford Wife. Don't tell me how to live my life like a good and proper woman. Seriously."

I'm not nervous about whether or not I'll be good at it, but about exposing the secret joy of the cards to the outside world, even if the outside world is only Gem.

Gem tells me she quit smoking in "sympathetic cocreativity" with me. I'm moved by this. She's working on a tall sculpture in the corner by the windows. She keeps it covered with a tarp and won't let me see. Open paint tubes are left on the floor and walked on, and there's a rainbow of a mess staining the floors. Part of me is terrified of the way she lives, and part of me wishes I had such nerve.

"I knew someone who used cards and divination to get you to do what they want, or to *be* what they want. Why isn't tarot used to tell you you're a great person, to just be who you are. Just say, 'You're spectacular, Gem. You're an amazing artist, Gem!'"

I'm trying to figure out where Gem had this experience where she was judged for being herself. I think it was from her mother, but she never talks about her family. I don't even know how she makes money. She often goes on what she calls "artistic walkabouts," and I don't see her for months at a time. I study her, look at her hard.

"Don't give me the death stare. I just don't like people trying to control me with their beliefs." She picks at wax encrusted on two candle holders, molds the hot wax into a small marble.

I throw a Celtic spread. Because of my doubts, I struggle with the difference between what the cards are really saying and what I wish they were saying. I fight to discern what's in my mind and what's intuition. When I'm alone, when the archetypes talk to me, it is something beyond intuition, something greater, a vast well of knowing. And when I can tap into it, it's a vast well of healing. But here, because I'm having doubt, I'm struggling. Gem notices.

"Sister, it's OK. Shouldn't this at least be fun? Don't sweat it so much."

Her words release whatever is holding me back. I start giggling as the cards stand up and begin to move, to dance, to gesture. A Queen confides in her Fool, who has issues with the arrogance of the Star. The personality of the play they're performing is so different from mine. There is more galloping and horseplay. It's wild, untethered. The Knight rides his stallion, wild and beautiful, unbreakable. I can see so many scars on the horse's belly from people enraged by its spirit.

"OK, so you're going to think I'm just saying this because of what you just said." I touch the Devil card. "Basically, the entire reading is just telling you to *be*, despite what your mother tells you, despite how society has tried to beat it out of you. You're wild and feral and it scares people. They try to tame you, but you will have none of it." I look at the Devil; Gem's reading is raving and untamed. I can see why she scares people. "By the way, you've never told me about your mother."

"My mother is pretty much like your mother," she says. And I think, *Yes, that's the problem with roles.* All "mothers" become one cliched person, become a role that society trains them to be, and they're not allowed to figure out their real identity.

"You scared your mother. You were so free," I say. "I actually have compassion for her after reading this. She had no idea how to manage such a wild child. It wasn't just the training her generation of women underwent to be 'good' women—you were truly two very different personalities. She was at a loss, so she either tried to control you or just left you alone. You reminded her of her father, and he never sat still, was always looking for adventure, and well, that scared her too. So it was a built-in ancestral fear that you triggered.

"The problem was, she didn't really try to get to know you," I say. "That's where the abandonment comes in. It was great in one way because you got to grow up to be the wild and wonderful force of nature that you are, but it was lonely." I look at Gem. "The person who was supposed to try and 'get' you didn't try hard enough."

Gem is leaning forward. Her hair is combed out straight today. She hides behind it, but the hidden eyes boil with emotion. She looks goth, ghost-like. Her snake tattoo writhes.

I say, "It says don't underestimate how damaged you are by all of this." I reach out to her solar plexus and move my hand like I'm turning a knob. "There's something serious that's been fucked with right about here. You did what you wanted, danced to the beat of your own drum. It just wasn't done to act like that as a girl. Whatever lodged in your solar plexus over that—it's why you're stuck."

"I'm not stuck," Gem says, low and dark. She's tense, her jaw set, her eyes full of anger.

"Oh my God, your mother was jealous. Your father was jealous." It comes to me so clearly. "Much evil is done in the name of jealousy, much twisting and darkness in that jealousy."

I feel so much love for Gem, big love, and *The Great Compassion* envelops me. Compassion for her, even for her mother, for her father, even for myself.

"My mother didn't fucking touch this," Gem says, pointing to her chest. She gets up and goes out, slamming the door. I've upset her. I'm going to have to learn how to couch this information. I notice a statue of the Chinese Goddess of Compassion, Kwan Yin, on a messy shelf. She isn't like any other Kwan Yin I've seen before, painted in so many different colors, like hippie tie-dye.

Gem storms back in, flops down in front of me.

"Sorry," I say. "I'm not that good yet."

"It's not your fault." She breathes raggedly and tries to get herself under control. In a softer voice, she says, "Don't underestimate. Keep talking." She puts her hands on her knees, cranes her neck to one side then the other like she's doing yoga or getting ready for a prize fight. "Just because I'm pissed off doesn't mean you're wrong."

I'm careful now, not sure what to say or not to say. "It's just saying the world wants to turn you into a stereotype, into Mother, or Caregiver, or Wife." I think about Rayne's explanation of Divine Feminine and don't know how these traditional female roles fit into that. Roles that Gem and I have always found offensive. They don't have anything to do with who you really are, but with what people want you to be.

"Do you know about this phrase, Divine Feminine?" I ask.

"Ugh," she says. "I hate the terminology. But yeah, I get it. I've always seen the divide between the 'Divine Feminine,'" she uses exaggerated air quotes, "and the 'Divine Masculine' as a divide between the two sides of the brain, the left linear side and the right creative side. And it's like there's a wall built up between the two in our society. And the right creative side is like this baby bird begging 'feed me, feed me'."

Her words affect me and I need time to process it, but not now. "Your reading is saying that you want to define the Divine Feminine for yourself, outside restrictive, society-induced roles. Does that make sense?"

She picks up the Devil. The black paint on her nails is chipped. I don't say anything for a long time. From behind her hair she says, "More?" I can see something opening in her eyes.

"It just keeps repeating that message about being your wild self in different ways. What if you could understand and break free of their jealousy? That jealousy has shaped how you expect people to respond to you.

"It keeps saying that's the message, and we can say it in different ways if you need to hear different renditions. And you're not to worry what anyone else thinks. And for a woman to be feral and wild is something the world needs really, really badly."

She gets up and paces catlike around her apartment. Gem always smells like sex, but now she's like a bitch in heat. Even I want to have sex with her. "You gotta take this shit on the road, Pearl."

"What?"

"I'm so fucking pumped up. I haven't been this pumped up, well since last night when I fucked . . . you know . . . " she points vaguely toward the bathroom. I do know, because I heard them going at it all night, the pounding against the wall like a primal drumbeat, a vibration in the belly.

"That's like a nothing reading," I say. "You don't need to be psychic to get all of this about you." I'm riding high on the magic. It happens every time, like I'm stoned. "It's probably a message you could say to a lot of people."

"I get what you're saying. But sometimes the truth is super simple and sounds stupid. Right? Like John Lennon, 'Imagine there's no heaven . . . it's easy if you try . . . ' Stupid. Simple. Deep. Sometimes the deepest messages are the most obvious. Even if that message could be said to everyone, the words you used, the vocabulary, seemed meant especially for me." She put a finger to her solar plexus and pressed there.

As Gem harangues me about reading tarot in public, I come down off the tarot high. This happens too after I read. It's like a drug, and when it wears off, I'm strung out.

She won't stop badgering me. She wants me to read at psychic fairs or metaphysical bookstores like some circus freak. I need a drink but can't have one. And I can't have a cigarette, and it pisses me off.

"You have to get out and share this gift with the world, Pearl!"

"No." I stand up. "No!" What have I been playing with? I throw the cards in my hand down. This is my worst nightmare. Psychics are losers. Why am I even going this direction? Who wants to be mocked, hated, even murdered? I don't care what doors it's opening. I shudder, scream too loudly, "What am I, a trained monkey?" I snap, "A circus sideshow?"

"Pearl, you just gave me an incredible reading! Why the reaction? It was beautiful. Powerful. You can travel the world by yourself, move to Japan, become a journalist in London, but you're scared of *this*?" She leans down and picks up a tarot card, the Sun.

"Some white-trash woman in a trailer park with a fucking kid in shitty diapers in a broken playpen nearby, drinking beer and reading people's fortunes? That's what you want me to be? Some redneck fortune teller?"

"Wow." Gem pulls her fingers through her hair. "No issues there."

Just then a guy emerges from the long hallway leading to the kitchen. I look at Gem surprised. She shrugs, sits on an upside-down five-gallon bucket in the corner, crosses her legs.

"I know you told me to make myself scarce, but I've got to motor," he says. He could be the twin of the guy I saw when I came back from the food bank. He has dark hair, an open shirt, low-riding trousers, suspenders, long ankles. There's something sensual about his ankles. I want to lick them.

He's looking at me watching his ankles and laughs.

"I'll get out of your hair," he says. I feel mortified and hope Gem doesn't think I'm after her man. He sits on the bed and puts on boots. I watch him.

"OK, ciao for now," he says, and as he passes me, he puts long fingers into my hair and cups the top of my head. It feels fantastic, like he's cupping my crown chakra. I'm enjoying it too much and look awkwardly at Gem.

She laughs heartily and winks as the boy opens the door and leaves.

Gem disappears for weeks. I don't know where she goes, but her apartment is dark. I miss her more than is normal. Daily, I go and knock, but she's not there. Nothing changes for me. I work on the boat, read tarot for myself, write every day, still see Rayne when I can afford it.

When Gem finally returns, I invite her over. She laughs at the cage beneath the desk and wedges herself at the small kitchen table.

I make split pea soup from scratch, the earthy smell fills the kitchen. Comfort food to combat ongoing nicotine cravings.

She's wearing a black leather bustier and crimson lipstick, and her nails are glistening tar. I ask her where she goes when she disappears.

"I go underground when I can't take it anymore," she says. "I get lost. I lose myself."

"Where do you go?"

She doesn't answer. I feel how much I don't want to lose her, and it surprises me. There is so much I don't know about this girl who lives on the other side of the wall.

As I stir the thick green soup I tell her how my sister and I used to make green pea soup, that we'd share it every Sunday after Mass.

"I had no idea you have a sister," Gem says.

"Half sister. Haven't seen her in ten or eleven years, and I'm not even really sure where she is, or if she's alive." Tracy Chapman is playing on the boombox. I got a box of old cassettes at a yard sale. *Sorry is all that you can't say. Years gone by and still . . .* "She ran away when I was eight."

"I can relate to the running away part," Gem says in a way that carries more weight than the current conversation. "Fight or flight, baby."

I revert to complaining about Seattle, one of my favorite subjects. "The only places of interest in any neighborhood are for shopping. Everything is about the almighty dollar." I stir my displeasure deep into the soup.

"It's not just Seattle, my dear friend," Gem says. "The entire spectrum of American culture is centered on the spending of money on knickknacks and baubles. Seattle is actually pretty much the best city you could've landed in. If you think the consumerism is bad here . . ."

"What do you think all this focus on consumerism is doing to the soul of the American?" It's difficult to explain all that I'm seeing. This is the power of distance that leaving a country and living abroad for years has given me, and the curse of being a channel—I can see so much. I can see how love is replaced with tchotchkes. How we have to keep making the tchotchkes that equal love until we destroy the entire planet for a mistaken notion of love. "Every relationship is somehow based on a financial transaction. It's just not like that elsewhere. It's this cultural way that people here don't even see."

The soup is thick and green, bubbling like a witch's cauldron. I look over and Gem is painting her toenails the same tar black as her nails.

"Of course there's consumerism everywhere in the world, and it's getting worse. But there's a flavor to it in the States I haven't seen anywhere else. It seems to me that people in other countries still remember that the baubles are the representation of the thing, not the real thing. But here the veil has fallen so fully, no one remembers."

Gem says, "For my part, I hate the politically correct shit of the West Coast. I hate when everyone says the *right* thing. One big platitude party." She stops painting her toes. She's letting her hair turn into dreadlocks, and she plays with a knotted strand.

"And don't get me started on all the American flags," I say.

Gem gets up and leaves the kitchen, goes down the hall.

I yell, "Why do Americans feel the need to fly so many flags? Enough with the freaking flags! They obstruct the view. This country is gorgeous and all of the flags are obstructing the goddamn view." I ladle out the soup and carry the bowls down the hallway.

Gem is sitting on the futon playing with my living room tarot deck.

"And there's no one I can talk to, besides you and Rayne. No one. I don't feel like this place is home at all. It's unbearable to come home to America and feel like it's not home at all. Where is home? I keep asking myself. Where is home?"

I need to make a change. The boat job isn't cutting it for me anymore. The previous week a worker shattered his foot in a dozen places kicking a rope onto a grommet—I'm fearful now. I don't want to crush my hand or maim myself for minimum wage. It's not a safe place to work. *Take. Take. Take.* I know I need to make a move, but I don't know which direction.

Something rumbles up from the depths, and one of the bowls slips from my grasp. It falls in slow motion and crashes to the floor, shattering on the hardwood. Peas and green goo spill everywhere. I stand over the mess. My pants are filthy. I start crying. I hand the good bowl to Gem and kneel, crying, and pick up the gob-covered broken pieces. I miss London. I miss my expat life. I miss Finn. I try to stop myself from thinking about him, but the images fly around me like bats. America disturbs me to my core, and no one else seems to see it. I want my old life back.

"Pearl, leave it."

"I have to clean it up."

"Leave it and come."

I stand lost in the mess.

She holds out her hand. "Learn to live with the mess, Pearl."

I sit next to her on the futon. I have green pea soup on the knees of my jeans, the cuffs are covered in the sticky goo, and I spy a gob of pea soup on the closet door.

"Listen to me. I know it's hard. Seattle will never be London. You need to connect the dots, OK, around why you've gone through everything you've gone through. First, the expat life, now repatriation, and now not fitting in Seattle. Why do you think all of this is happening?"

"I have no idea."

"It all makes sense to me. Each new experience makes you question your identity, right? What good is there in questioning your identity?"

I shrug.

"To find out who you really are. Isn't that the whole point of the life you've led? To question everything and come up with your own life and not some role that society thrusts upon you? It all starts with not fitting in, right? Maybe it's about finding home in here." She touches my heart.

"It's so hard."

"Nobody ever said it was going to be easy, my friend. So, first things first," Gem continues, "you've got to stop comparing it to London. Seattle has the soul of a medium-sized town. There's nothing wrong with that, per se. I know America is a tough nut to crack. It's not like I'm a big fan of this country either. But you've got to find something you do love about it, anything, and focus on that."

I start crying again. She holds up the deck of cards. "Let me read for you."

"You don't know how to read them!" I say. But I reach over to the trunk, move books out of the way, and light a candle and incense.

She lines up six cards in a row. She doesn't know what she's doing. She picks up each card and studies them. I notice a gob of green on the toe of her boot.

When she picks up the Tower card, a tower on fire, crumbling, her face changes. She stops smiling. A shadow crosses over her cheeks and she shakes herself. Some collective foretelling is in that shadow.

"Wow, that was disturbing. I don't know how you do this. This shit takes me down a dark rabbit hole. Or toward a future I'd rather not see." She puts the Tower back and puts both hands flat on top of the cards, obscuring them.

"The cards say you need to make more friends here, and to do that you have to stop talking about your international travel with new people you meet. Just stop talking about yourself. That's the only way you're going to make any new friends, and you *need* friends."

"You're that sick of me."

"More friends than just me."

"I can see that's not what the cards say."

She picks up a Page of Swords, puts it to her ear. "What's that you say? Tell Pearl people don't know how to respond to someone talking about Tokyo or the Himalayas?" Gem holds the card out to me and I take it. She uses a high-pitched voice as if the card is talking to me. "Stop. Talking. Pearl."

A thousand thoughts fly through my mind. Who *am* I if I can't talk about my experiences? It goes to the heart of my identity. I become invisible, a nobody. People who have never lived abroad think that you're bragging, that you've lived some magical life. They don't realize that the struggles of a workaday life are the same no matter what country you're in. Yes, it's exciting, but the challenges are great, greater than anything else you've known. Who you are *becomes* the global life. Who am I if I can never speak of that? I hold the card and look at Gem, and now I feel unable to speak even to her. Like my throat chakra has been clogged. Like I'm a little girl again and my reality is not wanted. It is a big trigger. I couldn't speak as a child. I couldn't talk about my visions. I couldn't talk about what I saw. I couldn't *be*. It wasn't allowed.

"It's more than just about me," I say finally to Gem. "It's about having a dialogue that's bigger than just one geographical place on the map. I want to have larger conversations that aren't just about this one corner of the world."

"I'm not saying it doesn't suck."

"I'm going to have to hide myself? Pretend? Hide my interest in the world?" I want to punch her in the face.

"Hey, calm your jets, I'm on your side. I can't stand it when women have to hide. It makes me insane." She is devouring the soup. Slurping. Making noises between bites. "This is fucking delicious."

I have to wait until she's finished the bowl, watching, waiting.

She wipes her mouth on the back of her sleeve. She licks the inside of the bowl.

"There's some more on the floor if you feel like licking the hardwood."

"Is there more in the pan? Damn, girl, you're a fucking good cook. Who'd a thought it?" She gets up to go to the kitchen, and I grab her wrist. Point to the cards. She sits down.

"OK, it says the people here are feeling judged by you, and that doesn't help. OK? Can I go now?" I keep holding onto her wrist.

"*They* feel judged? *I* feel judged," I say, "by every middle-class breeding couple that lives in the status quo and thinks that's the only worthy reality. By every person who asks if I'm married yet, or when I'm going to have kids. By every person whose greatest goal is to buy a house in Madrona. Far be it from the mainstream to have to question *their* realities."

"Soup!" She exclaims, pointing into her empty bowl. She gets away from me and heads down the hall. I follow her, still talking.

"There are conversations that we all need to be having. Global conversations. And we're not having them."

Gem fills her bowl up, walks back down the hall and sits on the futon. I follow her.

"I want to yell to people, 'You're going the wrong way!'"

Gem pulls the bowl up to her face and shovels the contents into her mouth.

"When I was a kid," I say, "I was at this school event and my mother came to pick me up. Some of my friends were there too. My aunt was in the car. This was so rare. I don't know why my aunt was there. I was sitting in the middle, between my mother and my aunt, in the front seat. My mother pulled out onto the highway, a divided four-lane highway with this massive grass median, two lanes going one direction, and across the median, two lanes going the other way. My mother pulled into the wrong set of lanes. We were driving seventy-five miles an hour into oncoming traffic. My mother was upset about something and she wasn't in her body. I think back and have no idea why she was upset. I'm pretty sure it had to do with my father."

Gem is filling up another bowl.

"Because it was two lanes, the cars moved over to the left, so you could think you were on a two-way street. I kept crying, 'Mom, we're going the wrong direction!' She wouldn't listen. My hands were in fists; I was bearing down on my fear.

"She said 'Pearl, this is the way to the house, you know that.'

"And I remember crying, 'Wrong way, Mom. Mom!' She wouldn't listen to me.

"We were going up a hill. Now there was no way the traffic on the other side could see us as they barreled forward. They were going to hit us head on, and we were going to die. Cars were honking. I kept insisting we were going the wrong way. I saw the wheels finally turning in my mother's mind as I looked at her profile. She looked over the median and could see the other lanes of the highway in the distance.

"She yelled, 'Oh my God, oh my God, Pearl!'

"She slowed way down. There was an exit up ahead, but she was going so damn slowly. A car came over the hill and veered just in time before hitting us head on. She slowed down even more. There was no way to drive onto the median because it sat higher than a normal curb. The anxiety in my body was so high I felt like I was going to explode. Inch by inch, cars veering, drivers screaming, we finally made it to the turn-off. I was sobbing. My mother was shaking."

Gem and I are sitting at the cramped kitchen table now. I rest my arms on my knees. Gem puts her hand on my upper back.

"She kept saying, 'Pearl, don't tell your father. Oh please don't tell your father.' Like I'd tell him anything, ever.

"My point is, Gem, we're going the wrong way. We're all going too fast the wrong way. I feel like I'm in Mom's old Chrysler Deville crying wrong way, and no one will listen. I just don't want to have the normal conversations, any chitchat that doesn't question a system heading for a full-on crash. Small talk makes me insane."

Gem licks some green off the tips of her fingers. "Who is the woman in Greek mythology who can foresee the future but is cursed and no one believes her?"

"Cassandra," Gem and I say together.

Gem stands with her bowl. "Even with all of that you still need human connection. Cassandra needed friends. No matter where you ended up living, these visions, this perspective you have, you'd still need friends, right?"

I say, "What about letting the bitch run free over the wild Serengeti?"

"You can let the bitch run free with me. But I think you've got to give other people time to get to know you first. I'm pretty sure over time you'll meet people you can really talk to. Hey, these are the consequences of traveling the world! Poor you. Now you have to try to fit in."

She's right, but I don't want to hear it.

"Anyway, don't give people so much credit or so much blame. Most people just think about themselves and their own lives. So when you're out, just keep the bitch tied up, and she can run free at home."

I'm disturbed. "Why the fuck did I move back to the States?"

"Look, I'm pretty sure there's a reason you're here in the Pacific Northwest. I'm not a huge fan of Seattle, and even I know I'm here for a reason." I wonder what that reason is for Gem. I didn't even know she didn't like it here.

"Sometimes we have to do things we don't like, live in places that don't suit us, because there's something else we're supposed to be learning."

Even though I feel the truth of what she's saying, I'm still upset. "I'll have to be invisible like when I was a child." It is my worst nightmare. "I'll have to shut up and nod like a dashboard dog."

She pats me on the back. "Nice doggie."

I growl at her.

"Can you make another batch of soup?"

I reluctantly get up. Gem skips behind me on our way to the kitchen, singing "green pea soup, green pea soup" over and over. She watches me prepare it. "You've got some serious magic in those hands."

I snort.

Two days later, I find a wrapped gift on the doormat. A tiny card says it's from Gem. "From one bitch to another." Inside is a bulldog, its head on a spring. I flick its muzzle with my finger, and it bobs its head like a good girl. I take it back and attach it to the corner of my desk.

I stare at it, morose, but then I realize something. Here, this space, this folding table in this corner of this kitchen, is where the bitch can run free. *Here. This* writing corner. My writing is the only place I can truly say everything I think, everything I've learned, everything I've experienced in my journey. Somehow I wanted this life. Somehow I asked for it. Just because you've asked for something doesn't mean you have to like it.

This rundown apartment near the whores, this rickety table, this old used computer. This is only place the bitch can run free over the wild Serengeti. This is the only place this dashboard bitch will have her say.

VI
THE LOVERS.

CHAPTER 6

The Lovers

I mull Gem's advice not to talk about myself and the rebel in me rears its head. No one tells me to shut up. *Be silent? Screw that! I'll talk more. Screw you, Gem,* you *shut up.*

I tell more stories. To the staff in the headquarters, the crew on the boat, the captain, the tourists. I talk about the poverty in India, the villages of shacks, the sewage, the naked children playing in the sewage, their bloated bellies. The woman with her nose missing from leprosy. The family I met in India who lived in a dumpster, the motionless newborn in the metal container I thought was dead but wasn't.

I talk about the boat boy in the Philippines who took Finn and me on an overnight ride through a dark sea, the sky dripping with billions of stars, like some magical movie, some fantasy, about the fish we saw snorkeling, this whole other world that lives just below the surface.

Often I turn as I'm talking and no one is there. They leave when I'm not looking. I can walk into any area and it'll clear out in less than two minutes. Nobody wants to hear it.

They just want ha ha ha and tee hee hee. My depression grows thicker and I wear it like a dark coat.

I stop talking, not because Gem says so, but because I'm brooding. On the boat I sit by myself and give the others the stink eye.

I spend a while in this dark place before I slowly start to notice what people are actually talking about. Conversations seem to revolve around TV and film. They quote something and laugh. They say things like "spoiler alert" before they speak. They team up to binge-watch TV, events to which I'm not invited.

I go out and get a TV, a small black-and-white set at a thrift store. Back at the apartment, I sit down and lean toward the scratchy images. *The Simpsons. Seinfeld. Judge Judy.* I have seen none of these shows. These gray players on the tiny screen, these archetypes of the American culture, become my doorway back in. This is repatriation. This is survival. Television becomes my re-enculturation.

I no longer talk about anything I have done or know or have seen. I talk instead about Homer and Jerry and Elaine, about Frasier and Niles.

And it works.

Months go by. I slowly, painfully start making friends. I even start dating.

A muffled world of weeping fecundity. Tree limbs drip with moss. The path slopes with mud. Our boots slip sideways on drenched rocks. Old growth towers like something out of a fantasy. Fat mushrooms grow near the slick trunks. The grass and moss glow neon green. Life sprouts from every surface, bark and stone and ground.

I'm with Red, a new boyfriend. We're in the foothills of the Cascades following a river, and the sound is so soothing I want to curl on the path and fall asleep. You never know how tired you are until you go where nothing is expected of you. And everything, simply by its nature, is given to you.

I think of the vision at Pioneer Square and know that what I'm seeing is but a shallow echo of what must have been here just a few hundred years ago. I look around and try to imagine the former glory.

Red keeps calling the river holy water. He is tall, ivory skinned, poetic. Sensuous. In Asia and Britain the men are small and thin. American men pulse with physicality. I call him my double-tall Americano. I haven't dated an American in a decade. He's eight years younger than me.

Nothing is for sale here. No one is in your face asking you to part with money. There's no work I have to do to pay bills.

We watch a black-tail deer take flight between branches and disappear. How long has it been since I last saw a deer? *Find what Seattle has that you love and focus on that*, Gem had said. I began asking myself what Seattle has that London doesn't.

Working toward what I love, focusing on that—it's a new concept. I spent so many years working against what I hated. Being a journalist meant working tirelessly to fix what was wrong with the world, rooting out evil, exposing it to the light, raining down justice upon it.

What did I love? I spent hours thinking about it, dreaming it, throwing cards on it, making lists. I believed in social justice for sure, the equality of every person, fairness, and women allowed their freedom, but what else? The tarot. Did I love the tarot? Was that weird? What did I love about it?

I love this forest. I love nature and always have. Mud and bark are the only places I've ever felt home. I couldn't think of what else I loved. What I loved became a lost memory from childhood. It was as if I'd forgotten my favorite color.

It was right after I realized how much I love the earth that I'd met Red, a hiker, an outdoor enthusiast. We go every weekend to the Cascades or the Olympics.

I don't say much as we walk. Not talking about myself is working. Red has a languid, dancing way of walking, a soft voice. He tells me we have a few miles to the hot springs. We come to a fallen log over the river. It is thick and slippery, rocks and rushing river below. If we fall we could break an ankle. Red prances across it.

I climb onto it, but I've been so in my head that I have little balance in my body. It feels like my head is four times the size of my torso, and it throws me sideways. My arms flail as I lose balance, but some force helps to right me, and I make it across.

Red is naming the trees, caressing the textured, hairy bark. Western hemlock. Douglas fir. Silver fir. The bushes are salmonberry and huckleberry—he shows me their berries in his palm. We pass rotting nursing logs, study the seedlings that germinate on the fallen trees.

I don't want to know their names right now. I want to simply exist in this permeable environment.

In London, Shirley used the word empath. She was right—I am a sponge, and whatever setting I'm in I absorb. The edgy, smoky, crazy streets of London wove into every vibration of every cell of my body. Now with Red in a dripping, mossy fairy tale forest next to a babbling brook, I become the vibration of the forest. My skin feels silky and wet likc the moss. I absorb roots and branch. My veins are filled with the water of the stream. I'm no different from a tree.

I stop to study deer droppings, small, round, brown pellets left by the deer. I grew up with deer. You think the type of deer you grow up around are the only deer, but they change depending on the ecosystem. This seems exciting to me. I pick two of the deer droppings up with my fingers. I've never been scared of shit. My childhood was full of the feces of dogs, penned-up animals, beasts of the forests. My last experience with deer was in the woods in Missouri, where we tracked game to kill. To survive.

"Why are you touching deer shit? Put it down," Red says. He takes my hand and flips it so the droppings fall to the mud. I don't tell him that I once tracked a deer, once killed a doe with the butt of a jammed gun. In a different lifetime.

Red shows me the difference between a lady fern and a sensitive fern. He won't stop naming things. I smile and listen. Nod. We're at the phase where the sex still outweighs the other person's annoying habits.

My legs ache. My muscles haven't had a workout for so long. I can feel the muscle memory and feel an urge, now that I'm no longer smoking and drinking, to find this fit self again.

We climb a steep slippery slope, roots as steps. At the top, at the first hot spring, three naked people sit in the pool. They look melted around the edges, so loose they can barely speak. We greet them and keep climbing. At the third pool, a girl with red hair is in water up to her waist, breasts bare.

"Hey Coral," Red says. They laugh with unfeigned affection. Something happens when two people genuinely care for each other. It fills up the world, it replenishes missing water. "Pearl, this is Coral. Coral, Pearl."

"Hi," I say. I like her energy immediately. She's probably in her late twenties but looks about twelve, with her long red curls floating on the water's surface. A dozen votives circle the edge of the pool, and she goes to relight three. Red and I strip.

From the water, above us are massive branches of old growth that drip, pitter pat on the pool surface, tap, tap on forest debris and earth.

"Holy water," I say. When a drop hits the top of your head, it is cold and sharp like a sudden idea.

Coral has a scar that runs from her breast bone down her stomach to her belly button. Looking at the scar is like looking into her soul.

She sees me staring. "Cancer," she says. "I was just about to graduate college."

I have a vision of her post chemo, rail thin, emaciated, sickly. Near death. Again that wash of *The Great Compassion*.

"I'm sorry," I say.

"It changed my life," she says with both a wisp of desperation and a wild jolt of hope.

We're so relaxed in the hot spring that none of us move when the sun starts to set. We discuss how we have no flashlights. How will we make it back through the woods to our cars? Still no one moves. Two by two, the people at the pools on the levels above us trek by, leaving before it gets too dark. Still, we stay.

Night falls. Above us the stars. I haven't been this happy since the Philippines, where being outside beneath the stars was part of normal day-to-day living. How many years ago was that now? My soul opens. Silhouette of a moss-covered branch of a red cedar, behind it the moon. Everything is dripping. Echoes of silver moonlight. Our whole world oozes sacred water. We're in the earth's womb, in vitro, floating down into the pool and up into the stars.

"I feel normal," I say. My head is resting against a rock. I can barely move it. "Human."

"Human," Coral says. "Being."

Red chuckles, low and throaty.

Well after midnight, we decide we either have to go back or spend all night here. Our heads are frigidly cold, and it's getting colder. We decide we must go. We dress in the dark, our loose limbs fumbling into clothes. No one thought to bring towels; our clothes become wet as soon as we put them on. We have no way to see where we're going down the steep path. Coral goes into her backpack, pulls out votives, places one in each of our palms, and lights them. Wet clothes, the pain in our palms from the dripping wax, three circles of light, a vast blackness, our breath like fog.

Coral takes the lead. I'm surprised by how short she is, nearly a head smaller than I am, and I'm not tall. We descend with blind trust, following her. I watch the top of Coral's wet curls as we descend the slippery path, marveling at the faith she has. Faith in the darkness is something otherworldly to me, something I want. We are blindly trusting her, but she's blindly trusting herself, a higher self, or a lower self, or something beyond that.

Our first challenge is to make it down the slippery hill to the forest floor. Slowly, slowly. One false step could topple the others down. When we make it that far, it's easier going, but we are quiet, focused. It's the middle of the night and we're in a black forest, and the only sounds are echoing animal calls and the shuffle of our feet. There is nowhere in the world I'd rather be. I haven't felt this good in so long. I don't want to leave here, don't want to go back to the real world.

Once I was in Southeast London visiting an actress friend. As I was walking down the main road from the bus stop, I became overwhelmed with the hundreds of aggressive cars, with the fumes and noise, no respite from the people, the concrete, the houses stacked one on top of the other. I was raised rural, in open spaces and vast, wild sky. I wondered as a woman walked by holding the hand of a child, how being raised around this many people and this much noise affected the psyche.

I felt a panic attack threatening like a storm. Looking back, I know my body was absorbing the chaos, my cells becoming the honking and sounds of construction, the water of my body being polluted with exhaust.

A blackened, crumbling church sat behind listless trees. I slipped off the main road and fled behind it to find a small, tumbled graveyard with weathered headstones. I felt such relief in the soil, profound release. For the first time, I saw the relief in death. All of us would end up together beneath the soil. All of the striving meant little, as we were led to the same place of rest. I sat on the ground next to a headstone and rested. No matter how madly we rushed the busy fairway, we'd all still end up here, beneath the soil, resting. Not just resting, but decaying back into the earth. No longer were we separated from nature.

I thought: *We go against that cycle to prove as a species we will somehow live forever in its hustle and bustle and hither and thither. It is all utterly exhausting.*

I left when the vicar came out the back door of the church and gave me a direct look.

"Rock," Coral says in a loud whisper. Our candles are burning down, our palms are burning, and besides small circles of light, we are surrounded by a vast pitch.

We lift our feet to Coral's commands.

"Root." Maneuver.

"Log." Climb.

"Hole." Skirt.

"Branch." Duck.

Our ancient sacred procession, specks of light in our hands, moves at a snail's pace beneath the massive arc of the darkened forest.

We hear it before we get to it. Coral stops. The river rumbles and splashes white in the darkness.

"River," Coral says and doesn't move.

Slowly, the three of us walk gingerly up to the water's edge. It's roaring now, tiny white caps flopping into relief in the moonlight. I go over and rub my palm over the log that crosses it. It's thick with frost and the wetness of nighttime, much slicker than the first time we crossed it. We will fall and break our ankles or crack our heads and be swept away by holy water.

Red walks up to the log and climbs it. I watch his shadow in the dark as he strides across and disappears into blackness on the other side. I need to muster his physical confidence. Any nervousness and my thoughts alone will push me off the log and into the freezing water. It is a lesson for life.

Coral climbs the log, stands with her arms outstretched. She crosses like a ballerina, toe forward with each step, candle held out like an offering.

I must follow her grace and Red's confidence. I step onto the log, stand, and can barely see it below me. I've always had trouble with my balance. I take one step. There is no way I will not end up in the freezing river. By the third step I give up and squat. I lie flat on my belly. I drag my torso across, grunting, a rough spectacle. Red and Coral laugh at me from the other side.

When we make it back to the car, I hug Coral ferociously. She's a friend.

She's like home.

My writing desk is filling up with talismans. The carved salmon, the freshwater pearl that my sister Meghan gave me so many years ago, my kitchen tarot deck, the dashboard dog, a striped rock I found with Red on Hoh beach on the Olympic Peninsula. Red and I spend every weekend in a wild place, leaping with our packs from boulder to boulder to access a hidden lake; walking miles with our packs through beach fog, rain driving at our faces; hiking hard up mountainsides to reach spectacular views.

The hikes add muscle and spit to my writing. Every morning at my desk, I open the cage and flick the dashboard dog under the nose. In the writing, I learn about myself, things I didn't know, things I once knew, or I recover memories that were once frightened out of me. The stories come unbidden on hiking trails, while I'm washing dishes—or they appear like ghosts in my dreams. They form one way in my head but completely transform once they leave my body and trot onto the page.

I was always a fast typist, clocked by disbelieving coworkers in the newsroom at one hundred forty words per minute. As I type, I think, *Oh, now this is what I'm doing with my hands, I'm telling stories.* This is alchemy, this is converting base metals into gold.

I'm sucked so deeply into the world of writing that I lose all sense of time. If I don't set an alarm, I can forget to stop and go to work. I can go months and lose track of time, thinking it is winter and surprised to see buds on the trees out my window. I forget to pay bills, forget to make money to pay bills.

As the purging calms me, as the buildup of energy inside me is released in the writing, I have an epiphany. All of the visions I've had and all of the intense emotion throughout my life needed to be expressed. All the soulful energy inside me just had no way out, so it would grab me and shake me. This force inside me was always just looking for a release, a way out. It just wanted to be listened to, to be heard, to be created from. The black dogs, the fits of depression, and the visions are just parts of me that have been chained up too long, like Lady Luck, whining and pacing a circle in the dirt. They just wanted out.

I have fewer and fewer visions. They're just stories that have not yet been told. My writing just needs off the leash. My soul only ever needed exercise, only ever wanted to be let loose to run free over the wild and pitted fields. I enter a different world, full of riches and intrigues, an abundance of realities.

When I finish my writing for the day, stand up and stretch, I'm surprised that I'm alone, that I have not interacted with dozens of people in the outside world. That I have in fact interacted with no one in one reality, but a host of characters in another reality. I never feel alone when I'm writing.

My life before was external. Now I'm entering the self, my focus solely on the inner world. Instead of reaching outward for validation, I sink inward. I have dreams of sinking. I have dreams of falling into water and going deeper and deeper.

Finding treasures there, depths of coral and multihued sea creatures, buried trunks full of gems.

When sheets of rain tap against the window, my tiny portal to the outside world, I feel I'm being cleansed. *What do you love?* Gem had asked. Finding what I love reminds me of what Shirley said back in London about finding the missing pieces of myself. Were these things I love the missing pieces?

Trips into the primordial forest with Red and Coral, this precious time at the folding table wedged into a kitchenette with a clunky computer, my deck of kitchen tarot cards. These things.

One Monday morning a year after I started this writing journey, I get up early to write. When I finish a few hours later, as I reach down to close the cage, I realize something about the monsters that have been haunting me.

They're *me*. The monsters are *me*. They're a pent-up, bursting-with-love-and-trauma *me*.

VII
THE CHARIOT.

CHAPTER 7

The Chariot

The goat is braying and the fool is skipping and the women are holding stars in their palms. As the writing comes alive, so does the tarot. Archetypes swarm my consciousness, let loose now from their restraints, every day a different theatrical performance, a perpetual vaudeville act, a different set of monkeys in a series of circuses.

I don't know what creates the shift, but I listen to Gem and take the tarot show on the road. I read for anyone who will let me: Coral, Red, drunk and stoned friends at Red's house parties, the boat crew, the boozy captain, the wait staff at pubs. Seeing inside so many people is a furious wake-up call, a call to arms. Tarot cards prancing on Formica tables, boat decks, front lawns, carpeting, on dirt around campfires. The archetypes pound a beat, throw a punch, beg a morsel, wail a blue note, belly a laugh—a darkest mirth. They face plant, stumble, and twirl with grace. They gorge and they starve.

I watch as the same card means different things to different people. For one it's heroic, for another it's an out-of-control ego. Each archetype has a core meaning, but how that meaning manifests depends on the personality of the person I'm reading for. The archetype is the outline of the thing, primordial energies like Mother, Father, Purpose, Hero, Love, but each person has a different set of crayons to color between the lines. As I read for boat captains and deck swabbers, receptionists and store clerks, I see how desperately everyone want to be seen, they want to be known, and how terrified they are that someone might see right through them.

Masks fall away. So many people think they are alone in their internal struggles. I learn that people are not alone in feeling alone.

At parties I'm put in back bedrooms for partygoers to come get their fix. There's a power to sitting across from a stranger, looking them in the eyes, witnessing their souls. I leave these events exhausted, barely able to bus home.

I buy a bike, black and clunky, for fifteen bucks. *Black Beauty.* I ride the hills of Seattle from Wallingford to downtown, up Capitol Hill to Fremont and beyond. Muscles in my legs harden. I become the fit and active child I once was. I find her again. *I love you ankles. I love you toes.*

It reminds me of being on my paper route as a child, riding miles through the Midwest countryside. It reminds me of Leo in India and flying in his cycle rickshaw. It reminds me of freedom. With my tarot cards in the bike's saddle bags, I feel like Mary Poppins, floating around the city creating magic.

One deserted early morning in Seattle's Fremont neighborhood, the streets are black and slick with rain, full of reflections of color and light. I'm biking to a new temp job. I pedal fast, purging sweat and breath. Pulling hard up the hills, popping up onto sidewalks, hands-free down long inclines. Lungs fill with air. Now that I'm not smoking, I'm breathing again. Face whipped by a cleansing wind. My favorite part is crossing the Fremont Bridge. No one around, lights reflecting off the waters of the canal. I love this predawn bike ride in Seattle before the people wake, before they turn beauty into a marketplace.

On this day, I bike by a small bookshop in a row of stores and stop. I must have passed it dozens of times. Dark behind the window, the reflection of me on my bike in my black rain gear resembles one of my tarot cards, the Knight of Swords.

I will be reading tarot at this bookshop. I bike away, knowing it's the truth.

That Saturday, I bike back and tie Black Beauty to a rack. Inside the bookstore, the front table is covered in Lamb, Estes, Carr, Angelou. At the counter a subtle, delicate woman asks if she can help me. Her blouse is incandescent blue.

"I'm looking for the owner."

"You've found her!" She laughs.

I introduce myself. Her name is Beatrice.

"Can I read tarot in your bookstore on Saturdays?" I ask in one rush. "Or Sundays?" I notice a bit of dried food on my sweater and cover it with my hand.

"Sure," she says. I look up, surprised.

"I can do a reading for you, if you like."

"Sure," she says again. She gets someone to take over the register, and we go to the back of the store, to a small alcove next to the toilet. In the alcove sits a little table and a love seat, and if we move the floor lamp, there's just enough room for two people.

I have her mix the cards. The Thoth are big cards, and they're difficult to mix. Her body vibrates with kindness. She's one of the first real givers I've met in a culture based on taking.

Her pure kindness surprises me like it's some kind of trick, like the other shoe will drop and I will need to be ready. The cards come alive on the small side table like a shadow play of Indonesian puppets, whimsical, haunting. I think I give Beatrice a good reading, because she agrees to let me read every Saturday out of this alcove. There appears to be no other shoe.

A red velvet tablecloth with a fringe, a fat candle, my tarot cards. A shelf holding used books. When you back up and look at the alcove, it is old world, circus, carnival. For the first time, this not only doesn't bother me, but gives me a rush. *I'm owning my inner circus freak.* The thought makes me laugh.

The first day, Beatrice has put signs in the front window advertising the tarot readings. I sit at the table in the back and wait. And wait. People pass by to use the toilet. I must remember to bring incense. One of the table legs jiggles. I try to fix it with a scrap of cardboard but the fix makes another leg jiggly, so I leave it.

From newsrooms in some of the world's biggest cities, from travels across Southeast Asia, to a rickety table in the back of a Seattle bookstore. Ladies and gentlemen, I've arrived! Finding the missing pieces of oneself requires being willing to go backward to go forward—apparently very far backward.

It's a long day of not reading for anyone until one of the staff comes back, short with a blonde bob and a post through her nose. She wants a reading but doesn't have much money. She asks if she can pay me with books. She can use her store discount that way. The readings are thirty dollars for thirty minutes.

Can you? Are you kidding? I want to hug her.

She's in grad school, a lit major. She's smart, edgy, and funny. We're leaning into each other and barking with laughter. We're running free here, and I don't have to be silent, and she can be fully herself, too. The characters on the table are prancing and dancing and telling a story of near madness, and this makes us laugh, too. For my troubles, I'm given the complete works of Shakespeare, an oversized, heavy paperback. That night, I carry the bard with pride upon my back as I steer Black Beauty toward home.

Over the following Saturdays, the staff starts coming back for readings one by one. Gay, straight, bi, sweet, intense, funny—we are a family of misfits here. I bike home with my pack full of Karr, Tartt, Le Guin, Woolf. The literature of the world jostles as I ride. I stack the books on the floor next to my writing table, and then later into bookshelf after bookshelf. I think, *In a country beset with buying and selling souls, I have finally found a sacred exchange.*

Word gets out. Soon there are too many people, and we start a sign-up sheet at the front. Banker types, women in business suits, rich housewives, poor artists, hippies, jocks, cheerleaders, nerds. They are not diverse in race—Fremont is too white for that—but diverse in socioeconomics. I assumed I'd only get the hippies. I feel honored to be allowed into the psyches and souls of such a swathe of society. It's like I'm traveling again, but this time downward instead of outward. It's like learning a new language. It's like visiting another culture, hundreds of other internal cultures.

When I'm reading for someone and tap into the sweet spot, I can feel it. It's light and hopeful and it is *all* me, and there is *no* me.

Many visitors to my table are square business types. I'm surprised by how metaphysical they are. Behind the business suit trappings are souls astral planing between solar systems. Some of the most conservative looking people are the wildest, and I look up from the cards into their eyes surprised, as if the suit is a wrapping that keeps all of the fractal parts cohesive, as if they'd fly apart if they didn't have their neckties.

And then there are the hippies who are conservatives. This surprises me nearly as much. Their unhappiness comes from trying to live an alternative life when all they want is stability. When I tell a goth girl with racoon eyes that she has two kids and a picket fence in her future, her face contorts, and behind that is a relief she won't acknowledge.

They come about grief and loneliness. About love lost and about love worn thin. They weep for broken families, for illnesses they can't afford, for jobs they can't abide.

Week after week, more and more people sign up. I sit for hours with no break looking into green eyes, blue, brown, and gray. People with big houses and people with tiny apartments. People with three children and people who never want to have children. People with PhDs and people with no education at all. Gay, straight, bi. Republican, Democrat, independent. Tall, short, fat, skinny.

Behind each question, no matter how wildly different the questioner, is a person who was never allowed to just *be*. This truth becomes so prevalent in every single reading, it's an epidemic. Every person seems twisted away from their true nature and forced into a world that values money over soul. This loss of self seems to be the reason for so much woe, so much war, so much personal pain. So many people are dying of thirst, begging for just one drop of soul. They turn to substitutes to quench the thirst—possessions, drugs, food, money. They try to fill the hole with more and more and more things.

All of the people I'm seeing in my metal folding chair in an alcove next to a toilet in a tiny independent bookstore in this sodden corner of the States have the same struggle I've had all my life. They cannot accept themselves. Again and again and again, I see this in the depths of their spirits. They are out of alignment with who they truly are. Everybody feels disconnected, alone. They feel judged for the sensitive beings they are, so they wrap themselves in accomplishments, in arrogance. In ego.

One Saturday, two young women come in for a reading. They're gorgeous, in low-cut dresses, heels, the nails, the eyebrows, the whole nine yards. Fremont is home to trendy bars, and this happens sometimes, two drunken friends walking by and seeing the tarot sign.

Beth wants a reading for her friend Sara. Apparently Sara isn't doing well in the dating scene. "She has so many opportunities with men. Guys are all over her. These great guys will talk to her, but then nothing comes of it. Look at her."

Sara is stunning. Unassuming. Straight hair, arched brows, delicate features, flawless skin.

Her friend is too intent upon Sara's dating life. There is something going on there, but I don't have time to figure it out because a book behind me flies off the shelf and lands on top of my feet.

"Whoa," says Beth. Sara jumps.

I pick it up. It's a lesbian book by a lesbian author. *Sara's a lesbian,* a voice screams in my ear, as if I didn't already get the message with the flying book.

"What does it mean?" I have no desire to tell this young woman she's gay if she's not ready for it. And she's clearly not ready for it.

"Let's do a reading."

She mixes the cards. Beth sits above us on a tall stool.

The cards give me clues as to how to address this without telling her directly. I spend a lot of time poring over them.

"Watch, look for who you are attracted to," I say. "The problem is, there is a certain type of person you're attracted to, and you just have to be clear on what type that is."

I can see the wheels in Sara's mind working. I can see she has held who she really is so deep, so very deep inside her for so long, and she's having a conversation with this other self now.

"Does it say when she'll meet the right guy? Like *when* it'll happen?" Beth asks.

"First she has to see it, then it can happen, so there's no real timeline. It says you're really hard on yourself. You want to fit in. Try not to be so hard on yourself, OK? You're great just as you are." It really says she beats herself up for being a lesbian, but I don't want to say this outright. "It says your parents were hard on you. They really want you to succeed. But their notion of success isn't yours." Her parents tried to mold the lesbian out of her, and their voices sit inside her too, telling her she's wrong for *being*.

Beth slumps on the stool. "We just want to know when she's going to meet the gu-uy," she whines.

"You're in your twenties, right?" I ask. Sara nods. I'm in my early thirties, but when I channel I feel ancient. "You'll go through a major transformation in the next couple of years, and as long as you are true to yourself, your real self, the life on the other side is brilliance and hope and love." Sara smiles for the first time. I smile back. She's actually quite a humble person wrapped in the flesh of a hot, cool babe.

There is really nothing more to say. I pull more cards but they say the same thing over and over. I tell her, "Write down what attributes you find attractive. Start writing it all down. It'll make more sense in writing."

I have her pull three final cards, a ritual I've devised to end the readings. It's like I open the flip top on my crown chakra to do the reading and the three final cards close it back down again.

"Let the chips fall where they may. You can say no to people. You have the right to be yourself. The word that keeps coming to me is faith. Have faith in who you really are. Have faith that you'll be loved for who you are."

Beth is in a boozy snooze on the stool and we have to rouse her. I give Sara a hug and wish there was something I could do for the child inside her who was never fully loved for who she really is. I wish there was something I could do for my own inner child, for the love she's now thirsty for.

Doing so many readings opens a portal of serendipity. I think it and it happens. Insta-karma, just add water. I think of a white rose, go outside to grab a coffee, and a white long-stemmed rose is lying on the pavement. Or after the readings, I'll bike home, think about a lamp I'd like to put on my writing desk, and it'll show up. Sometimes it's on my doorstep when I get home, a gift from Gem or Red or Coral, and sometimes I'm led to it.

One day, clad in rain gear, biking home from the readings through a sloppy Wallingford, I think about a chandelier to hang over the overhead light in the main room, a funky chandelier with dangling crystals that reflect rainbows when the sun hits them.

A voice in my head starts to direct me. *Turn right. Turn left. See the thrift store?*

I've never been to this thrift store. Didn't even know it was here. I tether my bike. As I walk into the store, the voice says, *Second shelf near the back wall.*

I go directly back and find the chandelier. It's exactly as I'd envisioned it. I purchase it for fifteen dollars and am back on my bike within five minutes. With the chandelier jangling from my handlebars, I wonder, *Does the object think about me and send out waves to enter my mind? Or do spirit guides plant the thought? Or does my thought create its appearance?*

I go through temp jobs like Gem goes through male lovers, a new one every few weeks. I can only stomach each job for so long. It's difficult to go from wide-open places of soul empowerment with tarot to a cubicle. It's difficult to be the lowest person in a hierarchy when you've just spent hours tapped into the divine. It's a bridge I find harder and harder to cross. I wish I could just do tarot, but I can't afford to live.

At one job, a man in his glass office picks the desk chair up, his suit hiking up his muscular frame. He holds it overhead, flings it over the conference table and toward the glass that separates him from me. The glass bends but doesn't break. At the reception desk I'm jumping out of my skin.

He flings papers against the wall. He throws folders against the windows, far below a view of Elliott Bay. This is an investment brokerage office. This is the fourth time he's had a fit since I started this temp job three weeks earlier. For the rest of the day, my body shakes. I go to the female manager and give my notice. She tries to talk me out of it. *You're the best receptionist we've found in years. That's just Frank. He just lost money on a deal. These guys are dealing in hundreds of thousands of dollars, sometimes millions. You can imagine what a loss like that does.*

I grew up with violence. I will not be around it.

Later, after the boss hears I've put in my notice, he comes out of his corner office and stands behind my chair as I type. I can smell his musky cologne. I have no idea why he's here. He's never spoken to me before.

He leans next to my ear. I freeze. "You think you're better than us," he whispers. "You think money is bad, and what we do doesn't do crap to help humanity. You feel superior to the work we do. Just go then. Who needs you?"

I say nothing. I don't turn around. He goes back into his office. Why does what I think matter at all to him? My father used to whisper hate in my ear, and here's another man in a position of power, whispering.

As I'm biking home, I realize how right the boss was in his understanding of me. All of the things he said were exactly what I feel. This investment banker is psychic! When he grows tired of his angry job, he could work as a full-time channeler! I laugh into the wind as I stand on my pedals and grind my way up a hill toward home.

I turn down temp job after temp job after this, sick of the normal world and all of its bruised egos, until I'm so strapped for cash I have to take whatever the job agency offers. The lumber yard is a twenty-minute walk from my house. I'm doing data entry. I enter lumber types and sizes into tiny boxes at an antiquated computer while a large woman in a muumuu stands over my shoulder and micromanages me. Oak, fir, hard maple, soft maple, walnut, cedar, two-by-four, four-by-four, plywood, four-ply, five-ply, seven-ply, nine-ply. I feel like killing myself. Rain pours in sheets down the windows, and rain pisses down in my soul.

On the last day of my second week, I leave the building and start walking to the bike rack in pouring rain. I'm crying. I don't know why I'm here. Is this the path to enlightenment the spirit guides were calling me to? I feel the dark night of the soul creeping up on me again.

A car pulls over. It's one of the managers at the lumber yard, a young guy in a suit.

"Hey, you OK?" he calls out his window.

"Fine," I say, clenching down on the sobs.

"Need a ride?"

"I'm OK." I hold up my helmet. "Bike."

"You sure you're OK?" He seems genuinely kind, and I have to grit my teeth.

I nod, wave him off, and continue my death trudge through slop and sludge toward my bike.

Rayne has a new office on Greenlake, a large space with purple walls, thick curtains, big plants, and paintings of women holding the moon. Somehow she makes this lifestyle work. I want to figure out how she does it.

I'm here because the people I read for are coming home with me. I'm here because I have no idea how to cross the bridge from spirit into temp world. I'm here because I'm trying to avoid the dark hole that's calling to me.

At a round table in the corner of the office, she first reads for me on the subject of temp work.

"Oh, I know that feeling well. Been there done that. I worked as a receptionist while I was building this business."

"You did?"

"I certainly did."

"I feel like offing myself."

Ten cards are laid out between us, upside-down cups and women holding too many swords.

"We're creating an entirely new system here, Pearl. We're rebuilding the Divine Feminine. If you're out there looking for a job, any job, it's going to be part of the old paradigm." She tells me she worked as a receptionist at an alternative healing clinic. I think about how something like that would be a better fit.

Rayne takes a look down at the reading. "It's saying here that you're right. Those jobs aren't for you. What's the plan then? What are you going to do to build your tarot business? And meanwhile, how can you make money in a way that's more in line with your soul?"

We move on to another reading. I tell her that sometimes a piece of the person's soul, a piece of their trauma, attaches and follows me home after a reading. Sometimes I have pain that is not my pain. Days go by, and I can't tell if the pain in my throat is mine, or if it belongs to a sales executive I read for. People attach to me, people thirsty for soul. They pull at me, their souls tugging at my collar, my hair, my shirt, my sleeve. I think of Jason's painting of his uncle and the tiny devil tugging at his mustache. I go to sleep being tugged at by thousands of tiny devils.

I also tell Rayne I'm ill prepared for the intense personal healing. The higher wisdom is pure energy pouring in through my crown chakra, and it purifies whatever isn't healed inside me. If someone has intimacy issues, the wisdom that comes through in the reading surrounds my intimacy issues and pulls them up like a toxin. Sometimes it smacks me on the side of the head like a Mack truck. I feel like a rag doll being shaken about by an unruly universe.

The worst part, though, is the exhaustion. I don't understand how it happens, but by the end of the Saturday I can barely walk. I bike home hardly able to keep my wits about me on the busy roads and fall helpless onto the futon.

I tell Rayne how it can take fifteen hours of sleep and rest, often more, to get back to even some semblance of normal. As I waddle to the bathroom to brush my teeth on Sunday morning, still in my day clothes because I had no energy to change them, I know in my gut I'm taking years off my life doing this, and I have no idea what to do about it.

I tell this all to Rayne, and we don't have much of the hour left to discuss what I need to do about it.

"Have you heard of hollow bone?" she asks.

"No." There's a whole new vocabulary for this lifestyle. Learning the ways of this "gift" is like learning how to navigate a foreign culture.

"It's also called empty reed in some traditions. It may sound new to you, but it's an old concept. The core of it is nonattachment. It's not something you do, more something you are." I think about my studies in Buddhism in Asia and the concept of nonattachment. Rayne continues, "It's about getting out of the way. Imagine the light coming from the universe through the crown chakra, through the center of you, the hollow bone. The information comes to you, and you pass it on, and it's released. The flow comes through you unobstructed by conditioning or even your identity." She runs her hands the length of her, breathing in and out. "No attachment."

"But how do I stop other people's pain from attaching to me?"

"Actually *you're* attaching to *it*."

"How do I stop that when I don't even know that I'm doing it?"

"Let's work with visualizations."

Rayne describes several protection visualizations. Light streaming from the universe, flowing into every part of me until my body is completely filled, then spilling like water out of my crown and flowing around the front and back of my body. The light then transforms into chainmail armor.

There is a decording exercise, too. I'm to imagine sitting in a chair across from someone I've read for, someone who won't let me go, or I won't let them go, whatever the truth is. I watch an energetic cord snake out from them and enter me, my solar plexus, or my heart. I'm to take the cord and sever it close to my body, hand it back, tell them they are not allowed to connect to me in that way, and send them on their way.

Rayne takes me to the center of the room, uses an eagle feather and sage, and cleanses me from head to foot. I wonder at how just a few months ago I would have grimaced at such tomfoolery and now I feel wrapped in the cushion of it.

It is the exhaustion, though, I'm most worried about. It is so bone deep.

We go back to the table, and Rayne pulls cards. "It's saying that you're living mostly in your crown chakra, and this is a result of abuse to your lower chakras. There is so much fear, even fear of survival, lodged in the base chakra. When that happens as a child, we're forced to live in the upper chakras, and when you have a gift like yours, this just takes up too much of your core energy. But all of this can be healed."

Whatever trauma Rayne is seeing in my base chakra I don't want to talk about. I have an aversion even as the subject is brought up. I may be opening the cage to write, but there are still many stories locked deep inside that have yet to see the light. I can see by the clock that the session isn't over, but I have to force myself not to end it early.

Rayne notices. "Let me show you a grounding technique." We go through a process of visualizing a root extending from the base of my spine, through the floor, and into the earth below, the root stem branching out until my whole body is deeply grounded. The root hairs collect nutrients from the soil that move up the root and back into my body.

I make a list of the visualizations and techniques before I leave. I don't really feel better. I know that I'll have to practice the techniques and it will take some time. I understand that there is damage lodged in my body, and this spiritual work isn't the panacea I thought it would be. I will have to heal.

As I'm saying goodbye to Rayne and getting on my bike in the relentless downpour, I remember the promise I made to myself as a child to be healthy, to heal.

As sideways rain stings my face and the back tire throws mud on my backside, I feel calm for the first time in a long time. So this is it. This is the healing. I feel I've found at least one piece of the missing puzzle. At a stop light, a young girl, a passenger in the car next to me, looks at me as I'm devoured by the rain. She rolls down her window and puts her palm out to the cup the rain.

I put my hand out too for drops of rain to splash in my already wet palm. She laughs. I laugh. Her mother yells for her to roll up the window. I wave to her and she to me. In that moment as never before, I realize in some weird way I've "made it." I'm finally coming home.

VIII
STRENGTH.

CHAPTER 8

Strength

Rabbits, birds, dogs, cats, a ferret, a piglet. A bark, a tweet, a mew, a snort. Coral's ramshackle house in Greenwood has weeds growing under the kitchen sink and cages of sick animals in the living room, her bedroom, the porch. The smell is gamey.

We sit at the kitchen table. Coral is resting a baby rabbit in her arm. She plunges a syringe into a teacup of goat's milk and squeezes it into the creature's mouth.

She's telling me about a mystical experience in the forest. She's just gotten back from camping with Red on the peninsula. Red and I have broken up—I want to date myself for a while, get to know myself. We split with no hard feelings.

Her blue eyes are big in her face, like she's still seeing the universe. I can imagine the rainforest scene as she talks, the branches heavy with moss, how the forest cover makes everything so dark, so cold, so dripping, so full of fairy tale and myth.

"Red was sitting beneath a tree. He was sick. We'd taken shrooms, but I've never had a trip like this. Whatever happened was crazy bigger than the shrooms. We were having this intense conversation but neither of us was talking. It was the purest telepathy." I look out the screen door to the screened-in porch, and the piglet is standing, watching us, a big goofy smile on its face.

"I remember thinking he's too sick, and we have to get out of here, and how are we going to do that? We were near a creek, and I went to look at it, and the water was flowing the wrong way. Or the right way, but not the normal way."

I cling to her words. This used to happen to me when I was five. I'd go out to the creek behind the house, put my hand in the water, and watch the water flow backward or upward. The pig snorts.

"Then this *being* shows up." She gets up, puts the bunny back in its basket, and takes an adult bunny from a cage. A kitten nearby cries. She sits, turns the adult bunny upside down and pets its belly. "It's hard to talk about. It was this being of light, but the weird thing was, it was so familiar. I just felt how familiar it was. Like I'd known it before."

In Coral's eyes I see sparks of stars and planets. She has the soul of an eccentric old woman and the face of child. I'm glad Gem encouraged me to stop talking about myself—I'm happy to have someone I can finally talk *to*.

"It saw me. Like right through me. Its existence validated me. I don't know how to put this into words." As she talks, her appearance changes. She seems to be made of liquid and not solid. She appears to me as a form created by millions of tiny shards of color, like hued polyps, merging to create a human collage. The effects stays with me, and looking at her makes me giddy.

"I felt in its presence that I could see right through to the meaning of things, to both the physical elements of a thing and to the larger beauty of it. Beauty was the word that kept coming to me.

"The feelings haven't gone away. I can still feel energy radiating through my body and going out each of my hands like electricity. It's like my entire body had been subjected to an electrical field. I asked Red about it and he looked like he had seen a ghost. He was having the same thing happen."

I tell her about the loaves of bread flying off the shelves, the framed pictures falling off the walls.

"Apparently people who have had some type of mystical experience have talked about that feeling of electricity running through the body," she says. She gets up puts the big bunny away. "It's like coming to some psychic edge."

I think, *Or maybe it's just a different language that we haven't learned yet, a language that will take a lifetime to learn.*

I notice the science books on her sagging bookshelves: a set of the Feynman Lectures on Physics, Carl Sagan's *Cosmos*, Hawking's *A Brief History of Time*, chemistry textbooks. She's taking classes to apply to grad school to work in a lab. This will take her away from Seattle, but I try not to think about that.

"What do you think about the intersection of science and mysticism?" I think about it a lot since I stopped doing journalism and started channeling. My life used to be based on hard facts, and now . . .

She says, "It's like looking into a microscope. You can parse down the physical elements. That's real. But you back up and there's this beauty in the design, and the beauty is real, too. There's the physical and there's something that animates it. Why is this so hard to put into words?"

"*Divine* design," I say, but Coral makes a face. She's a New Englander, and you just don't use words like divine and goddess. I get it, I still can't use some of the verbiage. I think of science as masculine and mysticism as feminine, and love the idea of both working hand in hand and not having to be opposed to each other.

We decide to do tarot readings for each other. Coral hands me her deck. Playing cards with black cursive script, obtuse prophetic messages written by some old lady. The cards are both plain and scary. She may not be woo-woo, but Coral certainly is psychic. She may not use the West Coast terminology, but she's as tapped in as Rayne, maybe more.

I tell her about how I'm picking up too much from the people I read for, about the protection rituals Rayne has shown me, how sometimes they work and sometimes they don't.

Coral tells me the story of a boyfriend who had cancer. "I put my hands on him and I swear I drew out the cancer. That's what it felt like. He didn't have cancer anymore, and then I was diagnosed right after that." His cancer became her cancer. This is exactly what I'm scared of.

I know without Coral telling me that because of the cancer she's not the same person, and this is the blessing of the disease. She carries with her *The Great Compassion* and sees people, really sees them, and deep down isn't judgmental.

She goes to a drawer, pulls something out, and comes back. It's a picture, an old rambling New England house. A younger Coral with cancer stands out front emaciated, leaning sideways like she might fall over.

Looking at the picture is like looking at a tarot card, some archetype for illness, for hitting bottom and coming back up again. An archetype for what is learned at the bottom. I know she wouldn't be the same spiritual person if she hadn't gone through it. That scar is what has made her the person she is today. I probably wouldn't ever have met her. How can one be thankful for cancer?

"That boyfriend is the reason why I won't read tarot more often," Coral says. "Anything can go wrong."

I've brought the bathroom deck, the Voyager, to use with Coral, collages of cranes and crystals, explosions, and winding roads. Coral is so tapped in—it's easy to read for her. It's only exhausting and like pulling teeth when you're reading for people who are shut down.

She wants a reading about the rainforest, but what comes up instead as I throw the cards is about all of the animals surrounding us. The cards show me a menagerie of mythical animals. In each animal is an archetypal wound. The scar on a zebra's brow. The gunshot in the leg of an orangutan. The poison that has burned the belly of the sow. How man's abuse of every animal is an abuse against himself. I see Coral like a white light with hidden rainbows, touching her animals; and as they are healed, she is healed.

"You're healing the animal body. You're healing your own scar that runs the length of you." As I read, the healing runs through me. I can feel every sick animal in the room. I sense the raspy lungs of the bunny, the broken ankle of the cat, the roiling tummy of the ferret, the dysentery of the happy piglet. I remember my own childhood of butchering animals and feel that lodged deep at my base. I feel the healing pulling up in my own animal body.

I pull the cards back and reshuffle them. The next reading is about the rainforest trip. I can see Red emerge from the collaged images on the cards, a deeply magical being, profoundly metaphysical. How lost he is with what to do with his metaphysical side and how to make money in the world. I can see that in another reality, he could be a healer. I'm moved that Red and I were more alike than I realized when we were seeing each other.

"There's a past life between you and Red," I say. "During like the Renaissance period in Italy, I think I'm reading this right, you were part of this group of intellectuals exploring metaphysical new thought or something. You decided to become lovers then, but it went wrong. So this lifetime you're just remaining friends.

"There was something that happened in the rainforest where it was a mixture of your metaphysical energy and Red's mystical energy that created the opening. Red felt sick, but behind it was the anger he's bottled up against a childhood that didn't let him be who he really is.

"I'll try to ask about the being you saw," I say, shuffling the cards and then dealing them. It's not really clear what they're saying. Sometimes it's like the message is in a foreign language and I can't understand it.

"All I can get is that the being appeared to remind you that you were once part of a great race of people, and although you can't go back, you can know that this powerful group exists somewhere, and you can be confident in your connection."

Coral's eyes are huge and inward looking, and I know she's processing on a deep level. I know how this works with the readings I get from Rayne; the awareness is on an ethereal level.

It's Coral's turn to read for me. The playing cards with their tiny words written in black ink seem more witchy to me than any deck I own.

She throws the cards on the tabletop. "OK." She leans back and wiggles in the chair. "It says as a child you weren't allowed to protect yourself without dire consequences." She has a way of shooting from the hip, and I like it after all of the political correctness of Seattle. She gets up, puts food in a bowl, mixes medicine with it, opens the screen door, and gives it to the piglet. We can hear it slopping up the food as we talk.

Coral sits back down. "Whenever you said no, or tried to do your own thing, there were serious consequences, violent threats."

She looks at the cards, shifts back and forth in the chair. "The info is coming to me so quickly, and I can't figure out how to say it all. A lot of what they're trying to tell you, Hillman wrote." She hands me the book. James Hillman, *We've Had a Hundred Years of Psychotherapy and the World's Getting Worse.*

"You can go down the path of how horrible this all was, or you can do what Hillman explains and figure out how this brutality was part of your training, how you needed to learn how to protect yourself in stronger ways than any other normal person, and how it's related to your purpose. You did learn to protect yourself, right? And it's given you a master level of protection skills. You just haven't tapped into them yet."

She's right. I learned early to keep my own counsel. I had to go deep to find my own way, deeper than I'd ever have gone without the trauma.

"How do I tap into that now? That's the whole problem," I say.

"How did you do it as a kid?"

"I simply negated everything my father said or either of my parents believed. I negated pretty much everything the nuns said at school. Anything that came out of any mouth, I negated. Some of it got in though."

She turns over more cards: the Seven of Diamonds and the King of Diamonds. I try to read the ink scribbles on each card, but they say things like "the winter is thin with ice" and "upon the roof a crow" and make no sense to me.

"Something about setting the intention and how that'll help. Your intention is to help others, right? If you say you're only here to help the person, then taking on their pain and illness doesn't help them at all, right?"

"And doesn't help me either."

She nods. I can read her mind. She's thinking about her ex-boyfriend and the cancer and taking it on herself. "Right. If it doesn't help, you set forth as an intention that it will not appear in your energy field."

I start to ask another question, but she puts up her hand. "OK, no more tarot. I'm exhausted."

"I know you don't like to read tarot often, but you could make extra cash if you did readings for the public," I say. I know she's working two jobs trying to save for grad school.

She makes a face. "That is never, ever going to happen."

Later, I'm at home with my cards and my journal and try to set an intention. All I can come up with for now is: "Let each reading be for the greatest and highest good."

East or west, I don't care. I bought a beater truck with a canopy from a friend of Coral's for eight hundred bucks. Despite my debilitation, I force myself out of bed early every Sunday so that I can drive deep into nature, the only place I feel grounded. All the visualizations in the world cannot make up for the real grounding of planet Earth. I go west to the Olympics or east to the Cascades, making the decision only when I'm in the truck, using my intuition to turn left or right.

I camp for one night and wake Monday before dawn to make it back to Seattle in time for my job. Perhaps the visualizations are starting to work, perhaps the psychic boundaries are beginning to take, but I need to be in the wild like I need food. Month after month these outings become obsessions; I'm hungry for spruce and brook and hawk.

Most people find edification in relationships with other people. My true relationships have always been with the land, with the earth. A copse, a field, a lake—each has a different personality, its ecosystem like the quirks of a good friend. Each forays into a different ecosystem; each Sunday outing is like the sacred meeting of a friend. This outer nature is as diverse as the inner nature of all of the people I'm meeting at my tarot table. The only difference is that when I go into nature, I'm replenished from the tips of my toes to the top of my hair.

It's the poetry that surprises me. I hike hard to come down off the tarot, to loosen the grip of the pain others feel. When I come down to earth in the midst of a forest or on a beach, it's as if I enter a magic kingdom and the ocean or the trees are an orchestra conducted for my pleasure.

Rounding a bend, a yellow leaf dances from a branch among a feng shui vista of shrubs and alders and sky. The movement of the leaf dances me, and I will spend weeks moving with the leaf in my memory.

The hikes are hot and cold and wet and hard. My legs ache and my hair is soaked, and I'd rather be here than anywhere else, surrounded by the elements.

Week after week I hike. Steep treks to plateaus with views of rolling blue hills; deep treks into thick-temperate rainforest, where I'm cocooned by moss and chill and darkness. Hikes along beaches, along snow-covered paths to high-altitude lakes. I push myself, hard breath, hard ache, hard sweat, and push and push until everyone residing inside me is sweated out. After so many years in big cities abroad, getting to know the land week after week on these Sunday forays is like getting to reknow a lover I left a long time ago.

In these wild places, wealth is the feel of rocks and roots beneath boots, the smell of mud and the musk of moss, and nothing is a transaction for money; no one is trying to sell or be sold, and it is the only place besides the pages of my writing that I feel free.

One Sunday, I hike too long and am back in the truck seeking a camping spot in the late afternoon—all of the campgrounds are filled. It's difficult to build a fire or set up camp in the dark, and just as the sun is setting, I grow desperate and pull into a scrubby place with a broken sign and a dilapidated office, a place I would never choose under normal circumstances. They have one spot left, and it sits right next to the dirt road that people drive through to get farther into the campground. It's far from private. These Sunday jaunts are my only relief from that other world, and I nearly cry at how close the cars and other campers are.

As I park and get out, I see that this stretch of scrub abuts a body of water. I haul out the cooler and pack of wood and start building a fire. It takes a while to realize that I'm camping at the edge of the Strait of Juan De Fuca. The low sun turns the water pure silver. I leave the food and fire and sit on the tailgate, surrounded by the silver glow, shocked to be in such a place of beauty.

As I'm sitting there, a pod of whales, large and small, wends through the water. One of the larger ones breaches, rising up like a god of the sea, dripping stars of water from its fin.

I move with the whales, feel the silken water, the sheer joy of existence, with no separation between us. I enter them and they enter me, and something moves inside me. I feel horny and alive and changed.

Some higher power got me here just for this, as if I'd hiked too long just to be forced into this one last campsite. As if I'm meant to be reminded that you can't judge where you will find grace.

On a Sunday in October, I'm in my truck heading east toward the Cascades. I'm trying to outrun a mother I read tarot for the day before, but she keeps pulling me back.

It's late afternoon, and I must find a campground before it gets dark. I watch for the brown signs, turn into one campground, into another, into a third, but there are too many people. It's nightfall, and I haven't even gotten a hike in. I veer down one rough road to another dirt road. Finally I find a hidden campsite, but there are still too many people. As I'm pulling out of the site, I spy a small sign, turn right, and head up a steep mountain road.

The mother at my wobbly table at the bookstore defied all of my protection visualizations. I push on the gas, trying to escape her, but she's following me, niggling at me.

I cannot remember her name. When she stumbled toward my tarot table, she was bent at the waist, about to fall over. I rushed to help, but when I looked more closely, she was standing normally—a trick of the mind or a psychic vision. It happens sometimes. I see the hidden emergency in the person. People didn't come to me when they were happy. No one paid money just to hear they're doing great.

I sat across from her and let her mix the cards. I knew something was very wrong. When I threw cards from the deck out onto the table, they became a two-woman show, a dark dance between a mother and a daughter. The card representing the daughter showed a girl who was being pulled, so far down. The mother reached to help her, but there was no hope. I watched the daughter die before my eyes.

I studied the mystical motion of the cards and looked at the mother hopelessly. I didn't know what she wanted. There was death and a hole in her heart, and I didn't know the words that could change any of that.

"Your daughter died?" I asked gently.

The woman started sobbing. I offered a box of tissues. Her cries were bottomless. I fell into her and I was bottomless inside her grief.

The mother told me in her cracked and crying voice that her daughter was a college student and had depression. As she talked, I fell inside the daughter's depression, felt its heft, knew it was because the college was turning her into who she wasn't. The girl and the mother didn't know this. The girl was doing her best to "succeed," but man-made success was killing her.

"It was the antidepressants. They put her on new meds. The meds put her over the edge," the woman said. Her daughter overdosed. The mother held the tissue box to her face and sobbed into it.

I held the story with the mother, and it was so very heavy.

The wet day is turning to ice on the road. The road is steep and heads up a mountain. It is narrow and rocky and the truck stumbles and jerks over the frozen rocks. At a steep and sharp turn, I go into low gear but lose traction. To one side is a deep ravine, to the other a rock wall. The tires spin, and the truck slips close to the edge. I'm not a wuss. I know how to drive. I put on the hand brake and slowly let the brake down as

I move off the clutch. My tires spin and slip more, and I slide backward a foot. I am getting too close to the edge.

I try to back up to get to ice-free ground and get traction, but with the turn in the road, I worry the truck will slide over the cliff, so I stop. I get out and walk around the vehicle. The danger of going over the edge is real.

I sit and wait. My gut knows something will happen if I just wait. It takes forty-five minutes. The sun has disappeared behind the ridge. It's colder now. A truck comes down from the other direction. A father and son. I tell them about the ice and how I don't want to tempt fate, and the son gets out of their truck and into mine. I think as I watch him that he could just as easily go down the ravine backward and this isn't fair to him. But he doesn't. He pulls the truck out.

The father says from the open window, "You sure you know where you're going?"

"No," I say, crunching the truck into gear. Then I add, "Away. Far away."

"Hope you got some long johns," he calls after me.

Rocky path and bad shocks up and up and up. My head bounces against the car's roof. The sun is setting; the ice grows thicker.

At the top, where the road ends, an empty campground flanks a lake and is surrounded by ancient trees, subalpine firs and lodgepole pine. The half-dozen camping spots are empty. It is old here. And frigidly cold. It's no place for wimps. The lake is frozen in places. The trees are warped, fat, and spread out. I park. I have a coat, hat, and gloves, but still I'm shivering. The sun has already dipped below the horizon, and I rush around and find branches on the ground before it gets any darker. Shivering now, I build a fire in a burnt-out circle. It's not just cold, it's bone deep and aching.

Soon the fire is a spot of orange in a vast blue-black night. The world cracks and shivers in the black, and even with the fire I'm not warm. Steak and potatoes in foil sizzle on the embers. The stars are holes punched into an arc of a big sky. I'm huddled near the flames, a tiny frozen speck on the breast of the land. The sounds of the night. An owl. A rustle in the underbrush. I'm not scared. I'm never scared in the bosom of the earth.

I asked Gem to come but she said it was my thing, that I needed it more than food. She seemed proud of me for doing these weekend forays. "We need places that scare us. We need places where there's a possibility we could die," she said. I didn't tell her I'm never scared. My only worry is that if I die, it will be a long time before someone finds me, because no one knows where I am.

It's the kind of cold now that feels serious. Like not waking up in the morning serious. I have to make a decision. I pace and cough out clouds of cold air. My snot is freezing. Should I try to go down the treacherous road? We forget how black the world is at night when there are no streetlights or lights of any kind. The leaving will be nearly as dangerous as the staying.

When it grows unbearable, I get into the cab, turn the engine on, turn up the heat. I have just below half a tank. I figure I can stay this way for about an hour and still have enough gas to get back down tomorrow. But is that true? I have no idea. I watch the gas gauge go down and lose my nerve after thirty minutes.

I jump out of the cab and into the back of the truck fully clothed, with my coat, hat, and gloves on beneath the sleeping bag. My bag is a good one and is supposed to keep you warm when it's below freezing, but the metal sides of the truck are like ice. The overhead canopy does nothing to keep out the frost. The metal floor creeps up through the sleeping bag and freezes my flanks. This is such a deep-in-the-bones cold, frozen in the bones of the land, too. I promise myself that if it becomes truly unbearable, I'll try to drive back down.

I don't sleep. I don't doze. I want to be aware if the cold is going to take me. I wait and wait. For hours. Lifetimes. A watched sun never rises. My body aches from holding it rigid for so long. Outside, the animals of the night pace and howl, and the sounds should scare me, but they're the only sounds now that make me feel safe.

Hours pass, a subtle lightening through the back window of the canopy, and the light begins its slow crawl across the land. When the sun finally begins to rise, I climb out, my legs and back stiff. I jump around for a while to get the circulation flowing. With all the biking and the no smoking and no drinking, my body is fit. I feel it strong and healthy as my breath comes out in gusts. I run around like Rocky, punching the air.

I build a fire to boil water and for some heat. After fruit and green tea for breakfast, the sun has fully cleared the ridge. I go to lie near the water, to put my hair in the water. This is a ritual. I do it every time I'm near a body of water, a full-bodied connection with the earth, the roots and rocks pressing against my back and ass.

At the frozen lake, I take my hair out of the band and put it into the cold water, just at the lake's edge. It is frigid. My frizz and curls sink into the brackish water. Rocks and roots on the bank poke through my down coat. Running fingers through my hair, all the people I've picked up, all the people whose woes stay with me, wash out in the lake. I tease out the woman and her dead daughter and return them to the lake.

Overhead, I look up at the canopy of a big-leaf maple, branches stunted and twisted, its growth from sapling to adulthood hard won in such a harsh place. It isn't pretty. It isn't a tree you'd photograph. It would never be a postcard. I think about growing up hard and twisted and cold. Solitary. And beautiful.

Afterward, I towel dry my hair, rebuild the fire. Today I don't have to rush back to Seattle, because I don't have to work. I'm between temp jobs. I spend the next four hours writing in a journal, steam rising from my head. I keep up my writing routine even when I'm camping. No one shows up. No one is around.

After a lunch of chili from a can, I strap on a backpack and take off down a hiking path. The vegetation is stunted. The smell is evergreen, sap, and dirt. I feel safe here. I feel less safe in Seattle around the starving hordes, less sure of my safety, more tenuously grasping my sanity, than I will ever be here, so close to the earth.

As I hike, I feel the mother and daughter heavy on my chest. I haven't yet left them completely behind. On the path, I see a small rock shaped like a heart. In my palm it's so small and fragile. It glitters in the afternoon light, sparks embedded in the stone. I cup it in my palm. The path leads out onto a valley of massive boulders. There is some energy here. I've always known that land has energy. The earth in Missouri is filled with the song of the Osage. You can't hear it if you don't have the ears to listen. It is sung in the leaf and stone. In the roots.

This has that energy, but different. The Osage are gentle. This is ferocious. Angry. Disturbed. Upset. Righteous. Or it is me projecting onto the boulders? I don't think so. The feeling from the earth is too strong. I was called here.

Whoever peopled this land before me were like lightning. I sit on one of the giant boulders in a sea of hundreds of boulders that stream down a hill to the valley below. Some energy is clearing out my body. Something is pulling the ugly out of me. The sun is up, and I take off a layer. I sit some more. I feel like an apple that's being cored, the energy is so fierce. I take off another layer, another, sit in bra and panties. I take these off too. I'm naked like a newborn here on this rock. Exposed. The only thing left on me the heart-shaped rock.

Around me the rocks are breathing. The old trees at the edges are expanding and contracting. They are communicating with each other. The grief inside me is overwhelming. It is the mother. It is the daughter. It is me.

It's more than that. It's all women, everywhere. All daughters. All girls who are not allowed to just be. Who are pummeled and twisted into who they are not. It's Mother. Earth.

I sob hysterically, a vomiting of tears. I'm this breathing rock, that treetop swaying in the morning light. The breeze hardens my nipples, and around my ankles I wear a ring of dirt.

I hear words on the breeze. Or are the boulders speaking to me? *You are upset, because it's upsetting. You're depressed, because it's depressing. You're enraged, because it's enraging.*

The hysterical sobbing will not abate; I heave up dryness because my tears are spent. The boulders tell me that I'm sobbing not just for myself, not just for the mother and her daughter, but for the whole world, for the daughters everywhere, for an earth that is our mother, now so toxic and abused that where can we possibly call home? I'm sobbing for the lost Divine Feminine.

Your sobbing is healing, you and others. Some people are asked to be cleansers of the world, and you are this. It's not easy. You agreed to it long before you came into this body.

The boulders, the trees, the clouds, we breathe together. The world and I are aligned in our inhale and our exhale. The sobbing quiets down. Drained, I fumble into my clothes. I stumble back to the campsite, sit at the base of the gnarly maple on the bank of the lake. I let the bark hold me as I curl up and watch the ice crack on the frozen water.

IX
THE HERMIT.

CHAPTER 9

The Hermit

It is time to visit my mother, to fly back to the Midwest and do what I couldn't do when I first landed in America. It comes to me in a dream. How can I heal the bruising of the feminine if I don't begin with myself? It's a journey back to find the missing pieces of myself.

I come off the mountain determined to do something. I want to heal something, heal a planet dumping toxins on its soil, or heal a mother and her dead daughter, or heal myself and my own mother, or heal it all.

"Aren't you a sight for sore eyes," my mother says, ushering me in. It's November in Missouri, and the trees are bare, and the light slants sideways across the land. She's a fairy tale mother with dark hair and milky skin, and the archetype takes hold of me. But we all know even fairy tales can be dark, too, and scary. "Where have you been all my life?" she says.

Kat, a young teenager now, is dressed in her Sunday's best, gingham with lace. She's chunky, tall, awkward, and big for her age. The last time I saw her she was a small child.

They crowd me into the living room. The boy Matt sits in an armchair playing a game and looks up once. His face is covered in acne, and he's not present behind his eyes. He's wearing a white shirt and tie. They've probably just gotten back from Mass at Holy Cross.

"Smile at Pearl, Matt," my mother says. He does an exaggerated smile without taking his eyes off the game. "Let me get you some hot cocoa. The kids have been having their afternoon cocoa," my mother says.

I left my mother's house when I was a teenager. Not this house—after my father was killed in a hunting accident, my mother remarried. She left that old life behind, the farm and the hard work, the gutting, the weeding, the planting, for this cul-de-sac life with a military man named Jack. They'd had twins, Matt and Kat, and I'd only met them once. They thought I was their aunt.

I sit on the sofa. Kat sits on the floor, looks up at me with big brown eyes. She leans against my legs. I keep having to shift because of the heaviness of her. The leaning is weird, and too much, and I don't understand it. The heaviness grows and deepens. I feel like I can't breathe, and I'm going to panic, and I keep shifting my legs, and she keeps scooting over to put her weight on my shins.

Kat leans her cheek against my knee. "I'm so happy I have a sister."

My mother comes in and hears the word "sister." She hands me the cup of cocoa and sits on the sofa next to me. She starts speaking rapidly. "We ran into Arleen at a family reunion. She'd just come back from seeing you in London, and she told us all about the work you were doing there."

I'd completely forgotten about the visit of the distant cousin who was in London attending some conference. We'd met for a brief dinner. She wanted iced tea and moaned when she had to order hot tea and a cup of ice and make her own.

"Where's Jack?"

"Daddy doesn't come home anymore until really, really late. And he doesn't go to church with us anymore either."

"That's not true, Kat," my mother says.

"Yes it iiiiis," Kat says.

From the moment my mother and Jack met, he'd decided what she felt about things, and she let him. I was a troubled kid who saw too much, a kid who had mystical visions, a kid Jack did not want around. And my mother let him want this. It was always something I hated in women, and why I avoided traditionally married women. The way they lost their sense of self, obeyed the man and called it love.

We have pork chops and apple sauce for dinner. Matt keeps his face in his game. When I first met the twins, I felt a deep connection with Matt. He was an empath, and we had conversations with the ants in his anthill. He was an artist who hid his artwork in case his father thought he was a wuss. Now there's no getting Matt away from the game to even see who he'd become. I feel such a soul loss for the boy.

I used to bake cookies when I was little. After dinner, I ask my mother for the ingredients and use the mixer to blend the eggs, butter, and sugar. It's a secret recipe; I've never told anyone how I make them. When we were little, if I turned my back, Meghan would steal the bowl of batter and eat it in great handfuls before I could wrestle it away. I'd have to take it into the bathroom with me when I needed to go because the dough would be gone by the time I got back.

Kat doesn't leave my side as I bake. She keeps grabbing my hand and my arm and tugging herself against me. I try to give her tasks, but she keeps glomming onto me, and I have to go to the bathroom to breathe.

Where is home? It's a question I've asked myself over and over for many years. Is home a place where you're a stranger to the people who spawned you, and you spend time in a bathroom because you can't breathe?

The smell of fresh-baked chocolate chip cookies fill the kitchen, memories now of love. I take a cookie and a glass of milk to my mother. She's sitting at the dining room table, which is now cleaned after dinner and gleaming in the light of dusk glowing through the window. I sit across from her, look into her mesmerizing green eyes. In them are so many untold stories. I have no animosity toward her, and I have no connection with her.

When I was young, if I didn't expect her to be "Mother," if I just pretended we were peers, we got along fine. Sometimes, like now, she would look at me as if I were the mother and she the daughter. She has her own history, my mother, long and hard like an icy road leading up a steep cliff, with gaping crevasses and spinning tires and near plunges into the depths.

She says things like "These sure are good cookies." And "Pearl, you have to give me that recipe you keep so secret." And "Tomorrow I'm thinking of making an apple cobbler."

And I say things like "I'll take the recipe to my grave." And "Cobbler sounds nice." And "Where is Jack?" This last one, I see in her eyes, I shouldn't have said.

Seeing my mother for the first time in many years, sitting here face to face, with the smell of vanilla and milk, it isn't the memory of the trauma that grabs me by the neck, it's the memories of joy and hope. It's the memory of love that sticks in my throat like a kitchen knife.

A confused mixture of love and pain brings me, of course, to Meghan. I ask, "Have you heard from Meghan? Do you know where she is?" Meghan is my father's daughter. He had her before he met my mother. Although Mother raised Meghan and me for years, I think in her mind she thinks of Meghan as a distant cousin.

She gets up, goes to a drawer, and pulls out a messy address book. She's always been this way, pristine cleanliness on the outside and messy on the inside. She pulls a bent card from the address book and hands it to me. It looks several years old. On the front is a rainbow-colored peace sign.

"The return address is there in the corner. I wrote her back but didn't hear anything. That was about five years ago. I don't know if she's still there."

I get up to find a pen and write the address down. This is my Divine Feminine. In my family, the Divine Feminine looks like a bomb went off, disconnected women scattered to the corners of the earth.

Later, when I'm preparing for bed in the guest room, I ask my mother for a second blanket. Her door is ajar. Jack still isn't home. She stands at her dresser lost in thought, her face slack, and a wave of depression washes like a waterfall over me. Her depression, not mine. Sometimes I can discern the difference.

Who is my mother? Does *she* know? She's had a long life, two or three lives already. With me and my father and Meghan, she had a life rooted in the earth, weeding, growing, hunting, gutting. And Jack took her away from it all after my father's death, to this suburb of repetitive houses and look-alike lawns.

In therapy Shirley told me that she'd counseled a lot of women who'd lost their identities in their marriages. After years of being married, many didn't even know their favorite color. Did my mother know her favorite color?

I go back to the room and make do with the blanket I have.

The next morning we have breakfast of eggs, bacon, and sausage. Kat asks if her dad is home, and Mother says we need to be quiet because he came in late and is sleeping. Matt's on his game.

That afternoon my mother and I look through a photo album of relatives I've never met on Jack's side, and relatives I haven't seen in years on her side. I know my mother is trying to share her life with me, but all I feel as I look at Easter and Christmas celebrations and family reunions, as I look at the faces of these strangers, is lost and alone.

I see Jack out of the corner of my eye get up and go into the kitchen. I watch my mother pop up to make him his meal. After breakfast he stops to say a quick hello, then disappears into his home office in the basement.

That evening I'm in the guest room packing. It's a long trip to get here, but I only have the time to stay two nights and must drive the hours to the airport early the next morning.

I feel more alone than ever, and I'm not sure what good it's done coming back here. What did I expect? Some sudden healing? I see a framed Polaroid on the wall above the bed. I was too tired the night before to notice. It's a picture of me. I know immediately that Mother put it up for my visit, that it doesn't normally hang there. Throughout the house there are no pictures of me, or of Father, or Meghan, just the new family.

In it I'm seven. It's Christmas Day. I was given a sleeping bag and a baton, and I'm in the bag, holding the baton horizontal and smiling. I'm so gentle. The gentleness nearly closes my throat.

This girl on the wall is a piece of me calling out to me. I put the picture in my suitcase. This is why I've come, to bring my child self back with me.

Kat opens the door and enters without knocking. "I want to show you my scrap book." I quickly shut my suitcase.

She sits on the bed while I pack, showing me snapshots of a normal girl's life. I feel the weight of her again. Or the weight of a childhood I would never have. Or the weight of the little girl now inside my suitcase. Kat looks at me, begging for approval, and I'm not sure I have any to give.

The girl chatters on about school and friends, holding up the scrapbook for me to see. As I fold a shirt, I look up to see Jack staring at me from the hallway. His eyes are hooded but there's something pleading about him. *Your mother needs you,* I hear him say. I look at him again, sharply, but he hasn't spoken. The voice comes again. *She needs you.*

The next morning over an early breakfast of fried eggs, tomatoes, and thick homemade bread slathered in butter, I watch my mother at the stove. The kitchen has always been her place of gravity. How can I help her? Why is it up to me to help her?

She talks as she works, inviting me to fly back for her family events. I understand she's trying to include me, but I still have so much rage.

It's more than that. Tradition is strong here. A woman's role is defined. I'm not strong enough in myself and my alternative path to withstand that suck backward.

I see what Jack means—I can feel Mother's darkness. She does need help, but am I the one to give it? A rage wells against Jack. Why isn't he helping her? Why is he disappearing?

I think about the concept of the Divine Feminine, my own healing, the healing that's needed for so many women I read for, the healing my mother needs. It is a monumental task; I see that now. We've been ignored and abused and seen as second-class citizens for centuries. We've been dismissed, dismantled, disturbed, and we've incorporated that into our psyches. The healing isn't just mine or my mother's, it goes back generations and forward generations.

I have no idea what my role in this healing should be. I do know it has to start with me. I'm still so bruised. So frightened. So disturbed. I know I can't do my own healing here, in the place where so much of the bruising occurred. I know I can't heal my mother. I feel bad, but I just can't.

Saying my goodbyes to my mother and Kat at the front door, I try to maneuver my suitcase between them, but neither will move out of the way.

"Pearl, don't be a stranger now," my mother says. I look at her, deep into eyes that once owned me. She looks so lost. She looks like someone whose past is haunting her.

I have to find myself, Mother. Centuries still to find myself back again. How can I help anyone if I don't know who I am?

As I drive away, I feel the girl in the suitcase cry out to me. I remember how when I was a girl, I committed to never having children. I remember it so clearly, a watershed moment. I stood outside the old farmhouse. It was September, a chill in the air, the sky dark with clouds. *I will never have children. I will have my own life.*

As I pull onto the highway, I know only this: I will focus on healing that gentle girl inside me. That's the best I can do.

★ ★ ★

The streets are thick with mud, London's outskirts, the buildings made of wood, ramshackle. Filthy. I'm old, an elderly woman in a long black dress. I'm trying to get home.

Two men fight in the mud. Their trousers are slick with muck. One climbs onto the plank sidewalk and is trying to walk away, but the other keeps grabbing him and pulling him back. They push each other. They fall back into the filth. They are slinging insults and fists.

I keep my head down and mind my business. I just want to get home. I'm old and my bones hurt. *People are so full of darkness,* I think. *This world is too full of darkness.* I walk out of the city. I keep walking down a dirt road for hours until I turn down a weedy dirt path and walk deep into a forest.

I have a hut in the woods. There are herbs growing as I approach, both wild ones scattered about outside the hut and ones I have cultivated. Just seeing the herbs fills me with joy. I'm one of them, I think. I'm an old dried herb. It makes me giggle. It is with them that I belong, not with those men throwing mud-encrusted fists.

The walls of the hut are made of tree branches, and there are gaps. I no longer stand up straight. The wet and the cold have twisted up my bones, but I wouldn't exchange this life for one in the city for all of the riches in the world.

I make pouches and poultices so they are at the ready. I pull from the bunches of herbs hanging to dry—lavender, dill, rosemary, St. John's wort, and sage, strands of each—and put them in different proportions in different pouches for different ailments and set them aside. I plunge rags into herbs soaking in rainwater.

I hear a woman outside. "Elinor," she cries. I open the door. Cecily has her baby with her. She's sweating or crying or both. She hands me the baby wrapped in a woolen blanket. I never know when they'll show up on my doorstep. They come at any time, day and night.

I place the child on the table in the middle of the hut and open the blanket. If he weren't so emaciated, he would appear like the Christ child, white and glowing in this dark place.

"He won't eat," Cecily says, wringing her hands. The baby was once so fat, so full of the force of life.

I take the pouch of sage and bergamot, but mostly my treatment is my intuition. I know the emotions behind the illness every time. I can see how the physical problems are passed emotionally from generation to generation. I can see that the physical is emotional, and the emotional is physical. This is my gift. They think it's magic, but I'm just a woman who can see. I'm just a healer.

Cecily was kicked in the stomach by her husband when she was pregnant, when this baby was yet born. I know that the baby is not eating because of this. The baby was kicked before birth by an angry father, and this has upset the child's stomach. It's as clear as day to me.

As I burn herbs and wash them over the child, I pull out the memory of his father's kick. I use my fingers as if I'm removing something from the gut of the child. I try to keep my back to Cecily—I know they think I'm a witch, though this doesn't stop them from bringing me their children to cure—but I can't fully hide what I'm doing. It's not just the pulling motion, it's the energy of healing that I send into the child, an energy that pulses in my palms. It's an intention of healing between me and the child and between nature and God.

The child is glowing as I hand him back to his mother, and he quickly falls into a deep sleep in her arms.

"Is he going to live?" she asks.

"I believe, yes." In the past, when I was younger and less wise, I would tell the people my insights. I didn't tell Cecily about the kick. It is best. They do not understand, and much confusion ensues, so it's better they think it's a mystery.

It's ten days later when Cecily returns. She has come with a basket of fresh potatoes, tomatoes, and squash. The child is gaining weight. Cecily laughs and hugs me. I give her a toothless smile. I have never felt I belonged, even as a girl, and it's these moments, when someone is happy with me, that I feel accepted and maybe even loved.

It is but a fortnight later that they show up for me at night with torches. The dark forest is spotted with the harsh light that throws unnatural shadows on the men's faces. The child's father is there, standing in the back, hiding. There are a dozen or so people. I know why they're here. We all know. They've come to take me to the church elders. Jeb is leading them, a man whose blisters I once treated.

I've heard of this inquisition, but I wasn't too fearful. Until now. I know it is over for me. Nothing I say or do will make any difference. I feel like Jesus at the garden of Gethsemane. His knowing. His dark night of the soul.

"Elinor, now don't make this more difficult than it needs to be," Jeb says. "You just come with us now, nice and easy."

"Jeb, Julius, Marcus, what do you think you're doing?" I point to different people in the crowd of men. "I have saved your wives, your sisters, your children."

"We have no choice, Elinor." Jeb takes me by the arm. "We don't have a choice."

"Shame on you," I say to Cecily's husband as I'm dragged past him.

I'm taken to the muddy city of angry men and placed in a cell. It's nothing more than an outdoor cage in a dark courtyard. I must relieve myself in the corner. My clothes grow filthy with stink; my hair becomes matted to one side. After a week, I'm brought into a courtroom. I would never show myself like this in an official setting, but they've given me no choice. They won't let me change clothing or bathe.

"She looks like a witch," a woman says in the galley as I pass. In the galley are dozens of people I have helped. I want to cry to the heckling woman that no one has allowed me to bathe.

They put me in the witness box and tell me I'm to answer questions. The barrister keeps saying that I don't love Jesus. Why do I not love Jesus? He's not really asking me, but preaching to the fevered crowd, to the judge.

"But I love Jesus. What I do doesn't stop me from loving Jesus," I try to say, but they won't let me speak.

"You have it all wrong," I finally yell in desperation. "Jesus is the reason I do the things I do." This he hears.

"Blasphemy!" he yells. "Where did you learn this evil?"

"I was taught by my mother, and she by her mother and so on and so forth. I'm just trying to do good."

"In the name of the devil."

He has it all wrong. There is no devil involved. There is only light. I want to say: *Jesus has been present at some of these healings. I have called on my Lord to help when it is particularly dire,* but I don't say it. There is nothing I can say that he will hear.

They sentence me to death. I look at the faces of the crowded courtroom, and they are full of blood lust and glee. They are the men slinging fists in the mud. They are the London I had always tried to protect myself from. This thing called civilization. They have lost the earth.

I'm not surprised I will be killed because I already knew it was coming. What upsets me is how wrong they have it. How they've twisted it up. I understand they're scared by what they can't understand, but I also get they can't understand it because they've given up the earth, they've given up earth wisdom for fists. If they studied the old ways still, they would understand.

As they lead me out of the courtroom, I try to catch the eye of the people I've helped. Cecily is there weeping. I want to say: *Now who will heal your children?*

I awaken from the dream. I don't know what day it is. I don't know where I am. Missouri? Seattle? Medieval London? The past is the present is the future here. Slowly, I remember returning from Missouri, passing out on my futon, dipping again into the dark night. I know this Elinor is me and that I lived this. I know it in my bones. The dream propels me off the futon and back into my life.

At my tarot table, I can now see how people's thoughts are making them physically ill, how the emotional, intellectual, spiritual, and physical are all one. It's as if Elinor has leapt from the Middle Ages into this lifetime. Her wisdom becomes my wisdom. I realize that in this lifetime I'm getting paid for a healing gift that got me killed in another lifetime. I realize I'm being valued for something that engendered fear and violence against me in the past. I realize also that my mother's path is not mine, and I can't go backward. This awareness changes everything.

The tarot intensifies, both revelations and retributions. More and more clients come to me.

A woman with gastritis can't stomach her husband's stealing at work.

A young man with ulcers needs to protect himself from corrosive parents.

A woman with back problems carries the whole world on her shoulders.

A majority of the corporate people tell me they're miserable in the competitive, manipulative environment. Many have physical symptoms, like migraines or stomach aches, or worse.

Your depression is your blessing. You're depressed because it is depressing. You come wanting an answer on how to fit into this culture. Your inability to fit is your greatest asset. Your not fitting is your very integrity. Your unhappiness with what isn't working is what is great about your soul. Can you rescript it? Can you see you're not a failure?

They come back again and again to drink the waters of the soul, but few leave the job. The money and the status are just too strong a pull. The handcuffs are too golden.

I befriend a yoga teacher who has a studio next to the bookstore. Sometimes we compare notes. She says people come into her studio and she spends an hour helping them align and get right with themselves, but then they just go back to their lives and get all twisted up again. She complains of how heavy the lifting is getting, trying to help them align even for a day, even for a moment. I understand. The same clients come back again and again to my tarot table, desperately wanting to feel OK, but consciously going right back into what ails them.

I'm starting to see what Rayne means about the Divine Feminine. I'm starting to see what the rampant, out-of-control, masculine world of competition, of ego, of hierarchy, of taking, taking, taking is doing to the human soul.

I can see through all of the chatter to the soul's magic. I can see the gem that each person is. I can read their purpose on this planet. I can see the blocks that stop them from their soul work. I can see it can take years for the person to see it for themselves, a lifetime. It's a heady way to spend time, swimming in such potential.

Weeks go by like this. Months. A year. The number of seekers increases. I do readings out of my apartment. I read for bridal parties, birthday parties, picnics. People far away call for a session, and I do readings over the phone. I fly so high, rarely touching the ground. I feel like a hawk soaring above everything. Like a tiny speck of a bird with the sun as my backdrop.

I'm eating dinner one night with Gem, a pizza she ordered and offered to share. "I'm not digging this trip you're on," she says. "You're so far outside your body all the time. It's been going on too long."

"Are you fucking kidding me? You should see the work I'm doing." I take a big bite of a pepperoni slice.

"You're gonna crash," she says.

"You have no idea of the power of what I'm channelling now," I say.

"Pearl, you're not listening."

I figure she just doesn't get it and devour another slice.

I meet other healers and tarot readers and we do exchanges. I'm ravenous. We are the Divine Feminine, women mystics channeling the sacred. I fly so high.

Gail, an acupuncturist in Fremont, asks for an exchange. We use her massage table for the reading, and then I jump on for my treatment. She is short and wiry, with dark hair, and has both light and darkness about her, and the mixture of it impresses me.

As she's placing the pins, she inserts one into the side of my right leg. The pain is instant and excruciating.

"Take it out. Get it out. Take it out!" I have never felt such pain in my life. I want to get up and run wailing down the street, but already there are six or seven pins all over my body. "Get the fucking thing out of me," I holler.

She's standing holding the pin as I'm screaming. She shows me she has taken it out. I'm still feeling it.

"What the hell is going on?" I scream.

"Let's let you go through the treatment and we'll talk. The pain'll subside. I'm going to leave you for about fifteen minutes and let the pins do their work. I'll explain what happened afterward, OK?"

She leaves, the room is dark. I feel fidgety and uncomfortable. The pain subsides, but what replaces it feels old and uncomfortable, dark energy I don't want to deal with. The fifteen minutes seems like hours.

She opens the door, turns on a soft light, and whispers, "How are you doing in here?"

I yell, "What the hell was that?"

She starts to take out the pins. "So Pearl, your reading for me was fantastic. First let me tell you that. It really opened up my understanding of the stuff I've been going through. So thank you for that."

"OK?"

"The pain you felt. The issue is that your crown chakra is so open, and you're sitting on an unstable base chakra." I remember vaguely Rayne saying something like this.

"In English?"

"You have a lot of trauma trapped in your base chakra. The imbalance of that trauma, along with how open you are to channeling, it's going to cause physical problems if you're not careful. The vibration between the two chakras when they're so out of whack like that, it can cause illness."

"How do I deal with trauma locked in my body?" I think about my writing. "I've been writing lately about my childhood. Surely that will help heal it."

"The trauma is so big and so deep, you may have to do more than write about it. Maybe seek out a therapist who does trauma work?"

I thank her. She leaves so I can dress. I'd already opened one cage to let the monsters out. The demons she's talking about with this next level of trauma—I just don't want to look at it. I can't look at it.

The "gift" continues to intensify. I no longer have visions that force me on tiptoe and show me a world losing its mind, but my days and nights are often like living inside a vision.

I'm receiving psychic messages beyond my clients, messages about the world. Visions like this have happened all my life—floods, earthquakes, fires—but now they are more specific; now they come to me with a little more peace.

In a dream, the banks of the Missouri and Mississippi flood, and I watch the water overtake the towns. A week later, this happens. People and cars and houses are washed away. My mother emails to say some cousin was washed away in his truck.

Another night, I'm transported to a plane that's going down. We're over the ocean, and the plane is nosediving. Everyone is screaming and crying. Luggage crashes from the overhead bins. We're all going to die. I cry in my sleep and wake up to news reports of the actual crash.

What did the gods want of me by putting me on that plane? Why am I seeing the flooding? What is being asked of me?

As I'm going to sleep one night, I enter the body of an elderly woman. I'm freezing. I can't feel my fingers. I'm sitting in the snow, my back against a fence. It's so cold out. It's too cold not to have a coat, gloves, a hat. If I stay out here, I will die. I sit on my bed.

In my warm bedroom and in the body of this freezing woman at the same time, I know there is a woman out there who needs help. Is she nearby? Should I go out and look for her? It's one in the morning, below freezing, so icy it's hard to walk without falling, and the neighborhood is sketchy.

I get up and pace and feel the cold getting deeper and deeper into the flesh of this elderly woman. I look out the window and open the door and see nothing. I send an email to Coral—I just need someone to know what's happening. Gem is gone on one of her art walkabouts. I know Coral won't get the message until morning.

As I go back to sleep, I feel the old woman again. I feel how cold she is, how close to death.

The next morning, I google local news reports. The woman was found frozen to death less than four blocks from me. She'd walked out of a halfway house without a proper clothing. She had mental issues.

I email the article to Coral. She shoots me back an email saying "Holy shit!"

Should I have gone out looking? Will I the next time I get the message? Is that why I'm receiving these messages? What could I have possibly done for the plummeting airplane? Why do these images come to me? What's the purpose? Is there no purpose? Is it simply that I sit here with a psychic door open, and this ability just "is"?

I tell Gem everything. I tell her that sometimes I want to shut this gift off. Sometimes I want to do something else and shut down this gift that's really a curse. Do I really have a choice? Do I have free will here?

"Always seeing so much," Gem says, putting her hand on my shoulder. "All your life. It must be so traumatic."

Oh Gem, you have no idea.

X
WHEEL of FORTUNE.

CHAPTER 10

Wheel of Fortune

For long phases, I have glorious, soul-enlivening readings full of epic beauty, and I forget the downside. My clarity seems to be increasing exponentially. It's like going to the gym: the more I channel, the stronger I get. I become a "potential" junkie. I can see the gift of every being that crosses my tarot path, and the power of the human soul is like a drug. I start to see the variety and diversity of the human soul as a tropical rainforest. I visited rainforests in Asia, and what amazed me the most about the dripping verdant environment was the variety of flora. How different each plant, and how all of this abundance coexisted. I start to see that people's problems arise because the world has become so standardized. That school systems and other systems standardize our thoughts and beings, and how painful for everyone it is trying to fit into a system that abhors difference.

I can see the stories each person has been told about themselves and the world, and the stories they've learned to tell themselves, and I see how these stories can either make or break them. The scripts often pull them off their center, make them wrong and bad. Sometimes the stories they've been told lift them up too high, and they can't move lest they shatter the expectation.

The word "rescripting" keeps entering the readings. Can they change the way they're perceiving the things that are causing them so much pain? Can they shift a stuck story to one that brings movement and evolution?

No, you lost the job not because you're not successful but because you're sensitive. Tell yourself the story of your beautiful sensitivity. Find a job that engages those sacred sensitivities.

No, your marriage failed not because you can't hold a man, but because you're being called to a more alternative life, a life that will make you far more fulfilled. Can you tell yourself that story, instead of the lie that you aren't lovable?

No, you're not wrong, you're seeing the truth about your abusive boss. Everyone else just refuses to see it. How do you hold your truth when no one else can see what you see, or refuses to own that they see it?

I see how so many people are missing their own purposes, missing their own plots. Again and again and again I look deep into the cards and see how the person experiences the world and how far away they are from living in alignment with who they are. I see how broken the systems are: family systems, school, work, and how we need a revolution.

Why aren't we speaking to the soul of the person from birth? Why aren't we providing each child with soul nourishment and a bridge from soul expression to the practical world instead of the other way around? I can see how depression and illness stem from this lack of alignment. And I see it will take a lifetime of rewiring the brain to get there. Their thoughts need to be more in line with what they love and not in line with what society expects of them.

A sales executive who is really an empathic energy healer but would rather die than become one.

A corporate program manager who has no idea he's a poet and visual artist.

A social worker whose soul screams musician but who won't do the music she used to love as a child, because how will that help such a messed up world as this?

For most people, their true natures are hidden from them, their bliss so deeply buried that it could take years to excavate. I tell them what I see, but I know it will take years of active participation on their part before they can begin to see it themselves.

Some Saturdays I bike home imagining a world where everyone is living their purpose, an explosive power of creative force, a rainforest of rich and exotic beings. It fills my heart to bursting.

I tell this all at some point to Gem and she says, "Don't forget about your own plot, Pearl, your own script that must be rewritten, your own demons. You have your own messages to unscramble, your own stories to rewrite."

The next thing I know I'm at a fiction writing course at the university. It's been a few years now of writing. What was once a practice of writing down snippets of stories in my morning writing routine had evolved to penning short stories, and I have no idea if they're any good. I do know the characters come alive on the page like the archetypes of the tarot, getting into all sorts of mischief.

I bike to class once a week and sit with the other adults and learn setting, characterization, plot, theme—I'm like a woman crawling across the desert, thirsty for the knowledge. As the others read their work, I see how all of our lives are story, all connected to the large archetypes: family, love, death, purpose.

The teacher tells me one day, as an aside, that what I have been writing is just scenes and not full stories. This opens a door. I go home and look at the scenes I've written, dozens, and they start to fit together like drops of water turning into a pond, and then a lake, and now an ocean.

My writing deepens, blossoms, expands. I have whole days now, weeks where I don't miss London, I don't think about my old friends. About Shirley. I don't even wonder about Finn, where he is, who is now getting to smell the sweat of him.

A few months after the writing course, I'm in my apartment with Gem and the phone rings. I don't pick up. It's the home phone and has an old answering machine, one where you can hear the person leave a message.

The voice comes on. It's a woman. Really, a girl.

"This is a message for Pearl Swinton," she says into the open room. "Ms. Swinton, we're pleased to announce that your short story 'Green Pea Soup' has been accepted for publication." I stare at the machine and cover my mouth with my hand. "Pick it up!" Gem yells. "Pick it up! Pick up the phone!"

"Give us a call back at your convenience at . . . " the girl continues. I look robotically at Gem and shake my head. It's too immediate. It requires more than I have. I cannot speak. "And congratulations!" the girl says.

Gem takes my arm and pumps it, not like she's shaking my hand, but more like my arm is a wing and she's flopping it up and down. "Green pea soup! Green pea soup!" She laughs and swings me around the living room. I want to curl up on the futon and sleep, for hours or generations. How exhausting it is to finally get what you want.

We do an awkward chicken dance. "Let me read it," she says. I look at her. "Please, oh please, oh please." She folds her hands in front of her, faced upturned like a small girl.

We go back to the kitchen and I open it on the computer. Gem sits down, knees spread, facing it full force like she does everything.

A woman is sitting at a kitchen table with her head in her hands. She sits back up and her head doesn't come with her. Green pea soup simmers on the stove, then burns. The husband is annoyed. The soup is ruined. He builds a shelf in the kitchen so she doesn't have to hold her head while she's cooking his meals. The darkest part is at the end, when he's horny. He's never been this horny. His wife without a head is his horny man-dream.

I watch the back of Gem's dreadlocks as she reads. Her profile is soft. I realize how much I love my friendship with her. She finishes and sits back.

"It's dark, I know," I say. "Sorry."

"Dear God, don't apologize. You're pissing me off with all the times you apologize." She stands up. "Come. I want to show you something."

We head to the crooked front porch and into her apartment. She makes her way over boxes of art objects to the sculpture in the corner. She's been working on it for months. It's covered in a burlap sack. I still haven't seen it.

She takes down the burlap. "Viola!" she says.

She's carved a face into a tall tree stump. A long braid of painted twine runs down the back. The tree is painted with bright red and orange checkers, like a country girl's blouse. She used old seventies handle bars for short arms.

"Pull the hair," Gem says.

"What?"

"Pull it!"

I reach around to the braid and pull it, and the head tips back. I startle because I think like my story, that her head is falling off, but it stops on a hinge. At the front, something has emerged from the throat. A slip of cardboard. It's a life-sized Pez dispenser.

"Read it!" Gem says. She's standing with her shoulders around her ears, wringing her hands.

I take the cardboard from the throat. It reads: "Time Wounds All Heels."

"I call her Platitude Patty. Politically Correct Platitude Patty."

I bark a laugh.

"When she loses her head, she spews platitudes all day long." Gem points toward the wall that separates our apartment. "Great minds, eh? We're basically both dealing with women losing their heads."

There are pieces of cardboard with different sayings around the figure. I pick them up like a cards from a deck.

"I'm trying to figure out how to make the cardboard messages come out one after the other. I can only insert one at a time now," Gem says.

Hold a grudge and remember.

What doesn't kill you still hurts.

There is no 'I' in 'Me.'

No man waits for time and tide.

Be careful what you do not wish for.

God doesn't give us more than we can bear, but man does.

Gem pets Platitude Patty's braid. "I love your pea soup story, Pearl. This is what I love about art, any art! It gets to be dark. It doesn't have to wear a bow and say all the nice things and make everybody happy.

"We need the expression of the darkness. I'm worried about the way this world is going. Everybody thinks if you say the right thing then all will be OK. Where does the darkness go then? When we don't own our own shit, we project it, making all sorts of people the 'enemy,' creating all sorts of depression. Both sides of the political spectrum do this, right? You've seen this, right? As artists, we have to own the dark. It's our job."

She puts another piece of cardboard in Patty's throat, closes the head and pulls her hair again. "Who was it that said art should comfort the disturbed and disturb the comfortable?"

★ ★ ★

No matter how hard I try, I can't make enough money to support myself reading tarot. The exhaustion always catches up with me. I wonder how the perpetual need for money defines me, directs my destiny, rules me, changes my brain chemistry, morphs my cells.

I take Rayne's advice finally and spend concerted effort looking for a job whose values I can align with. I finally land one at a nonprofit foster care agency in their communications department. I'll still do tarot at home and on weekends, but no more temp jobs! This is not a typical nonprofit. They have money, some kind of legacy left by an ultra-wealthy donor. They offer me three times the amount per hour than anywhere else I've worked. I bike home laughing into the spitting rain.

My celebrations are short-lived.

Because it's a foster care agency, I imagine it'll be progressive, but this doesn't prove true. Toxic hierarchy. As the new person in the department, the shit drips down to the bottom of the totem pole, where I sit swimming in it.

When I arrive for the day, fresh off my bike, my hair is wild and unkempt. I'm sweating, panting. I nip into the bathroom to change and wash myself off. Other women in their business suits are there. My feral green eyes meet the mascaraed blue, and there is no connection. It's like we're on different planets.

My job is to write the articles for the company's newsletter. Sometimes interviewing the offsite social workers touches me, but these enriching assignments are few and far between. Mostly I write fluff that's handed down to me from the "editor." It's impossible not to be depressed by this job—such a wide gap between this and the journalism I'd been doing for years, where articles changed lives and affected government policy. Again going from the wide-open divine of the tarot readings to a place of hierarchy—it's an excruciating dichotomy.

The newsletter is marginal to the work done here, so my editors have other, real jobs; the newsletter is something they do on the side. I have to send my copy to an assistant editor, the guy who heads up the IT department. Every time I send him one of the finished articles, he shoots back a poem he's written. They're sappy and obtuse, and he corners me in the break room to see what I think of them. I smile. I nod. I play the dashboard dog.

One day he takes me into a conference room to go over one of my articles with a red marker. He's tall and thin and acts too young for his middle-aged years. He speaks to me in a soft, politically correct tone, using one hand to mark up the article I've written and the other to fondle my knee. I scoot my chair back, hard. I feel the hopelessness of this toxic workaday world, but I don't quit. I've bounced to enough temp jobs to know none of them are much better than this. His behavior sparks poetry of my own when I get home that night:

Red streak on white
Knuckle on knee
You old man.

I think about the Divine Feminine, about the imbalance, about how I've had to deal with men like this all my life, how every woman I know has. How toxic masculinity has become. How the denigration of all of the feminine traits has created such a twisted world. This is the needed rebalancing act that Rayne has been talking about.

I'd imagined I'd be helping children, but this is the corporate headquarters, and there's a vast chasm between our air conditioned offices with a view of Lake Union and the children who need help.

I spend time meditating on the work. This feels like the end of the line. Whatever the next step is, it can't be in this direction, but I'm stuck with this job for now. I see what Rayne says about building a new system. I'll have to come up with something on my own; the answers to what I want don't exist in the existing paradigm. I simply can't read enough tarot to survive without losing my mind.

One day I'm leaving the foster care agency clad in bike gear and carrying my helmet. As I unlock my bike at the front of the building, a social worker pulls up to the front. Two girls emerge from the car—one about ten, the other seven or so. They stand holding each other's hands desperately, dressed in clothes that don't fit, waiting for the social worker to collect her things.

I can see these girls and the difficult home they've been taken from. I can read it on them just as if they'd told me. I know the older girl is protecting the younger. She is fierce. She's looking for a new mother for them, a good one this time, somewhere they'll be safe. She looks at me. Our eyes meet. I can feel her trust.

Are you my new mother? Could you be our mother? I hear the words as she thinks them. My heart breaks. I tear my eyes away. She looks desperate when I look back. Does she think this building is a place full of new mothers? I tell her with my mind, *I'm sorry. I can't be what you want. I wish I could. I can barely take care of myself.*

The social worker takes them into the building. I don't know why they're here. You never see the children at the headquarters. We have wall-sized images of the foster kids, but few ever visit the building. I watch the three of them disappear into the building and send as much good energy as I can muster to the little girls.

I think of my mother and Kat and their desperate need for mothering. I think of all the women I've met all over the world, from developing countries to rich countries, and how much we need Divine Feminine guidance.

Rayne wants to try something new. She asks if we might try shamanism, an earth-based healing spirituality. I can't believe how much I've changed in just a few years, how I thought all of this new age stuff was just mumbo jumbo, and now I come to it like a thirsty woman to a tall glass of water.

We're going to use the shamanism, Rayne tells me, to focus on trauma still trapped in my base chakra. I've been doing some research on the base chakra, how it has to do with survival, and how it might help this journey I'm on around money.

She sits beside me, eyes closed, hand on my ankle. I'm in a Barca lounger in the corner of her office with a lavender-scented eye pillow over my eyes. She shakes a rattle and emits something between a song and a hum. I can feel the soulful pull of her. I'm not journeying with her. I'm meant to stay alert, be present, and not fall asleep. She sits beside me shaking the rattle in active meditation and is gone for a while. I feel her in my guts poking around. She rattles quickly when it's time to come back.

"OK," she says. "Ready?"

I take off the eye pillow. When she opens her eyes, they are dark and deep and somewhere in the land of the spirits.

"I have to do this first," she says. She stands up, leans toward me, cups her hands, and blows into my heart. "The first thing I did was a soul retrieval," she says, sitting back down.

"What's a soul retrieval?" I ask.

"There are parts of each of us that are lost, soul parts that leave because of trauma. In a retrieval, we go in and retrieve the lost parts."

I'm excited to the core. This is exactly why I came back to the States, to find my lost self.

Rayne explains how the journey took her down into the earth, through a tunnel that ended at a place where two mighty rivers met. She found a black panther there, protecting a girl of about four or five.

"The colors were so vibrant, Pearl. Like I'd fallen into a painting."

She spoke to the panther, told him she wanted to bring the girl back with her, asked the panther what was needed for the child to return.

"The girl came out from behind the panther. I was entranced by the flow of the two rivers, the way the streams merged. It was so powerful and epic. The girl comes up to me. She's terrified. I can see the terror in her body, running up her legs and into the base of her torso. I felt like I so desperately wanted to protect her. She hands me a delicate painting. It was so beautiful. She told me she needed art. That if she was going to come back, she had to have art."

I can feel the girl, and I feel like crying. "What does this mean?"

Rayne explains how she took the girl and brought her to the surface and blew her soul into my heart. "With soul retrieval, the only way the soul part will stay with you is if you honor their wishes. Pearl, you have to do art."

The thought of it terrifies me. Rayne sees this.

"Do it even if you're terrified."

I think about how my entire life has been filled with artists, from Jason to my friend Yuriko in Tokyo to my landlord Sala in London to Gem now. I think about how every free moment I had in London was spent at the galleries. Sometimes who you are is staring you in the face and you just can't reach out to her because she scares the shit out of you.

There's more, Rayne explains. She tells me she carried the young girl with her and jumped into the current of the rivers, was carried over a waterfall, and farther out into the ocean, where they sunk to the depths.

"I was being led to your unconscious. I was shown that so much is bursting forth and flooding you from the unconscious that it's threatening to break you."

I tell Rayne how I've been going into what I call mini comas. I feel overtaken by the dream world and just go to sleep. Usually I make it home, but not always. I fell into a mini coma in a recliner in a furniture store once and woke to people staring at me, and another time I was lying across a path on Mount Si outside of Seattle, a couple stepping over me.

"We're going to surround you with power animals to protect you," she says. "Sea creatures came up to me and told me they would surround and protect you from all that you're picking up psychically."

She stands, circles her hands above my head. "A stingray will watch over you from above." I can see the stingray, wings spread, swimming there.

She does the same circle below my feet. "A sea turtle will be your foundation." The turtle's shell is as clear to me as the lines on my hand.

"To the front, a school of iridescent fish. To the back, a gray whale. To the right a seahorse, and to the left a dolphin."

She tells me they'll keep me protected from the onslaught, but I will have to invoke them daily, visualize them. I'm to use them with the other visualizations she's already taught me.

As I pull myself off the recliner and get ready to leave, I look at Rayne. She's like the images of women in Italian Renaissance art, women like the ones Botticelli painted. Opulent body, flowing clothes, long mussed hair. I wonder at how many people she reads for. She has just started an earth-based temple, and her following is growing. How does she manage it? She's such an abundant person. There's so much life and exuberance in her. I admire her for what she gives to women and to the world. I know in the depths of me how much she believes in women, loves women. I know that on some level she's saving my life.

"How do you do it?" I ask.

She tells me about how she used to be an actress in New York, but she always had the second sight, and when she moved to Seattle, she knew she had to use it for the greater good. How this lifestyle marries her desire to perform with her love of the mystical.

"This way of living isn't for the faint-hearted," she says. "But I wouldn't change it for the world."

"I think a lot about going back to my old life in London."

She narrows her eyes. "Don't forget the message you got from that child, to do art. Can you pick up art supplies on your way—"

I interrupt her. Something is triggered in me. I don't want to hear about the art. I want to run. I want to go back to London, to the life I had. Artists are broke. Artists are crazy. Artists become bag ladies. I don't want it. "I have a choice, right? Free will and all that? I can choose to do what I want."

"Sure, but then you have to deal with the consequences of those choices."

As I leave her office she hugs me. "Pearl, be careful what you wish for."

XI
JUSTICE.

CHAPTER 11

Justice

The woman shapeshifts. I'm sitting two people away from her. Fur seems to warble in and out of focus around her body, animal guts become her guts, her face elongates. The wolf is there and gone so quickly.

This isn't a dream or a journey or some metaphor. This is real life, in a conference room with ugly matted carpet near the Seattle Center. I'm at a weekend shamanic workshop. Gem brought the ad for the workshop to my attention and practically dragged me from my apartment, shoved me out the door, and forced me to go.

We're all standing up one by one and talking about our experiences with the metaphysical. The woman speaking is Rachel. She has a strong New York accent, lines on her face, and straggly black hair, and she wears skinny black jeans, high-heel boots, and a black turtleneck. If you just saw her, you'd think she was a harried, hip New Yorker, and not someone who has traveled the world looking for help because she can't stop herself from transmuting into animals.

Mostly it's a wolf, she tells the group, but other beasts too. It's happened all her life.

Seventy-five souls create a circle in the massive conference room, seventy-five people who don't fit into the normal. My people.

The organizer sits in a metal folding chair at the head of the circle wearing an oxygen mask. He's sick. He has an assistant with a clipboard who is telling us his story: He was an anthropologist and taught at Berkeley, Yale, and Columbia, then took a trip to the Amazon, met a local shaman, and asked to be initiated.

You can hear his labored breathing through the assistant's microphone. I'm sure this lifestyle, meeting so many of us who are plagued with living with one foot in the normal world and one in the not-so-normal world, has not been good for his health.

The assistant explains that he had been a man of science, but inside he felt the call to this other wisdom. He was sure he'd been a shaman in another life.

He went deep into the Amazon to meet a well-known shaman. As part of the initiation, he was given ayahuasca. The shaman and others took him to a spot in the rainforest and left him with nothing but a big stick. If you see something huge and something scary, they told him, go up to it and poke it with the stick. They left him there, high out of his mind, with nothing but a stick.

Alone in the Amazonian rainforest, he saw giant bat figures. They kept appearing, kept saying: *We are the rulers of the universe.* He poked, but they kept coming back. Later, he asked the shaman about them. "Oh, them. Ignore them. They're always saying that."

He came back full of the earth's mysteries and started a shamanic foundation. He traveled and studied tribes all over the world and distilled down their shamanic practices. He brought this dying tradition to the West, revived it.

"What Yogananda did for Hinduism and Suzuki for Zen, this man has done for shamanism, introducing it to the West," the guy with the clipboard says.

The head guy waves away what the young man is saying. He takes down his oxygen mask, takes the microphone. "I'm not a guru," he rasps. "This is an independent spirituality." He takes a heavy breath. "Each of you can go directly to the source." Stops, breathes. "If you think *you're* important as you do this practice, you're not getting it."

The floor is reopened for people to stand and talk. A big man in a flannel shirt stands. He's weeping. He can't stop weeping. Great gulps of air, his face the color of a beet, and snot on the back of his hand. He can't get to the bottom of it. This sadness. It comes from somewhere else, he says. He can't stop it. It's a long song, a crying of a pod of whales, a small child's tears, a father who has lost his inner little boy. He's an immigrant who's lost his country. His tears are like the poetry of despair.

A teenage girl holds her mother's hand as she talks about all of the spirits who have always surrounded her since she was born and how she can't be with her friends or stay at a normal school or think of a future. The young pale hand clasped in the weathered one, to have a mother hold your hand through such a thing. This is shocking and moving to me, a mother who would stand by your side.

Women in business suits sit sideways, smoothing down skirts. A man adjusts his Akubra, looking like he's walked in from the Australian outback. Hippies with long hair and military guys with crew cuts. Body builders, anorexics, middle-aged spreaders. If you saw any one of us walking down the sidewalk, you'd never guess the theatrics of our divided souls.

The assistant explains a basic shamanic journey. We'll close our eyes while he drums. We'll do a sort of creative visualization. We'll imagine a passageway into the earth, something we've actually seen with our real eyes, so that it will be easier to imagine—a mole hole in the forest, a well, a drain in a basement. We'll step into it, and we'll be pulled into the earth until we come out into a light, into a field, onto a beach. We'll look around in our visualization for an animal or a figure and ask them if they are our teacher. We'll keep asking until we find our teacher. We'll ask the teacher for wisdom. It all feels so familiar. Like it felt when Rayne did the soul retrieval. Like I already know this. Like I've lived this already so many times in my dreams.

We lie back and close our eyes. The drumming begins, a thump, thump, thump. I can feel my heart merging with it, feel the energy of the other heartbeats around me, until we are one force, one communal heartbeat.

I visualize a hole at the rotted base of a massive red cedar and step into it. Sucked hard into the earth, I go deeper and deeper as dirt and root swish by me.

A desert. I'm thrust out from the earth into sand. I never knew deserts could burst with such color—lemons against purple, orange, and crimson. I roam and look at the tint of the dunes and scrubby vegetation, mountains like a wash of watercolor in the distance. When has color ever been so mystical, so full of magic? I reach down and grab a handful of sand. Each grain a gem of a different hue. They fall like silk through my fingers.

A snake slithers toward me. Its skin is translucent, red that glimmers and bleeds and mixes with gold as it parts the sand and undulates toward me.

"Are you my teacher?" I ask. I'm scared of its cold blood.

"Yes," she hisses.

She slithers up my calf, circles my thigh, enters me. She climbs up my spine, uncoils until she's straight with my spinal column, from the base of my skull to the base of my ass. She is longer than that, but she adapts to me.

"What is it you want me to know?" I ask.

She says nothing but seems to be ingesting my toxins. Like a snake that's swallowed a mouse, I see the darkest parts of me enter her and bulge her belly. I see this toxin travel like a rat down her body and down my spine.

"What is it you want to tell me?" I ask.

"Death."

My stomach gurgles and I belch.

"Rebirth."

I bear down to hold off the fart. The snake is stirring things up. She's joining the different centers of my body, parts of me that have been living in isolation. The throat reaches down to the heart, which holds its hand out to the intestines, then reaches for my sex. So much is being released, and I worry which orifice I'll need to clench next.

"As inside you, so outside you," she says as I squirm with the visceral feeling of her inside me, gassy but so sensual, so sexual.

The assistant is beating the drum faster, calling us back up from the journey. I don't want to go! The snake crawls out from inside me. No, snake, stay!

I'm being pulled back up the way I came. The colors bleed up like clouds, and wisps of each attach to me. Like multihued lightning bugs they alight on my body. The colors journey with me as I travel back through the soil. I open my eyes.

Some people share their stories. I don't want to. It's something just for me. It's mine. My stomach rumbles as the others speak. I drink from my water bottle until it's empty, and I'm still thirsty but don't know if it's OK to go get water.

After a few people speak, we're directed to tell our stories to the person next to us. My partner is short, stocky, and freckled and has hair that sticks up. He tells me he met a mouse.

"A mouse," he laments. "How manly."

"What did the mouse tell you?"

"I entered him and became a mouse myself, and we scrambled along the forest floor. There was so much magic. Every mushroom, every blade of grass, the insects. So real. I've been hiking a lot lately, so it seemed relevant."

I feel the power of what he's saying. "That's beautiful. Even a mouse has a lot of power. Maybe that's the point."

He smiles and nods.

I tell him about my snake, about missing my sensual, sexy self. I have tears as I'm telling him. I don't realize how much I miss myself until I'm talking to him.

He puts his hand on me. I look at the mouse with my new snake eyes, and he jerks back like he's been burned.

"I'm not sure a mouse and a snake are a good partnership," I say, and we both laugh.

After a break for lunch, we're instructed to do a partner journey. We're to go in and do a journey for another person, to ask their question of a teacher and bring that wisdom back for our partners. The goal is to learn how to use the gift of journeying to assist others. I turn to Mouse, but the assistant says we must find someone new.

I turn to the woman on the other side of me. She looks like Tammy Faye. Short and round, a tight perm, pearl necklace, pearl earrings. Her perfume overwhelms me. As I look her over, she looks me over. My skinny jeans, tight concert t-shirt, combat boots, and rat's-nest hair that won't behave in this humidity. We are an odd couple. We are two people who would never hang out.

The assistant says we must give our partner a question, and we will go on simultaneous shamanic journeys to ask the guides.

I ask her what her question is and she says, "How can I expand my work as a Christian missionary?" How odd and wonderful that she's Christian, and she's here doing this shamanic workshop, something so pagan.

"My question is, when will I meet my next significant other?" It's a dumb question. I don't even know why I'm asking it, because I actually don't care. I don't think I trust her enough to ask her a real question, to be that open and vulnerable.

We're told to lie back and have the sides of our bodies touching. The drumming starts. I find myself immediately transported. The visuals are clear. Others in the seminar talked about how hard it is to do the journeys, but for me, it's easy. It's the way I live.

I'm at a river bank. The grit and mud, the sparse grass like balding hair, it's as real to me as anything in normal reality. A guide comes up beside me; he looks like Jesus. In front of me is a small pool of water. Beyond the small pool is a narrow strip of land, and beyond that a wide river with a strong current. It's muddy and reminds me of the Missouri.

Jesus hands me a wafer, the body of Christ. I know it well from Mass. He tells me, "Put the wafer on the ground, in the grass." I do so. He traces around it with his finger. "This is the extent of the space it takes up," he says. "You see the space it occupies?"

I nod.

"Now put it in the pool."

I do so into the tiny, still pool in front of me. It breaks apart and dissolves.

"Now, in this small pool, it has dissolved, and see what space it takes up." The pool is less than two feet in diameter. I nod.

"Now watch this." The river swells up, breaks the bank, and swirls into the tiny pool. The river absorbs the pool and the tiny particles within it, and the current pulls it out and away. "Now see the space the wafer takes up. It flows in vast directions."

I nod.

He says, "Tell her to bring her Christianity into every area of her life, not just church. Tell her to dissolve it into the waters of her soul and have it permeate her every breath."

I hear rapid drumming in the other world and visualize myself traveling back and up and out of the meditation.

I give the woman the message word for word, with all of the visuals. She melts. She cries. She hugs me. I don't see her as "other" anymore, like I did before. I realize we are both just people, just living, just doing our best.

"Yes, I keep my Christianity at the church. You're right. It needs to be everywhere in my life." She has the bluest, most gentle eyes. I didn't notice them before. She thinks for a while, then looks at me with such trust until *I* melt. "Thank you."

She tells me about the journey she did for me. "I meet a woman who glows blue. She takes me to a clearing where a girl has just had a baby. A newborn. The woman guide picks up the baby and hands her to me. She's beautiful, the child.

"I'm told to come back and give you the baby." The woman pretends to hand me a child, and I pretend to take it.

It's a younger version of the girl Rayne blew into my heart.

"The guide says that you have to raise up this child in your own way. Don't rely on anybody else, or any system or institution. You can't meet anybody now for any serious relationship, because you have to raise up your girl. She has to be raised the way you would raise her. Ask yourself, 'If I had a child, how would I raise her?'"

I look at the imaginary child in my arms, and she starts to grow. Soon she's a toddler, and then she's four, and I know she's the same girl that Rayne met on her journey. I want to cry and laugh. I'm terrified. How does one raise a child? I have no idea, never learned, have no one to emulate.

We share our stories with the group. But I can tell that everyone is elsewhere, deep in thought, needing to process. The day ends, and I stumble out and onto my bicycle.

The child is with me on the way home, and my mind keeps going back to the desert, to the magic of the colors, to Rayne's story of my girl at the bottom of the ocean. How would I raise a child if I had one?

When I get to Wallingford, a few blocks from the duplex, there's a sign for a yard sale. I feel pulled to go to it, despite the fact that I'm wigging and just want to get home and close the door on the rest of the world. I find a folding table, a pad of paper, and a giant box of broken crayons.

I put the supplies in my pack and walk my bike and the table home. In the living room, I set the table up in the corner, put the paper and the crayons on it. I sit down and run the crayons back and forth in squares of tangerine, maize, apricot, and tickle me pink. That simple movement of producing color with my hands creates a wellspring of joy. The multihued desert comes to me again, and I try to recreate it with my crayons.

I have a Chagall print on the wall that separates my place from Gem's. As I'm coloring, the print falls to the floor. I pick it up, study it. The mystical flying people and soft colors. I take it as a sign. I will raise up my little girl with art. Something inside me, like a wall, feels like it's crumbling. It feels terrifying and exciting all at the same time.

I go to bed thinking of Jesus, the pool of water, and the river. I think of the colors of the desert, the broken stubby crayons on my table. How can I bring those colors into every area of life, into the pool and into a current, so that they rush everywhere and touch everything?

I dream that the ceiling above me crumbles, and at first I'm scared I'll be crushed, but I'm not. The ceiling is open now, and I can see the universe from my futon. The stars are sentient, and light travels from one to the other as if they're speaking to each other. Constellations are created above me, my personal mythology, connecting the dots of my soul.

The River Academy, a center that offers art classes to adults, is on Capitol Hill. I drive the truck instead of bike. I'm here to apply for art classes, but I keep missing the street. I drive past it and see it but somehow forget to turn. I turn around and drive past it again. And again. And again.

Something is being knocked down inside me, and I can feel it, and it makes it hard to focus. It takes me forty minutes of circling the block, running over curbs, and nearly side-swiping a car before I just give up and drive home.

On Gem's urging, I try again a week later. This time, I make it directly into the parking lot, but I'm shaking and can't remember the last time I was this nervous.

At the front desk, I find it hard to speak above a whisper, but I finally explain I want to sign up for a beginner's painting class. The guy behind the desk is young with piercings. He says they have an opening for an assistant they want to fill. I'm not here for a job. I just want to take a class. I look at him confused.

"Assistants set up the easels and the lighting, help the teacher create the still lifes, break the studio down at the end."

"I just came to sign up for a class," I say.

"If you sign up to assist the teacher, the class is free."

"What?"

"You'll get to take the class at no charge."

I grow dizzy.

"It's an intermediate class, though," he says.

This makes me dizzier, and I can't seem to speak.

He says, "You'll be working with Saint Harbor. Write your name and number here."

I do as I'm told, and it's as if the universe is moving my hand across the paper. "What's a Saint Harbor?" I ask.

"The teacher's name."

I laugh. I go to my truck and shake.

A week later, I'm wearing a painting smock, standing at an easel and trying to paint a naked man along with several other female students. The naked man is our model for the session, and he's lying with his arms above his head on a settee with silk fabrics draped about.

Saint, the teacher, is shockingly handsome, tall and fit, with salt-and-pepper hair. A white V-neck t-shirt is stretched over his biceps, and his jeans are covered in speckles of paint. While I assist him before class, setting up easels and taborets and wiring lights to the center stage, it's hard to keep my pants on.

I find out the next week that the other women feel the same way. They come back with new hair styles and makeup and wear low-cut dresses and heels.

This is way over my head, this intermediate class. I'm the worst artist by far of all of the other students. Saint is talking about the color wheel—tone, hue, line, shape, composition—and I don't even know the vocabulary. I have no idea how to hold a paintbrush, how to put paint on the brush, how to push the brush across canvas. I don't even know how to buy a canvas. To save money, I search for and find a piece of canvas in a clearance bin at the art store and bring that in, and it's so rough it tears my brush up. Somebody mentions "gesso," and I have no idea what they're talking about.

Saint notices I'm struggling and over the weeks comes to help me hold the brush. He smells like sweat and sex and someone who's been around the block six dozen times. I don't want to feel what I'm feeling, don't want to go there, but dear lord the pheromones.

"You've got this," Saint says. "You're an artist. I can see it even in the way you walk. Just keep going. Try it all. Do it wrong. Just keep doing it."

He's a stellar teacher; I can feel his passion for his students' progress. He highlights blocks of orange I've painted in the corner of my canvas and tells me why it sings. He knows how to inspire. He does this for all of the heaving and giggling women in the class.

As I'm setting up for class one day, he hands me a book. It looks like a children's book. It visually tells the story of

Little Red Riding Hood using the elements of art he's trying to teach. Using rectangles to represent a forest, and triangles for the wolf, and incorporating color, it shows how tension and unity are brought together by shifting these simple shapes. It's fundamental and is exactly what I need. Within the pages are the fundamentals my inner artist needs. To have a man nurture what I need to grow—it's heady.

I thank him shyly and place the book in my backpack, where I study it every night for weeks. Art, it's a foreign language, and I must open my mind to learn it.

At night I dream of hands. Hands moving through space, pulling purples from the sky and crafting magic. I dream of hands painting and sculpting, creating pottery. I dream of the same psychic energy I use to channel, and instead of using it to read tarot for people, this energy moves from a higher place through my body and out my hands, and it forms the color of the rainbow on a stretch of canvas. I dream of hands creating beauty in an ugly world.

Awake, the art brings up tremendous fear. The fear is interesting to me. It's palpable. I stand back and observe it. I hear a siren nearby on Aurora and fear they'll come and arrest me because I'm doing art. It sounds absurd, and I know it's ridiculous, but the fear when I hear the sirens is so real. Saint gives us "homework," and sometimes the fear translates into dark muck, and I can't seem to crawl through it to the canvas. I bring muddy ugly paintings to class, and it's clear the other students don't even get why I'm here. Saint does, and I'm moved how he can see through me to the potential.

It becomes clear to me that I have a lot of work to do on myself, a lot of debris to clear to get to this place where I can channel beauty and light.

★ ★ ★

The shamanic workshop, the art class . . . the idea for a full-blown metaphysical walkabout comes to me in a dream. *Go across the city and beyond. Find the people and groups who are doing art and mystical healing. Try everything.*

I go to energy circles, psychic fairs, metaphysical seminars, intuition conferences. I visit crystal healers, energy healers, shamans, astrologers. You can't swing a black cat in Seattle without hitting someone or something metaphysical. I try mask making, collage, mandala making. I find myself in expensive living rooms of rich houses, in the basements of churches, in rented spaces over massage parlors, in conference rooms at the Seattle Center. I'm around novices and experts and everyone in between. People are loving, bitchy, warm, cold, beautiful, ugly, sane, insane. Some think too much of themselves, and some think too little. There is nothing perfect about this walkabout; it's messy and flawed and full of frustration and hope.

I do group energy healing with my hands, join a shamanic circle in a yurt, sit at tables at psychic conferences giving readings, and much, much more. I do group art with young girls and old women. I'm still trying to figure out where I fit.

At a past-life workshop in Issaquah, a dozen people sit on the floor in a circle next to a bank of windows that look out on trees. The room is wet and musty and dark.

A guy with a ponytail and a beard named Rob guides us in meditation. We're doing a form of self-hypnosis to explore our past lives.

Rob leads us down a set of stairs, deeper and deeper until we we're at the bottom, where we are to visualize a hall of mirrors. To our left is a series of mirrors in a row, and in each mirror is one of our past lives. To our right is another series of mirrors in each of our future lives.

We're focusing on the past lives today, the mirrors to the left. Again I have no problem with visualizing—I can see figures clearly in each mirror, in a line, in period clothing, bonnets, helmets, scarves. Women, men, girls, boys, black, white, Native, Asian. I'm full of spit and excitement for this process. If all of these people are me, I hold within me a vast multiculturalism that goes beyond even global traveling.

We are asked to see which life takes a hold of us. We're asked to visualize reaching our hand out to the mirror. I do so, and someone pulls me hard, and back and back I go.

She's just sittin' there, playing. Lookin' at her, I can't stop weepin'. Just a child. Not even a toy—just some funny-shaped rock. She says Hi Grandpa and I can't stop blubbering. I'm crying all the sadness that's built up in me a long time. I can't stop it. I know it ain't safe, but I can't stop. The girl, he'll take and rape her. Like the others. I can't stop any of it.

I look down at my hand, and it's black and large. I'm wearing threadbare trousers, sitting on a log that's just a bench outside a low shack.

"Sisters, he's on one of his crying jags again," Betta says. I look over and see Sary and Peg jump up. They come up and grab me under the arms, off the log bench.

"It's a Sunday. Nobody's around," says Sary.

"I'm not taking chances again," Betta whispers.

We go into the house that isn't really a house but a bunch of wood nailed wrong. They put me in the bed. I'm still weepin'. I'm weepin' for before I was born, and I'm weepin' for after I was in my grave.

"They'll beat him again. One of us gotta stay here and make sure he don't go back out."

The little girl runs in. "Grandpa's crying again," she says, and stares at me with big dark eyes.

She ain't really my granddaughter. They took her people away before she could talk.

I had a woman, Elsie, so many years ago now. I loved her. She was my heart. I knew what they did to the babies, selling them out of the womb. When she had our baby, I didn't want to see it. I was standing outside the room where she delivered. I was nineteen, but I had no desire. I didn't want to know it. Why love something they're just gonna take away?

They made me come see the child. I looked at the little child. I took it up in my arms, and I held onto it fiercely. Blood of my blood. Blood ties meant nothin', and here was my blood and it meant something. I held it with almighty muscle and tenderness. I wanted to crush it, to save it. I loved it.

They sold off the baby. They sold off Elsie, too. And other folk, related, unrelated, it didn't matter after a while. Children sold off. Nothing to protect them. Families torn up.

The little granddaughter now next to my bed, she puts her little hand on me. I grab her hard in a hug. I sob against her little dress. He'lll rape her, like he already done all the girls, and I'm an old man and there ain't nothin' I can do!

I come out of the hypnotic state, blinking up at a line of thin fluorescent lights. Beneath me is tightly woven industrial carpet. The room goes in and out of focus. I'm so upset I have to bite down on my lower lip not to cry.

As others share their experiences, I think about this black man in the American South during slavery. In Seattle, if you're white, you're not supposed to have an opinion on race issues, because how could we possibly know what racism is like? But is that true? If you believed in past lives, haven't we all lived the lives of others? Haven't we all been many nationalities, many races, and different genders? Haven't we all been desperately poor and insanely rich?

I think of how this man's family was torn apart in a system that tore all families apart. How much this echoed my ambivalence about family this lifetime. I have no trust in it.

Everyone in the room is so emotional that before Rob guides us to meet one of our future lives, he has to guide us on how to deal with what we're experiencing.

"Try this," he says. "Instead of entering the body of the person you were in a past life, stand beside the person, witness her, without fully embodying her. That should help with the emotions."

I think this is a metaphor for my life, for how not to embody the people I'm reading tarot for, how to stand outside them and witness them, without falling headlong into them.

We're out of time, but Rob tells us to go home and practice and to try to follow the past life until death. To leave the past-life body and follow the spirit ascending, to come to an understanding of what we've learned during that lifetime.

On the bike ride home I think of Elinor, the herbalist who was killed for her beliefs, a past life brought to me in a dream. Now, finally, I know how to control the process, how to meet these past-life selves on my own terms.

At home I close the curtains, turn off the phone, light a candle, and do the past-life regression, eager to meet the old man again. I want to be there when he dies. I want to know what he's learned from his lifetime.

After the self-hypnosis I find myself at the mirrors, the same immediate connection. I'm pulled back, and then out, coming awake on a plantation. This time not outside their shack, but outdoors with green fields to one side, a barn on the other, and the big house behind me.

I'm being beat up. The foreman is smashing that stick in my back hard. Again. Again. Just cause I took a break. I'm old! I did everything they said all my life, and I wanted a damn break. The stick is breaking as it comes down on my back. That foreman got to prove something to the folks, the white folks and the black folks.

It ain't that the beating broke my body. It was the final break of my spirit.

In the shack now, in bed, Betta and De-De are carin' for me now when they can, but they gotta go out into the fields. We know there ain't nothing left of me. I see Elsie like she's sitting beside me, holding my hand. That other little grandbaby girl? The one I was crying over before? She was shipped off somewhere when she was eight. Lord knows what kind of life she has.

I weep all day, and it ain't for me. It ain't any of the cryin' for me.

I'm pulled forward in time to his deathbed. I watch him die in the cot a broken man. I watch the soul leave his body, watch it hover, looking down at the body. Up the soul ascends. Me as him—we leave the earth plane. We're in a different reality now, surrounded by comforting presences and a cocoon of colored lights. A voice asks us what we learned this lifetime.

I see the foreman who beat me. I see how a whole system twists things up, puts people in the straitjacket of roles, one role is the beater, and one the beaten. I learned that the way you break a whole people's spirit is by splitting up their family. The way you break a whole race is by tearing apart their blood kinfolk.

I go back to the Issaquah group a week later. I love this work, feel like all of these lives that surround me, and them, and us, have been there all along, and the veil between worlds has always been thin for me. Today we're learning future-life progression.

We do the meditation, and I'm thrust into the hard seat in a beat-up truck in a desert landscape.

Next to me, driving, is my father. My father this lifetime is my father in this future. I look at him shocked. He is half ape. At least I think it's ape—it's some monkey-like creature. I look down at my arms and they're covered in long, dark hair. I look back at my father, and he has long hair on his face, but he has the nose and blue eyes of a human.

We're driving through desert. All around us the world has dried up and become sand, dust in the throat and eyes that scratch.

I understand that we're human-ape hybrids, that the first of us were created in a lab, in a test tube. We're part human, part beast, and we've been created to be a labor force. They give us some freedom—to drive, to go home afterward—but we're underclass, and we're slaves. We aren't human, so they believe we don't deserve the rights afforded humans. How people will always find a class of others to describe as sub-human so they can use them.

We come across a sandstone town center, a few buildings in the vast sea of desert. I wait in the truck as my father goes in to get the supplies we need. I'm beaten down by this life we're forced to live and look hopelessly out the window. There, one building away, is a woman who's giving me the lust eye. Some of the rougher women like to have sex with us, with the animals they think we are. I recognize her and look away, sick to my stomach.

Rob pulls us out of the progression too quickly. There's so much love in the truck, love for myself and even for the father I found it hard to love this lifetime. Rob tells us that future lives are not givens, they are potentials, possibilities. We stand in a circle as a group to release these other lives, to give gratitude for them. As I hold the hand of a hippie woman with long gray hair on one side and a boy in spandex bike gear on the other, I think of how many stories surround each of us, how exciting that is. How we're all a progression of tales, not just the incidents of our childhoods, but the legends of the past and the potentials of the future.

As Rob does an incantation, my past stories, my current story, and my future story take on the rings of a tree. The first rings start near the center, and more lives and more rings, and I'm a tree. I am a whole, with circles that build and build upon each other. That night, I sit outside looking at the stars. Seattle lights obscure many of them, but I can still see a smattering. I think about this past me. All of the past me's and future me's. I think about all the people I'm meeting while reading tarot, all of their past selves. I think about the guides I'm meeting doing the shamanic journeys. The vast wealth of the spirit, the individual, the collective. The variety, the music, the glory, and the pain. We are trillions of stars in a mosaic. I see the potential way above, so far above, riding high above this pain.

I think about my writing and all these vignettes that come out of me on the page. I think about how someday I hope to get this all down, to weave it into a web so that I can see. So that we can all see.

XII
THE HANGED MAN.

CHAPTER 12

The Hanged Man

The sheet of loose-leaf with the address is crumpled in my fist. The taxi driver drops me at the top of a steep road in Haight-Ashbury. I want to walk. I need to get my head clear.

I've come to San Francisco to find my lost sister. Meghan is a missing piece of me. I'm the old man who lost his family years ago, and I'm here today to find my family this lifetime.

It showed up in my writing. After I put all the stories together that I wrote, after I fit the puzzle pieces, there are gaps. Meghan is missing. I'm here to find her and mend the fabric of my blood.

A man defecates in front of me. He clings to a lamp post, his pants tethering his thighs. Shit pours from his bare ass. He slides down the post. He's muscular and tall. I stand transfixed. In all my years in Southeast Asia, in poverty-stricken countries where people live in sewage, I've never seen anything like this. I've seen women in India lift their saris, squat, and defecate on the streets, but this . . .

I get as close as I dare. He's drooling. His eyes roam around in his skull. His pants are still around his thighs. Shit is smeared on his legs and butt cheeks. A group of nuns in full habit emerge from a house a few doors down. I move toward them to ask for their help. But they see the man, turn the other direction, and rush down the street.

The man falls backward into his feces. I walk around him. I have no idea what I can do to help. Should I help? Whom do I call?

I keep walking. The address says my sister's house is just a few blocks farther down. Someone else leaning against a garage door staggers and falls. I pass others lying on the sidewalk, old and young, men and women, mumbling, drooling, groaning, defecating. They're all on something, or many somethings. The juxtaposition—the abundance of the souls I read tarot for, and this soul loss. It yanks at me like a rabid dog. It takes my breath.

I find Meghan's house finally, a rundown Queen Anne, flaked siding, a turret that teeters as if it's about to collapse, and a row of dirty bay windows going up floor by floor. One of the windows is boarded up. Still, it's actually nicer than I expected.

When I was little, Meghan gave me a pearl, a black river-water misshapen thing. I have it in my purse, dig for it, hold it hard in my palm. Meghan gave it to me the day she ran away.

I ring the bell, stare down at the cracked tile of the front porch.

"We don't want any," a voice says, then a laugh and a cough.

I push the button. "I'm not selling anything."

"Who is it?" A different woman's voice.

"Um, I'm looking for Meghan."

"Who is it?" This time a desperate shout.

"Pearl."

"Who?"

"Pearl, her sister. Half. Sister."

I wait a minute. Another minute. I'm about ready to leave when the door buzzer sounds and I open the door and am inside.

It's one of those apartment buildings where you can't be sure what's going on behind the closed doors of the other apartments. Unusual smells. The once-regal wallpaper scratched up. No decorations, no doormats. Desperate sounds behind scarred doors.

I climb the stairs, find the apartment. The door is ajar.

"Hello," I call, knocking. "Meghan?"

I enter a hallway that opens to a living room and feel a dense, hard energy. Walking down that entryway is like a past-life regression, but this time the regression is into the darkness of my childhood.

Meghan is leaning back on the sofa smoking a cigarette, eyes narrowed against the smoke, staring at me through the fog.

I say breathlessly, "You're alive!"

How long has it been since I've seen her? Ten years? She left when I was eight, but I found her again when I was a teenager. She was scary then in her devastation. And now? She's skinnier, harder.

She snarls in response.

"What are you doing here?" It's another voice, and I turn, and there's a woman sitting on the arm of a chair. She's long and stringy. I try to look at Meghan, but the force of this other woman keeps pulling me sideways.

"This is Pauline," Meghan says. The woman moves to the sofa, sits shoulder to shoulder with Meghan.

"Who are you?" Pauline asks.

"I'm here to see my sister."

"Half," Meghan says.

"I just came to check in on you," I say.

"It's like a once-every-ten-year thing with you, huh?" Meghan says. The last time I saw Meghan in Missouri, she was heading off to California for a new start. We've had a lot of water under both our bridges since then.

Pauline asks, "Where are you staying?"

"I'll get a hotel."

"Stay here," Meghan says. Pauline shakes her head. "It's settled then," Meghan says.

"Pauline, get her a beer." Pauline gets up and goes into the kitchen. She hands Meghan a beer.

"I'm on call."

"One won't hurt."

"It's never one," Meghan says, and takes the beer. Pauline hands me one, too.

"You work?" I ask.

"Yeah, I've got a fucking job," Meghan says.

I hold the beer like a precious object. How long has it been since I had a drink? A long time. It's cold and sweaty in my hands.

I learn that they both work as aids in old folks' homes. I want to find out how Meghan went from turning tricks back in the day to this new life as a nurse's aide, but I can't figure out how to ask it.

"I need to go to the ladies," Meghan says. She's slurring her words. Obviously she's on something stronger than beer. She stands, loses her balance. She gets upset, starts tearing up.

"I need to call my sponsor. I have to call Beth." She falls back on the sofa. Pauline looks away and rolls her eyes. Meghan struggles up again and swerves to the bathroom. No one calls Beth.

Pauline leans in and whispers, "You may just want to leave before you make things any worse."

Meghan comes back, uses a side table for support. "Pauline, I need to go to a meeting," she says, whining.

"I know. I know." Pauline is slurring her words too. She stands and goes to Meghan and brushes her dark hair away from her face. "Sit. I'll get you another beer. Come on. Sit. Good." She goes into the kitchen and calls, "It'll all be OK in the morning."

I don't know what to say so I tell her about the man pooping on the street. Meghan says, "So many people shitting on the sidewalks now."

I tell her about the nuns. "I didn't know what I could do to help."

"What're you going to do? Hand him toilet paper?" She laughs but it sounds like screaming. "Wipe his ass for him?"

The man pooping is an omen for me, not just about Meghan, not just about San Francisco, but about an image of modern America, and I can't shake it. The energy here with Meghan is heavy and dense and pulls me backward, into the old world I've spent my life running to escape.

"Shit, I have to make a beer run," Pauline says. She looks at me. She keeps staring until I figure out she wants money. I give her a twenty, just happy she'll leave for a moment so I can talk to Meghan.

As soon as the door slams, I ask Meghan about her life since I saw her last. She doesn't want to talk, so we sit in silence for a while. I'm leaning forward in my chair, still holding the beer, which has gone warm.

When she starts talking, I can barely hear her. From her slurred, disjointed narrative, I cobble together the story. She hit bottom a few years after she arrived in San Francisco. For a while, she was on the streets.

"At least back then, they had programs. Somehow I got this good guy, this mentor, Jerry, and he got me into a program. I got my GED." She said this with such pride and smiled, and I noticed two of her back teeth were missing. "He got me into this nurses aid training thing." She throws out her arms. "The rest is history."

"What happened to Jerry?"

"Died," she says.

"He fucking committed suicide," Pauline said. She's standing behind me. Apparently the liquor store isn't far from where they live. "Like two months ago. She hasn't been the same since."

Meghan cries, sniffles behind her hand. The phone rings. Pauline answers it. "Is it them?" Meghan asks before Pauline hangs up.

"No, all good," Pauline says.

"I'm on call," Meghan tells me. I already know this. I also know she can barely walk. "If they haven't called by now, probably they won't?" Meghan asks Pauline. Meghan starts crying. She keeps saying, "I'm sorry. I'm sorry." I can't tell if she's sorry about being drunk or sorry about crying over Jerry.

The Great Compassion enters me, and I see Meghan as a girl, a child I never knew, before I was born, a scared girl dealing with the ogre that was our father. I want to go up to her, but the booze is like a muck I can't swim through.

Pauline takes out something. She lights it, drags deeply, exhales. She holds the pipe to Meghan's lips and repeats the process. It doesn't smell like weed. Pauline offers me the pipe, and I decline. "Ooh, little miss goody-goody," she says, blowing smoke.

I look down at my beer and it's almost empty. I realize I've been drinking it. I have been clean for years, and I'm so disappointed with myself. Pauline goes to the kitchen, gets another beer, and replaces the empty bottle in my hand with a full one.

Later, when they're stoned out of their minds, they ask me what I do, and I tell them about the tarot. "Holy shit, she believes in unicorns," Pauline says, and she laughs until she goes into a coughing fit.

It's past midnight when it's finally time to go to sleep. I'm given Meghan's room; she's sleeping with Pauline, a fact that makes Pauline a little too excited.

There's just one small lamp next to the bed. Black-out curtains on all the windows. Even with the lamp on, I can barely see. I'm drunk. I lost count of the beers. I'm sick with myself for being drunk. How family can pull you back, so far backward.

As I'm getting into bed, I kick something, a glass, and it rolls under the bed. I reach under to get it. I have to hold it up to my face to figure out what it is. It's an empty rum bottle. There's so much clanging under the bed that I reach again. Find another empty rum bottle, and another, and another. I open the closet door. It's filled with hundreds of empty rum bottles. In their overwhelming sweet smell, in their sticky emptiness, I see the soul of my half sister, a casualty on the sidewalk that everyone veers to avoid.

In the middle of the night, I go to the bathroom. The toilet is full of bright-orange piss. I've never seen urine this orange. It's thick, too, like soup. It's Pauline's or Meghan's, and it's full of poison.

The piss seems to get inside my veins. I think of the pooping man on the street. I get dizzy, but this is more than just the beer I drank. I'm picking up Meghan's addiction—it's in my veins. It's the kind of empathy that's physical, the kind of relationship with the world where things lodge themselves in my flesh. I slide to the floor, curl around the base of the toilet. I'm so dizzy I can't lift my head.

I takes me ten minutes of being curled up like this before I'm able to sit and use the toilet, before I'm able to go back to the bedroom decorated with empty bottles of rum.

Before I left Seattle, Gem was worried I'd choose to move to San Francisco. The thought had crossed my mind. Seattle felt like a backwater compared to London. I rarely met anyone from other countries. I just wasn't making enough money. I despised the foster care agency. And no matter what I did, I couldn't kickstart my journalism career.

"Don't do it," Gem begged. She'd grabbed me by the upper arms and stared into my eyes. "Don't do it, Pearl! Don't move to San Francisco."

As I stumble back to Meghan's room, all I can think was how much I miss Gem, how much I miss the Pacific Northwest.

The next morning, I'm in the kitchen looking for some coffee. I open curtains to see better. The kitchen is filthy, encrusted, the stove top more brown than its native white. Someone has thrown pasta against the wall to see if it will stick, and a single spaghetti strand dangles there. Dishes in the sink. Flies.

I know that I have to leave. I have to go back to my own life. I want to help Meghan, or save Meghan, but I can't. I can barely save myself. I don't know how this fits into my story, into the missing and lost pieces of the puzzle. I don't know how any of this fits into the Divine Feminine.

I find some instant coffee, a pot in a cupboard that looks vaguely clean, boil some water and make a cup. Pauline and Meghan come out of the bedroom.

"OK, I'll be right back. Going to get smokes," Pauline says. She leans in to kiss Meghan, who shakes her head and moves away.

The phone rings. Meghan answers it. Her hands shake, a thousand vibrations in her drug-addled body. "OK. OK. Got it," she says. "I got it," she snaps, and hangs up.

She goes into her room and comes back in scrubs. As Meghan stands in the living room, surrounded by morning light full of flying dust particles, time seems to slow down. I have an opening in that moment, and I see her again as a girl. And I see how abused she was by Father, the hole inside her from the abuse. Father broke her spirit. That's why she ran away. And then my own treatment at the hands of the man who was supposed to protect me starts to rear its ugly head.

"I have to leave," I blurt.

She grinds through her purse looking for something. Her energy is frazzled.

"See you in ten years," she says without looking at me.

I move around until I'm looking at the side of her face.

"Look. We're both recovering from the same toxic man."

"Oh, please, you're doing just fine. Ooh, I lived all over the world, ooh, I'm so damaged."

"You have no idea what I've been through."

She looks me up and down. "Oh please, little miss goody, with her goody life."

I shake my head. "Forget about me then, Meghan." I take her upper arms and turn her to face me, and she's surprisingly fragile in my hands. "You've done it once and you can do it again. Pull yourself out of it. The Meghan I know is strong." I squeeze her upper arms. "Strong," I say, squeezing. "Strong," like a mantra.

She moves out of my grip and for a second I think she's going to punch me. She puts her hands out flat and swims them in front of me, up and down my body. I notice her hands. Beyond the quivering, they're so expressive. Thin, long fingers with chipped nails. "You're so special aren't you? Good little Pearl. Always the hero."

I think about her hands and how she's using them, the drugs, the quivering fingers. When we were kids, we used to butcher animals. She had blood running through her fingers at eleven years old. I remember thinking even then that it's not good for Meghan to have intestines dripping from her hands. This isn't good for Meghan's fragile psyche. She also once used her hands for making art, transforming found objects into masterpieces, like Gem, like Father.

She takes a small bottle of breath spray and squirts it in her mouth. "See ya," she says. "Have a good life, half," she pauses. "Sister."

Pauline comes in, sees us, and pulls Meghan away.

"It's all right, she's leaving," Meghan says, looking at me. "That's what she does, leaves." I don't point out that she was the one who ran away from home first. She grabs a pack of cigarettes from Pauline. "I've got to get to work."

I want to tell her that she needs to leave here, this place, and this part of San Francisco, because the culture itself is too drug addled. She needs a clean break, but she's heading for the door, and I don't say anything.

When she's gone, I gather my bag and take off as quickly as I can. I have no idea what I've accomplished. I wasted the little money I had on this trip.

At least you know she's alive. You know there's hope. I don't know whose voice this is whispering in my ear as I make my way back to the airport, but as the plane takes off for Seattle, what stays with me is not that message, but the man shitting on the street and the deep-orange piss in the toilet. As I watch the waterways below shrink until they're snakes slithering along the earth, I think of the addiction of a planet, the toxins running through the veins of our world.

I wake up to Gem on the edge of my futon. She's saying something, but it's like she's whispering, as if she's a ghost made of smoke and mirrors.

"Glad to see you made it back alive," Gem says. She's wearing black lipstick and black eye shadow, and she's the one who looks like a death mask.

"Meghan's alive," I say.

"I was worried you'd never come back," she says. "I'm worried that someday you'll get on a plane and I'll never see you again."

"Other people talk about fun visits with their families. My bar is set at 'lucky to make it back alive.'"

"Platitude Patty would say you have to go forward to go backward. Oh, that's a good one." She finds a stack of Post-its and writes it down.

I go in and out of consciousness, mini comas. My body drowns in waves of the unconscious, and it all seems to do with Meghan, with mending a broken family, with a whole world of broken families needing mending, centuries past of broken families. When I wake up, Gem is still there. She's sitting on the futon watching me.

"I'm so depressed," I whisper.

Gem's voice fades. "You're depressed because it's depressing. You're upset because it's upsetting."

I'm somewhere between asleep and awake. It's an hour or two later. Gem is there, or she's not there, I can't be sure. I slide into a past-life regression like a dream, like a vision, like our lives are lived in layers that most of us fail to see. I know even as I fall into the past life that I'm going to meet Meghan again from another time, a long time ago.

The grass is frozen, hard and white. My hands are little boy's hands, feet in worn boots with holes. The ground is cold on my big toe. We're in a fishing village somewhere in Scandinavia. My father is there, bent shoulders, torn-up hat. I can see the hut that we live in in a village of shacks.

Something's wrong with my brain. It won't think right. Oh it makes Father so angry. I try to think but lose my train. Thoughts go foggy. It's like a whiteout in a snowstorm.

Born with a brain that won't work, I've spent my life with my father's rage. Sometimes fear. He can't understand. My foggy brain won't harm him. Others are scared too. They are scared somehow that I'll cause them harm. It is true that I'm too handicapped to do the normal things, but I wouldn't hurt anybody.

It's my twelfth birthday. My father leads me by the hand away from the village, several hundred yards to the rocky coast. He's going fast, and I keep stumbling as we walk over tide pools, ocean debris, and rocks. We go up to a large fishing boat at the sea's edge.

My father speaks to the captain. The crew are rough, unshaven, in torn clothes, weather beaten. They stare at me. I expect them to laugh. Everyone is always laughing. Father hauls me up the plank onto the boat.

"This will be your home now." He won't look at me. My father cannot abide me, so he's giving me away.

"Go!" And when I won't move, he shoves me from behind. "Go." I watch him disappear across the shore, back to the village, and I know I'll never see him again.

My regression jumps to years later.

I'm now a grown-up. It's my job to move the ropes so the crew won't trip, to tidy them up and wrap them around the grommets. They no longer yell at me. I can do what's asked now as long as they keep it simple. My brain's fog has never lifted. I can't process anything but the most simple tasks.

One of the men is my friend. Really my only friend. He has a face bloated up by alcohol, deep pockmarks in his cheeks, a scraggly black beard, bushy eyebrows. I love him.

Fast-forward again.

I'm middle-aged now, weather beaten like the rest, an old half-witted sailor. I'm not unhappy, generally. But now my friend is sick. This hurts my heart. He's still working the fishing nets, but he's sick, and he's not getting better. One night it's raining, and I know he's on deck because it's his turn to keep watch. I feel a strong intuition to go to him.

The rain is cold and blowing sideways. I can't see him. The rain is hurting my eyes, but still he's not there. Finally I find him on his back lying on top of coiled ropes, the ropes I tidied up earlier. I've made him a bed of ropes. His death bed. I try to help him to stand, but he's too sick.

I sit with him. I put his head in my lap. The only person I've ever loved. The only person who ever loved me. He never once was angry at me, never laughed at me like the others, was never frightened. He saw through the fog to my soul.

He opens his eyes and whispers something I can't hear, or my brain can't think about. He dies in my lap. From the heavens, a blessing of sharp rain upon both of our faces.

I come out of the regression knowing the sailor who loved me in that seafaring life is my sister Meghan in this life. Rob taught us that many of the people in the old lives are still with us now. I have no doubt that sailor was Meghan. The connection my sister and I have goes way beyond this lifetime, has so many layers you could cut them with a knife.

I look around and see that Gem has left green tea in a delicate cup on the side table. She's written me a note, "What goes down must come up," with a smiley face as a signature.

The past life on the fishing boat reminds me that love is there for the broken, the ugly, and the sick. That love isn't politically correct, isn't some hipster version of fit and correct. I think love must include the shadow, but I have no idea how.

Someone asked me once at the foster care job if I really believed these were actual past lives. I told them there's been proof: People have done a past-life regression and received enough information to find a person of that name in that time period in old ledgers, someone they couldn't possibly have known about. Or they find a gravestone or descendants, or they recall facts that are then verified.

I say, "There are more things in heaven and Earth than are dreamt of in your philosophy." It was much more exciting to believe there are other dimensions, and spirit guides. What was the alternative? That this reality was the only one?

I told my coworker I didn't even mind if I was simply tapping into a collective consciousness and being visited by the memories of souls who once lived. It didn't matter if it was *my* past life or just something I was privy to, some channeling of other dimensions. The effect on my consciousness when I did a regression was just too real. I tied these past-life lessons to real issues I had today and used it for healing. It didn't matter to me what one called it.

I once felt a death as it was happening. My mentor and friend Usui in Tokyo. When he died, I felt his soul shatter into thousands of pieces and shoot out like stars, landing in trees and sky and earth. A thousand pieces of my friend entered and *became* these entities. I didn't worry that I could experience this shattering and that I could see my sister in a past-life sailor. Perhaps just part of our souls reincarnated, and it was just a small fraction of my sister there. Still it was familiar. Still it was part of me. I knew even as a young girl that the multiverse contained layers of reality, and it was far beyond the comprehension of our linear minds. This knowing was so clear as a child and it was systematically denied and shamed and scared out of me.

XIII
DEATH.

CHAPTER 13

Death

Gem and I are at the Canterbury (AKA the Kinda Scary) on Capitol Hill. A suit of armor leaning at the front door, coats of arms askew on the walls, drunkards falling off bar stools. The room is perfumed with sweat and stale booze and smoke.

I plop the pile of cash I made doing tarot readings that day next to the ash tray. "I'm buying."

We order pints of Alaskan Amber. I'm drinking again. And drinking. And drinking. We're talking about money, about poverty, about American consumerism.

"When I first got back to this country," I tell her, "the grocery stores were so huge. So many products, so much fake food. I'd have this intense visual of breaking things. I wanted to take everything off all the shelves and smash it into smithereens."

Gem lights a cigarette.

"It's like all these things they have for sale are more important than people, more important than the earth. Buy and take and take and buy, and throw away and keep throwing away and dumping on the earth. Ad nauseum."

Gem's hair hangs in flat, black sheets by her face. She's watching with intense dark eyes, and I find myself falling into her. The snake on her arm quivers.

No matter how hard I work at the foster care agency, or how much tarot I do, by the end of the month I may have just enough money to live, but none to pay back the debt I accrued when I first moved here.

"I actually came back to this country with zero debt and didn't even own a credit card. But the big American suction started happening, the good ole American Way of Debt, and here I'm running like a gerbil on the proverbial wheel and not even able to keep up."

I tell Gem about the impact that traveling through third-world countries in Asia and India had on me. "How can I possibly live a life of comfort in a dominant, rich culture that takes advantage of other countries for its wealth? I choose instead to live in sympathetic poverty."

Gem plays with the cash on the table. I tell her how I went to Rayne to have a reading because I wanted to see what was wrong with me, to heal my poverty consciousness, and how that night I had a dream.

"I was shown this dirt path through the woods that led into this mist and fog. It was beautiful. In the dream I was made to understand that these woods and path were what was really of value to me. And that's exactly right—deep down that's the thing I value, nature and walking in it, above any crap they sell at stores, or any car, or any house. And in the dream, I was made to understand that my views of money were actually quite healthy."

Gem picks up a twenty-dollar bill from the top of the pile and starts folding it. As I talk, an origami heart emerges in her hands.

"We're questioning and blaming the individual for their money issues when the whole system is toxic," I say.

"Trees don't grow on money," Gem says, holding up the heart. The waitress comes over and I order a Maker's Mark, neat. I have no idea how Gem makes money. She doesn't talk about it, and I've stopped asking.

"Anyway, I'm sure I do have some healing from my past around money," I go on, "growing up in poverty, but I just feel we blame the individual about money issues, when it begins as a cultural issue."

"Love can't buy money," Gem says, fist on cheek, looking bored now.

She unfolds the twenty, flaps it back and forth.

"I'm more important if I have more of these pieces of paper than you," I say.

"I'm bored." She fans herself with the bill.

"Sorry I'm boring you."

"It's all so boring," she says as she waves her hand toward me and out into the pub.

"Thanks."

"I'm tired."

"Of?"

"Waiting." She sighs.

"For what?"

She doesn't answer. She seems to get an idea and sits up straight.

"Watch this." With a flick of her wrist, she holds up the twenty dramatically. She takes her cigarette lighter from the table with a flourish. She holds the lighter to the corner of the bill. She clicks it and the flame licks at the edge. It catches fire. Everyone looks. The drunks at the bar are gaping. The hipsters are aghast. She drops the burning bill into the ashtray.

The waitress rushes over, stares at the green flames. "Um, is everything OK here?" She sounds like she's about to cry.

"Everything is excellent," Gem says. She's no longer bored. I know what the waitress is thinking. That could've been her tip. I'm thinking, I live paycheck to paycheck and that could've been for food or more booze.

"That's illegal!" a drunk older woman at the bar yells.

I'm mesmerized by the flicking flames, the way the paper curls, the fire at the edges, how it eats into the middle, leaving behind black ash. I look up and notice every person at every table and on every bar stool is looking over and watching the bill burn. They're all so uncomfortable. Not a single person in the pub is unmoved by this. I'm psychically open after a day of reading and I can feel their agitation, their fear, their need.

Gem has her face against her fist again. "All this fucking fuss over a fucking piece of paper."

"This is an act of art, of pure art." I'm so impressed with Gem right now. "You're a genius."

"Bored genius, that's me," she says. She motions to the waitress for another round.

There are some actions that work as rituals, that have an archetypal effect, that trigger a manifestation.

Something happened when Gem burned that bill.

The next morning I awake to thousands of dollars in my online tarot payment account. Thousands.

I sit at my computer in the kitchen, hungover, trying to figure out what I'm looking at. I open and close the account and log in again. I pour another cup of coffee. Yes, several thousand dollars are in my account when yesterday there was none. I think it's some trick or that I'm still sleeping.

Opening email, I find dozens of messages from people I don't know. I click one. Then another. And another. They all wanted readings. They're from all over the world, and they *all* want a tarot reading.

Be careful what you don't wish for, I hear Gem say.

Sometimes we think life occurs in a linear way, but it's not true; the future can happen first, followed by the present. And sometimes the past is so far up in the future's business it's hard to tell the difference.

I finally find an email that gives me some kind of explanation. They mention someone who referred me, a name I don't recognize. Someone has written about me and sent it to their massive following. I search for the online newsletter that discusses me and finally find it, and the website. I look at the picture of the author and then remember.

I'd read for the woman just the day before at the bookstore, right before I met Gem at the Kinda Scary. She stuck out because she was too well dressed, too hip to be at my table. Too aware. She told me she was a self-help book writer from New York visiting Seattle to see a friend. I have absolutely no recollection of the reading itself. Her website called her experience with me "life-altering."

"You've received money," says an email that pops up from my account. Another. Another. Over the next few days, my account fills up and fills up and fills up.

You would think this would be a good thing, but I spend the week in perpetual hyperventilation. With the readings every Saturday and those during the week and the parties, I already can barely function. If I read too much on a Saturday, I can't even go on my Sunday forays into nature.

I spend days answering each email and setting up readings. I don't think I have the right to say no, and besides, I need the money. I stop going camping and fill up my Sundays. I set readings over the phone for the people who are far away. Every day for hours now, well into the night, I read the psyches of people all over the world.

Abandonment, divorce, depression, cancer, drug addiction, lovelessness, loss, kids causing trouble, husbands causing trouble, sick wives, sicker bosses. Fear, lust, hatred, envy. The seven deadlies in all their iterations. They don't come to you with their joys. I can see the golden light of their beautiful souls, but we're all so overtaken by the problems. I raise the conversation up to their gifts, their beauty, but it's heavy lifting to keep the energy there.

There's no boundary between their voices and my psyche. I sit with them in my ear. The voices stay with me long after the call, build upon one another layer after layer.

I learn I'm better at channeling when the person is not visible to me. I'm more fluid when I can't see the person's face. The spirit unattached to the body has more clarity for me. I travel the world over the phone lines, flying with the souls of others. Every day, I barely come back down to earth.

Months go by. I'm a zombie. I'm a dehydrated husk of a person. I awaken one Sunday to Gem sitting next to me. "Hard day at the office, dear?" she says. Her eyes are large and brown and full.

"Such neediness," I say. I'm hollowed out and my voice sounds empty. "Everyone's soul is starving. We're like shipwreck victims, drowning in water made of salt, and we're so thirsty but we can't take a drink."

"Not your job to save them all, Pearl."

I tell her how all night, while I sleep, I'm flying. I never touch down anymore. I take the wind and soar across the country, and farther, beyond oceans, across continents. I fall into and out of the psyches of so many all night long. How I'm still trying to keep the pain at bay, keep it from entering the flesh. How I feel like Wonder Woman with the magic arm bracelets, flinging my arms upward to block this sickness, block their trauma, block their rage, but I don't have enough arms to keep it all at bay.

Gem plays with a strand of my hair and hums something. "You need to find another way."

"I know." I feel like I'm taking all these people into my body and it's taking years off my life. I know that Rayne taught me "hollow bone," but it doesn't seem to be working, or it just doesn't work for me, or it *is* working and this is as good as it gets. When I'm not channeling, all I do is visualize self-protection.

"I need the money," I say. I tell Gem how I keep thinking about the women I read for who have husbands who take care of them financially, of all their struggles with identity and self-worth. I keep thinking about my mom. How it was a given for her generation that you found a good man to take care of you. I don't want a man to take care of me. *I* want to take care of me. But how can I keep doing this?

I scoot over so Gem can lie on her back next to me. She's still humming.

"It's like the women's movement never happened. I'm always shocked by how many women still depend on the man's money and don't make any of their own." Gem's humming is like a lullaby. I continue, "Some people say I'm not good at relationships, but it's that I can't stand the unconscious entitlement of the man and the unconscious passivity of the woman and how I end up standing by my man, smiling and nodding like some bobble-head dog."

Gem hums.

"It's not just about money, you know. Finn was the artist, the musician, and I was always the audience. When is it my turn to be the creative one, the one *with* the audience? Coral calls it 'being eclipsed by the man.'"

Gem says, "You're preaching to the choir, sister."

"I feel like we're living in a fascist heteronormative state," I say. "This whole man-woman-two-point-five-kids thing, it's so boring. I'm so goddamned bored. It's so old world, so caveman. Cavewoman and cavebaby scared of big bad wolf. Big strong caveman come to protect them. It's old brain-stem behavior, and aren't we far beyond that?

"What if relationships and marriage are also part of this big systemic change everyone is talking about?" I continue. "What if in a hundred years we don't even recognize anymore how people have relationships? I promise you, the world and love are more exciting and diverse than anything we're living now."

Gem goes back to humming.

There are thousands of ways to live a life. *I want to use tarot to give people the freedom of their innate variety.*

"I read so many tarot readings for so many women who think they're wrong for wanting something different, or they have this primitive terror that if they don't find their caveman they won't survive," I say. "And then once they do, they're all too ready to subsume themselves. It doesn't matter if they're independent. Professional. They want the man. They meet the man. Then they pick up after the man. They cook and clean and wash and scrub. And no one even questions that role?

Really? Ok, that's not right. Some women do, but they *still pick up after the guy*!"

"This is why I'm a serial sex enthusiast," Gem says. "I get what I need, give them what they need, and get out early. Get in. Get out. I don't have to deal with the bullshit. They say I have *intimacy* issues," she says. "It's not that. Or maybe it is, but it's more like intimacy issues with a society that puts me below the man. Intimacy issues with an entire toxic system. When you don't want them, *you're* the bitch. When really *society* is the bitch. The guys don't even see the entitlement, and they'll nice you all the way to the grave."

Gem stretches her arms and toes toward the ceiling. "So the system isn't really great for men either, right? The roles thrust upon them? The fact that by the time they're in middle school, they're forced to conform or get the shit beat out of them. Don't cry! Don't show emotion!

"I'd rather the guy be angry, pissed off that he's being boxed in by society's definition of what it means to be a man. That's a start. That requires some level of consciousness. But they're the difficult ones to date. I've tried. They're up against a wall, and they come out punching at who they're told to be. These are the guys I like. But it's a fine line. As a woman you represent a whole pit of expectations, and they can be hard on you. But they're honest. At least they're honest with themselves."

I'm falling into unconsciousness, and Gem squeezes my wrist. In a low, tired voice, I say, "So exhausting, Gem, the dating. I'm hungry. I need food, and I go out and aren't I promised food? Instead the guys suck off my teats. I get hungrier and hungrier. It's great to talk to you about this, because most people make me wrong."

"Sister, you're you. A gentle giant."

Sharp tears come to my eyes with her words. An exhausted giant at a rickety table in a wet corner of the world.

She says, "We can talk woo-woo and hypotheticals all day, but still we live in this capitalism. Something is wrong with all of it. No system should require us to push ourselves until our bodies can barely take it. Just to survive. I'm not just talking about you reading tarot. Think of the factory workers. Think of the single mothers with three jobs. Successive generations of parents push their kids to get educated so they can at the very least get out of the three-job syndrome and just work nine to five, but it doesn't really solve anything, right? There are still all of these people working too many jobs and dying inside to survive."

"Divine Feminine," I say. It's all I can say. "We're all out of balance. It's all out of balance." I'm slipping again. For a moment, as I go, I see Gem as me, and me as Gem. We're the same person, as if our boundaries are porous.

I hear Gem through the fog: "I don't like seeing you like this. It reminds me too much of when I first met you. Come on. Get up."

I whisper, or Gem does—I can't figure out who's talking anymore. "It's the dawn just before the dark."

One day Gem and I get stoned, and I walk by myself to the store to buy chocolate. On the way, two middle-aged women point at me from across the street, run through traffic to get to me, then grab and hug me.

"It's you. It's you!"

"Yes," I say. I'm so high I can't keep my eyes straight.

"What you said. Oh my God. I love you. It was true. So true. Thank you."

I don't recognize either of them. I don't remember anything that I channeled. I often run into tarot clients on the street who rush up to me, desperate and excited like this. I often don't recognize them. I've lost count of how many times this has happened.

"What you said saved our relationship. We're talking again."The woman has tears. I just want to get to the store and buy my Kit Kat and a Diet Coke, my white-trash stoner treat.

"Thank you. Bless you. Bless you," she says, her hands grasping mine. "My friend wants a reading. When can you read for her?" Her friend is glowing at me with expectation.

Her friend spreads her arms and says, "Read me now!"

I smile and nod. Nod and smile. I do my best dashboard dog impression. I mumble something about checking my schedule, and the two women laugh and run away, skipping through traffic like children holding hands.

It keeps happening everywhere. People I don't recognize rush up and thank me for words I don't remember saying. The thanks would be OK, I suppose, if it wasn't for the guru-ing. I have no desire to be a guru. None. I don't have the answers. I'm just the channel. Don't blame the messenger, and don't guru them. I want people to find their own power and not rely on my channeling. They keep thinking that power is outside them when it's inside them. I want them to know they can channel this stuff too—it's just a muscle that needs to be built.

I can't go to parties without people I've never met coming up to me and saying, "So you're the psychic, go ahead and read me. I can take it."

"What do you see in me?"

"Oh I'm so embarrassed about how much you're reading me right now."

Or they avoid me like the plague; some even stare daggers at me. As if they have something to hide, as if I'm even interested in whatever they're hiding. As if I care.

I'm losing my sense of being a person. I'm becoming a magic eight ball. People are shaking me and turning me upside down.

The cards on the table are acting out a play in another tongue. It's like trying to understand a foreign language. It's another Saturday at the bookstore. It's not like I don't love the work. When the energy travels through me it's pure love; people I don't even like I'll end up loving after a reading.

The woman sitting across from me looks normal. Short brown hair, a bright, fresh face, an expensive turquoise purse matching low-heeled shoes. The cards are standing up now, but they're acting out a skit I can't understand, and their words are coming out in consonants and vowels that make no sense, in the formation of a language that I don't think exists. Either a new language I haven't heard or one that doesn't exist anymore, an ancient tongue.

I hold up my hands. I can't read the reading.

Finally I say, "The way your mind works, it's so far outside of anything I've ever witnessed. I don't know how to translate this." I point toward the cards.

Tears well in her eyes. "I've always felt like an alien," she says. "Like when I'm myself, my real self, there's no one in the world who is like me." I hand her a tissue and she carefully dabs at the corner of her eyes. I feel different, too, and have read for so many people who don't fit into the mainstream, but her mind is at an entirely different level, otherworldly in its difference.

She seems to change before my eyes. Before, she was rigid and standoffish, and now she's relaxed and her face is opening up. Before, she was hard and difficult, and now she's soft and beautiful. I look at the tarot spread between us and realize that the fact I can't read her *is* the message she needs to hear. The information the spirit guides want to give her is that the way her mind works is foreign, different, outside the box.

I've noticed this again and again in readings. People just need to be seen for who they are. The moment they're seen, a transformation happens.

The cards break out into song. A theater production is underway, operatic and with its own rules. The language is translated so that my mind can understand it.

"I've got it," I exclaim excitedly.

She laughs.

"As early as you can remember, you were different from absolutely everything and everyone else. You've spent your whole life figuring out how to create a bridge so you can be who you are, and at the same time reaching into the modern world so you could survive." She's dabbing at her eyes furiously now. "It's an absolutely necessary bridge, but it's fragile, so you work hard not to rock it, or it might break. If anything too difficult comes up in your life, it challenges the structural integrity of the bridge. Change becomes so risky."

I've learned with all the readings I've done that sometimes as the reader you can get too excited because you're given the information. You can blurt out inappropriate information with excitement. Like one time when a young woman wouldn't tell me what was wrong and I suddenly saw with great clarity that she was grieving an abortion. I blurted with excitement over knowing the information, "It's an abortion. You've had an abortion!"

The information seemed to hit her across her face. I've since learned that it's got to be about them, and not my own excitement. I see something clearly for the woman sitting in front of me and want to approach it carefully.

"You're planning a big move?"

She nods, with tissues covering one eye. "To the other side of the country."

"Well, of course you'll have tremendous fear taking the risk. More than most people. You're worried about the structural integrity of the bridge you've built."

She takes my hand and looks at me with her real face. Nervous, I pull my hand back, pick up the cards, mix them, and throw another reading.

"You've done an incredible job of creating that bridge. Astounding. Where you are right now is a testament to that. Now the cards want to talk about making adjustments to the bridge. What we can add to it, metaphorically, to help it withstand the transition." We talk about abutments, arches and beams, about bearings and cantilevers.

Something deep is resonating with this reading, something about how different *I* am, something about recognizing it, owning it. It churns my solar plexus until I feel sick. Some bridge is being flooded, and I'm being called to build a new one.

Meanwhile, someone is pulling my attention in the bookstore proper. There is no door between the alcove and the rest of the bookstore, and I can see down the fiction aisle straight to the front. I try to focus on the reading, but a young man standing sideways is pulling at me; I can feel his energy fully focused on me.

The woman is asking me something and I have to ask her to repeat it. She wants to know where to find her purpose with such a different way of thinking. I keep feeling the guy pulling at me, and have to throw three different spreads before I come up with an answer.

The artist card comes up. I point it out to her. "But it's not like being a painter or anything. It's about creatively bringing these eccentric aspects of your different way of thinking into whatever work you do. You think you can't. But you can. You'll actually see much more success this way. The world needs different ways of seeing things. Badly."

I watch her leave after the reading is over, her shimmering blue purse glowing with beauty, a chain for a handle. Tomorrow, or the next day, if I see her walking down the street, I might not even recognize her, an average person with a spectacular handbag. But inside is an exciting and exotic creature.

I gather the cards just as the guy I noticed before walks up to my table. Light shines behind his head and I can't see his face.

"Pearl?"

"Yes? Do you want a reading? There's a sign-up sheet up front." He stands there, the shadow of him. I say again, "You need to go check the front desk. There may be people already signed up."

"You don't recognize me?" he asks.

"Sorry?"

He moves forward a bit into the light. "It's Dave." I stare at him blankly. "From the *Kaze*."

"Dave!" I stand up and we do a loose hug. We worked together at the daily newspaper in Tokyo for a couple of years. "What are you doing in Seattle?" I ask.

"Oh, I had one of those atrocious five-hour international layovers, so I thought I'd check out the city." He looks down at the table. "What are *you* doing?" He starts laughing and picks up the Devil.

"Oh, nothing. Just goofing," I say. "Just between jobs. It's just a goofy hobby." I'm Peter denying Jesus, and I know it.

He narrows his eyes and looks at me sideways. "Oh Mystic Meg, what fortune do you see for me?" He fingers the cards, flips some over, laughs again.

I reach down and collect the cards. I don't like the way he's poking at them. "What are *you* doing these days?"

"I live in Hong Kong, working for *Time's* Asia office."

While I sit at a yard sale folding table with a wobbly leg reading people's fortunes.

"The last I heard you and Finn were traveling through Southeast Asia. Didn't you guys end up in London or something?" On a tiny side table are a stack of my business cards; Dave reaches over and takes one. "Creative Tarot?" he reads from the card.

How can I tell him about this psychic call that I don't even understand? How can I tell him that Finn and I had to break up so I could follow this crazy calling, that I had to come back to America and find the missing pieces of myself? He's staring at me, waiting for me to speak, but I'm voiceless. I know none of it will make sense to him. There is no bridge between his reality and mine.

"Excuse me?" A young woman's high-pitched voice comes from behind Dave. He moves to reveal a young brunette wearing a bikini top and short shorts. She says in a small voice, "I just paid up front. Is this where I go to get my reading?"

Dave smirks. He puts out his hand. I take it. "I've got to get back to SeaTac. You take care of yourself, OK?" He holds my hand too long. His face is back in the shadow, but I can tell he's trying to convey something to me with his eyes. "Let me know if I can help. I'm here," he says. He hands me a business card.

The girl scoots around him, sits in the chair. "Omygawd, I can't believe you were free. My boyfriend is driving me crazy. I need some advice, like bad. Like, he's a total idiot."

Dave gives a wan smile and takes the paperback he's holding up to the front desk. I see him look at me one last time. I watch him move away from me and am filled with remorse over the life I've left behind. I can't look for long because the needy girl with the bad boyfriend commands all my attention.

A few days later Dave sends an email. The subject reads "Thinking of you." There's no personal message, but he's pasted three links. Each is a journalism job opportunity in another country. Under each, he's added a few sentences of description.

One is a job opportunity at *Time* magazine in Hong Kong where he works; another is for a news service looking for a reporter in Singapore. The third is a work visa program in Europe. I close the email quickly, like moving away from a pack of cigarettes, the temptation too great. My old life, beckoning.

I've become the sort of person who other people feel sorry for. I tell this to Gem later, and she says, "Every silver lining has a cloud."

XIV
TEMPERANCE.

CHAPTER 14

Temperance

Dave's reaction has disturbed me more than I thought possible. There's a whole world out there I'm not seeing, a whole life I'm not living, and for what? For exhaustion? For poverty? For hoards of the needy?

I'm pissed off, and everything annoys me. The people and their perpetual complaining, the endless rows of shops selling useless knickknacks, how big and loud Americans are. The job at the foster care agency becomes untenable—ridiculous, disempowering, hierarchical.

One manager steals my ideas and presents them as her own at meetings. This has been happening for a while, but now it makes me murderously angry.

I don't shine here. I'm not wise here. I'm small and beaten down. I don't know how to bridge the two worlds, the power of spirit and this job. I don't know how to bridge my old life traveling the world as editor and reporter with this frustrating job on Lake Union.

The managing editor of the foster care's newsletter is Suzanna. A former social worker, she's now assistant director of one of the departments. Every two weeks, before the newsletter comes out, Suzanna commands that I come to her office and sit behind her as she adds her opinion piece to the newsletter. Every two weeks, it's the same thing.

She positions a chair a few feet behind hers, motions me to sit in it, and then sits in front of me with her back to me and writes her piece. I'm not beside her. I can't see what she's writing. She'll ask me a question or two over her shoulder, but I'm just expected to otherwise be quiet and stare at her back. The office is dark. The window is behind her desk, and she keeps the blinds drawn. It's claustrophobic. The view of the lake is spectacular, but here we are trapped.

If I move she says sit.

One day she receives a phone call. She's harried and upset on the phone, and when she hangs up tries to focus again on the newsletter, but she keeps clicking her tongue.

"What happened? Bad news?" I ask from my chair far behind her. In hierarchies, you're not allowed to ask or to talk or to be. In other times, she would've ignored me. You're only listened to if you're at a certain place in the hierarchy.

She starts talking, softly, as if to herself, still staring at her computer, her back to me. "They grow older, and no matter what you do, these bad things keep happening. Even after we get them out of the home, even after they're with foster parents who really love the kid, who take advantage of all the programs we offer to help the kid. And it's not even about the decision the kid makes. They don't get into drugs or steal cars or anything. Something tragic always happens anyway. The tragedies pile up, and they can't get out from under them. It's like there's some kind of hard wiring to tragedy."

These are the kinds of conversations that would make this workplace vibrant and healing. I ask her more questions but she goes back to normal and ignores me. I sit quietly and stare at her back.

What a difference it makes if we're all allowed to talk, to be, to share. How humanizing. I can't understand hierarchies. I've always just been myself at jobs. Is it America? I don't know. I think about all my corporate tarot clients on the verge of despair because of the corporate atmosphere. What potential for abundance exists but is twisted and held down. We live in ego when we need to live in spirit.

I stare at the edges of blinding light around the stuttered slats of the darkened window.

She's Latina, small and round. Something dark moves behind her eyes, some personal oppression, some universal depression. When the whole world beats you up—that kind of darkness. She's jumped the queue, or someone didn't show and there was an accidental opening; I don't know how it happened, but she's there. I feel unready for her.

As she sits down, it's like she's already inside of me. Not her, exactly, but the black pain. It moves through my blood.

I've read three readings that day and before that did my protection ritual. This darkness is not her fault. I try to do an extra protection meditation, but the energy coming from her keeps throwing me off my game.

The cards are slathered with darkness. A blackness grabs at them, invades them. There is abuse here.

What are hands used for? This keeps coming to me, as I see hands where they shouldn't be, and they reach out of the cards and try to mess with me. I don't want to think about this, don't want to feel this. I don't like how it's attaching in my base chakra, where my own abuse resides. The half hour passes, and I have no idea what I've said. She's crying, and I'm calming her, but I'm so relieved when she leaves that I too cry. It's not her fault. I hope I've helped her. I do another reading but feel sick.

I go to the bathroom during a break and see blood in the toilet. The toilet paper comes back red. This is not my period—the blood is in my pee. It's a flood of blood, a testament to the demons stored in my womanhood.

Someone is driving me to the emergency room, and the doctors tell me what I already know: I have a urinary tract infection. A bad one. One of the worst they've ever seen.

That night I wake from one of those dreams, the starving, the needy, hands begging, but this time I feel their need invade me, take over my blood stream. There's no separation now between me and the rest of humanity. There's a memory here, the infant me, absorbing it, no distinction between me and the world, no protection for me against a brutal father, a mean world.

I can't sleep, get up and pace. So disturbed. So sure there's no way to protect myself from my pain, our pain, *the* pain.

I sit at my computer, open Dave's email, and click the links.

It's two months later, and Gem won't answer her door. I pound with the side of my fist. "This is ridiculous. This has nothing to do with you," I shout. I've been knocking on and off for days. I know she's in there.

"Fuck you!" says an echo from somewhere deep inside her apartment.

"That's progress," I yell back. "That's the first thing you've said to me in a week. By the way, nice mouth!"

I hear pounding footsteps. The door flies open, and I nearly fall into the apartment.

"Wrong way!" Gem yells. "Wrong way!" She slams the door.

I knock. No answer. "Look, I don't want to leave like this. You're a good friend. We can still be good friends."

"Wrong way!" she screams through the door.

I applied for and received the work visa that Dave sent and am going to London for six months. The plan is to take a job in a newsroom, prove my worth, have the newspaper extend my work visa, and stay beyond the six months. I'm going to get my old life back—get away from this trauma, this neediness, this relentless consumerism.

I leave the next day. "I'm tired of being this broke in a country I don't even want to live in. I'll have my old life back. You can come visit. We'll take the Chunnel to Paris!"

Silence.

"Don't you even want me to be happy?"

"Don't *you* want to be happy?" she mocks back at me through the door. "What do you want, Pearl?" she asks, sounding defeated. "What do you want out of life? You've got to ask yourself that. I'm so tired."

Exasperated, I turn to leave. The door flies open again. She looks young and fragile in her rage, in a t-shirt and cut-off camouflage pants, covered in paint, her hair two braids hanging beside her dark face.

I should feel awful about leaving her, but I don't. This is my life. *Mine.* I'll make the choices I want to make. Period. She knows I hate the temp job, knows what the tarot reading is doing to me, knows how physically sick I'm getting, how broke I am.

"You're going to give up everything. Like that? Just leave? Are you fucking kidding me with this shit?"

I take her hands and she doesn't resist. "We can talk on the phone, every day if you want."

"The answers are not out there, Pearl," she says, pulling her hands back.

"Well, they're not here in Seattle, either," I say.

"Wrong way!" she yells, and slams the door.

After this, no amount of knocking brings her back.

The next day, I wake from my sleeping bag on the floor. My apartment is empty. I gave most of the stuff to Gem earlier when she thought it was some kind of joke and took them thinking I'd change my mind. She said she'd give them back when I came to my senses. She had my throw rugs, curtains, futon, my extra tarot decks. Everything else wasn't worth keeping and went back to the thrift store from whence it came. I also sold my truck.

My writing is backed up. In my suitcase, one tarot deck, two pairs of pants, two shirts, seven underwear, seven pairs of socks, a jacket, two pairs of shoes. This is the fourth time that I've gotten every possession I own down to two medium-sized roller suitcases.

I wait outside on the crooked porch for Coral, who's driving me to the airport. I knock on Gem's door one last time but the apartment is dark.

It's a heavy rainy day, and as Coral and I drive the city feels encased in shadows.

As the plane climbs through the perpetual dark cloud cover that falls on Seattle and we break through into bright sunshine, I try not to think of the bookstore, of the staff there, of their love of books and their love of each other. I don't think about Coral, who is leaving anyway for graduate school in Canada. I feel Gem go underground and fade into darkness as I fly. In my imagination, I reach out to her, but she fades and fades.

The foster care agency threw a going-away dinner party. The office manager gave me a stunning blown-glass quill pen and a bottle of ink as a gift. It was beautiful and unexpected. The surprise was how much they seemed to like me.

I'll spend the next nine hours crossing a bridge. I'll leave one reality, one culture, one set of values behind and open to a new way. I've done this so many times before, left one country for another, that I'm now a master at turning one culture off and another on.

I know how to lock down emotions. I learned a long time ago how to leave what isn't working, how when you leave the wrong, you also leave the right. You leave the love. I learned to cram it into a box and put it on an upper shelf where you don't even see it anymore. Feelings get you into trouble.

I need the separation, the distance. I'm crossing a corpus callosum between two realities. I think of all the different realities I've known, every country I've visited and lived in with its own set of truths, my own savage psyche and its reality, the untamed ecosystems of the psyches of so many I've channeled for, the realities within writing fiction, the cultures within the past lives I've led. There are so many truths, layers and layers of it.

Gem asked me what I wanted. I want to be free. Free from it all, the people and their need, their soul sickness invading my body, my own sickness in my own animal body.

Free from being a guru, from having to live a correct life. I'm not good at playing the role of the all-knowing one. I'm not good at acting so good. I want the dark and the light, the yin and the yang, the ugly and the beautiful. I want dimension and texture. I don't want to have the answers; I want to pose the questions. I want to be free from Seattle's political correctness, yes, but it's more than that. Free from anyone or any culture telling me who I'm supposed to be.

I nod off into sleep and dream of Coral and Gem and the love and wake up crying. A woman next to me offers me a tissue, puts a hand on my shoulder, and I wish she wouldn't, because any kindness right now is going to crack me wide open. Just because you're the one who makes the decision to leave doesn't mean it doesn't hurt. Just because you're good at crossing a bridge doesn't mean you don't miss the other shore.

As we come in for the landing, London like a village of steeples, attached houses and tiny trains on minuscule tracks, I think of all the past lives I've uncovered where I lived London.

Prostitute, medieval herbalist, nanny, geologist. The prostitute was the one who lived most on the surface when I lived in London before, lipstick on the teeth and the smell of rot between the thighs. I loved this whore. I met her in London's alleys, heard her whispers and her wisdom even before I really knew what a past life was.

From the moment I met London, I knew her in my bones. I knew where a building was located, or the geography of where I was in places of the city I'd never been before. I just *knew* that if I turned this corner, and that corner, I'd come to something I was looking for.

I was also a high-brow boy in the eighteen hundreds near Kensington Palace who loved rocks and would grow up to be a geologist. The boy and his family were invited to all of the royal events. He lived a charmed life, and I wonder if he's the reason things go well for me in London.

In another regression, I was a nanny to a fancy Hampstead family in the seventeen hundreds. The regression haunted me for months. In it, I was in a three-story attached London house, long and narrow. The family was wealthy, and the room I was in had tall doors, wallpaper that was painted on the walls, and deep, narrow windows. I took care of two small privileged children. I often stared out one of the windows, down at the street, at the poor who labored below, wondering at the arbitrary nature of those who are rich and those who are poor, and feeling such depths of compassion for the poor.

The mother of the children never thanked me for the good work I did looking after her children. When asked by someone once why this was so, she responded: "One doesn't thank the help."

Then of course there was the medieval herbalist me, the one who was put to death, the one with mad healing wisdom that still imbues me today.

Each of these past lives remain like ghosts in my psyche. These past me's, once drawn to the surface, become friends, spirits circling me. I have lived all over the world, not just this lifetime, but through many lives. I've been rich and poor, woman and man, black and white, Asian and Native American.

When I land at Heathrow, the hordes of people send shock waves through my system. I remember when I moved to Seattle, I kept wondering where the people were. Here, the buses, tube, and streets teem with all walks of life, different cultures, and a cacophony of sounds. In the years since I've been gone, London has changed. There are more Russians in heavy jewelry now, more Eastern Europeans since the Soviet

Union collapsed. I read their psyches as they pass me on the streets, how they're trying to survive in a capitalist world when all they've ever known is communism.

I realize as I'm roaming the busy London streets why I like living abroad: the anonymity.

The job I land on the six-month visa is for one of the most respected newspapers in the world (this, after years of not being able to get a journalism job in Seattle). When I go to get my visa processed in Croydon, the clerk can't believe I've gotten such a lucrative position on such a visa. But that sort of thing happens to me in London. It's like the city and I have some kind of mutual vibration.

Before my job begins, I gorge myself on London's teats, devouring Blake and Turner, Matisse and Monet, ingesting the art at contemporary galleries in Chelsea, Covent Garden, Camden. Feral, I sit hunched over the kill, great art dripping from my eye teeth, dribbling down the flesh. *Feed* me.

Everything is faster here, everything is sped up, eating, shitting, walking, thinking. Soon, I'm going so fast it spins Seattle right out of my head.

I'm sorting photos for a series on depression. Another thing that has changed about London since I lived here is that depression in young people has skyrocketed. We're writing a special insert on looking for the signs, causes, and treatments. The new job is good, and I'm surrounded by smart, hard-hitting professionals.

I look up to see a mousy woman. She tells me she's from HR and to follow her. The offices are at Canary Wharf, and I look out the massive windows at the snaking Thames and the docks as we cross the open-air office. At a desk in the corner, a petite woman stands as we approach her. She has light-gray, straight hair, delicate features, porcelain skin, in her early fifties.

"Salacia Brown-Evington, this is Pearl Swinton," the HR woman says. I shake Salacia's hand. My hand feels huge enveloping her small fingers.

"I go by Sala."

The mousy woman says, "Pearl is seeking a living situation, and we understand you're looking for a lodger. Sala is one of our longer-term editors."

"Lovely t-shirt," Sala says. *Viva Las Vegas* is stretched over my boobs. You have to weave your head to read it. I laugh, run my fingers through my hair to try to tame it. The London weather has sent it into a wild circle around my head. Sala laughs. "You're very obviously not British," she says, and laughs again. "You'll do just fine."

I take the tube to Chalk Farm after work and find her attached house on a cul-de-sac that sits in front of a massive old building of reddish stone. It has arched windows and turrets at the top that sport small metal flags. It's something out of a fairy tale.

Sala meets me at the door. The room she's letting is up a narrow set of stairs. When she opens the door, the room is glowing. It's white with a white duvet and white curtains over tall windows. This woman has some kind of magic, and I feel some other force has led me here.

She shows me the rest of the house, and I catch my breath as we enter the kitchen. It's an addition, built out into the garden. In the ceiling, a skylight. Sala tells me the turreted building is a school. It looms above us, through the skylight, as if it's bending forward and looking in on the kitchen table, tiny flags quaking in the wind.

We go down another set of stairs to the basement. The entire basement has been transformed into a master bedroom, with a big bathroom and an office that leads out into the garden. The home is gorgeous. I tell her this.

"Well then, you must see the attic."

Up three flights, a door topping off the stairs. Inside, angled ceilings, a dormer window, a beam of light like a beacon in an otherwise dark room. She walks around turning on studio lights. An art studio. Of course. What did I expect? I'm perpetually drawn to artists.

I move among the paintings. Studios are sacred spaces, more holy than churches. Salacia paints water. Droplets magnifying the colors of a flower petal. Ice cubes floating in pure, clear glasses of water, the only color a splash of red reflected on the glass. Sixty-inch paintings of swimmers in pools, the abstraction of water over human bodies, swirling arms and legs, as if the bodies themselves are liquid.

I sit in the middle of the floor. In every direction there's another study of water. I think of Red—of our hikes and the holy water of the rivers.

"Water is the only substance in the world where the solid can float in the liquid," Sala says, running a finger along her canvases. "It has three distinct forms: gas, liquid, solid. It's a universal solvent. But there's something about the sheer amount of water in the world, right? It falls from the sky. It fills oceans. It makes up our bodies. It's both ordinary and extraordinary."

I merge with the water, become it. Salacia starts to turn off the lights. It's time to go. Of course, it's her space, and just as with anything sacred, we are allowed a glimpse, but we must always leave.

I call Gem daily. She won't answer. I leave her messages. Coral and I stay in touch through email, but Gem would never bother with anything online, which always made me like her even more. I leave Gem long messages about Salacia and her water art and the drizzle of London. About the times I just sit on the edge of the dirty Thames and watch the boats. She never responds. I'm talking to myself.

One weekend Sala invites me to an exhibition. Her love of water has her constantly seeking out anything to do with it. We're in Oxford Circus, a borough of neon and nerve-jangling consumerism.

At the Photographer's Gallery a dozen images that look like snowflakes grace the white walls. The show is called "Water Consciousness," and the artist is Dr. Masaru Emoto.

The photos are magnified images of water crystals, no two alike. The typical white pentagrams with stars at the corner, ones that look like delicate lace work, and then darker, fisted-looking monstrosities. Each photo is paired with a saying like "You disgust me" and "Evil" and "Thank you" and "Peace."

Emoto exposed water crystals to words and used magnetic resonance analysis technology and high-speed photography to take photos to see if the intentions of the words transformed water.

"Thank you" and "Peace" look like gentle quintessential snowflakes. "Evil" is a snake skin around a black pit.

He also took photographs of a polluted lake in Japan before and after it was prayed over, the first a pitted rock, the latter a crystalline masterpiece.

A quote is stenciled on the wall: "For a long time, I have been giving water many pieces of information and making ice-crystal photographs. We have given water as many pieces of positive information as we can think of—beautiful words, beautiful scenery . . . and beautiful music . . . But the most beautiful one to me was the crystal that formed after the water was exposed to the words 'love and gratitude.'"

I notice Sala is riveted by the crystal photograph above the word "Beauty," a hexagram with six glimmering crowns. I roam over to "Love and Gratitude," a diamond ring circled by pearls. "What is it you love?" Gem's words haunt me.

On our way home in Sala's old Jaguar, I worry. If water is so profoundly affected by a negative or positive word, how much are humans and other animals distorted or empowered by words, thoughts, intentions? I think of the corporate clients I read tarot for in Seattle, how they're bombarded by toxicity at its worst, and at best, organizations whose bottom line is only the mighty dollar. What does that intention do to the water in their bodies, and to them? The animal farming industry has been bothering me on a deep level—what's the intention of using and abusing these animals solely for human edification? What is it doing to us when we eat them? Since I started reading tarot, I can no longer watch violent movies. Seeing rape and murder as entertainment has become nauseating to me. How much are these movie messages reshaping the liquid in our collective body?

I worry about how the job at the newspaper is affecting me and everyone else. I worry about how reporting so much trauma will alter me. Besides the series on depression, I've been covering the increase in stabbings in the city, the devastating challenges for immigrants, financial corruption of big corporations, people directly affected by climate change, and much more. Who knows how these stories are reshaping the crystals of my body, their bodies, our bodies?

I notice Sala has been quiet as we drive. I look around and see London at night, somehow through her eyes, the lights, the steeples, the magic. I'm usually traveling on the tube, and I miss this beauty above ground.

She looks at me and smiles, and there's a light in her eyes. Where I'm worrying post-show, she's electrified. Finally she says, "You know how they compare consciousness to a single drop of water in a larger ocean?"

I know what she's talking about but want to hear her talk. "No, what do you mean?"

"Darling, you must have heard about this. How we're all individuals like single droplets, but we're also part of the whole, just as water can be a droplet and be the ocean."

"Oh, yes," I say.

"But I think it's more than that." She's so short she has to crane her neck to see above the wheel. "I believe when we left the ocean to be born into a droplet, when we became an individual, it left in us an urge, a great desire to find that ocean again, to feel like we're not separate, to dissolve back into the whole. And our whole life, we're searching for that impossible ocean."

Now *I* feel electrified.

She turns into the cul-de-sac and parks a few doors down from her house. "And that's what being an artist is, do you see? An artist is just searching for the lost ocean. Every work is an attempt to find and to feel that connection we lost at birth."

I feel like she's handed me a jewel and it's glowing in my palm. And for some reason, all I can think of is Gem.

It starts with dizziness. I feel like I'm going to fall over. I've been in London two months. It's overstimulation. My body vibrates with engines, horns, music, chatter. I grow moody. Anxious.

At first I don't realize I've been reading people's minds and souls all day—on the tube, in the office, on the streets. I've been moving so fast that it takes me a while to even hear the low-grade chatter, and even longer to understand this is why I'm dizzy and growing increasingly tired. I've flown halfway around the world to rid myself of this psychic self, this sensitive self, this empathic self, and of course she has followed me here. Wherever you go, there you are. Or to quote Gem: "Wherever you are, there you go."

What I'm hearing in the psyches of people on the streets and in the underground is *doubt*. So much doubt in so many, the pain of doubting the essence of who they are. A doubt so deep that no one seems to trust themselves, or even really *like* themselves. It's like the readings I was doing at the bookstore, how no one is allowed to just *be,* but just with a different cultural flavor.

Sometimes there's joy—a child with technicolored glee, new lovers flooded with serotonin—but the overriding energy is confusion. People worry about everything. They question every move they make, have ever made, or will ever make. There's no past, no present, no future that has *any* peace in it. As I walk down busy London sidewalks, I'm swept up in a deluge of uncertainty, like I'm being held just above the earth and I'm swinging my legs trying to walk.

I'm not just picking up their inner world, though—higher truths are being passed on by higher selves, or guides, or whoever's passing the info. Messages come to me. I see a woman walking with her son and know the child has a heart murmur that no one knows about. A young man who stands regularly at the corner of the Chalk Farm station is dangerously close to killing himself. A girl on the train doesn't want to tell her mom the truth about the male neighbor who babysits her.

So many people means too many messages, all lapping over each other like waves at the shore. *You're right, he is cheating on you. Your wife is sick, and it's serious, more serious than you realize. There's an auto accident in your future.* I grow jumpy with the influx, twitchy like an addict. I use beer and cigarettes to massage the overload.

Still, I'm able to do my job at the newspaper. Being an empath all my life means I've learned how to receive psychic messages and still function. I'm able to multitask, edit copy, find photographs, write headlines, *and* read millions of souls. This is my superpower. And I know it has its limits.

My managing editor, Brandwin Houser-Blakely, is a public school man, a nice upper-class guy with a drinking problem. I try not to let the trauma we're reporting on invade me, warp my crystalline body, but I'm pretty sure I'm not succeeding. What *is* working is the regular paycheck. I have enough money now.

I meet people at the newspaper and we hang out. We go to raves and do ecstasy. I can afford to go to expensive, trendy restaurants. A few times we spend weekends in Amsterdam or Italy. I purchase clothes from a normal shop instead of a thrift store. My old London life is slowly being resurrected.

XV
THE DEVIL .

CHAPTER 15

The Devil

Sirens in my dreams in Sala's room of light. Not American sirens, but the two-toned shrill of British cop cars. I bolt upright in bed. Something is wrong. Someone is in trouble. The phone is ringing.

I snatch it up. "Gem? Are you OK? Where are you?" I'm sure Gem is missing. I'm sure they're calling to tell me she's dead.

"Pearl." It's a man's voice. I'm fading again, going back into a dream world where Seattle and London are both illusions.

"Pearl, fuck me, wake up!"

"What?" I say into the phone. "Who is this?"

"It's Brandwin."

"Who?"

"Pearl, sit up. Now."

I swing my legs over the bed. I can't shake off the dream world. Remnants of the dream comes back to me: Gem is missing, and I'm searching desperately for her.

"There's some news." Brandwin. Brandwin. Yes. Yes. My editor. He's in the South of France. I remember now. He took off on an extended vacation in Provence. Brandwin is still talking. He's talking about something that I can't take in. What is he saying? What's going on? It can't be real!

"What?" I scream, not sure whether what he's saying is reality or dream.

I hear him this time. I scream again. I slam the phone down, jump headlong out of bed. I have no clean clothes. I smell the shirt and trousers on the floor and throw them on even though they stink of exhaust and London grime. Brandwin calls back and I hold the phone with one hand while running a brush through my ratty hair. He's barking orders.

"I know what I have to do," I yell at him, and slam the phone down again.

I run to the tube station and catch the train. I can't quite fathom it. I think of the two boys. I should be thinking of what I'll need to do when I get to the newsroom, but I can only think of the boys. Around me on the tube, there's a pall, a train in trauma. People are weeping. This news is setting an entire nation to shock.

At the newsroom, people have lost their minds. They're running, screaming to each other, yelling over the sound of hundreds of ringing phones. This is the biggest story in most of our lifetimes. I go to my desk in the Special Sections department. I sit for a moment in the chaos, the yelling, the panic, the glee, even. I can't stop thinking about the boys.

Diana has died. Killed with boyfriend Dodi Fayed in a paparazzi chase in Paris. Behind glass partitions, a group of male editors is meeting to make the big decisions about covering her death. (It's a liberal paper, one of the biggest liberal papers in the entire world, and I no longer even fathom what liberal means when there are so few women involved in the decision-making, when it's almost always men, and they're always white, and they're always running the show.) One of them keeps belting out "Candles in the Wind." The meeting breaks up and he roams the newsroom, singing and raising his arms in operatic flourish.

It's a coincidence. Serendipity. For the last month, Brandwin and I have been working on a special supplement on grief, on types of grief, support for it, personal essays by well-known journalists on their journeys through it. Grief brought on by disasters, by death, by aging. It was my idea. This is why I've always been a good editor: my psychicness allows me to choose subjects that in time attach to reality.

Freelancers had been commissioned weeks ago to write articles on dealing with death, cancer, divorce, breakups, anything that sends people into mourning. We'd commissioned the paper photographers to get pictures to go with the articles.

I have just a few hours to rewrite the entire supplement to focus on Diana's death. I try to breathe, but I pick up the hysteria of the rest of the office.

I call the freelancers. There are twelve articles that need to be rewritten with the angle focused on the grief of a nation in the wake of the Diana tragedy. I'm screaming into the phone and plugging one ear to hear them. The freelancers have to be able to turn around the new piece in a few hours. If not, I'll need to pull the article and find another freelancer who is home and willing. I'm sweating bullets. The pace is breakneck. I run to the archives for photos of public collective grieving. The rest of the newspaper will have plenty of photos of Diana and Dodi, of Charles, the queen, and the boys. Oh the boys, the boys. I have to control my heart—there's no time for emotion.

For the next ten hours, I don't stop. I'm fielding calls from writers, editing, rewriting, penning captions, making headlines. A writer falls through and I'm calling down the list of freelancers frantically, finally finding someone, and she has only one hour to whip out an article and send it. Editing, more editing, layout, proofreading, more layout.

At six that evening, the paper goes to bed. I made it but just barely; I didn't have time to look the entire supplement over one last time from a distance. Sometimes errors are big and missed in the study of the minutia.

A sudden wave of release falls upon the entire office. I flop back in my chair. We're all too wired, jumping out of our skin. I'm surrounded by half-full coffee cups and smashed pieces of paper. A bunch of the journalists are going out to drink, but I need to be alone. I've soaked up a lifetime of energy in one day and I need to purge it somehow. I go out and walk to the tube, and there are so many people, so many souls, and it's all too much.

The man next to me on the train whispers to his female companion, "We're bombing other countries. Children are starving. So what we had a princess die. Not even a princess. She lost that title. A lady. Why is everybody so up in a snit about it?"

I want to say: *Because she's an archetype. A society needs their archetypes, their heroes and heroines, their villains. They are symbols, something bigger than themselves, a larger-than-life energy that pulls them up and out of the mundane. And is anyone really considering the boys?*

I get to Sala's house, go up to my room, close the door and hide. And all I can do is hope that by morning I'm able to purge enough of these other people, alive and dead, to function.

I smell it before I see it, heady sweetness mixed with rot. Around a corner and there it is, the lawn stretching before the gates of Kensington Palace. It's covered in millions, tens of millions of long-stemmed flowers. It's a few days after the deaths. Bouquet piled upon bouquet piled upon bouquet stretching for hundreds of yards. This is collective mourning. This is the photo that should've graced the front page of the supplement.

The first mourners put their blossoms on the lawn, on the grass, and those who came after placed theirs on top, and so on and so on, until there grew a lawn of flowers four feet deep. The sweet rot is overwhelming. Roses, tulips, daisies—stem and petal turning brown and gray and into mulch. The decay enters my flesh. Everywhere, in shops and pubs, in museums and offices, a collective heartache. I think again of her boys. About who is helping the boys handle their grief, and what this means.

At home, I find Salacia upstairs in her studio. The rest of the room is dark, and she's using a studio light like a halo on a canvas. She's painting dying flowers on their side, a vase of water nearby. The flowers get no liquid. I'm covered in the rot of Diana's death as I sit on a crate and watch her. Sala has spent the past few days at the newsroom as frantic as I've been, writing articles of the reactions of the UK's top brass to Diana's death. We've all heard the conspiracy theory that she was killed by the royal family.

The room is dark except this spotlight, these withered petals, that blackened stem, the untouchable clear water shining sacred. I realize suddenly I'm the student and she's the mentor; she's teaching me art. I sit up and pay closer attention. It's not just brushstrokes and the mixing of paints on the layered, stuttered palette. It's soul speak. It's a channeling from somewhere else, through the body, mixing with her personality and coming out of her hands. *This is what she does with her hands.* She's handing me a cup of water and asking if I want a drink. I'm the withered flowers being offered the sacred water. I sit with my mouth open and don't say a word.

In less than a week, Mother Theresa will die. Again the newsroom will be in chaos. On one of the vehicles at the funeral procession in Calcutta, the word "Mother" spelled out in flowers. One of the vehicles in Diana's funeral also had the word mother on it.

Diana, a modern woman, a woman who was finding her voice. Theresa, a traditional woman, a voice for a nation. The Divine Feminine in a world hungry for its archetypes.

She lives beauty, creates beauty, is beauty. Sala. I've never been around anyone for whom beauty is such a core value. My life, except for within the grandeur of nature, has been about folding tables, second-hand furniture, boots with holes in the toe.

In my room, the lamps throw halos of light on the ceiling. It's a surprising joy to lie in bed and look at this light. I have rarely had such joy from lamp light. It complements the white shades of the deep, narrow windows, the white down comforter. Everything ties to everything else in subtle song.

When I tell this to Sala, she claps with delight. "Yes, darling. I actually bought the lamps with that in mind." Beauty as intention. "I'm delighted you can see it. No one who's stayed in that room has ever noticed."

In the mornings there's often a spray of flowers in a vase on the table in the kitchen. The flowers throw a beauty into your soul. When I tell her the joy of it, my breath catches, and she claps her hands again.

"You see it. You see it," she says, like a giddy child.

One day she's passing me on the stairs. I'm lumbering up to go hide in my room and see if I can't shake myself of another day of too much stimuli. Like the sickly trees that pepper the side of London's streets, I'm turning gray.

"Shall I put the kettle on?" Sala asks.

"Ugh," I say, shoulders drooping.

"I'll put the kettle on."

We sip earl grey next to a spray of wild garden flowers beneath the massive school building. I must use a coaster. The table is blonde wood, handmade, and when I first moved in, I left a ring with my coffee mug that she's still trying to get out. Apparently beauty requires coasters.

She tells me that early in her editing career, she too would get burned out. She'd only gone to art school at age fifty, only truly learned of her sensitivities to the world then. "I found beauty to be the only thing that calmed my soul. It fed me when the world took so much."

I study Sala. She's so small. Like most sophisticated London women, she's a size zero; she told me she buys her jeans from the girls department. Her spirit is full of joy, a joy you don't often see in modern humanity.

"Darling, you're going to have to start looking at what you find beautiful, and why."

I've heard more about Sala in the newsroom, how she was known to take the homeless in to give them a place to sleep for a night or two, how she worked with the migrant community. There's so much to her.

"What do you find beautiful in the world, Pearl?" she asks.

"I like the old school," I say, pointing above us. "The old crumbling London."

I tell her how much I loved camping in the Pacific Northwest, the wild and unkempt nature, of roots so massive you have to climb over them, of trees dripping with moss, of the dance of river over rocks. The earth in London has been so manicured. I find beauty in art, I tell her, at the art galleries here. Unlike Seattle, London is an international city, and I'm still gorging myself three to four times a week at the Tate, the National Gallery, the National Portrait Museum, the British Museum, the Victoria and Albert.

"I think I'd like to be an artist," I say to Sala in a soft voice. I think of Rayne's prophetic reading, of the message from the dark night of the soul. How the love of art seemed to be outside myself; how the love of art were the others I met who did art, and for the first time as I sit here with Sala, I own it inside myself. I want to be an artist. I feel five years old saying it. "I'd like to go to art school. I think at the end of my life I would be proud then of the life I lived."

Sala pours the tea and looks at me. "It's difficult to live in such an expensive city as London and be an artist. I had to go back to editing at the newspaper." I know she's right. You can't step out the front door here without money flying out of your pocket. I've been shocked by the expense, lucky to have a well-paying job, but unable to save. *Is she telling me I have to leave London?*

I tell her about my walk to the tube station. "The direct way to Chalk Farm tube is so ugly. Cheap shop after cheap shop, too many people, and the traffic."

"Finish your tea, darling." I take a sip. She stands and walks toward the front door. "Chop-chop."

We walk down her street. "I want to show you something," she says. She lives on a dead end. I've never gone this way, didn't even really know there was an outlet past the dead end.

"Where your house is located is super quiet, Sala," I say.

"Why do you think I chose the house, darling? Beauty is a series of choices."

We take a left at the end of the cul-de-sac, head down a side street, and come to a main road. We use the zebra crossing, passing honking, stinking cars. We move onto a side road that I've never taken before. A peace descends; on both sides, weathered classic attached houses with bright shutters, vines crawling up old brick, crumbling lions at gates, chaotic shabby-chic front gardens. Through the windows are glimpses of stained-glass lamps with glass tassels that reflect back stars of light. Through one window, an antique wooden hobby horse, through another a sculpture of a dancing girl.

"Plan B," Sala says.

We walk past roses climbing trellises and bright plants in massive stone pots out front. My mood is lifted, and we're laughing and have a skip in our step. Salacia is a big soul. We turn the corner and I still don't know where we are until we turn another corner and come out right next to the tube station.

"Voilà, darling, a way to find beauty even on your walk to the tube."

After this, I make it my sworn duty to find beauty every day, to cultivate beauty, to engage and create it. Beauty as a way of survival in an otherwise ugly world. I position my chair at work to see out the windows, to watch the slow, arcing movement of the Thames, and I take breaks sitting right at windows and watch the tugs and other boats plying the waterway. I seek different paths from work to the train station.

I often went to the art galleries before work but now make it my duty to go every day before my shift.

I still write my stories daily. In the mornings, I rise before dawn to get in four hours of writing before taking the hour tube journey first to see art, and then to the newspaper. My small table at the window in Sala's house looks out over rows of attached houses and behind that, the turreted school. I look down at the small rectangular back gardens, the grass and trees gray, the land, too, overwhelmed by the weight of the people—but still there is peace here.

What mesmerizes me the most are the crooked lines of chimney pots on the roofs of the attached homes. They're in disarray, tottering, stuttered, like some kind of fairy tale. There's something that happens to the view when you're a writer. In Seattle, it was that red barn-like shed and the way the moss grew over it, and how the branches and leaves that bordered it changed season to season, went from green to red to barren, how it was like a living painting. Views for writers become vistas that stay with them for a lifetime; it's something about the writing process where the tang and tenderness of the visual mixes with the openness of the writing soul. Beauty out the window, a writer's portal to the real world.

I've been writing for hours a day for years now and am slowly getting to know my long-lost self. I'm writing myself into authenticity. This is beauty too, this writing. I'll sit back from something I've just written and think, *Wow, that's what I really think*, as if I'm just now remembering beliefs I lost a long time ago.

I'm writing more and more stories of my life, resurrecting bits of myself from the ashes like collecting found objects. Here a knob, there a piece of colored glass, over there a swirled marble. I raise myself from the dead with each word I type.

Memories start out as hazy, like a child playing in the fog, a hint of green in her shirt, long hair flying in and out of the mist. I can't quite see her, can't quite capture her in words. As I write she comes more and more into focus until she's standing right in front of me, begging to come home.

Memories come where at first there were none. I try to fit the puzzle pieces together, but one piece of my story is so lost in the fog that I won't even have a hint of it. Then, within twenty-four hours, the memory comes to me, vivid of tint and hue, running out of the darkness to me. Perhaps it's given to me by one of my guides. Are muses just our spirit guides hard at work? This resurrection of self comes simply because I focus on it. Simply because I ask her to come out and talk to me and play.

On the days I have to be at work early, I'm up at three in the morning, huddled under a single lamp. Only when the darkness yields to light across the chimney pots do I come to the end of my writing session.

On days off I write all day, the sounds of the children arriving and leaving at the big school echoing, the sounds of them playing on the pavement at recess entering my dream world, becoming the soundtrack of the childhood I'm trying to recover in my writing. I want to go to Sala's studio and watch her paint. But I'm afraid I'm not invited. I'm afraid she'll throw me out.

For now, I know that the only way to raise myself up, the only way to be the parent of my lost little girl, is to keep writing consistently—that it's a process, and it'll take time. I'm learning that it'll take years. When I first started writing my stories in Seattle, I was still in my journalism mind, where I wrote stories and had bylines within days. Here in London, I realize it'll take a lot longer, that this writing myself back to myself is a lifetime pursuit, that this process is almost more important than the product. In some ways, writing has become my home. Whether I'm in Seattle, in the woods camping, or on a cul-de-sac in Chalk Farm in London, writing is always there, is my safe space where I am free to *be*.

I write about bike accidents and plucking chickens, about paper routes and teachers with closets full of books. I write about scary things too, about terror and helplessness, about fear. About a girl who just kept getting up, about a girl who never gave up.

I'm walking home from the Chalk Farm tube, down the back streets that Sala has shown me, and I'm drawn to an overgrown, narrow lot beside an old house. As I'm standing there, the lot transforms into the forest it once was. Perhaps I'm seeing the vegetation from the seventeen hundreds, but I'm not sure. It's a full forest, with earthy smells and the sounds of small creatures. It's so moody, full of fog and mystery, rich and green and edifying. I stand within it, being washed by it.

Slowly the vision disappears, and the streets, the crammed houses, and the parked cars reappear. I walk home as if on clouds. I miss being next to the earth. I miss the camping. I miss my body freezing and cold-hair washes in frozen lakes. There's something about being next to the elements that keeps me inside my body. I love London, but I find myself inhabiting just my head. But when you're on a new adventure, it's best not to be honest—to push the memories back.

Sala isn't home. When I unlock and open the door, the alarm system beeps. I'm supposed to deactivate it but I've never had to do it before. I'm too far gone into this other pastoral world and key in the number wrong once, twice, and the alarm blares like it's the end of the world. I'm holding my hands over my ears as a voice comes through the speaker, but I can't hear him over the screaming alarm. The neighbors are screaming and I'm trying to get Sala on the phone so I can deactivate it, and I'm screaming and she's screaming, but I can barely hear her.

Later, shaking in my bedroom, I think, *It isn't just artists who find it hard to afford living in London. Empaths too find it hard to "afford."* It's harder in a big city to be psychically open. Nearly impossible.

My six-month work visa is about to expire, and I'm hearing nothing back from the HR department at the newspaper. I'm assuming they'll keep me on, but how do I know they will? You can't be without a job in London. Beyond the visa, it's the sheer expense. I ask Sala for advice and she promises to keep her ears open.

In a panic, I look at classifieds but find nothing. It's Sala who refers me to another newspaper, a major financial daily. I apply, go through interviews, and get the position, with another six-month visa attached to it. If I work out, they say, they'll extend my employment.

I call Gem. This times she picks up.

"I hear you breathing," she says. "I know it's you."

I'm quiet on my end because I can't believe she answered.

"Are you coming back?" she asks.

"How did you know it was me?"

"I'm psychic."

"I can't believe you finally picked up. I haven't spoken to you in months." I feel such relief after all of the dreams where I've searched for her to no avail.

"When are you coming back?"

"Sorry," I say. "I just landed another job. I wanted to tell—"

She hangs up.

"I'm so sorry," I say to the limp receiver in my hand.

The financial newspaper is all about business and money and not about emotions, and I find it easy, perhaps even boring. The Chinese bank raises millions with a new convertible bond, German car makers make record profits, Boeing constructs a new airplane. I sit at a copy desk with about six other subeditors, and it's our job to check the copy after the reporters submit their stories. I befriend a young man who has a public school education that's the British equivalent of Ivy League. We chat daily, and I think we're both feeling a connection. I'm pretty sure it's not romantic, but who knows?

The schedule at the new paper gives staff the normal two days off per week, and then five days off in a row every three weeks. I bond with the other subeditors and we take trips to Amsterdam, Zurich, Berlin.

One day I receive a package at Sala's. It's from my mother. I'm not sure how she got my new address. I haven't been in touch with her. I think about who in the States has this address and whom she might've called to get it, but I give up.

Inside the package is a binder. My mother has written a letter explaining that one of my cousins is researching our family tree. The binder is a family tree—dozens of pages of names, dates of birth, marriages, deaths—going back to a few ancestors in Ireland and Germany. A darkness swallows me up looking at it, as if these ancestors have followed me here to London and are trying to suck me back. They are all peasants, the poorest of the poor. There's no sudden discovery of ancestors who did something great. No past women writers, no female or male ancestors who traveled—just bruised, beaten farm housewives and their daughters, hardworking farmers and laborers, and a handful of men who've committed murder.

I become mesmerized by the binder, its chronicles of sickness, of death, of twelve, fourteen, sixteen children per family. I take it to work to study during breaks. I notice a number of suspicious-looking entries for young women back a few generations. They seem to die as teenagers. Someone has written "possible suicide?" after several of them. I keep looking and there's a pattern of it. There's a series of young women who just couldn't take it.

I show it to Sala. She looks through it tentatively, turning the pages as if they're something fragile that might crumble in her fingers.

"Darling, I didn't know."

I didn't know. She sees where I come from, the depth of the hardship, the devastation. There's nothing soft about that binder: a legacy of back-breaking work, of rural poverty, of brutality. I want to curl up. I want to go up to the attic and sit in the dark and watch her paint water.

There's one other letter in the entire binder. It was written by a great-great-grandmother who crossed America in a covered wagon. She was almost illiterate, but I keep rereading the letter for clues. It's nothing more than six sentences with errors and misspellings and half the words missing. It tells of how they were going from Pennsylvania to Missouri and gives what ground they covered that day and how one of them is sick in the back of the wagon. There isn't any more, despite how much I keep reading it.

If I were still in Seattle, would I want to look at the binder? It's all just too close. In London there's some distance, and I can think of my past as some quirky and edgy bio of an expat writer living in London. In America the reality of my heritage cuts too close to the bone. For the first time, as I hold the binder, I realize why I moved to London, why I spent most of my adult life living abroad. It's for the distance. It's for the distance created externally that I can't seem to create internally.

As I study the binder at work, the public school friend comes over to my desk to see what I'm looking at. I turn the pages and explain what it is while he looks over my shoulder.

"My family tree," I tell him. "With very few branches, if you know what I mean."

I show him the letter. I flip through and say, "My ancestors, voilà!"

In addition to the few times "suicide?" is written in cursive, typed beneath some of the men is their stint in prison, and the word "murder."

He turns pale. He looks mortified. He scurries back to his desk.

Later I try to talk to him, but he won't look at me. He won't speak to me. This day or the next or the next. He never speaks to me again. I know what he thinks, that I'm at one of the biggest newspapers in the world. I'm American. I must have gone to an Ivy League school, been from a good family—otherwise I wouldn't be here.

I want to say something to him, to stand up for my people, but I don't have it in me. I've barely pulled myself out of the muck myself; I'm barely on dry land. I want to say, "I contain multitudes, can't you see that?" I want to give my ancestors some kind of credit for their hard lives. I want to feel some kind of gratitude for these people who suffered so much so that I could be here now. But I'm not sure he'd understand, and I'm not sure I do either.

The work at the financial newspaper is dry. We look through articles for typos or problems with logic, and re-add the numbers to make sure everything adds up. The building is at the end of the Southwark Bridge and is old, with tall, deep-set windows that only give the slightest hint of a view of the Thames.

There is rarely, if ever, anything wrong with the copy. These are some of the world's top financial journalists. They don't need fixing. A monkey could do the work I'm doing.

I wake up, do my writing, take the back way to the tube, stop at an art gallery, come to the office, do my work, and go home. I spend every few months in another country, drinking wine in a village in Cyprus, going to clubs in Poland. I have everything, but something is missing.

XVI
THE TOWER.

CHAPTER 16

The Tower

I'm waiting on a friend in the newspaper lobby so we can go to lunch. I knew Charlotte when I first lived in London years earlier. She was my feminist mentor, feeding me books that changed my life about the plight and power of women.

Charlotte has just returned from the VSO, the Volunteer Service Overseas, the British equivalent of the Peace Corps. She worked in Nepal with kids with cerebral palsy. She told me on the phone how she'd gone into the Himalayan villages to take care of the severely handicapped children. Most of the time, the adults would go out to the fields and lock them in a back room. Charlotte would craw through the windows to get to the children. They would be on their backs, often lying in their own excrement, unable to move or speak or cry out. I could feel the Himalayas in her voice.

As I wait for her, I look at the lobby through her eyes. Steel and leather design, the low sofas, the subtle front desk reception off to the side. TVs hung around the lobby show graphic multicolored lines giving the financial reports from around the world. DOW, Nasdaq, S&P, NYSE. The lines remind me of an abstract painting, the only color against the minimalist gray backdrop. I know what Charlotte will make of it, having just come from the poorest of the poor.

When she enters, she says before she's even close to me, "Let's get out of here."

She's wearing a Nepalese orange-and-blue handmade vest, and when she gets close I can see this other world in her eyes. Something is happening to me as I look at her. I'm flashing back to my time with Finn in the Himalayas and the spiritual awakening I had there years earlier, where I felt the call, where I felt I was meant for bigger things.

One of the stitches on Charlotte's jacket is glowing and pulling me to it. It's a crooked stitch at the top-left side on the striped trim.

Love. The stitch is glowing with love. But it's more than that. The creator was an artist, because there's art in the stitch. Beauty. It's like someone has flipped a switch in the lobby, because it seems like the building is flooded with light. So much love from that single stitch grabs me by the throat. There's a call in the stitch and in the light, a call to great beauty. Such unbelievable beauty. Higher than any beauty I've known before.

At the top of my head, the crown chakra, a lightning strike flies down and tears into my soul. Love is not a trifling thing. It's hot and searing, and it burns away illusions. It's as if I'm on the road to Galilee and a lightning strike is commanding that I become another person.

None of this I say. The only thing I show is my inability to move. Charlotte is dragging me by the arm, and I'm following. We stumble out of the building.

"Sorry," she says. "Finally, I can breathe."

I nod and smile.

"Are you all right, Pearl? You're so pale."

I'm dizzy. The world is stripped of illusion. How am I supposed to act without illusion? I need some time to integrate what is happening to me, but I don't know how to tell her or ask her. I'm flooded with this knowing that I'm meant for something bigger, that I'm bigger than all of this. It's not just an idea in my mind—it's a turning point, a place where I can't go backward, and it terrifies me.

Charlotte pulls me into a low, dark restaurant. It's an Ethiopian place. I'm thankful it's so dark. I can't explain to her what's happening, so I ask simple questions so she can talk. I ask her about Nepal. I nod, but I'm not in my body. It helps to eat with our hands, to be an animal again, and not this soul who has just met the Creator.

Charlotte glows, and her hands in the food glow. The light is strong around her, but elsewhere too, out the window and even in the napkins on the table.

Somehow we make it through the meal. Somehow we hug and agree to meet again. I walk back to the office, and I'm too open. Before, I could read people's minds or souls, yes, but now it's a clashing orchestra of chaos. If before it was a six on a scale of ten, now it's a ten. The walk through the teeming hordes to get back to the office is like going through all the stations on the radio dial, and all I can capture is words and phrases—of fear, of hope, of hate, of shattering things. Even the sickly trees breathing the fumes of the traffic speak to me as I walk.

Yes, this has happened before to me, but this is an entirely new level. It's beauty, but it's everything that's the opposite of beauty, too.

I'm like a ghost in the newsroom. *What am I doing here? What a waste of time. Why am I focusing life energy on money, on financials? I'm not needed. This has nothing to do with who I am.*

When there are no articles in the queue, I wander, not just in the newsroom, but between departments, to the archives, to the HR department, to the sales department. I'm a traveling minstrel with nothing to say.

The feeling doesn't go away the next day or the next. Depression hangs like dark moss on a tree in a petrified forest. I no longer jet to Amsterdam with the work group. I barely make it to and from work. After work, I try to shut down as I get on the tube, then, when I get to Sala's, I take beer upstairs and drink. I spend hours soaking in the bathtub. I get under the covers. No lamp, as dark and unstimulating as I can make it. I remember Rayne's advice on getting back into my body and tell my body parts I love them. *I love you elbows. I love you nose. I love you finger joints.*

It becomes clear I can't be a journalist. It becomes clear that I'm being called to use this channeling, and to use it for beauty. That all that's required of me is beauty. Like the dark night of the soul in Seattle, this dark night is a warning. It becomes clear that I can no longer keep running from who I am.

I can't bear to leave London, but I can't afford to live here unless I work a mainstream job. Everything I want is *here*. European travel, great pay, connection to what's going on in the world. People I can *talk* to. I feel like the gods are against me, forcing me out of what I love, always forcing me out, a whole lifetime of being forced to leave what I love. They say you have free will, but it's not true. I don't feel free to choose this psychic lifestyle at all.

Part of me holds on for dear life. Part of me, the ghost part roaming around the newsroom, knows I must let go—for dear life.

A month later, my work visa is up for renewal. If they don't renew it, I can't stay. I can if I go searching for another journalism job, but as a ghost I don't see this as feasible. I'm invited into the managing editor's office. He tells me the newspaper is not going to renew my work visa. I'm not surprised. I'm a shell of the person I once was. I would be more surprised if they *did* renew it.

When I get back to my room, I need to talk to someone. I'm straddling two worlds. Do I talk to Sala? Will she just try to help me get another journalism job? Do I want that? Charlotte isn't a good candidate for a chat because she hates everything that America stands for. She'd wonder why I would even *want* to go back to the States.

I call Gem. She picks up.

"I'm coming home." I start sobbing.

"Finally," she says, a relief like *her* life depends upon it.

"Home, whatever that means," I say, unable to stop the tears.

"The whole world is about to change," she says. It sounds like she's channeling, like she's pulling this message from somewhere else. "Get your ass home."

"I'm so depressed," I say. "I don't like Seattle. I want to stay here."

"You can be depressed here. Sometimes it's not about *your* wants and needs, it's about the world. It's about the whole world being turned on its head and where you need to be while that's happening. But you also haven't finished finding the missing pieces of yourself. There are still some shards of you lying around here. Come home."

I get off the tube at Elephant and Castle and walk the dirty streets to see Shirley, my old therapist. She was shocked to receive my call; she'd been the one who'd urged me years earlier to go back to the States. She had no idea I was in London.

As I walk toward her office I get again that soft feeling of home I always get when I move near to her. At the door she smiles broadly. She's still wearing long, loose pastel dresses; her ankles are still hairy. The room is low-ceilinged and nondescript, with white walls and white blinds, but it feels like the most beautiful room in the world.

I fill her in quickly about the years in the States, learning tarot, studying reiki, the fiction writing.

"I can't wait to read your books."

I start crying. Why am I crying?

"I'm just saying that I'm looking forward to reading your books when they come out."

"My books?"

"Oh there are *many* books," she says.

There's something about someone wanting to read the stories of my trials and tribulations, of my soul's journey across the planet, that touches me so deeply I can barely acknowledge it.

I tell her the reason I'm here—the lightning strike that happened with Charlotte, the power of the love in that stitch, the massive opening. The ghost-like feelings and now losing my job. I'm realizing as I tell her this that she's actually the only person in London that I *could* tell such a story to. With all the talking I can do with Sala or Charlotte, this is not something I could *ever* tell them.

"Your gift," she says.

"What I need to know is how to survive with this gift. I don't want to leave London, but I'm just bombarded. I just can't stay in my room under the covers for the rest of my life."

"*You* don't want to leave, but maybe God wants you to leave."

I don't say, *What about what* I *want? Whatever happened to free will?* "Yeah, I'm going to listen to a capricious god who's given me nothing but a shitty upbringing, a psyche I can't handle, and abject poverty. Thanks, God!"

Shirley leans back and closes her eyes. She's quiet. I don't know what she's doing so I survey the room. It really is quite an ugly room, with an outdated floral love seat and mismatched floral cushions on the chairs. One wall is a closet covered in old-fashioned, mirrored sliding doors. I avoid looking at myself. I haven't been able to eat, and I've gotten too thin again. I don't understand this feeling of home I get coming here and the beauty I feel, when in reality it's such a tacky environment.

Shirley takes a deep breath and opens her eyes. "My guides keep using the word empath. But you know that, right?"

"Your guides? You never talked about your guides before. Are you channeling now?"

"I've learned to speak to my guides since last I saw you. I don't know if I'd use the word channeling, but yes, I find great comfort in speaking to my guides, and I use that power to help my patients."

I smile at this.

"Back to the question," she says. "You know you're an empath, correct?"

"Yes, I'm an empath, but mostly I'd say I'm psychic, right?" *What difference does it make what we call it?*

"It's my belief that the word empath is most relevant. Have you read current literature on what it means to be an empath? There's a growing number of books on the subject."

I shake my head.

"So, with empathy," she says, "it isn't only about sitting and reading fortunes for people, and it isn't only how you can read people when you walk about London. It's more all-encompassing than that. You absorb like a sponge whatever environment you find yourself in. Is that not correct? If you're in a busy city, you absorb that frenetic energy, and if you're near the ocean, you absorb the tide's energy."

"Yes, absolutely." This surprises me. I'd never realized this before, but it's so true.

"You pick up the emotions of the people around you, and sometimes you don't know what is you and what is them."

"Yes." I lean toward her. "I can feel when someone is sick. I can feel where it's happening in their body."

"This is the very definition of the empath."

"Why is it important to define myself as an empath? How does that help?"

"It's a matter of accepting who you really are, all of the time. Not just part of the time. Fully owning and working with your authentic self and not working against her."

I'm quiet for a while. "What confuses me is that other people don't see and feel what I see and feel. It's like we're on different planets. That's what's most frustrating to me. Like I constantly feel wrong—and it may take like five years for anyone else to see what I've been saying all along."

"Your challenge will always be learning to manage this empathy," she says.

"Why do I have to do all of the hard work? Why? Why can't I have some kind of normal life?"

"OK, so how to look at this." She grows quiet again. "So let us say you're an incredibly beautiful woman, a drop-dead gorgeous woman. Heads turn wherever you go. You cannot be in a coffee shop without creating a fuss. Men are surrounding you all the time."

I nod.

"Do you not think a woman like that has to manage herself? People tend to think someone with such beauty has it made, but imagine every man coming on to you. Imagine trying to be taken seriously."

"OK. I can see what you're saying."

"Think of your empathy as incredible beauty. It has to be protected. Honored. But first of all it has to be owned."

I sit with an image. A ruby held in the palm of the hand. I want to protect it, value it, and only show it to people I trust.

Shirley stands. "Let me provide you with some books to read."

She gives me three, and they all have "empath" in the title.

I go back to Sala's and read the books late into the night. This is a turning point. I'm not alone. Not. Alone. Yes, I'd been around other psychics, but this was different. This was not just a part of me, but all of me.

The next week, I'm early to see Shirley. There's a "do not disturb" sign on her office door. I wait outside in the rain until the other client leaves.

I launch in before she even sits down. "Does this empathy mean I can't live in London? Does it mean that the psychic crashing will keep happening? How would I manage it?"

"I imagine there are empaths living all across London. I'm an empath."

I nod, smiling. Hope!

"I have to be honest with you, though. I think the work you're doing on yourself in the States isn't finished."

I feel like deflating a balloon. "I've worked on myself for years, Shirley."

"I know. It's a lifetime pursuit, Pearl."

"So I'll spend the rest of my life broke and doing my healing in the States. It's like a death sentence."

Shirley closes her eyes and leans back. I know enough to keep quiet. She nods as she listens to her guides.

When she opens her eyes, she leans forward and clasps her hands. I look at the left and right hand, and it's as if she's holding her own hand, as if she's her own best friend.

"There's a lot you don't see, Pearl. None of us see. There's something happening in the world. And part of the reason you're being called back to the States has to do with this global shift. You're needed there. You need to be there, and you're needed there. But it's more than that . . . something else is going to happen in the world, but they won't give me any more information than that. Or maybe they would, but I just cannot understand it."

"I feel overwhelmed when I think of having to go back there again."

"From what you said, there was a lot of good in that lifestyle, too."

"Yeah, but it feels so small, so isolated."

"What if you have it all wrong? What if the financial newspaper you are working for is small, and the tarot you were reading and the people you were helping was big? Very, very big? What if London is really the small thing in your life, and the forests you camped in were the big thing?"

I shake my head. "Everything is upside down."

"Yes, yes it is," Shirley says. "The values of this world we live in are very upside down."

We don't speak for a while.

"Well, I do know that the arc of our lives spans many lifetimes," Shirley says. I laugh and tell her about my past-life regressions. She looks delighted.

"You've come a long way, Pearl, from when I saw you years ago. These pursuits in the metaphysical are really good for you. So you understand, yes, that this life you are in now is part of a much larger arc of your soul over many lifetimes? You can fight it, or you can live it. Relish it. Warts and all. What was the name again of your spiritual mentor?"

"Rayne."

"Did she ever tell you about how many people are being born right now who are highly sensitive, and there's a reason for that?"

"Yes, she did."

"Our global systems aren't working. You see this, yes? I mean this has been going on for generations. Using too many resources and not giving back."

"Oh yes." This feels so deeply true to me. If I'm honest with myself, this is why I was bored at the financial paper. There was nothing evolutionary about it, at least from my perspective.

"All of these sensitive people are being born who cannot abide the way things are. You're one of a growing tribe. We're required to build a new world to the point where the old-world rules will simply not apply. A world that is more in tune. So we are pioneers. And the change you want to see may take generations. You just have to do your part."

A flash of understanding comes to me then, on why I moved to Seattle, why Seattle is a good thing. The West Coast offers up the metaphysical to anyone who wants to learn. It's accepted, like a mystical Disneyland.

"Still, I have no idea how to do this, not really, just vague ideas about vibrations and energies, and no clear practical steps. I keep coming to people like you for help. I keep seeking. But I don't seem to get answers, just more questions. Where are the answers? What are the answers?"

Shirley looks like she's about to speak, but then holds up her index finger, closes her eyes and listens.

"I keep getting the phrase Zen koans. Does this resonate?"

I nod my head. "I love Zen koans."

"Do you know the concept behind them?"

I nod. "It's used in Zen practice to create a great doubt. I studied Zen Buddhism when I was living in Japan. The idea is that a Zen koan can break your brain, break it open, because we get too stuck thinking in certain unproductive ways. The whole 'What is the sound of one hand clapping?' is a Zen koan." I burst out laughing and think of Gem's Platitude Patty and all of her upside-down phrases.

Shirley smiles. "So all of this seeking isn't supposed to be providing answers. You see that, yes? Any answers given will lead you more deeply into illusion. So it is not for us to answer, but question. Everything we see in reality isn't real; there are only questions. And we all know the answers aren't outside of ourselves. All answers are found in here." She places her hand over her heart.

"What am I supposed to do? Just continue to question everything?"

"Yes, pose the right questions. Then be of service to help others pose the right questions." She takes a sip of green tea. "But don't be fooled. There are a lot of ways to be of service. One must not be fooled by that phrase and think it means being a caretaker. Women become caught in this trap. Dancers are of service when they share their gift. Writers. It's your job to figure out how you want to share your gift."

"I'm just trying to figure out how to survive it," I say.

★ ★ ★

Saying goodbye as an expat is never easy. Sala and her beauty. Charlotte and her passion for helping handicapped children. The friends I'd made at the newspaper.

Salacia and I say goodbye at her front door. I have everything again in two roller bags. In the time I've known her, I've given Sala a smattering of tarot readings. The cards always transformed into ballerinas, and her readings were always elegant ballet performances. As I stand with her in the doorway to her home, I feel honored that I had the joy of getting to know the beauty of her spirit.

She gives me a quick hug. "You were never meant to be here long, darling. Even I saw that. This was always meant to be a temporary jaunt. You're a traveling minstrel, and minstrels never stay in one place. They gather up the stories and they leave. Don't think of this as a failure. Think of this year as a sabbatical. It's all in the way you define it, you see. Beauty is in the way you define it."

She hands me a parting gift, a small canvas. I unwrap it there on the doorstep because I can't wait. It's a single drop of water. Hovering.

XVII
THE STAR.

CHAPTER 17

The Star

When I get out of the airport van in front of the old duplex in Wallingford, Gem is standing with her arms up against the door frame to her apartment, the light behind her a silhouette.

I roll my luggage up the walk and burst into sobs.

"Asshole," she says. Her hair is longer now, and she looks thinner. "Well, come on. You're getting soaked."

I walk into her apartment, and at first I'm confused. It looks like my old apartment. I walk in on my throw rug, look at my wall hangings, sit on my futon. I remember then, this is all the stuff I gave her before I left. Gem's familiar found objects are scattered around, but I see no new art. I'm surprised. Every piece of art I see is what was here before.

"Why no new art, Gem?"

"Dry spell, but I can feel the moisture returning to my process as we speak."

"I have a surprise for you," she says. "Not in a million years are you going to believe it." She looks like a cat that's eaten a canary. She grabs something from her backpack, grasps it tight in her palm, holds her hand out.

"Can you guess now?"

"Oh my God, I've just been traveling for fifteen hours straight."

"Follow me." We go outside to the porch, and she does a little spin that makes me dizzy in my overtired place. She opens her palm. In it is a key. She opens the door of my old apartment.

"What are you doing?"

"Come on . . ."

We walk in. It's empty.

"It's yours!" She hands me the key.

"What did you do?"

"That's for me to know and you to find out!" She spins. "Your old home is now your new home!" She goes down the dark hallway and comes back wheeling Black Beauty. "I saved your bike for you, too."

I'm not sure how I feel about coming back to this place. It feels like I'm going backward.

Gem reads my mind. "Sometimes you have to go backward to go forward. And anyway, who ever said there was anything wrong with where you were?"

Me! I want to scream.

We move the futon and blankets over so I can sleep the night. Gem gives me a pan, the coffee maker, and some coffee. I don't want anything else. I'm seeing the place with new focus, a vision inspired by Sala, and I want to take it and transform it into as much beauty as possible in such a run-down place. I begin by hanging Sala's painting of water on a nail already in the wall.

After Gem leaves, I lie on the futon, looking up at the same cracks in the ceiling. I'm moved by Gem's gesture but feel weird—crazy, even. Wouldn't it be better if I moved on from this place? I grapple with the thoughts all night until near dawn, when a small voice inside me says, *Yes, but you're not ready*. So I'm not meant to be traveling Europe or living with Sala or making a decent living. I'm meant to be here in this falling-down duplex next to the hookers. Wonderful.

I was in the UK for about a year, and it takes a while to purge the streets of London. It takes a while to recover my energy, to get up, to create as much beauty as I can in my apartment, to get back to the woods to hike, to consciously surround myself with beauty. I'm determined that this return to Seattle will go well. I make a list of what I love, of what gives undeniable beauty to my soul. The forests here, art, my writing. I go back to being of service with tarot readings and try to manage it better. I must do temp work to survive, and I try to be OK with it, but deep down I'm not.

Rayne rattles with one hand, her other hand resting on my ankle as I sit in the recliner. I can hear the traffic outside her office window on the road that separates her space from Green Lake. I'm here asking her about my writing, how to evolve it, how to see it as more of my purpose. In the back of my mind, I think I can get a book published and become famous and rich, but I also know this may just be a pipe dream.

She returns from the shamanic journey and tells me there are owls around me.

"Lots of owls. Barn owls, screech owls, horned owls, snowy owls."

"What in God's name do owls have to do with my writing?"

"They all fit together," she says.

"What fits together? The owls?"

"I traveled inside an owl's eyes and watched rain drops fall and become a stream."

"OK, and?"

She looks at me, confused. "Your stories. You asked about your writing."

My stories. I have hundreds of pages of stories.

"Put them in order. Put them together."

"Put what together?" I'm still thinking of the owls.

"Your stories. Put them together in a book."

I sit up. Click. Click. Click. All of the stories I've been writing fall into quick successive place; they build on each other. It's as if all the puzzle pieces of me, all the missing pieces, were there all along. They were all floating in bubbles, and in my imagination, the bubbles pop and they drip back to earth and flow together.

I grab Rayne's hand. "Oh my God, thank you."

"Thank Goddess," she says.

I've paid her and I'm getting ready to leave when she says, "There's one more thing. I keep being told to tell you this. You're crossing over to another plane now. The old ways of the world can no longer satisfy you. You're already noticing this, but there will be more. You won't fit into the old paradigm anymore. You're leaving behind the old archetypal masculine and really now entering the waters of the Divine Feminine. If you try, it'll just bring you frustration, or worse."

Biking home, I can only think about my stories and how they fit into a book. It's like I'm in the wash cycle agitating. My body vibrates like something wants to get out. The cage is being rattled.

That night, I wake, startled by a noise, and sit up. Above my third eye, hovering there, are five novels. This is not a dream, and I'm not asleep. Glowing books are floating in front of me in the darkened room.

I'm shown each book in quick succession. The first shows me planting and weeding and gutting, living with the soil as a girl in the Midwest. In the second I leave America and float above a foreign culture. The third is the phoenix rising from the embers. In the fourth, I'm healing. Finally, the fifth book is something about collective consciousness. Each book is deeply entwined with natural elements.

The first book flies toward me and enters my third eye. I'm shown the entire storyline. I can see theme and plot, characterization and setting. It's the story of my childhood and so much more. It's not written in stone, but is alive, a living document.

The second novel flies up and toward me and enters my third eye with a force that pushes me backward. It's my expat story with its pain of separation and growth of perception. The third follows into my third eye, the fourth, the fifth. The fifth book remains the most vague to me, speaking of something I don't yet know. The themes of all the novels enter my bloodstream; plot lodges in my bones.

With each book comes visions of a future I don't want to see, a heavy load of knowing. It seems I can't open to these books without also opening to a knowledge of a toxic, disturbed out-of-balance. The future I see reminds me of the visions I had as a child in the family garden in the Midwest, when a Native woman came to warn me. I see her warnings coming true before my eyes, soon, too soon: killer storms, deadly droughts, global disease, man's greed and rage and fear. I knew this inside me somewhere all along. This is the source of my years-long despair. The reason I can't fit and live a life of pretending.

Over the next few days, the future sits heavy in me as I print out my stories, sit on the floor and mix and match them. These are some of the missing puzzle pieces I've come back to the States to find. When I'm finished, still so many pieces are missing. It'll take years to write the whole series. A voice says, *No, a lifetime.*

What I find interesting is how many of the stories involve visual art. I feel an urgency now to follow this calling to art more than ever, before it's too late. How am I to be a visual artist if I'm a writer? The questions draw up a well of confusion.

I run into him at a grocery store. We're under florescent lights and standing beside suction-packed slabs of cow. The smell is gamey, bloody, cold. He stands coiled and leaning toward me. In his basket is just one item: six carrots with the bushy green tops attached.

"How's the academy? How's teaching?" I ask him. It's Saint, the art teacher I assisted years ago now.

"Good." His hands are covered in paint. He keeps looking at his fingertips and flexing his fingers.

I tell him I've just returned from London. I talk about the newspapers, about Diana's death, about the field of rotting flowers.

"Have you been doing art?" he asks, and I shake my head and again feel like crying. "Can I take you to lunch?" he asks.

I swipe the tears as I nod. I haven't eaten out in months, since London.

We walk to a nearby pub. I order a pint of Fat Tire, and then another, and then an Alaskan Amber, and I drink them like the rare desserts they are for me these days. At home, Gem and I drink cheap beer—Miller Genuine Draft. Saint and I order fries and burgers, and I eat half his fries, gobble them like a starving person. The biggest thing I miss about London is the social life that working at the newspapers gave me. Sitting across from Saint, I feel normal again, social.

"I'm thinking about doing some freelance journalism articles," he says. "Would you mind giving me pointers?"

I stare into his eyes, look at his thick lips, at the muscles in his arms straining against his shirt. I feel like I'm in a Harlequin romance. I imagine few women say no to this guy.

We discuss generating story ideas, pitching stories, conducting research, doing interviews.

Despite what Rayne advised, I still pursue a journalism job. I have to make a proper living and refuse to go back to tarot. I tell Saint how I'm looking for a newspaper position but having no luck, and how I'm now seeking an unpaid internship. "I haven't been in the American journalism mainstream much," I tell him. "They have a sort of hierarchy that your path is supposed to take. Small-town paper, then regional paper, then city paper. If you're outside of it, no soup for you!"

"What about freelancing?" he asks. "You should be able to make money freelancing, right?"

"It's a hard row to hoe," I say. I think of my early days in London freelancing with Alex and Eileen, and the lack of money. "I think if you're aggressive and build a career, you can build a proper income over time. But you have to work at it, hard. It's great, though, to be able to pursue whatever subject matter you're interested in instead of being told by an editor what to write."

A heaviness overcomes him. I see through him and into him. He's an artist who has spent his life trying to make money but failing, the kind of person for whom abundance is art and creativity—but these don't necessarily translate into strong finances. *The Great Compassion* floods over me and into him. I can see what it's like to be a man, with all the expectations society and women put on you to be the breadwinner, to be a forty-something male artist in such a system. He visits the world with soul. It's a challenge for those who live through the soul. I want to take his long, spattered fingers into mine.

Afterward at his car, I lean forward and kiss him on the mouth. He moves back, but the car is behind him and he's stuck. The kiss is cold and muscular, and I feel nothing, and I'm pretty sure he feels nothing, too.

He says in a monotone, "I've wanted to do that myself all day." I think, *He thinks he's supposed to say that.* He's squirmy as I stand too close to him, so I back up.

He opens his car door. I lean to look in, and I feel a pull to enter the dark, warm interior. The car interior is like Saint, cold and warm, both. Hard and soft.

"Come with me," he says. I imagine again few women saying no to this guy. It'd be like entering a deep cave, like entering Saint's skin. There's something pulling me, but I don't know if it's a good something or a too-comfortable something that may be hard to extricate myself from, that may expect too much of me.

“Next time,” I say, and he leans forward and kisses me, hard and warm, soft and cold.

From out of the blue comes a call from a local public radio station. I have an internship. Twenty hours a week, no pay. I’m already working thirty hours doing temp work and fifteen doing tarot to survive.

On a whim, I take the internship.

“Why are you going back to journalism, after everything?” Gem asks me. I’d told her about the sacred stitch on Charlotte’s jacket. The intense light and love I felt after that encounter with Charlotte in the newspaper lobby. I’d told her how journalism felt so wrong afterward.

“What choice do I have? I refuse to go back to reading tarot full time. I can’t.” I tell her how much I hate my temp jobs, how deadening they are, how I’d do anything to have an interesting job. “How do you suggest I make a living?”

“You’re thinking of only black and white, either I make money as a journalist or I’m a temp. Surely there’s a more dimensional way to transform this.”

“I’m all ears.”

“It’ll come to us,” she says.

Every night I meditate before I go to sleep, asking for the answer. I can see that blinding light there, but I can’t seem to understand what’s being said to me.

The office is smaller than I’m used to, with about twelve women and a half dozen men. I’m given an on-air personality to work with named Gus. I take the news off the wires and rework it, rewrite it for radio. They train me on how to do this, but it's not hard. Gus reads what I give him on air. Within a week I'm all caught up. It's brutally easy. I'm bored. I'm a decade older than the other interns.

My own stories are coming to me in a flood, all the missing pieces raining hard upon my head. They appear like visions during my workday at the station, like tarot readings, characters in some kind of mythological play, swarming me and demanding to be heard. I'm in the kitchen at the station when the first one hits. I grab a marker from the white board and scribble it furiously onto napkins. Soon my backpack is filled, and my desk is strewn with napkins covered in black cursive. Almost everyone ignores the temps, so no one seems to notice—except Gus. He asks me what I'm doing, and I pause long enough to tell him about a girl who was tied to a plow in her family garden because they couldn't afford a donkey.

"Cool," he says.

Because the job is so easy, because I'm on the outside looking in, because I can focus on my own writing, I don't seem to find this place psychically overwhelming, but I do find it confusing.

The women sit hunched forward at desks, sweating over the keyboards, barely emerging all day. The men strut and guffaw and only sit when they feel like it, and a few of the men spend an inordinate amount of the day lounging on leather sofas against one wall. The bosses are male. Most of the on-air talent are male. I expect this in London—it's still part of the old world. I don't expect it on the West Coast of the U.S. There's very little Divine Feminine here. They do shows about equal rights for women, when in their own newsroom it's so out of balance it's shocking.

In the kitchen I run into a foreign exchange intern. I think he's from India. I don't know because he won't speak to me. He stands in the corner of the kitchen or the corner of the office watching and looking frightened.

If I mention the sexism in the office, or that the one foreigner in the entire room doesn't look comfortable, it'll be like insulting the holy grail of liberal journalism. I'm an outsider here. I sit on the sidelines, write my stories and observe.

It's a week later when I do get into Saint's car. We drive across a bridge to a rambling apartment complex he manages. He uses a remote to open the garage. The place looks like a paint bomb went off. His art studio. I walk into the garage like something's yanking me, sucking me up, swallowing me whole. It's like walking into a painting. Spattered color on every surface. The canvases merge with the walls and bleed into the floor.

By the time he clicks the remote to close the door, *we* are merging, lips and tongues and hip bones and thighs, hard and strong and animal. We roll across a blue tarp against the concrete floor. The tight muscles of his arms and chest and the relentless rigidity of the floor.

Coral and I have a term for a guy like Saint: "rutter." Coral is a milder version of Gem, sleeping around. But unlike Gem, Coral gets emotionally involved with the guys. Mostly they fall head over heels in love with her. When telling me about this guy or that guy, Coral will say, "He's a rutter" or "He's not a rutter." Rutter is a good thing. Like rutting animals, physical and wild, not wormy. A rutter is a guy who has sex like a jack hammer, a guy who likes sex and isn't afraid to show it. Saint is a rutter, and I suppose by extension so am I.

On a tarp crusted with the colors of the rainbow, we rut. We buck. We bruise. We stain.

At the station, one of the hotshot on-air guys, Devon, is on his back on a big leather sofa against one wall. Arm flung over his head, he calls out into the newsroom, "I'm looking for anyone who has any contacts for local psychics. I'm putting together a piece on psychics. I need contacts, people." *Hotdogs. Get your hotdogs here.*

I write Rayne's number on a Post-it, as well as info on a couple other psychics I've met. I don't give him my name and number. I'm careful not to mix my journalism self with my psychic self. I don't want to sully my professional reputation. Somewhere inside me, though, I'm desperate for this journalism life I'm leading to accept the metaphysical. I want to see if they'll take it seriously, treat it as sacred, before I step up to the plate and open that side of myself to this old male world. I know Rayne is strong enough to take on these guys. I am not.

Devon moves from the sofa to his desk. He's tall and skinny and his corduroys and shirt are wrinkled. His desk is positioned in the center, at the head of the room, facing two lines of desks where hunched women do their work.

I go up to his desk. He sees me or doesn't see me—I'm an intern and a ghost. He picks up the phone. Talks to someone named Roger who doesn't seem to know any psychics. He puts down the phone and I'm still there, but he acts like I'm not.

"Hey," I say.

He's bouncing up and down in his chair. "Did someone take my chair? Is this my chair?" Bounce. Bounce.

"Hey," I say louder.

He looks at me. His face is gray, and he looks like he spent the previous night on a bender. "Yes?"

"A list of legitimate metaphysical healers," I say, and hand him the note.

He looks at it, puts it to the side.

I would love to hear a well-rounded radio show on how psychics work, on channeling, on how there exist energies in the world beyond the everyday. I actually think that would be one of the most interesting shows I've heard in a long time. I don't say any of this.

"I've worked with Rayne for years. She's the real thing."

He bounces in his chair. I go back to my desk.

The next day, I hear him on the phone doing interviews, and he's obviously found quacks and is making a joke of it. When the spot comes out on the radio, I try to listen, but it's hackneyed and cliched. His goal is to prove them all wrong. Worse—to prove them all ridiculous. I shut off the radio. I'm glad he didn't call Rayne. I remember what Rayne said the last time I saw her, how I wouldn't fit into the old paradigm anymore, and how frustrated I'd get. I can't believe how often women are in the subservient role, even here. I've traveled the world looking for a place where women are treated fairly, and I can't find it.

At home, disturbed by the radio show that mocks psychics and feeling I'm the butt of the joke, I empty my pack of napkins covered in handwritten sprawl so I can transcribe them into the computer. I've spent my life holding all sorts of positions: editor and travel writer, boat swabber and key cutter, tarot reader and data-entry person. I don't see one person as higher or lower, just that each person has their own path.

Worse, I hate the mockery of things metaphysical. I used to mock it myself, but now I'm sick of it, over it. It's not just the station. When I was in London, one of the other journalists invited me to a dinner party. I'd mentioned that I read cards in Seattle, and he asked me to bring them. At the dinner, fat old candles dripped wax onto a beat-up table. A massive bowl of pasta and another of mixed greens, several open bottles of wine. The host asked me to break out the cards. Laughing, I did. It didn't go as planned. There were so many skeptics. People looked at me darkly. I felt ashamed.

Of course there are readers in London, but in the old world, they're still seen as hokey. I lost the respect of more than a few other journalists at the dinner party that evening. All over the world, you still find people who will mock things spiritual. I used to be one of them. And now I'm done with them.

I'm assembling my stories into my first book. An hour goes by before I see the flashing light on the answering machine. I get up and check it. There's a woman on the other line telling me that another one of my short stories has been accepted by an anthology. She gives her phone number.

"Congratulations," she says. "You're a gifted writer."

I push the button again and stand with my head bowed as she repeats her message.

Saint is smart and engaging and social. So social. We attend art shows, fiction readings, the opera. His friends have dinner parties. His students invite him to parties where people dance through the night. I'm more of a homebody, an introvert who's happier by herself or in the woods, and now every week,

I work hard to keep up with Saint. Finally I have a social life in Seattle.

Women come at Saint from every direction. They gather and snake and slither. We show up anywhere, and within minutes he's surrounded by gaggles of giggling gals. My ex Finn was handsome, but Saint is a whole new level, a whole new degree of grappling with my self-worth. I watch seventy-five-year-old women turn into schoolgirls. Worse, I see hot women become predators. By his side, I don't even exist.

I have no space inside me to manage this. I don't have enough belief in my looks or my sexual prowess to stand up against these women in their heels, with their sharp, polished nails. Even at the best of times I'm not good at relationships. I read tarot for women whose only goal is to get a man, and I've never understood this. It's never been my goal. I think this intrigues Saint, my lack of interest in the traditional relationship path. Or perhaps it's because I don't desire for him to carry the role of "man." I just want us both to be able to "be."

I've never known how to follow the rules, to pick up the pile of expectations put upon the shoulders of a girlfriend. I can't fulfill the role, and I find it all ridiculous and mainstream. When I was with Finn, we'd argue endlessly because I wouldn't keep house. Why was it my job to keep house?

Saint triggers me, too. He's not my father, but he's a manly man and that's close enough to be a trigger. Finn and Red were softer men, and the triggers then were more gentle. With Saint, the triggers are like infants screaming at the top of their lungs. We fight—over the women, mostly—and the fights are me crying out as a child. I can see it even as it's happening and can't seem to stop it. I don't trust men, so I pick a man who is unbearably untrustworthy.

Still, there's love. I watch him one day take my clothes out of the dryer, and my shirt looks fragile in his fingers, and I feel the love in the way he folds it. Long into the night, on many nights, we hold each other. I hear from one of his friends that his mother was depressed, that his mother didn't hold him enough. There were rumors that his mother was abused. So many women abused.

My heart fills again with *The Great Compassion*. I turn to see him standing by the stairs at his apartment, and he's a four-year-old boy who was never fully loved, and my heart breaks. When love is real love, it's universal, and when I see him as this child and *The Great Compassion* floods me, I see also my own father as a four-year-old, every bruised man as a four-year-old who just needs love and guidance.

Other times, though, too many times, I'm so angry at him that I look at the same man at the same stairwell, and he becomes every many who has hurt me, an archetype of an abusive man. In my mind, I have a cardboard cutout of such a man, and I visualize that cutout instead of Saint. I can't see him; I only see every man who's hurt me. If the cutout doesn't fit, if there are places that don't apply to Saint, I color in the blanks with metaphorical markers until he does fit. Until he becomes every man who has done me harm. I know I'm doing this, and can't stop myself.

Saint is a man with a reputation. I know that, knew that going in, and I *still* went in. I'm never sure what he's doing on the side. Bored housewives take his classes in droves. They show cleavage. They call him up just to talk.

I know, because I answer the phone.

XVIII
THE MOON.

CHAPTER 18

The Moon

There are cracks in the foundation, cracks in the driveway, cracks in the ceiling. We're at a house on a hill in Seattle's Queen Anne neighborhood, sitting on the deck and having a barbecue with Saint's friends. Every weekend there's a new social event; every weekend I meet a group of new people; every weekend I'm nearly invisible, the second string, the back-up to this man's artistic genius. I think of Coral and how I'm being eclipsed.

The husband is a veterinarian and the wife a professor of medicine. He's tall and thin and she's tall and thinner. They both look like they've had work done on their faces.

He's pointing to the crack in the house's foundation. He's crouching and pointing and walking along the crack. For some reason, this makes me want to kill myself. At a dinner party where everyone else seems to be having fun, I want to die.

There's a ruckus on the street below. We hear a man yell, "Baby girl, stop, no!" I run over to see. The others follow. We stand high above the scene, looking down on a steep street.

A little girl is running wildly up the middle of the road, hair swept out behind her, arms pumping; she's no more than four or five. Her grandfather is old and chasing her, or trying to chase her. His legs are bowed, and he's wobbling toward her as she barrels up the street. She screams with delight, her legs covered in dirt. The upturned dirty-girl face, the look of wild freedom. The feral child imprints on me. I'm this girl, this wildness, this lover of freedom.

The wife is standing next to me. She's beautiful, with plucked eyebrows and carefully styled blonde hair. She has a runner's body beneath a silk pantsuit.

"There's the stain of Satan in that girl." Her voice is low and she's whispering. "I've been watching this child. There's the stain of Satan in her. Do you see it?" She looks at me. Her eyes are blue, and tiny lines radiate out on porcelain skin. I excuse myself and go and hang on Saint's arm.

The child runs, the grandfather stumbles, the girl's cries bleed up from the roots.

"Ugh. Those people," the wife says. "I can't bear it."

People like what? Running children? Laughing girls? Grandfathers trying to catch little girls before they hurt themselves? Who is Satan in this picture? If the girl is the devil, then so am I.

We go back to the table, where the woman delivers a berry crumble and the man goes back to outlining the snaking crack in the driveway and the girl over the edge continues screaming with a fury of freedom.

I don't fit with Saint's crowd. This makes me sad—further proof of my inability to fit. I feel like an expat in my own country. I only fit in with the fringe community, the psychics and wackadoodles, but barely even there.

The moment Saint and I began sleeping together I knew we'd be together for only three months. I told this to Coral and she thought I wasn't being open to the potential of the relationship. It wasn't that. The same thing happened with Red. I'm psychic. I can see how long the thing is supposed to last. After the dinner party with the satanic child, we're making the drive back to Saint's and I tally it up. It's been two and a half months. It's nearly time to pack up and leave.

Gem opens her door. I haven't seen her in a while. She goes back to sitting on the floor, working on a project. At first she won't look up from what she's doing. When she does, she looks like she's holding herself back.

"What? Say it?"

"You're so pale. You're so skinny. You're not healthy."

"I know."

"Don't abandon yourself for some guy, Pearl. It's feminism 101."

She's right. There's something about being with Saint that drains me to my core. I've been abandoning Gem, too. "Sorry," I say, but I'm too tired to mean it.

I tell her that I think Saint's sleeping around. The women who call his house act too familiar. He's too hot to have so many women friends.

Gem nods like she's known all along.

"Hey," I say. "You sleep around."

"Yeah, but I don't let the guy believe I'm being exclusive. I let the guys know up front what they're in for. I think these days they're calling it ethical nonmonogamy."

I try to figure out what Gem's doing with her hands; she seems to be stringing some kind of beads.

She says, "What if you wish you could be like Saint, have the same license to be that sexual? What if you resent it in him? What if you wish to *be* him? What if you were an artist like he is, and all of these people were attracted to you?"

I shake my head.

"Seriously," she says. "What if you're sleeping with him because you want to be him? I always say, never sleep with someone you wouldn't want to become."

"Never become someone you wouldn't want to sleep with," I say back to her.

Gem goes to the kitchen and comes back with a cold MGD for me. I expect some tall hipster to pop out from behind a closed door, a current amour, but this doesn't happen.

"Maybe he does represent my animus," I say. "My inner male is wild and free, smart and muscular, and a slut."

Gem is twisting the string of beads and it looks like a double helix.

I ask her, "How do women go around having normal marriages with normal men? You'd kill yourself, Gem, if you were forced to be normal, right? I feel like I'm on a completely different planet. Like the heterosexual coupledom is some kind of fascist way of living. Like there are no other ways of living. And I don't just mean gay. Because there are a lot of gay couples in the same sort of forever relationships. I feel like there are millions of ways to live a life, and being coupled is just one of them. It's like everyone can't stop drinking the Kool-Aid."

"You're an artist. That's the way a lot of artists think," Gem says. "Give me your wrist."

I extend my arm. She takes the beads she's been working on and ties the bracelet around my wrist. It looks exactly like a DNA strand. It has Gem's energy, and the vibe tingles my skin.

We're at another outdoor dinner party. This time in Ballard. Saint wants me to go hang out with the women in the kitchen. I'm sitting at a picnic table with the men, but when I speak they act awkward. I want to be part of the conversation but they won't let me in. I don't know if this is what middle-class dinner parties are like, or if it's just Saint's friends. The men outside talking, the women inside cooking. I might as well be back in Missouri. Seattle's supposed to be one of the most liberal cities in the country, and still all of these ancient, unchallenged paradigms. Saint's an artist, and it surprises me his friends are so square. Especially after Saint was such a good teacher and saw the potential in me, I don't expect him to be so normal. But he is.

When I again try to enter the men's conversation, Saint says, "Pearl, come with me." He takes my hand and leads me through a back door. In the kitchen, five women of various ages are cooking, stirring, chopping, and drinking wine. Saint introduces me.

The hostess is taking vegetables out of the oven. "What do you like to cook, Pearl?"

"I don't cook."

"You don't cook anything?"

"I don't cook," I say again. I learned a long time ago that if you let anyone in a newsroom know you're a fast typist, they'll give you more work. It was the same with cooking: don't let them know that you cook, that in fact you have a gift for it, or you'll be stuck in the kitchen for the rest of your life while the men lounge outside.

Saint tries to pull his hand away from mine, but I hold onto it tightly. He works until he extricates his fingers and turns and goes back outside to be with the men. Holding a big glass of wine, I watch them stew and stir and sauté. I grew up with this. Rural American women did all of the cooking, all of the housework, all of the childcare. Roles that felt like ropes strangling me to death. I ran hard and I ran far to get away from it, but here I'm in a middle-class home in the middle of Ballard facing it again. And again. And again.

The women are too nervous to talk to me. Finally I excuse myself and go outside. In the backyard, there's a tree. I go to it and climb it and hang upside down from my knees. The family dog runs up and circles my head, barking.

"Saint, is Pearl OK?" the hostess says as she pops out with a basket of fresh bread for the men. No one at the men's table has noticed me up to this point.

Saint shakes his head and turns back to his conversation. I watch them all upside down, the men sitting, the women serving them, the earth as the sky.

I think of a quote from Philip K. Dick: "It's sometimes the appropriate response to reality to go insane."

The eggs are burning. I'm sitting at Saint's dining table with my laptop doing my daily writing. It's Sunday morning. The smell keeps interrupting.

"Saint?" I peer into the kitchen; he's not there. It's his turn to cook. This has been happening a lot. He creates situations when it's his turn to do the cooking, and he starts but then goes missing. So I'm required to pay attention, notice that he's not participating, and rush in to save the eggs. I refuse to move. I meet myself in the writing and forget about the stove top.

We have other issues. He doesn't like my depressions. That isn't true—that's too much of an understatement. He can't abide them. They send him spiraling. They trigger in him something deep and dark. He's angry at his mother for the neglect and angry at me by extension. Like most of liberal Seattle, he can spout support for the feminist movement. Like the journos in the newsroom, he can intellectualize compassion. Finding it for his nearest and dearest is another matter altogether.

Saint doesn't know how often I try to beat back the depression, how often I wear fake smiles and go to events when I'd rather stay home. Does it matter that I was also once four and never hugged? Does it matter what happened to me or to his mother, or to all women throughout time? *He's* not happy. So let's just make Saint happy then.

He comes in the front door, rushes to the kitchen. "What the fuck?" I peer sideways as he grabs an oven mitt and takes the frying pan off the flame.

"Pearl?"

"Yes, dear."

"Well, breakfast is ruined." He stands in the doorway to the dining room holding up the pan for me to see.

"Oh no, what did you do?" I ask.

"Didn't you smell them?"

"Where did you go?"

"I was in the garage organizing my paintings for the show."

"While you were cooking?"

He gives me a hard stare. I don't care. It's not my job to be hypervigilant. I do my share of the cooking, and often more than my share. Balance isn't just important to me—it's a deal breaker. He knows this. I've told him this. We're closing in on three months.

We're not talking to each other as we sit at his kitchen table, which is covered by a table cloth decorated with bees and salt and pepper shakers shaped like chipmunks. His whole apartment is stuck in the late seventies, his entire living room filled with rattan furniture with floral cushions. We share a piece of toast because it's the only thing that's not burned.

I decide to break up with him. I want to have sex one more time before I go but think better of it, so I decide to break up with him before sex.

"We need to break up," I say.

His face transforms to that of a small boy as he sits on the edge of his chair. He starts crying. "Please, Pearl, please."

He takes my hands, his fingers covered in oil paint. It's not just the eggs and the ghosts of girlfriends past and the specters of other lovers whispering in my ear as I pick up the phone. It's not just having to smile and nod. It's not just feeling so drained all the time. Our values are too different. I say none of these things. I feel burdened and bent forward by his expectations, and bent forward by guilt because I no longer want him on my shoulders.

"Pearl, please don't run away." He's kissing the side of my face and my cheeks are wet with his tears. "This one time, just don't run away."

It's too much for a girl so starving for love, this handsome, gifted man begging her to stay.

We go upstairs and have sex.

Daily, with the public radio station, writing my first novel, the tarot, the outings with Saint, there's this other love pulling at me, this memory of beauty. That tiny stitch on Charlotte's jacket and the opening to divine beauty that happened in London. I can't seem to keep it in a box, whatever that was that broke me open in London. It's still there, nagging at me, waiting.

Saint's art show is coming up, and I sit and watch him paint in the garage. It's nothing like watching Sala paint water. He scratches out nudes in hard lines, the curve of the line like cutting through flesh, splashes of red paint like blood. With Saint, painting is an argument, a fight he's having with himself. He struggles with the nudes so passionately he forgets that I'm there.

Meanwhile, we go to art shows, galleries, museums. He introduces me to Kandinsky and de Kooning and Dubuffet. He leans into paintings and talks about composition and brush strokes, color, tint, and hue. It's not just what he says—I enter him and see the paintings through his eyes. My vision shifts, and I see the layers of paint as molten lava, and I see the hands of masters with their brushes.

It's these times and during sex that Saint and I are good for each other. I wonder if Gem is right—maybe the only way I know how to become an artist is to fuck it.

We write together. He still wants to learn freelance writing to make extra money. We decide to cowrite an article. He comes up with an idea for sanctuaries for wild animals, birds of prey mostly. Bald eagles, red-tailed hawks, peregrine falcons, and ospreys and their ilk, who have broken wings and other injuries and need rehabilitation.

We spend weeks traveling around the edges of Washington State and into Canada, going from sanctuary to sanctuary. We watch an owl being stitched up and study an eagle whose wing is damaged, and I think of Coral and healing the animal body. I teach Saint how to interview, the who, what, when, where, and why. I show him how to write an intro and a nut graph and how to quote a source. He has a natural talent for it. He's heavy and hard with the process, though. It doesn't need to be that laborious, and his process is hard to cocreate with. But we finish the article. We contact publications to place it and find an airline magazine that's interested.

The night of Saint's art show, I wear a silk suit I had made in Bangkok on my trip with Finn through Asia. It has a long jacket and a short skirt and is silver blue. With high heels that Gem lends me, my hair back from my face, and makeup on, I could pass as a beautiful woman. Saint keeps staring at my legs as we enter the large hall where his paintings will be shown. Another man in a business suit passes us and stares at my legs. It must be all the biking. *I love you thighs. I love you calves. I love you ankles.*

We're met in the presentation space by the gallery owner, Bev, a short woman with wild gray hair and cat eyeglasses. Saint is nervous, and I run my hand up and down his arm to try to comfort him, but his nervousness is too great right now for comfort.

Twenty of Saint's paintings grace the space. Male and female nudes, as if they're chasing and struggling around the circumference of the room. Often the figure isn't fully realized, just a few lines to suggest a body, black, white, crimson. Red vaginas. Red penises, studies in the base chakra. I'm already sleeping with him, and even I want to do him right then looking at the paintings.

As the people show up, as the hall fills, I try to stay by Saint's side, smile and nod. The shoes hurt my feet. High heels are the modern equivalent of Chinese foot binding. Soon so many people are asking Saint questions, pulling him here and there, that I become less and less visible, pushed to the edge of the gallery, standing against a white wall and holding a glass of wine.

I stay this way for an hour, watching. The paintings are brilliant. Saint is good. He deserves the attention. But I'm just the audience again. I was this with Finn and his music, perpetual audience to the man's giftedness. Always the audience, never the artist.

Some storm is brewing in me, something big and fierce, something frightening, something so bright it's blinding. A new layer of monsters unearthed, breeding in my gut.

I land a paid journalism job. It comes out of nowhere. How many years have I been looking? Before London and after—six years? Full-time pay and benefits, and for the first time in Seattle I won't have to worry about money. I'm now a copy editor at a major Seattle daily newspaper. Saint is over-the-moon excited for me. I wonder, not for the first time, if like I'm with him to learn visual art, he's with me to break into the world of journalism.

On the night shift at the paper, for a month I sit at whatever computer is available in the news department.

Usually the only open desk is next to the editor's desk. Soon I learn why.

Below the editor's desk, the police scanner keeps up a perpetual litany of bad news. While I edit stories on a tiny screen with tiny lettering—the computer system is old here—I'm regaled with tales of violence and abuse, of drugs and prostitution. It's like listening to a book on tape, but all the stories are wretched and disturbing. It's like growing up and my father whispering insults. Sitting next to the scanner is like a horrible patriarch whispering nastiness into your soul.

On my way home, I thrust my bike against the wind and driving rain to dispel the auditory trauma, popping up on the sidewalk and swiping between cars and buses, ass off of seat, head thrust forward, sweating out the hate. I come to work the same way, too, in bike gear, covered in mud, hair in all directions, sometimes half-wet strands stuck to a sweating neck—feral as I leave sweat trails on the way to my computer.

It's worse than seeing it. There's something about sound, about the voices, something about how they weave like smoke deep into the psyche.

One night, while working on a story on shipping tankers in Alaska, a little boy cries in my ear. *Help! Help!*

He's under his bed. He's on the phone with the police. "Daddy's going to kill Mommy." His voice bleeds from the scanner. I can see him in some psychic part of me. He's wearing a white t-shirt and PJ bottoms with images of small dogs. He's curled up beneath the bed as far back as he can get toward the headboard and the wall. It's a craftsman house in Southcenter, the walls a sea blue. I can see it all while the boy whispers unbearable tragedies that float up like smoke.

"Daddy's going to kill her. Please!"

"What's your name?

"Hurry. Oh, hurry!"

"It's OK. It's OK. We're going to help. What's your name?"

"Nathan!" He's crying. "Nathan. Nathan . . . Michael Nettle."

"Nathan, do you know your address?" Crashing sounds come through the phone line and through the scanner.

"Ooh, ooh, he's hurting her. Mommy!"

"We need to come help you, Nathan. And we need your address. OK? Can you give us that? Do you know it?"

"Mommy! Mommy! Mommy!"

"Nathan, your address. Now."

"Bend Road. One, four, five, nine. Oh no, he's hitting her. One, four, five, nine!" he screams. "Mommy. No. No. No." He's scooting his feet to back himself up against the wall into a tiny ball. He's curling up against the sound of voices that will stay with him a lifetime.

"Somebody's coming to help, Nathan. Stay with me. Where's your daddy, Nathan?" the disembodied voice asks.

I'm staring at the shipping story trying to remember which paragraph I just edited.

"Ship and barge freight move millions of dollars of goods between Alaska and the lower 48. Millions of pounds of goods go by sea and land, from fresh produce to seafood."

My arms grow heavy. I can't find the point of the story. It just seems like a list of *the, the, the, the, the.*

"He's in the kitchen. He has a gun. He's so mad at Mommy." The boy starts sobbing. He can't talk. I feel his cry in my throat.

Something about new Canadian regulations for shipping over land. I try to lift my left arm to fix a typo, but it won't move. My arm is dead. I send it a message to move, for the hand to come up to the keyboard, but it just hangs by my side. Something's also going on with my back—it feels like a rubber band has broken between my clavicles, between my wings. My back feels loose, like it won't support my sitting up. My right arm too starts to go numb. Soon it's hanging by my side and won't listen to my commands. I'm terrified. I don't know what's happening.

I hear the police on the scanner. They've made it to the house.

An official's voice comes over the scanner now. He's talking to someone, not the dispatcher. "Where's the boy?" Nobody is answering him. "Where's the boy?"

He's under the bed, I want to yell. *He's under the bed!*

I go to the editor and tell her about my arms. I'm emotional. Distraught. About the boy, about my arms. Both. Someone has to help me to the car service, which drives me home. I have to leave my bike. I have no idea what's happening to my body and it scares me more than any vision or anything else that's ever happened to me.

I can't open my door, and the driver has to get my key out of my pack and do it for me. I don't know what's happening. What's happening? To go to the bathroom, I have to rub up against the doorknob on the open bathroom door to pull down my pants. I'm scared. I've never been so scared.

Later, Gem says, "You just couldn't *handle* it anymore. You couldn't hold onto it anymore." Gem is beside me and then gone, some days there and some days not, like a ghost. I stare at my lifeless hands. What will my hands do, now that they can do nothing?

"You wouldn't listen to the universe, so they *made* you listen," Gem says.

Doctors run test after test, and the best they can surmise is that I may have thoracic outlet syndrome: nerves pinched at the collarbones. The physical therapist tells me my condition is more complex than issues with my thoracic outlet. They won't give me the official diagnosis—they can't find one that fits.

It isn't just my arms, but my back too, and the hardwood is the only thing that makes it feel better. As I lay counting the cracks, I have to admit that my arms have been going numb for a year, maybe longer. The complete numbness and lack of all feeling had already been waking me from a deep sleep for many months, even in London. I couldn't admit it to myself before, though, because how can you admit that you're losing the use of your body?

Physical therapy brings back some use, but not all. I'm stabilized for a few weeks, and something tweaks my upper back and shoulders, and I'm on the floor again for three to five days.

The elderly doctor doesn't think I have anything wrong with me. They've done test after test, and nothing is strictly conclusive. I break down in his office, crying because I don't know how I'm going to survive. I can't work, and the Labor and Industry claim brings in so little monthly. He must be in his eighties, old-world eyes sunk deep into his skull. As I sob, he looks at me, annoyed. He writes in his notes that he can't find anything wrong with me, and I'm hysterical. I know because I ask for copies and read it myself.

I do intensive physical therapy several days a week. The physical therapist tells me that if we don't see stabilization in my back and arms within the first three weeks, the prognosis isn't good. Months go by without full stabilization. I have days where my back and arms are fine, but never whole weeks.

When I'm stabilized I try to keep seeing Saint. I can see he's trying. I stay at his place, and every morning he cooks breakfast. Watching his meaty hands cut onions, I feel the love in his thick fingers. It scares me. What does it mean to have Saint love me? The power of it, but the weight of his unresolved pain, too. The responsibility. What does love like that mean when you're so fragile? I learned at a young age that love is something you must be able to protect yourself from. I can't use my arms. I can't protect myself from Saint.

It's no use. If Saint thought my depressions were bad before, welcome to severe depression in physical form. I can barely fend for myself; how can I possibly hold it together for him? And I don't trust him enough to allow him license to fend for me.

He suffers greatly from the breakup, as if he's fallen into a river of darkness, into a deep and fast current that's taking him out to some stormy sea. I'm surprised by the depths of his reaction. This is some trigger—this is more than just me.

I tell Gem I don't think it was love.

"Oh, he was in love with you, Pearl," Gem says.

"Wait, he was?"

"Two souls, a single body," Gem says. "It was there."

Were we a single body inhabiting two souls? Were we? What is love? I know there's a difference between special romantic love and universal love. I know I have flashes of universal love for Saint. I think of the love in that single stitch. I think of universal love that's for the greatest and highest good for everyone, and how selfish romantic love can be. I think they must be two different kinds of love.

Love wasn't something that was demonstrated to me as a child. When you're surrounded by anger and threats of violence, you grow up confused. You grow up having no idea whatsoever what love looks like.

I'd promised myself I wouldn't be poor again. This broken promise is the universe's fault, and I resent it. I resent my sensitivity, my visions, my psychicness, and the entire world. The universe's abandonment bothers me more than not having enough food to eat.

Something happens when body parts don't work like they're supposed to. A deep grieving, a physical mourning as if for the death of a loved one.

Still, I have to work. I have to eat. I can't use my arms, but I must work. The Labor and Industry claim won't even cover the rent.

With what little arm power I have, I call an eight hundred number for psychics to try to work for them. Even in the psychic world there's a hierarchy. There are the phone psychics and the real ones who do healing. It's like the difference between being a street walker and working for an escort service, or maybe the difference between being a hooker and being a wife.

The assistant at 1-800-PSYCHIC schedules me to read for the boss. On the day of the interview, the boss calls me, a woman who sounds very New Jersey. The cards become punch drunk like a group of Irishmen coming out of a pub. The boss snorts when she laughs and guffaws when I'm right and hollers at the end, "Sister, you got the fucking job!"

I have enough arm strength to turn cards over. Every day, I sit cross-legged on my bed taking calls. Sometimes I'm on my back taking calls. These are rough customers, nothing like the professional, gentle people I read for at the bookstore. I feel like I've fallen backward yet again. Like the universe is punishing me for not listening to them the first time.

"Hello, you're speaking to Pearl. With whom am I speaking?"

"This is Addie," she says. Then she pauses and adds, "Ma'am."

"And to what do I owe this honor, Addie?"

"What? Ma'am I'm not sure what you're saying, you talking fancy like that."

"How can I help you?"

"Well, ma'am, to be honest with you, I've got myself a frying pan and I'm waiting for my cheating husband. And I'm going to bash him over the head with it."

"Addie."

"I'm going to kill that motherfucker." Pause. "Ma'am."

"Addie." Silence. "Addie?"

"Whadda yer magic cards have to say about that?"

"Put down the frying pan, Addie."

She snorts.

"Put it down. Have you put it down?"

"Nor for long."

I flip over cards. Her archetypes look like a Goya painting with dark, shadowed faces and jester-like haunted characters. But there's a depth there, too, a beauty in the darkness. "Now, you love him, right? It says here you love him."

"Yes, ma'am. And right now, I hate him too."

"It says you've got to try talking to him. And remember you have to love yourself, too. If you love yourself you don't want to put yourself in jail, right? So you have to set limits and tell him your limits."

"I'll give him limits right to his head." The words belie her voice—she's softening.

"Are you ready to hear me?"

"I'm listening, ma'am."

"Good, now tell me what's been going on, and let's see if we can't get your spirit guides to help us."

Day after day, the question I get most often is "Is he coming back?" The question came when I read at the bookstore too, in many forms and guises, but here, it's the predominant query. Women spend hundreds of dollars to ask if their cheating boyfriend or abusive husband is coming back.

Why do you want him back?

I love him.

What is love? Define it for me.

The people are so hungry. Starving for love. Card after card, reading after reading, the guides show me the difference between universal love and romantic love. I'm not sure which we're all starving for, feelings of love for ourselves and the rest of humanity, or to feel special, or both.

You get the liars. They'll call and see if you'll catch them in the falsehood.

"I think my boyfriend is cheating on me," a woman says.

"What's your name?"

"Babs."

"It says in the cards, Babs, no. It says no. He's not cheating on you."

"I DON'T EVEN HAVE A BOYFRIEND," Babs screams and slams down the phone.

They're paying per minute, so if you don't instantly cry, "It's a lie. You're testing me," they move on to another psychic.

Sometimes for several days in a row, I can't even do the telephone readings from the floor, as my back and arms have no strength. To get to the fridge for food, I cling to the wall for support. I hold my bladder for as long as I can to avoid the bathroom.

One night it comes to a head. I'm scared. I'm crying. I've had enough. I can't go on like this. I can't survive being myself. Feelings boil up from the depths. It goes on all night. It's like another level of the dark night.

Live.

Or die.

Near dawn, I cry to the cracked ceiling, "I surrender. I surrender."

Just tell me what to do, and I'll do it, God or Higher Power or Creator or Goddess or whatever you want to be called. Guide me and I'll listen. I'll never doubt you again. Just tell me what to do!

XIX
THE SUN

CHAPTER 19

The Sun

From this day forward, I listen. Overlisten. Hypervigilant. I listen to the spirit guides, to the messages. I listen to my body. I have longer phases where my back is stable. I eat healthy food. I stop sneaking cigarettes. I drink more water. This is a big message I keep getting: Drink more water. More. More. Your body is water, and your soul is fluid. I stop drinking alcohol again. I take long Epsom baths by candlelight. I thank my body parts.

I've been working hard since I was ten years old, and the inactivity induces boredom. Witless. Mindless. Boredom. I can only sit on and off for about four hours to do the phone tarot.

Most days I have eight hours to fill. I try walking the neighborhoods but can't for more than an hour because the movement starts tweaking my back, and now that I'm listening to my body, I refuse to push it. I can't really go out anywhere without the option of being able to lie on my back with little notice.

I go stir crazy. So much space around me, a great quieting. Space from other people, space from the trauma of the news in the newsroom, space from going out even to shop, space from boyfriends, space from hot sex. The boredom stretches, evolves. As weeks become months, my mind settles like murk in a stream. There's something going on behind the chaos. Some wisdom. Some knowledge. I wonder if the illness, the boredom isn't some kind of blessing, the loss of the use of my arms isn't some kind of miracle. My mind has never been so quiet.

I stare at my hands, these often useless appendages now hanging from useless arms. You don't realize how deeply important your arms and hands are until they are no more.

How do we use our hands? Rayne's bejeweled fingers throwing tarot cards. The hands of the women in the newsroom working a furious keyboard. The labor of my ancestors, the weeding, the plucking. A woman across the country holding a frying pan as a weapon. The hands that do healing with massage or craft pots out of mud. And in my darker moments, I think of the hands of abusers. The hands of the addicts. My father. Meghan. Hands that do harm.

My hands are idle. I'm from peasant stock, and idle hands are the devil's plaything.

I come across an old piece of cardboard. I sit on the floor and trace one of my hands. I curve the pencil around the bone in my wrist, up my thumb, around every finger, a caress. I cut out the cardboard hand and stare at it for a day.

I tear up some old fairy tale books. Elmer's glue. I collage the hand with fairy tale symbols, the princess and the pea, a castle in the palm, a pea up the pinky, a crown on the thumb.

There's a sudden noise. I move my project out of the way just in time for plaster to fall from the top of the wall and crash to the hardwood. There's a hole now up toward the ceiling between my place and Gem's.

"Holy shit!" I scream.

"Hey neighbor," Gem says. She raises her hand and I can see it through the hole.

"You're home!"

"Yes, I just got back."

"I'll call the landlord," I yell.

I hold the Princess and the Pea Mystical Hand up for Gem to see through the hole.

"Fuck, you *are* an artist," she calls.

Day after day, I trace fingers, thumb, and wrist, collaging a dozen hands, two dozen, waiting for a landlord who never shows up.

Gem comes over with clothespins and string. She runs the string across the walls and over the windows. She uses the pins to hang the hands around the studio apartment. The Mystical Hands like a baby's mobile dance in the breeze from the ceiling fan as I lie on the floor and watch them.

Gem finishes and says, "Your apartment is starting to look a lot like mine."

Two weeks later, there's a knock. Finally the landlord to fix the wall. It's Gem with some guy. She lets herself in with her key so I don't have to get off my back. He's different from the rest of her men. His own person. He emanates something into the room. His hair is actually blue black and flows down and hides his face.

The young man swims among the mobile hands. The way he moves his body is like a fish, like someone who lives in water. I want to know him but he's Gem's.

He takes down one of the hands. Fish in the sea on the wrist, land mammals in the palm, and birds flying up each finger. I had Gem pick me up some shellacking fluid to harden and make the hands shine.

When the boy leans over to show me the hand, I catch a glimpse of his face. He has the high cheekbones and coloring of someone who is possibly Native American.

"How much?"

"You don't need to do this," I say, wanting to lift my hand and touch the liquid brilliance of his face. "Gem, you put him up to this."

She puts her hands up. "I didn't. I swear."

"You have something against selling your art?" he asks. He's looking at me, and I'm falling into the black puddles of his eyes.

Gem says, "Two hundred fifty."

"Gem!" I cry.

The guy takes out his wallet. It's filled with cash. You never know how much you love looking at piles of cash until you don't have any. He counts out the money and puts it beside me, and the bills brush my cheek like a kiss.

"I may want another one. I'll get your number from Gem."

He turns at the door to say goodbye. He has the Mystical Hand pressed to his heart. Gem is behind him mouthing, "Wow," and doing fist pumps.

As the door closes, another section of the wall crashes down. The hole now is about the size of two hands.

I call the landlord and wait, but he never comes.

Over the next few months, I try to make more money. I take other online jobs, any telecommuting job where I can talk to people on the phone, customer service, that sort of thing. But the computer is hell for my back and even the most well-meaning boss can't keep me on when there are days I simply can't show up at the computer to do my work.

I go online. It's so much paperwork, too much for my arms. Only thirty percent of the claims are approved anyway, and it'll take a year for anything to happen. I decide applying for disability isn't really an option.

What I really miss is my writing. I long for the parts of me that come out in the writing process, the parts that have nowhere else to go. I long for my writing like a missing lover. On the hardwood, I cry for this loss. *Am I a writer if I can't use my hands? Am I a writer if I can't write? Who am I if I'm not a writer?* I stare at the cracks in the ceiling, counting and recounting the cracks.

On the floor, I daydream of flying. I see myself skydiving, remembering the year I spent in Missouri jumping from a plane. This was before tandem jumping became a trend. We weren't attached to an experienced jumper. This was solo, chutes pulled by static line. You had to climb the plane's strut and dangle from it until you were told to let go. I freaked out the first time and wrapped my arms and legs around the strut and wouldn't let go and the jumpmaster thought I was going to die.

I jumped though. In the end, I jumped. I spent a year jumping, a year flying. It was what gave me the courage to leave the soil I grew up on, to leave my ancestors, to travel the world.

I learned to fly, I think. *I learned to fly!* A story comes to me in full poetic force. I can't get up to write it down. I can't even scribble it on napkins. It's my skydiving story. Not just memories, but poetry and metaphor, a short story. I know this feeling, this urge. It happens when a story is ready to be born, and all I have to do is push, but the baby's coming too fast and I have no arms to carry it.

Story, slow down! I demand. *Please, slow down.*

The first sentence comes to me. *"Get your feet out and stop," the jumpmaster said over the rumbled scream of the engines, over the howl of the seventy-mile-an-hour wind.*

I memorize it word for word. Repeat it again and again. Now, the second sentence.

The three strangers in the plane's dark belly watched me with deer eyes.

I repeat out loud the first and second sentences. And repeat again. And again, until they're etched into my flesh.

Then the third sentence.

In slow motion, I swung my legs out. The wind took my boots like misfit toys, flew them backward and knocked them against the plane's metal. Rat a tat tat. Rat a tat tat.

I repeat the first and second sentences and add the third. I repeat all three out loud until they're embedded in my memory. I keep going. These aren't just verb, subject, object, but a song of the soul. I memorize four sentences, five, six, twenty-five, sixty, repeat and repeat them.

Hours and days later it grows to a full story: "I Learned to Fly." A story that's not on the page but memorized now in my soul.

Would that story even have emerged if I was able-bodied? Did the soul need the body out of the way to speak with such purity? I fade into sleep, promising myself that someday I would type that story up, and someday I would get it published.

I break down and call my mother. We have no relationship. I try to ease into the conversation. I ask about Jack. The twins.

I never call her. I didn't call her after I saw Meghan. What would be the point? But I'm calling her now, and it's for money, and I know how wrong that is.

When we're ready to hang up, I tell her about my arms, about not being able to afford food. She isn't particularly sympathetic or she doesn't really hear me. I'm not sure. We have no connection. You need connection to be heard. Out of sight, out of mind. I'm just a voice from the past who refuses to stay in touch. She has her own problems.

She asks for my address. I give it to her. I hang up, knowing what she's thinking: *Pearl never calls me. She only wants money.*

Six days later I receive a letter from her. The envelope is thick—there's more than a just a letter inside. As Gem hands it to me, I say with a cracking voice, "My mother finally came through."

Gem sits next to me. "Yay, mama bear," she says. I stare at the letter for a long time. "Well, open it."

I have enough arm strength today. I rip the envelope and the contents spill onto the floor. Photographs. Eight of them. A handwritten note. I shake the envelope. Nothing else. I pick up one of the photos and Gem picks up another. They show my mother outside with a white sedan. She holds the door open, smiling toward the camera. She leans against the hood. She sits in the front seat. She has her arms out, stretching bumper to bumper.

I read the letter out loud. Jack bought her a new car. A Chrysler Prowler. Leather seats and cruise control. There's no other message.

"You talked to your mother about how you couldn't afford to eat, and she sent you pictures of her modeling with her new car?" Gem asks.

"Welcome to my mother," I say.

I know my mother. She's showing me that I'm poor, but she has Jack. She has a man, and a woman who has a man will never want for anything. A woman who has a man gets a new car, while a woman without a man starves.

"OK I get it now," Gem says, but I barely hear her. I'm falling into some kind of pit. "I don't think I got the level of massive head fuck going on in your family before, but I get it now. Pearl? Pearl?"

I'm sinking. My arms have stopped working. I'm a baby wanting to lift my arms to my mother, to be held, but she won't lift me; she won't hold me.

Gem brings tea. "I can help you figure out the money," she says.

This is about more than just money. And she knows that. And I know that. All the money in the world can't fix this.

One morning I wake, and my back is fragile, but I'm relatively OK. I turn on the small black-and-white TV for some companionship. In the kitchen, I look for food. The fridge is bare.

I have no more money coming in for a week. I open a cupboard. There's only one can. I take it out. Black-eyed peas. I hate black-eyed peas. Black-eyed peas remind me of being poor in Missouri. It's the food of the rural and the redneck. This can of black-eyed peas is all I have left in the world. And I hate it.

I wrap my hand around the can, take it down the long hallway, carry it to the bathroom, into the living room. I sit on the steamer chest, holding the can like a baby.

I start crying.

On the TV, an announcer says, "Ladies and gentlemen, let me introduce the amazing, the incredible, Black Eyed Peas."

I think it's a joke, some cosmic farce. Or that I'm hearing things. That I'm making it up. Through foggy eyes, I watch a band enter. They start to play. I listen to the music. They're incredible. I have no idea if they've been around for long because I don't keep up with trends. I know that I've never heard of them until this moment.

I hold the can toward the TV and burst out laughing. I stand up and dance to the music with my can of peas. I laugh and dance. I lean forward in great belly laughs full of dancing gods and wise jingling fools and cans of odd-tasting legumes.

"I get it!" I yell. I can still be great. It has nothing to do with money. It doesn't even have to do with the body. Money doesn't define me. Even my body doesn't define me.

Greatness is voice and expression and love. Greatness is soul. Love is found in a single stitch.

"Are you losing your mind in there?" Gem yells through the hole in the wall.

"A mind is a wonderful thing to lose," I yell back.

Since I cried uncle to the universe, I'm trying to listen to every spiritual urge and follow it. The term "purpose" keeps popping into my head.

You want me to explore purpose, universe? Sure, whatever you say!

I get books on finding purpose. I tarot on the concept of purpose. I journey on purpose. I do past-life regressions on purpose. What is my purpose on this planet? Is it to read tarot? What does purpose mean as a writer of fiction? The word "voice" keeps sounding through me. For weeks, voice comes to me on dry land and floats to me on the water of my dreams.

Days later, the phone rings. The man on the line keeps using the word "voice." It's synchronicity and serendipity and I can't quite figure out if I'm in a dream. He tells me he's from Labor and Industry. They have a word processing software where they can train me to use my voice.

He comes to teach me the software, and I'm an infant learning how to speak. Step by step, I speak words into text. I voice in words that become sentences that turn into paragraphs.

I'm used to my thoughts traveling through my fingers, onto a keyboard and onto the screen. Thoughts going through the hands create a certain story. Now that I sit with headphones, speak, and watch words magically appear on the screen, I'm learning how different the flow of the writing is when it travels directly from the vocal chords. I'm seeking my authentic creative voice and finding it now even more as I speak. Dialogue becomes nuanced and giddy and sometimes even cruel. It's like I'm singing my stories into being. My stories loosen up. My stories become my body. I become a torso of plot, fingers of characters, toes of setting. My body opens.

I voice my memorized story "I Learned to Fly" into the computer. I realize it's the last story of my first novel, and I use my voice to cut and paste it into my first book.

What is voice? What does it mean to find or recover our voice? Especially as women, what does it mean to have a voice? I know from the deep work of the tarot that some women think it's being loud like men. But I know that the voice of the Divine Feminine is often gentle and soft, full of beauty and spirit.

How might I use my voice? If I can't use my body, how might my voice support me? Poet? Songwriter? Novelist?

Artist? Teacher? *How can I use my voice to make a living?* Day after day I implore the universe. *How?*

★ ★ ★

The older woman leads me to a gleaming wooden table in the dark library full of tall wooden shelves and thousands of books lined to the ceiling. The aroma is of musty ancient texts. Stained-glass windows tint the light the color of rainbows. A beam of yellow light falls upon an open ledger on the table. The woman extends her hand toward it as an invitation.

I lean over it and study the markings. They seem to be in another language, an alphabet I don't recognize. She comes beside me and reads it for me. As she does, I can read it too. It's a program that I'm to teach to others, written out for me step by step. The ancient words are like a life I've lived before. In this tome is the essence of unlocking the creative voice.

I wake from the dream. How the spirits answer your pleadings in dreams and visions. I go to my computer, voice in the curriculum I've been given: eight practical steps full of soul. Storytelling as personal mythology. Storytelling as excavation of voice.

I spend the next few days contacting university extension programs. A local university is interested. I set up three evening classes a week, two hours each. I pray and pray that my back and arms can handle standing up for two hours. The money won't cover everything, but it's at least something. *This is what happens when you listen to your guides,* I think.

Men and women, young and old. The first class is full, and I stand before them, humbled. I have them introduce themselves. A recently homeless kid sits next to an elderly woman in a pillbox hat. There's a wealthy woman, the daughter of English professors, on one side of the room, and a white-trash woman (her words) who was raised in a trailer park on the other. I feel overwhelmed with love. Inclusive is just a word until it isn't.

We're in a sixth-grade classroom, and the adults are wedged into kids' desks. I think it's appropriate because we all need a reeducation based on nurturing instead of competition. Around the walls, inspirational words are written on pieces of construction paper: Help Someone, Don't Bully, Be Kind.

The lecture comes flowing out of me as if from somewhere else, as if I'm just the channel and all I have to do is get out of the way.

"Think of three events that happened to you before the age of twelve that you can't get out of your minds. An event you tell at dinner parties, to friends, one that's become family folklore. For the purposes of this exercise, we're looking for an event that lasted a few hours. For example, we're not talking about how every summer you went to your grandmother's farm and helped out, but rather something that happened one day during one of those summers. Write a brief paragraph about these three events." I warn them not to choose a traumatic story because it may shut them down. Someone raises their hand. "What if it was all traumatic?"

"Choose a more recent story, then. Too much trauma at first, and you could block your whole creative process. That doesn't mean you can't write about the trauma later, when you're more grounded."

I've never felt so confident. I tell them to pick one story, turn to the person next to them and tell it.

The storytelling begins, the classroom a cacophony of voices. I walk around. In the corner of the room is a large aquarium that houses a snake. It's supine when we start but begins moving as the class heats up.

I overhear the trailer park woman tell the story of her mother, who chained the refrigerator so the kids wouldn't eat all the food while she was at work. One of her brothers wedged it open enough so that the tiniest sister could climb inside. The student's memory is of a tiny hand popping out from inside the fridge holding a piece of bologna.

The elderly woman remembers sitting shiva for her father's funeral. The tattooed boy with a crew cut talks about traveling from coast to coast with his girlfriend and the day their cat disappeared.

The daughter of English professors tells of being a child on a small pond in a rowboat all by herself because her father for the first time allows her to row out alone.

As I walk around between the desks, I notice that many of the women are telling stories that happened to their fathers, grandfathers, and brothers, stories where they were just the witness. Most of the women aren't choosing stories about themselves.

I go to the head of the class.

"Everyone, could you stop for a moment?" The storytelling continues, and I have to repeat my request. "Everyone. Hello!"

"As women, we must tell our own stories. Not our father's stories and not our brother's stories. Let's take a moment and make sure we have a story we were actively involved in. Choose a story where you were the key player."

A middle-aged woman raises her hand. "The only stories I have are about them."

"Are you sure? Maybe the boy stories are the only ones that became family folklore, the only ones that were repeated over and over. Is that possible?

"Let's take five minutes more for people to ponder their stories. What you choose is important because we're going to spend eight weeks developing it."

I walk around. A few of the women show me sentences they've written down about events in their lives. They're starting to get it. I kneel by one woman and help her figure out a story to use. What does it mean for women that even our stories aren't our own?

"OK, let's get back to sharing our stories. And I want the women to note how often the events of their lives aren't seen as family mythology. How we go through these times and there's no oral record of events. This is what we're trying to change. Women's lives and stories matter."

The class goes back into wild multilayer discussion of their stories. The students are like excited puppies, tumbling over each other to be heard. I notice the snake is writhing up the sides of his glass cage and think, *The snake knows something's going on.* Five minutes later, a woman opens the classroom door and summons me.

"Yes?" I say.

"Could you guys please keep it down? My class can't focus from all the noise."

"Everyone, OK, let's end our discussion. Apparently our stories are so raucous they're bothering the other classes. That's how powerful your stories are!" The class bursts into laughter.

I ask for hands to share their stories. One young man raises his. He looks like a typical Pacific Northwest guy in his late twenties: flannel shirt, boots, beard.

"It's a story about the time my dad and I went hunting."

"Good. Go on."

"I was about eleven, I guess. We went up into the Cascades looking for deer. Snow up to our knees. We didn't see anything all day. When the sun was setting, we came to these hunters' cabins. Any hunter can use them. I guess my dad led us there for the night. We built a fire in a wood stove with some wood left over by the last hunter. The sun went down. We went to sleep in our sleeping bags on these slat bunks. Me on the top bunk.

"I woke up in the middle of the night. It was so dark, but I could just make out my dad in his white long johns. He was kneeling by the window. I moved the curtain and looked out. The moon was glowing everything so white, and there was a doe in the moonlight between these massive red cedars. It was so amazing, like a painting, silver and peaceful.

"I heard a gunshot and jumped. The sound in the cabin was like a bomb going off. I looked over and Dad's gun was pointing out the window. He'd shot the doe. I looked out and the deer was down. The whole time, I was thinking it was like a dream."

I want to jump and clap my hands. This is what I'm finding in all of their stories, locked inside are the themes of a lifetime. The love for a father, a boy being shown what it means to be a man. His father has his own story to tell, the deer its truth, the landscape a narrative, too. I tell them that as the class continues over the next few weeks, we'll be exploring what was going on with the other characters in the story, too.

We listen to a few more students' stories that are just as good. Authentic. Delving. It's working. The program is working.

The subjects they choose to write about are archetypal: love, hope, family, children. The first time she rode her bike.

The birth of his brother. The birthday gift he got from his mother. Some are sad. Some are happy. All are full of the pathos of a life.

I tell them, "Go home, sit down, and in one session write out your stories beginning to end. Don't worry about grammar, spelling, or punctuation. This is a rough draft."

I give them two other assignments: Find photos from the time period to refresh their memories and explore the social context around the event—what else was happening in their lives or the lives of any of the other characters in the story? In their parents' lives? What was happening in their town? In the country? In the world? How does that context affect the story? Do some research. If you can't find actual pictures of the event, go online and find pictures of that time period. We want to immerse you in the imagery to bring back the memories.

All night the students dance in my dreams. I dream their stories, their souls, their mythology. I realize that I'm a good teacher.

The next week in class, the students are back and they're excited. The daughter of professors has her hand up immediately. She holds up a photo. I go over and take a look. A little girl sits in a boat in the middle of a tree-lined pond. Just her small, white face in a sea of green.

"I was looking at the photo, and . . ." she starts to tear up, this woman in her forties in cat-eye glasses and sensible shoes. "I saw the rope." She passes the photo around. "The boat was tied up all the time. My dad let me go on the boat by myself for the first time, and I thought I was out there floating by myself, but I was tethered."

"Why does that make you emotional, Katherine?" I ask.

"It wasn't the photo alone. When I started researching the context, I put together a timeline of events at around that age." I find tissues on the teacher's desk and hand her one. "I realized that this picture was taken when my parents were going through a divorce." She's smiling. "I realize the rope was a metaphor for how my dad was going to be leaving the house, but he would still be there for me."

I turn to the class. "This is a perfect example of how context can shift the telling of our stories." We go around the class and have others describe their contexts.

I split them into groups of four so they can share their photos and discuss their stories. As they talk, I can see their stories fly up and out like angels and join some greater collective story, their voices joining lyrics of some bigger song.

I discuss characterization, a different level of context. We often tell our stories first just from our own perspectives, our own points of view. I pass out characterization analysis sheets and have them take them home to start to process what's going on with other characters in their stories.

To the hunter's son, I ask, "Who is your father? What was going on in his life? How will that deepen or even change the story around his shooting a deer from the window?"

I'm learning just as much as my students. Teaching the lessons teaches me. I sit at my computer, thinking of my own father. His rage. His trauma. And I start to wonder, *Who was he, really*?

A few weeks later an envelope arrives.

"Open it," Gem says.

I turn it over and over.

"Oh my God, open it," she repeats.

Finally I rip it open. I've been accepted into the MFA program for fiction at the university. I applied a couple of months earlier. They received 1,500 applicants and chose only six people.

The stress of excitement seizes me up. I lie on the floor to celebrate.

This is what the universe was asking me to do. This is my purpose: to be a writer and teacher. I feel intense pangs of emotion that I've finally found myself.

I set up meetings at the university to speak to one of the professors. I want to find out how to go through the program if my arm problems flair up. I want to make sure I'll be able to complete the assignments using voice software.

I bike to the campus. My back and arms have been stable now for a few weeks, and I'm tentatively biking again. The exercise is necessary to keep me sane.

I can see the university at the end of the street when the panic attack hits. Every foot I inch forward on my bike intensifies my panic. I would laugh if I could. I can see the campus but can't get to it—it's like some cosmic joke.

This would be a great time to listen to my body, but I don't. It's trying to tell me something, but what it's saying is against what I desire. I press on. I'm going to be late. I'm never late.

I pull over, place my head between my legs, gasp for air. I don't have the time to stay this way, so I get back on my bike and start pedaling, but the panic attack comes on with such force that I have to pull into a gas station. The panic will not subside.

While I'm staring at the building from a couple hundred yards away, I call them. I'm looking at the lawns of the east side of the university as I tell them that I'm sick and I can't come. They reschedule me for the following week.

I get home and tell Gem what's happened.

"I think the universe is trying to tell you something. Haven't you made a promise to listen?"

"What are they trying to tell me, do you think?"

"It doesn't sound like rocket science. You shouldn't go to graduate school."

"It's the only way as a writer I'll have a proper career!" I almost scream. "They told me to explore my purpose and that's what I'm trying to do, goddamnit!"

She says tentatively, "Maybe your purpose is something different?"

"Being a writer is already different enough," I holler. "I'm trying to follow my soul. Why can't I have what other people have?" I'm enraged at her, or the universe, or both.

"Normal." She does an exaggerated shiver.

I have so much rage at being the person I am, I want to punch a wall.

"There's nothing wrong with *not* being normal, Pearl," she says. "Maybe the fiction program is *too* normal."

The next week I make it to campus. I'm determined to push through. Besides meeting the professor, I'm sticking around afterward to meet a former grad student in the program, and after that I'm attending a student literary reading. There are no panic attacks this time, and I push away any feelings that arise—mostly a dullness that fogs my brain.

The professor is a hot guy in his forties in too-tight jeans. He reminds me of Saint: men who are artists who are aging and full of raw energy. His office is a train wreck, books and papers in pile upon pile. An entire section of the office, the only area with windows, is blocked off by bookcases, with no floor space for your feet. The light's blocked and the room is dark. He tells me he used to be a garbage man. He spreads his arms as if to say "and look where I am now!" He teaches short-story writing courses.

When he speaks, I hear what he's not saying. I can tell he doesn't like the metaphysical. Most of my stories are metaphysical. I sense he voted against my acceptance. Writing is such a personal process, and I don't feel he's rejecting my literary gifts, but me personally.

I can't imagine being taught by someone who hates the core of my voice. I can't imagine ending up with forty thousand dollars in student loans for the luxury of being ridiculed for who I am.

I talk to him about my arms, how I use voice software. He points at the sign hanging on the wall behind him. I look up. "No Whining," the sign reads, with a red circle around it and a red line through the words. I don't point out that the sign is a double negative.

As I leave, I think of my students, how fragile they are sharing their truth, how important a nurturing environment is. I could just imagine what being around someone who doesn't believe in them would do to their creative voices. What would that do to their spirit? When I was little, no one told stories. We weren't allowed to talk. I knew so little about Mother's and Father's childhoods. I promised myself then that in my presence, everyone would be allowed to speak, to voice their truths no matter what they were. I promised myself even as a child I'd hold the space for people to tell their stories.

As I look back at the professor, I wonder what the system is like that's created this energy. Is it that competitive? Is there not room for every voice?

I find the other professor I'm scheduled to speak to around the corner. Her door is open, her back to me as she works on her computer.

"Hello, Ms. Hill?"

"Yes?" She turns around briefly to look at me but then turns back to her monitor.

"We had an appointment."

"Yes, come in." She points to a chair, then turns sideways and looks at her computer, and then at me. Beside her a pile of papers.

"You look busy," I say.

"You have no idea," she says.

She has blonde curly hair with just a hint of gray.

"Go on," she says, but she's looking at her computer.

"Me?"

"Yes."

I tell her about my arm condition. "What I'm really worried about is the workload and whether or not I can manage it."

She's reading paperwork now beside her keyboard.

"We have a computer lab, perhaps they can help you."

She looks up at me, but her eyes aren't present.

"Where's the lab?"

"Oh, it's on campus. It's not hard to find. Just ask anyone."

I sit without saying anything as she turns to type, click, click, clack. She looks down to read papers next to her keyboard again, puts a finger on the paper to keep her place, and turns her head to me.

“Is there anything else?”

“No.” I get up and stand at the doorway, wanting to see if she’ll turn around, just look at me. I think of Rayne telling me about the old paradigm and how frustrating it would be for me.

I find the computer lab, a small building with old machines. The guy in charge has no idea if voice software will even work on them or how I’d manage it. He’s busy and doesn’t have much time to talk.

The coffee shop is on University Ave, rundown and stinking of antiseptic cleaner and urine. A murder of homeless teens gathers against the shop’s wall, dreadlocked, tattooed, dark, exhausted. “Ave rats,” as Seattleites call them. I give a girl with a broken guitar a dollar.

A woman sits alone at a table in the middle of the shop. “Are you Samantha?” I ask. She nods. “Pearl,” I say. I hold out my hand and we shake. She’s large and wears a shirt that she tugs at because it doesn’t fit her well.

I grab a latte. The barista created a heart in the foam and it’s the first good feeling I’ve had all day. All I know about Samantha is that she went to the university’s fiction program. It was Coral who suggested I talk to her.

At the table we talk about the program.

“I lie about it,” she says. “I say I graduated, but I didn’t finish. I dropped out midway through the first semester of the second year.”

“What happened?”

She tugs at her shirt. “It was like I didn’t exist. Like everything I thought and felt, everything I wrote, didn’t fit, and I didn’t exist.” I pull tissue-paper-thin napkins from the dispenser just for something to do. I think of the professor's "No Whining" sign.

"I now have to work overtime to pay back my student loans, so I don't have much time to write. That is, if I could still find my voice." She tugs her shirt furiously, like she's fighting to get someone off of her.

Information channels through me as if I'm reading tarot. I feel a great need to help this woman.

"Did you know I used to be a journalist?"

She shakes her head no.

"If you're a reporter on hard news stories like rape or hate crimes or politics, you're thought of as a serious journalist. If you're a features writer and you cover art, you're soft news, less than. This same concept is at work here too, I can feel it, but I'm just not exactly sure how. Feminine truth not just ignored but actively dismissed. I know that a lot of women succeed as fiction writers, so I'm really talking about this on a deeper level. Divine Feminine is about cultivating and not comparing, something about art as process instead of art as product. It has to do with hierarchy versus a holistic approach. It has to do with how the patriarchy has decided what is and isn't storytelling. It has to do with the commodification of creativity. It has to do with an old system that goes by the rules of special, elite, exclusive. It has to do with a new system of inclusivity and oneness that no one thinks matters but is the only thing that will save us."

I'm given this information in one brain dump and now will need to spend the rest of my life figuring out what I just said.

Samantha is kneading a napkin into pulp. "I've been meditating on what the hell went wrong at that school for two years, and everything you just said is what I came to understand, too. I just can't stop feeling sad all the time."

I tell her it's probably not only her own sorrow she's feeling, that she's probably feeling the heartache of centuries of women.

"I have no idea where we fit, Samantha. I just don't know how to make it in this world that seems so upside down to everything I believe."

Later I go to the university building where they're holding the fiction reading by the second-year MFA students. I desperately want to go home, so tired I feel like crawling back to my bike, but I promised myself I'd see this day through, no matter what.

There are about fifteen people in the audience in folding chairs, grad students in a row of chairs in front of us. The lights are too bright and the shadows too stark. The first reader is a young woman. Her story is about her boyfriend. She's in her dorm room, lying on her bed, thinking about her boyfriend, waiting for her boyfriend. It goes on and on, this waiting and pondering, this dry dorm room, this boring subject. *Get off the damn bed and do something,* I want to yell at her. I think of my tarot clients and their perpetual question: "Is he coming back?"

I've already traveled the world. I've already had a career. What do I care about this girl and her boyfriend? It's not just her story. The energy in the room feels oppressive. Worse, it feels "special." Like only the few on the dais are the elite, the writers, the chosen few. I don't want to be one of the chosen few. I believe everyone has the right to tell their stories, everyone has a right to have their voices heard.

I stay for all the readers but nothing touches my heart. And then I go home.

XX
JUDGEMENT.

CHAPTER 20

Judgment

The battle in me rages for days and then weeks. I'm going to say no to the university, but how dare I? I can see my writing career stretch out in front of me, and without an MFA, where will it lead? Why do I not fit, even here with other writers? It's so confusing to me.

I feel pulled out of my body when I think of joining the university. I feel pulled out of my knowing. That's the sense I get, of a pulling, a yanking, of someone above me taking my power from the top of my head. It feels like I'd have to give them my inner knowing in exchange for a place at the literary table. I have dreams of published writers around a conference table, looking at me over their shoulders. There's no place for me to sit, no place for the real me at the table. I'm invited in, but only if I give up being me. Even here, I stand outside, looking in. Why?

I go to Rayne. Outside her office an ice cream truck is circling the block. It passes her window at intervals, with the haunting sounds of "Turkey in the Straw" playing in a loop, then fading, then loud again and full of hope, like a childhood dream.

She throws a Celtic Cross spread, gives me a rose quartz to hold onto, and I clutch it in my palm.

"Do you remember the last thing I said to you at our last reading? That the old ways are not good for you anymore, that they just won't work? The program is too critical. The people will be too critical, too brain focused, and not heart or soul focused. It won't be nurturing. Do you understand?"

I think of Samantha. I think of her shirt and how it bothered her, but how she was like a flower and just needed to be watered.

"You're like a plant emerging from the soil, and they would critique how you emerge. How does critiquing a plant while it grows help it grow? It just grows."

"It doesn't make sense to me," I say. "Lots of women go to grad school for fiction and become successful novelists. What is my problem?"

"Some of us are called to be part of a new paradigm. How many ways do I need to say this so you can hear it?"

"OK, so what *is* my path then?"

The ice cream truck has parked directly outside the window and the music fills the room.

"It's going to present itself over time. But it says to look at the writing workshops you're teaching now. You're doing amazing work there. And with your tarot readings. You're already helping a lot of people. Look at what's working well now."

I think about inclusivity. Process. Cultivating and nurturing. Authentic selves being allowed out to play. The power of storytelling not just held in the hands of the few, but carried by the souls of many.

"I can't have a proper career teaching in extension programs. I make so little money. There's absolutely no career track."

"What if you just enjoyed it? What if you just kept teaching the way you're teaching and said screw the career track? What if you let it unfold?"

"I'm tired of being broke," I say.

She pulls more cards, starts laughing. "Don't yell at me, OK, over what I'm about to say. It says the good news is that you're an artist. The bad news is that you're an artist."

I snort. The ice cream truck pulls away, the music of our collective childhood fading.

We go to the Barca lounger for the shamanic journey. I close my eyes to the sound of her rattle and fall into a meditative state as she journeys. Even the cars honking outside seem to fade to silence.

When she returns, she says "OK," and I open my eyes just as she opens hers. Her eyes are big and round and shrouded in a mist, a mystery.

"I was in an African country, centuries ago. The guide is a dark-black man, tall, over seven feet, thin. We're in the sand at dusk next to a body of water, a bay, a lake, maybe the ocean. He's drawing in the sand with a stick."

I'm right there with her. I see him. He's so familiar to me, like he *is* me.

"He's saying to me, 'The sand has a voice. The ocean has stories. This is the true nature of storytelling.' His limbs and cheekbones are sharp. I hear the lapping water speaking next to him. There is no separation between this man and the ebb and flow of the sea. The way the moon pulls at the waters, the way it pulls at him. He says, 'The earth is telling stories all the time, the ocean's voice, liquid and moved by the moon. Water caressing stone, petting scales, mirroring the night sky. There are tales in the cadence of the rain.

"This is the art of storytelling, this ocean's voice," Rayne says, but her voice is my voice and his voice. "The words I'm giving it, Pearl, don't come close to the feeling coming from this man. He didn't say it, but I got in a deep way that he wanted to impart that there is a way of wisdom that has nothing to do with this world. This world is built on illusion—there is a wisdom that has nothing to do with university programs. Follow this old way. You already do, just stay rooted in it."

I let out an exhale. I have an unbelievable urge to write. My desire to write makes me feel like I'm going to burst out of my skin.

I get home, voice an email to the university. *Thank you, I cannot attend your program.* I know in my psyche now that someone else will be allowed in, and that's the right thing.

A reply is shot back within seconds, just one line. He isn't happy. "Well, have a good life then."

Something is off. I wonder why my decision to go another direction is so painful for *him*.

For the next two years, my life slowly turns around. There's something in saying no that creates a transformation. I learn to manage my body better—even though I still have episodes—and everywhere there seems to be healing. I take Rayne's advice and turn toward what's good in my life, acknowledge and nurture it until it blooms. I stop worrying about the word "career"; I own my meager income and no longer fight it. I make more friends, meet more healers, finally settle down.

My tarot work is flourishing. In my writing classes, I'm amazed by how much growth is happening for my students. I'm discovering a gift and passion for helping people excavate their authentic voices.

Still voicing in my first novel, I see all of the puzzle pieces come together, growing into seedlings and then flowering. The process pulls me in like a lover, my heart, my sex, my brains, my soul—everything is engaged in the writing like a full-bodied dance. I could see how this novel is my purpose, too, how one woman telling the journey of her life can change the world.

One day an editor from an airline magazine calls, the same editor Saint and I had worked for before.

"How'd you like to do an article on spas along the Canadian West Coast?" she asks. "I was supposed to do it myself, but I'm unfortunately scheduled for a minor surgery." She explains I'd be flown on a small plane to remote spas, receive treatments, and then write about each for the magazine.

"No!" I shout into the phone. "Sorry, and thank you," I say in a calmer tone. "I don't do journalism anymore." It's been years since I've done a journalism assignment.

"Are you sure?" she asks.

"Yes!" I don't tell her that I have no desire to rock a boat that's finally floating.

We hang up.

The phone rings again ten minutes later.

"Do you know what you're throwing away here?" It's the editor again.

The room around me seems to fill with light. I burst out laughing. Since I've been nurturing my life, whenever I have to make a decision and it's a good one, the room will fill with bright light. I've been following the light like it's a voice giving me directions.

"OK, I'll do it," I say.

"What?" I'm sure she expected a bigger fight.

"I'll do it. I said I'll do it, and I'll do it!"

I can hear her smile. "I'll have my assistant contact you with the details."

The small plane bounces among dark and bulbous clouds over the Pacific Ocean. Below us, the Canadian West Coast, tumultuous seas, rugged outcroppings, speckled inlets and islands, waves of vegetation-covered rocks that fade far into the distance.

There are six of us and the sky is stormy and there are sudden air pockets that send us and our stomachs up in nausea. I've been on a small plane like this a few times—the times I skydived in Missouri before I left, and once when Finn and I flew up into the Himalayas, both experiences life-altering.

We disembark at the small landing strip. We're in the middle of wild forest. The air is shocking in its clarity as it brushes against my face. I breathe like I haven't taken a breath in months. And I'm inexplicably sleepy, the way nature can remind you how tired you really are. I roll my luggage to the hangar, where a car is waiting, and have to stop myself from curling up on the nearby grass and sleeping for centuries. Sometimes we're tired from overwork, and sometimes we're tired because we're empaths and the toxic world is such a relentlessly tiring place.

I have my massage itinerary. What will follow are days of massages, wraps, indigenous cleanses, warm rocks, cold-water therapies, detox mud therapies, paraffin wax therapies, and something called chromotherapy.

I'm in the first treatment before I even have time to unpack. It's called The Elements Wrap: Fire, Water, Earth, and Air. It begins with a seaweed exfoliation, and then hot and cold water therapy. The treatment ends with warm stones lined up on my back. I lie there only now realizing how much I need to be touched like this, how needy I am for it.

A woman gives me a massage. I choose from a basket of massage oils, an oil infused with rosemary, lavender, and ylang-ylang. She first massages my hands and fingers. I grow emotional. How long has it been since someone has held my hand? Saint wasn't really a hand holder, and neither was I. Touch for me has always been confusing. As a child, I learned touch was conditional. I worried my hands carried the physical rage of my father. And when I touched someone, it seemed to double and even triple the psychic information I got from them.

There are other treatments. I'm slathered with mud, wrapped in linen. Essential oils envelope and hold me, lavender, cedar, sandalwood, patchouli, and citrus. Shirley sometimes had an essential oil diffuser going in her office, and I feel the love of her in the room. I can't imagine a life of using your hands this way, to bring comfort and healing to others. I grow weepy with the gentleness of therapist after therapist.

I can't drink enough water to refill what's being pulled out of me. That night, I finish by five, and I go to the hotel room and just want to go to bed. I have to remind myself that I'm writing an article and that I'm supposed to be taking notes. I've only gone to spas twice in my life before, both in London with Charlotte. Each time, we could only afford one treatment each. As a journalist, I would have never considered covering spas. I wrote stories about the disenfranchised, gave voice to the voiceless. I didn't believe in luxury journalism. I didn't even know how to write about it.

By the end of two days, and after traveling to different spas nestled deep within forests, I've been poked and wrapped, massaged and detoxed so much that I fear if another person touches me, I'll punch them.

One thing is clear: I need to do this physical healing. Desperately. My shoulders live up near my ears and are like twisted roots as the therapists massage the knots out. Trauma is locked in joints and tendons. My arms and back are damaged from all the fear I carry in my body. It's all just detoxing at once, and as I walk, I feel like I'm spewing toxins.

The third day, at another spa closer to the coast, the aesthetician starts by giving me a questionnaire that asks about color and my moods. Apparently this is chromotherapy, color therapy. I have to put a leash on my cynicism. For some reason, the notion of it brings up my orneriness.

"What colors do you see first thing in the morning?"

Gray. I live in Seattle. But I say instead, "Orange" and don't know why, and she writes it down. I tell her yellow is the color of midafternoon, and blue midmorning. Red is the hue of Sunday. Green the vibrancy of dawn. My name is lime colored. The month of October is purple. I laugh as she writes down what I'm saying. I feel like I'm losing my mind. *A mind is a wonderful thing to lose.*

She "calibrates a device" to reflect my answers. They lead me to a large room with a deep bath. I'm told to take off my clothes and immerse myself.

Hilarious, I think. My sardonic journalism brain starts a full-on laugh fest in my mind as I disrobe and lower myself into the bath. I don't know why this process is bringing up the cynic. I'm already so open to the metaphysical.

Yellow is flashed in the water, along my torso. An orange spotlight appears at my stomach. Then something happens. The entire room fills with light. It's like someone has switched on a bright light, and I think of that tiny stitch on Charlotte's jacket.

My perceptions break open into a kaleidoscope of color. My being becomes fractals of lemon, crimson, mauve. I'm not a physical body anymore, but a combination of color that's so porous my skin lets in light.

I feel van Gogh in the room. I think it with surprise: *van Gogh is in this room!* No longer are things made of lines, but of blocks of color, of dark and light. The color breaks me apart and redefines me. Do others have this reaction to chromotherapy, or is it just me? I think of seeing the art with Saint and how this is so similar. It's like a door that was slightly ajar in my psyche is suddenly thrust wide open.

It feels like I'm on an acid trip. The room shifts. It's no longer made of matter, and instead, energy and vibrational variations of the color spectrum. Everything breaks apart and dances in millions of molecules. I look at my hand and arm, and they're no longer flesh, but colored vibrating light. It's difficult to capture in words. It's preverbal. It's van Gogh's thick strokes, which alone make no sense, but layered on top of each other create a reality.

I am an artist. I am an artist. I am an artist.

Is it happening because I've been so emotionally and physically worked over by so many people during the past few days? I think of my initial skepticism—who was it who said the more true something is, the more the ego will rise up to resist it? Here in this bath, with blues washing up over my breasts and reds caressing my thighs, I'm not just an artist. I *am* art.

I'm stoned and babbling when I emerge from the magical room. The director is waiting for me in her office so I can do the interview. Through the window behind her is the spray of the rowdy sea, and when it hits the rocks, the water flashes red, yellow, green. I'm blown away by the sheer magic of our world.

I don't know how the interview goes. I'm so giddy. I keep slipping sideways in the chair. I scribble notes that later I can't read.

That night, I'm without borders or function as I lie on my hotel bed. I need to be writing but can only stare at the ceiling. What stays with me is how I was so sure when I called bullshit to the editor and when I called ridiculous to the color therapy. I was so *sure*. And I was so *wrong*.

Something else is going on here. I told each spa about my arm and back problems, and something is coming up. I can't put a finger on it, but something's ready to rear its monstrous head.

It's all *too* good. It is as if this editor who doesn't know me was directed to send me here by a benevolent universe so that I'd meet my artist self. It's like every treatment beforehand was set up to break me down so that these colors could transform me. *I am an artist*, I think, and I'm so terrified I feel like I might faint. This isn't a one-time decision, to own your purpose. The challenge to own it has come up so many times already, each time provoking fear and joy. It's scarier to think the universe is benevolent than to live in cynicism. So much more is at risk.

A miracle. I've spent my life calling bullshit to miracles. "There are none so blind as those who will not see." The problem is you have to learn to see. It takes new eyes.

Layla has a soft face and natural brown hair, and she looks like a thousand rainbows. This is the final spa. A driver brought me here, hours from the middle of the forest to this wild village in a temperate rainforest on the edge of a wilder ocean.

I had treatments at the spa, but now she's walking me down the beach to my final treatment of the entire trip. The wind whips our hair sideways, the ocean in a dance of cresting whitewater waves. The white-sand beach stretches for miles ahead and behind us, and the frothy Pacific Ocean leads out to scrubby islands bombarded by spray. It's fifty degrees and we're bundled in coats.

I merge with her as we talk. We go beyond the interview, discussing gardens and composting and sustainability. She tells me where the essential oils they use in the spa are farmed. Other voices echo as we talk. It's as if I'm speaking not just to her, but also to the land, conversing with the wide stretches of beach and the islands in the distance. I think of the tall, thin African man in Rayne's shamanic journey and how the waves themselves are telling us a story.

Layla is awash with color that bleeds and dances and forms and re-forms. I'm not sure what she sees, but for me the place is alive with color; the sand and sea and far-off islands swell with burnt orange and turquoise, browns and forest greens.

We come to a hut right on the beach. Two young men in white shirts and trousers greet us. Layla introduces them and tells me they'll give me a Lomi Lomi massage.

She leaves, and while we talk, I sit in a wicker chair facing a wooden door open to the ocean. The spray carries on the wind and tickles the flesh. The men explain Lomi Lomi to me.

"It is massage with intention and prayer," one says.

"Sacred work to exorcise the dark," the other says.

"If you were a plant, what plant would you be?" the first asks. I'm hypnotized by the ocean.

"Wisteria. I like how its beauty crawls and surrounds."

"What animal would you be?"

"Black panther," I say. "Physical and ancient in feline wisdom."

I'm surprised by my answers.

The young men are forms of color, too, one more purple and dark, and the other a green yellow.

"We use palms, forearms, elbows, sticks, and stones," Green Yellow says.

Purple hands me a basket of emollients, and I'm to choose one. I choose sage and peppermint, and he laughs but doesn't explain why. He asks me, "What kind of tree are you, if you are a tree?"

"Weeping Willow," I say, thinking of the tree whose arms I slept beneath when I was a child, when I ran away to find Meghan.

I undress behind a screen to the sound of crashing waves, and I think, *What if all life could be like this, a dancing wind, a poetry of thought, the land as flesh? How would our lives be different?*

The massage is so sexy, both men mixing color into my flesh, that I'm in pain with how turned on I am. I'm writing an article. I need to be professional, and I do all I can to not groan, although two or three escape my lips before I can stop them.

"You are holding on so tight," Green Yellow says. "So tight to the pain, so tight to the past." He moves hand, forearm, and elbow the full length of my back. He says again, "So tight. You're holding on so tight."

I feel like crying, but that would be taboo. *Be professional.* It gets so bad, I'm so on edge, that I keep repeating *be professional, be professional, be professional* to myself over and over.

Afterward, they give me a robe and leave, and I sit by the open door and watch myself be turned over by the waves, turned and turned, until I'm nothing but water.

Somehow that evening I find myself in a trailer farther down the beach. Somehow I'm here getting Reiki certified. There's such a magic to this place that things happen, and you're guided and you don't even know how you got there.

When I went on my metaphysical walkabout years ago, several people told me to pursue Reiki certification. They said I don't have to practice Reiki on others but that the certification has a way of aligning all of this energy that's coursing through my body.

Maya is part Jamaican, hair like a halo, skin warm and rich. Colors pop and dangle from the rugs and fabrics thrown over sofas and chairs. I feel the residuals of the old depressed Pearl lingering, and at the same time I'm as giddy as a little girl at a birthday party.

I'm sitting on a sofa, a handmade mug full of fat green tea leaves in my lap. Maya is describing what Reiki is, and after the first few sentences, I can barely hear her. There's a noise like the ocean in my ears. This happens sometimes when something is big and powerful.

She tells me how the founder of Reiki traveled the world to learn how Jesus did healing by the laying on of hands, and how he wanted to share that process with others. She gives me reading material to take back to the hotel.

"For the next few days, we'll be studying Reiki symbols, Kanji that are used as sort of power symbols." She hands me a workbook so I can practice them. I realize I need to find the pilot and put back my departure. I'm going to be here for days.

I find the symbols easy because of my time studying Kanji in Tokyo. It's dark when I finally leave Maya's trailer. She gives me a flashlight. I hear coyotes howl as I walk down the deserted beach, stars overhead, the tang of the sea. I've never felt so animal and so alive.

I find a cabin to rent in the middle of the temperate rainforest, the ocean a ten-minute walk away. I can't stay at the hotel because the magazine's no longer footing the bill. Everything out of doors is perpetually wet and strikingly old. Over me in the bed is a skylight that looks out on branches and stars, and I feel like I'm in an old Japanese scroll painting.

The second day after the training with Maya, I wake up beneath the skylight and sit up suddenly in bed. It's like when the novels came to me all at once, but now, I feel like there are spirits around me, and they're lobbing white balls of light at me that are entering my chakras.

In the light are the Reiki symbols. Spirits are lobbing sacred symbols into my flesh. Symbol after symbol enters my heart as a ball of light.

When it's over, when the room grows dark again, I lie back down. I feel full of spirit, but something deeper, something in the roots, some healing that goes beyond me, that branches out to Mother and Meghan, that flies backward in time, to grandparents and great grandparents, and further and deeper than that, too.

I tell Maya the next day what happened in the night, and she's so pleased.

"You've already been attuned, but let me do it anyway," she says. She gets behind me and prays and moves her hands, drawing the Reiki symbols in the air. The room grows bright and I see white light, and I think, *Jesus.* Jesus seems to be in the room. I'm not a Jesus freak; his appearance is not my doing.

Maya finishes and I tell her about Jesus showing up.

"Oh yes, he's been showing up a lot lately."

I have a small sore on my upper chest, and when I go to the bathroom I notice it's gone. Healed.

"My seeing Jesus—it doesn't mean I'm suddenly Christian," I say to Maya.

She laughs. "No, you're not suddenly Christian." She laughs again.

I tell her how I see myself as one size but often get a feeling of a larger self that's right behind or above me. She laughs and runs back to the small bedroom and comes back with a diagram. It shows a large figure, a higher self, and the lower self is a person, and the goal is to grow into the higher self.

That night I dream of my grandparents. I dream that I hear their hearts beat deep inside the earth, *boom, boom, boom.* I understand that if I don't tell their stories, if I don't heal them, they'll be lost forever in the soil.

I go back to Maya's. Today I must practice Reiki on a person. Maya's friend lies on her massage table, and I'm sweating bullets. I don't want to say to Maya that I'm no good at touching people, that I worry my father's abuse will somehow come out of my hands.

I hold my hands above the woman, hover. Maya tells me that I need to put my hands on her. I do this. I don't know how I can possibly be any good for her, with my sweating and my anxiety. She goes into a deep trance and comes out later and says she's never felt such a shift. I know that I have a power, and I know that I'm terrified of it.

Maya takes me outside. As the sun sets, she asks me to help Reiki the ocean.

"So much is being dumped into our waters, Pearl. When you go back to Seattle, Reiki the water whenever you can. Even the reservoirs."

We stand in the sand, ocean spray peppering our faces. We draw the Reiki symbols in the air over the waves. We put our hands flat out facing the sea, streaming love energy through our palms. I think of Emoto's water crystals and say the words "love and gratitude" over and over again. I think, *This is what our hands are doing now. It's like a prayer, but the opposite. Instead of hands folded, asking for something, our hands are out, giving something. No longer taking, now giving.*

After the sun sets, I hug Maya goodbye and walk along the beach. She told me we're not supposed to be on the beach at night because of the mountain lions, but we both feel it'll be alright. It's pitch black and I can feel the animals in the forest. And I'm an animal in the forest, and the world is made of a deep crimson and a royal blue.

After the attunement, I feel like all of the wild and sad and glorious and crazy energies have been brought together in the center of my body and given a purpose.

A day later, Layla finds someone driving to Vancouver who can give me a ride. From there I can take a train back to Seattle. I don't want to leave. I have to leave. I look out the rear window of the car as the village disappears and my heart fills to bursting.

Back in Seattle, months go by and it's difficult to stay in the gentle light. I have ups and downs. The chromotherapy and the Reiki seem to mix together in a matrix of colors. Still something stirs below the depths. Still I have episodes where my back and shoulders and arms become jelly. Still there is something in me hiding.

I do a shamanic journey, a soul retrieval. I feel a child inside me who wants to come home. There are so many lost girls inside me.

In the journey I go into a visualization. I can see a waterfall. I jump, falling down, down, down with the water, splashing at the bottom, swirling into a whirlpool, thrust down beneath the water and out the other side to a calm pool. The pool is fed by a waterfall surrounded by subtropical flora.

A woman is standing in the pool next to a small naked child. The girl has her back turned, and I can only see her shoulder blades. I come up to the child and she's scared. She's terrified. This upsets me greatly. I know the woman with her is her guardian.

"Please, please, let us put some clothes on the girl," I beg. She hands me a shirt and shorts, and we put them on the child.

"Why are you so scared? What's wrong?" I ask the child.

She won't answer. Her teeth are chattering, and she's clinging to the edge of the pool, still with her back to us.

"How did this happen?"

She won't answer. No one will answer. I know it's something to do with my father and his rage. That is a given. She feels no one will protect her. She's terrified he could kill her.

"I need you," I say. "Without you, I can't live my best life. What do I need to do to help you come back to me?"

The girl turns to me. "You need me?"

"Yes," I say. "Yes." I bend before her.

"I just need gentleness," she says. "Maybe a stuffed animal that I can hug. Just something gentle and not so mean."

The girl takes my hand. Her eyes are large, freckles on her nose. The subtropical landscape morphs into one of vibrant greens and reds and the swirling blue of the water. It's like the chromotherapy.

She points to the colors. "This is what I take with me," the girl says. She's an artist. I've come here to retrieve my little girl artist.

I take the child's hand and we swim up and up the way I came, up and out of the journey.

I open my eyes and blow the soul of the child into my heart. I feel her as warm energy that travels down into my body. I go out and buy a teddy bear.

★ ★ ★

The easel at a yard sale is surrounded by blinding light. It screams at me as I'm walking by, a siren song. *Buy me. Now. Take me home.* I have the guy running the sale carry it the few blocks home for me. I show him where to put it beneath the hole in the wall, and when he places it there, another chunk smashes down.

"Whoa, dude," the guy says. He spins around and sees all of the dangling mystical hands and says, "Cooooool," then runs out the door without saying goodbye.

I bike to a thrift store and buy two ugly paintings on canvas for a couple of bucks a piece. I purchase gesso and cheap paints and brushes from an art store. I tie the paintings to the bike rack and dangle the bag from the handlebars and bike them home. I gesso over one of the paintings.

The next day I put one on the easel. This is what that terrified girl has brought back to me: an insatiable desire to do art. I spend a night or two grappling with the issue of wanting to be a fiction writer and now wanting to be a visual artist. I think I have to choose one. A voice says in the middle of the night, *Why do you think you have to choose? Be both writer and artist!* And the artist is let loose like a wild beast once in a cage.

As I stand at the easel, I pick up a brush, slather it with paint. I throw the paint against the canvas, and the feeling is something close to bliss. I paint for a while, a chaos of color with no form.

Gem gives me a thick piece of charcoal and a newsprint sketching pad. I tear up. It's one of the nicest gifts I've ever received. I find out where they hold live drawing sessions in the city and go once a week to an open art session at the university.

A dozen students, a nude woman, from deep-set windows a stream of light that falls upon her shoulders like grace. I feel spirit animate my fingers as I draw with the charcoal, powdery sketches that disappear with a strong breath. This is church to me, religion. I realize while I'm drawing how much Saint taught me when I first took his class, how much Sala taught me, how much every artist I've ever known has shown me, and send them all a silent holy moment of gratitude.

I see the model's spirit and draw her flesh. I go into a sort of vision as I work; greater forces are present. It's like my old vision, but I'm conscious, and I'm working, and it feels beautiful and not scary at all. I feel bliss here. I love tarot, and I love my writing, but charcoal in hand, sketching on newsprint in front of a live model, it's only here that I feel true bliss.

At home, I work at my easel when I can, and I'm happy in this simple place. One evening, after a day of painting, I'm on the front porch and have feelings I can't understand. A voice says, *This is happiness.* I'm surprised. It's a new feeling, or an old feeling I just haven't had for years, like an old friend you hardly recognize.

When my back goes out now, which is becoming more rare, the ceiling is my blank canvas where I paint my heart and write my stories. I paint my life like a fresco upon the cracks. I connect the dots and mend the cracks, and even though I'm in pain I can feel the bliss that also feels like love.

XXI
THE WORLD.

CHAPTER 21

The World

It's early morning in September. I'm painting a rooster on a large canvas. The neighbors out my writing window with the moss-covered shed have added a chicken coop, and the rooster has caught my fancy. I think of the chickens I knew as a child, the chickens I butchered, and I know with each paint stroke that I'm healing my animal body.

Gem starts screaming. The hole has grown so big that now it's the size of a door. The landlord never showed up to fix anything. Gem keeps screaming. I look through the hole and can't see her. Brush in hand, I scream back, "Gem, what's wrong now?"

She runs into her living room, trips on something, puts her hands against the broken wall, talks to me through the hole. "Turn on your TV," she pants. I'm scared now. She's not laughing and her face is pale.

A part of the wall where Gem is leaning gives way. She falls forward and gets angry and rips off another large chunk of the drywall. I turn on my television.

We stand at the hole in the wall in silence. At first I can't understand what I'm looking at. A building, debris, a lot of people running.

The announcer explains: "A plane has just flown into one of the World Trade Center buildings." The white dust turns the people into ghosts. It's like a Hollywood film. It can't be real. I struggle to understand.

Gem and I watch as another plane flies into the second tower. A camera on the ground shows people screaming, and then the scream grows and it's now Gem and I screaming. The small dots are people jumping to their deaths, tiny black specks on the tiny TV.

Gem grabs my hand. It's covered in paint. Something is happening, not just on the TV, but to Gem and me. Great chunks of the ceiling and wall fall with a thud around us. Drywall tumbles. Gem's arm becomes my arm. I look at her and she looks at me, and it's like we're looking in a mirror. She's being pulled into me, and me into her. Her hand becomes my hand, Gem's face, my face. Her torso enters mine. We're the dark and the light, together now.

"Finally," I hear her whisper as we become one. "This is what that little girl brought back to you. Me!" Gem's voice is like mist and fog.

I walk around with Gem inside me and see that the wall has disappeared. The apartment is one big room. I am Gem and she's me. This is our apartment. This is our art studio. I feel the found-object art of her mix with my paintings. "We're like a found-object painting ourselves, aren't we?"

Gem as me and me as Gem sit on my futon and watch the drama unfold on the television. *The Great Compassion* overtakes us—for those killed, those going in to help, those who are losing loved ones, and for a world where we could even get to this place of horror. As a journalist in other countries, I perhaps know more than most how we got here.

"They're going to need us," Gem whispers.

"Yes." I feel something rumbling at my base, some force, some reckoning that still must be resolved.

"We'll have to figure out a new way of being. We'll have to come up with a whole new way."

"Yes," I say.

That night is another dark night of the soul for me and for a nation in grief. We are skeletons walking on the bleached bones of the dead in a fog of debris at the base of the twin towers. Bones give way to dust and we crumble with the others in the detritus.

The sky grows dark. If it would just rain, just one drop of holy water. We look up, pleading.

A single raindrop splashes. Water mixes with dust. A hand emerges from the clouds. The fingers work the liquid scatter, form us into clay. From the clay a new people emerge, a new us.

Around the country that night, many on their knees, still as dust, still looking skyward, begging, oh pleading. Just one single drop.

ACKNOWLEDGMENTS

A book begins many lifetimes into the past. I must start by thanking my ancestors. I'm from brutal stock, generations beset by poverty and pain. In there, men and women (my people) worked hard to claw their way upward. Because of their efforts, one of their progeny has gained the education and freedom to do what she loves, to write this book. Most importantly, they gave me the freedom to tell the truth, and I am grateful for it.

These are my roots. Then there is the intangible help, the guides and muses who have spent the past four years showing up in the yurt as I light candles and incense. They have been guiding my hands as I write. These muses have dropped books and recordings in my lap that have taken the writing to a whole new level. They have guided this book much more than I have.

Then there is the physical plane, and the people who have shown up to make this all possible. Caroline Clouse is such a spectacular editor. She reads between the lines. She asks the right questions. She can feel where an idea can be expanded to bring the writing up several notches. To Designer Greg Simanson, who worked with my vision closely to realize the fabled cover design. I'm so grateful. To my early readers, Lisa Mehlin, Ellen Newhouse, Judith Laxer, Gail McMeekin, dozens of gems flew from your mouths and landed in these pages. Thank you for your time, your soul response, and your excitement with this project.

To my book clients via my coaching business, every day as I teach you, I learn from you. It's not just about deepening our understanding of characterization, setting, plot, and theme, it's about us helping each other have the real courage to speak our truth, in a world that desperately needs honesty and transformation.

To the forests, lakes, rivers, and ocean of the Pacific Northwest. Camping and hiking within your corridors changed my life. The beauty of the Pacific Northwest has transformed me, and I'm so grateful for it. To Seattle, thank you for allowing me to wrestle my demons and play out my drama in your neighborhoods. I'm pretty sure you deserve more credit and love than I'm giving you in this book. You're a special city.

And finally, to every reader who has brought their wisdom and understanding to the reading of this book—thank you.

READ ALL OF THE BOOKS IN CAROLINE ALLEN'S SERIES

Earth

Winner of the 2015 Independent Publishers' Gold Medal for Best Midwest Fiction. In rural Missouri in the 1970s, thirteen-year-old Pearl Swinton has just had her first mystical vision. There is no place for Pearl's "gift" in the bloody reality of subsistence farming and rural poverty. As her visions unfold, she must find her way in a family and a community that react with fear and violence. When Pearl discovers that her Aunt Nadine has a similar gift, she bicycles across the state to find her. That trip unexpectedly throws Pearl into a journey to save her runaway sister and sends her into a deep exploration of herself, her visions, and her visceral relationship to the earth. Told with fierce lyricism, Earth is a story about the importance of finding one's own truth and sense of self in dire circumstances and against the odds. It is also a story about the link between understanding ourselves and our relationship with the earth. In this first of the five-book Elemental Journey Series that will follow Pearl across continents and into adulthood, Caroline Allen introduces a form of storytelling that is unflinching in its honesty, filled with compassion, and underscored with originality.

Air

Winner of the 2016 Independent Publishers' Silver Medal for Visionary Fiction. Turbulence opens this second book as Pearl, now in her twenties, uproots from the Midwest and flies to Tokyo, where she has no job, no friends, and no home, a place where she hopes to live floating above the culture. How will she survive with her mystical visions in a country so foreign from everything she knows? Pearl lands at a Jesuit mission and is magnetized to the ethereal missionary Usui. After she is forced to leave, she is thrown unprepared into the complicated world of Japanese culture and must learn to maneuver friendships, understand love, and balance the intensity of working at one of the city's largest newspapers. When she stumbles upon Usui living as a homeless man, a journey begins that draws Pearl deep into Japan's hidden homeless underworld. Having given up any connection to civilization to "find himself," Usui brings Pearl face to face with her own homelessness and challenges her to begin the painful journey of understanding her visions and finding herself. In the end, hope flies on the paper wings of thousands of origami cranes. Pearl is called to her own mysticism, not just for herself, but for a world where the loss of magic may well be the real threat. A fundamentally radical work of art, Air tackles core issues facing individuals coming of age in today's world. How can anyone feel safe and at home on a planet threatened by escalating violence and devastating climate change? Where, truly, is home?

Fire

Winner of the 2018 Independent Publishers' Gold Medal for Visionary Fiction. Twenty-something Pearl is on walkabout for a year across Southeast Asia with her boyfriend, Finn. Pearl is a travel writer and encounters a host of dynamic characters, from a boat boy in the Philippines, to a penitent in Nepal, to a rickshaw driver in India, each challenging her world view. In search of her life purpose, Pearl is being pulled more deeply away from all that is familiar on this journey, a path that began when she moved to Tokyo from the U.S. years earlier. Who is the self behind cultural conditioning? Who is she when no one is telling her who to be? What is her calling? The couple ends up in London, where Pearl finds some semblance of home, while Finn struggles to belong in a place he left behind years before. Pearl ultimately realizes that before she can go upward and understand this illusory "purpose", she must journey down into the self and heal. In the end, she is faced with a decision that could reduce to ashes the life she has built, and destroy all that she holds dear.

Made in the USA
Monee, IL
30 November 2020